3 9082 09492 1 ✓ W9-AQM-209

A LOVE SO STRONG

KENDRA NORMAN-BELLAMY

MOODY PUBLISHERS
CHICAGO

AUBURN HILLS PUBLIC LIBRARY
3400 E. Seyburn Drive
AUBURN HILLS, MI 48326

© 2004 by
KENDRA M. NORMAN-BELLAMY

All rights reserved. No part of this book may be repro-
duced in any form without permission in writing from the
publisher, except in the case of brief quotations embod-
ied in critical articles or reviews.

ISBN: 0-8024-6834-9

1 3 5 7 9 10 8 6 4 2

Printed in the United States of America

Norman-Bellamy, Kendra M.
  A love so strong / Kendra M. Norman-Bellamy.
    p. cm.
  ISBN 0-8024-6834-9
  1. Birthfathers—Fiction. 2. Married people—Fiction.
    3. Illegitimate children—Fiction. I. Title.
  PS3614.O765L685 2004
  813'.6—dc22

                                    2004003859

"In every thing give thanks: for this is the will of God in Christ Jesus concerning you." (1 Thess. 5:18)

Thank You, heavenly Father, for blessing me beyond measure and for counting me worthy of Your favor and Your grace. Thank You for placing so many wonderful people in my life to love and encourage me in the capacity in which You ordained them. Thank You for . . .

Jonathan—My strong rock, my biggest fan, my dearest friend. Thank You for giving me such a God-fearing, ambitious, talented, loving, patient, and supportive husband to share my life and the lives of my children with.

Brittney and Crystal—Lord, You gave me highly intelligent, beautiful, and gifted daughters to love and nurture. I give them back to You to be used according to Your will.

Bishop and Mrs. H. H. Norman—I thank You, Lord, for giving me to them and them to me. I am who I am and what I am because You gave me ever-loving parents who brought me up to know You and Your will for my life. I am eternally grateful.

Crystal (Albert), Harold (Gloria), Cynthia (Terry), and Kimberly—Every sibling that You gave me has played a vital role in my life, and I'm appreciative of every emotion that we've shared through the years. Thank You for the closeness we share.

Jimmy (1968–1995)—Lord, I'll forever cherish the time You permitted me to share my heart and life with such a wonderful human being. Thank You for allowing his memory to continue to live inside of the children that You gave us.

Shunda & Jamill—Thank You for the literary company You blessed them to establish, and for allowing me to share in business with them from the ground up. Even more invaluable is the bond of friendship that You've given me with them both.

Terrance—Thank You, Heavenly Father, for keeping us close through the years and allowing us to be there to encourage one another to stay on the straight and narrow. Blood made us cousins, but hearts made us friends.

The Bellamy family—Charles (Ossie 'Sweetie Pie'), Reggie (Adrian), Sonya, Angela, Stocky (Pamma), and the Holmes family—Dad, Mom, Kenny, Jeffrey (Tina), Timmy (Tonja), and Andray . . . Thank You for genuinely loving and supportive in-laws who remain family no matter what.

Mildred, Courtney, LaMonte, and Jon-Jon—God, You have given me wonderfully blessed godchildren, and I thank You for each of them and the joy that they bring to my life.

Heather, Gloria, and Deborah—Thank You for childhood friends whose bond still holds true in adulthood and whose support holds strong no matter how far apart we live or how few times we get to see each other.

Aunt Joyce and Uncle Irvin—Lord, I'm forever appreciative for my godparents who have been great role models in my life.

The memories of Elder Clinton and Mrs. Willie Mae Bellamy—Lord, thank You for allowing me to share in the lives of such beautiful parents-in-law.

Revival Church, Inc. (Bishop H. H. Norman) and Church of God by Faith Ministries (Pastor Wayne Mack)—Sometimes spiritual families are just as important as natural ones. Thank You, Lord, for giving me divine guidance through these vehicles.

KNB Publications—The Company that You gave

Jonathan and me the vision to establish. This is only the beginning, and I thank You in advance for our amazing future.

Circle of Friends II Book Club—Lord, You knew a better bunch of reading sistahs didn't exist, so You placed me among the best. For that I feel highly blessed.

The employees of Genesis Underwriting Management Company (Atlanta, Ga.) and The Care House (Valdosta, Ga.)—Lord, thank You for allowing me to have worked with such nice people who've given me memories that I will hold dear for years to come.

The many literary inspirations You have provided for me—Thank You for Maya Angelou, Victoria Christopher Murray, Carmen Green, Stephanie Perry Moore, Travis Hunter, S. James Guitard, Donna Hill, Vanessa Davis Griggs, Michael Baisden, Patricia Haley, Jacquelin Thomas, Pearle Cleage, and many others You've allowed me to meet who have shared words of experience and encouragement with me along this journey.

Booking Matters (Decatur, Ga.) for my first magazine interview; Rejoice (Valdosta, Ga.) for my first newspaper interview; Divine Eloquence (New Castle, Pa.) for my first online interview; WJEM (Valdosta, Ga.) for my first radio interview, and WATC-TV (Atlanta, Ga.) for my first television interview—Thank You, Lord, for people who believe in me and help me share this gift with the world.

Rudelle Thomas, Alvin Romer, Shon Bacon, TJ Jackson, LaShaunda Hoffman, Marilynn Griffith, Ruth Bridges—Thank You, Lord, for supplying valued and sometimes unexpected support from so many avenues.

Cynthia Ballenger and the Moody Publishers family —God, I give thanks to You for allowing them to see in me the gift that You have instilled.

Last, but not least, Brian McKnight, BeBe & CeCe Winans, Men of Standard, Take 6, Commissioned and Boyz II Men—I thank You, Heavenly Father, for supplying, through these talented vessels, the powerful, positive music of love and inspiration needed for my thought flow as I write stories of passion and romance in the Christian community and . . . The Williams Brothers, John P. Kee, Donnie McClurkin, Fred Hammond and Shirley Caesar—For the "shouting music" needed once my work is complete, Lord, thank You for these vessels too.

For all these and countless more blessings which will go unnamed, but not unnoticed, that You have showered upon me in my life, I thank You. All praise, all honor, and all glory belongs to You, Lord. Amen.

CHAPTER ONE

The sunlight broke through the window blinds as Nicole stirred beneath her satin sheets. She opened her eyes as she felt the emptiness beside her. Slowly sitting up, she looked beyond the vase of drooping roses that her husband had given her for Valentine's Day one week earlier and glanced at the clock on her nightstand. She realized that she had somehow overslept. It was 10:00 AM. She had slept four hours longer than she had planned.

"Bryan," she whispered with a chuckle.

Just the night before, she had told her husband of five years that she was going to get up early Saturday morning and go to church to help the other members who would be there cleaning and getting the sanctuary prepared for Sunday's appreciation service. He had made it clear that he didn't want her to be overworked.

"You're always working," he'd said. "Let some of the others do the work sometimes. You've worked late into the night, and now you're talking about going back again tomorrow morning? You're trying to do too much, baby. I don't need you getting sick or burning out. I'll make some phone calls and make sure everything is handled. You get your rest."

Looking at the clock more closely, she noticed the alarm that she had set the night before was turned off. Bryan was such a sweetheart. She really did desire to help prepare the church for the upcoming appreciation service, but he was right. She had needed the extra sleep.

The service was to honor one person in each of the church's ministries. The honorees were voted upon and chosen by the more than five-hundred-member congregation. In some ways, Nicole felt obligated to help out as much as possible since Bryan had been chosen as the honoree of the Ministerial Counseling Ministry. He'd been a part of the ministry for nearly the past ten years, becoming the youngest counselor when he joined the ministry at the age of twenty-one.

"Good morning, beautiful," Bryan said as he opened the bedroom door carrying a tray with a delicious-smelling breakfast that he'd prepared.

"Good morning." Nicole beamed as he sat the tray on the bed and bent in close to kiss her gently. "You let me oversleep," she said as he sat next to her.

"Guilty as charged," he said without apology. "Do you feel rested?"

"Yes, but I really needed to be there this morning."

"No, you didn't," he said as he uncovered the plate of grits, scrambled eggs, hash browns, and sausage links. A small saucer on the side was filled with fresh-cut strawberries. He disappeared for a few seconds and returned with a glass of orange juice. "Hope you're hungry."

"Thank you." She kissed him again. "I am, but I'm sure that I can't eat all of this."

"I know. That's why I brought two forks"—he smiled as he held the second fork up in the air—"and two straws," he concluded.

Even after five years of marriage, his presence still stirred deep emotions in her.

"I told the others last night that I'd be there to help them again today. I keep my word, you know, Bryan."

"I called Sharon this morning and told her that you were going to sleep in," he said as he fed her a sausage link and sipped from one of the straws. "She told me that she'd make sure everything was covered and that they could handle it without you. Whether or not you're dependable isn't the issue here. You needed your rest."

"I should have known you'd get Sharon on your side." Nicole laughed as she spoke of her best friend and joined Bryan in enjoying the food.

"She agreed with me," he said. "She said that you stayed after everybody was gone last night. An hour after she and Melvin had gone home, she called and found out that you were still there. They actually came back to the church and insisted that you leave."

"It's a special service, baby," Nicole defended. "I just want everything to be perfect on Sunday. Everybody is just so slow about getting the annex cleaned and the sanctuary decorated."

"Nicole," Bryan said as he placed one finger on her lips to silence her. "There are eight honorees for the service. All eight of us have family and friends. You don't have to try and do it all. Melvin and some of the fellas are taking care of the yard work today, and Sharon said that several of the ladies are helping her set up in the annex, pulpit, and choir stand."

11

"I know, but . . ."

"Nicole." He stopped her again. "I know you want everything to be flawless because your husband is being honored, and I love you so much for that. But I needed you here with me today. Maybe I'm just being selfish."

"So that's the real reason." Nicole smiled as she relaxed her head against his shoulder. "You wanted us to spend some time together."

"Like I said," he said as he kissed the top of her head, "call me selfish. We've both been so busy lately. You've been managing the day care center, and I've been spending days at the bonding company and evenings counseling. It's been a while since we both were home on a Saturday. I thought maybe we could take advantage of the opportunity."

"Mmmmm," Nicole murmured softly. "I like the way your mind thinks, Mr. Walker. That's why I married you."

"For my mind, huh?" Bryan removed the tray of half-eaten food from the bed and placed it on the nightstand. "I thought you married me because I was tall, dark, and handsome."

"To me, you're all that, baby," Nicole flirted as he slipped under the covers with her.

"No, sweetheart, not *to* you," he whispered. He looked at her lovingly as she lay looking up at him. "*Because of you,* I am all that. You make me the man I am."

"Then somebody ought to give me a medal," Nicole whispered back as the lips of the man she loved covered hers passionately.

Bryan and Nicole Walker shared a beautiful marriage. As with any marriage, they had the usual problems along the way, but their union never lacked love, communication, and fresh passion. Every year seemed to bring them closer and make their love and desire for one another stronger. When she moved from Orlando to Jacksonville, Florida, six years ago, Nicole never imagined her world would be turned inside out by one of the church's most eligible and sought-after bachelors. Nicole and her friend Sharon Baker attended college together at Florida State University in Tallahassee. They earned their degrees in early childhood education and, upon graduation, moved to Orlando and opened their own day care center.

With a lot of prayer and hard work, the business was successful. It was really hard on Nicole when Sharon and Melvin Gibbs, who had worked with the construction team that built the day care center, decided to get married after a year and a half of courtship. Melvin and Sharon decided to move back to his hometown of Jacksonville so that he could accept a partnership in a thriving construction company.

Nicole carried on the day care center for another year but found it impossible to turn down the offer to join her friend in Jacksonville after Melvin and his construction team built a brand-new center. Not wanting the responsibility of two centers, Nicole sold the Orlando business and partnered with Sharon in Jacksonville.

Just as in Orlando, in Jacksonville she found herself having to start a new life. This time, though, life was given a whole new meaning. She struggled with getting used to the new church she joined in Orlando, but the Christ Center of Hope was heaven-sent. Having been a part of small churches all of her life, including the mission her father pastored when she was a child, the Christ Center with its hundreds of worshipers was a new experience.

She remembered the conversation that she had with Sharon as she and Melvin were helping her move her belongings into her small one-bedroom apartment.

"Girl, do I have the man for you," Sharon had announced.

"Sharon, I didn't move here to find a man. I didn't like the one you set me up with in Orlando, and I'm sure I won't like this one. Don't get me wrong. It's nothing really wrong with the men. I'm just not looking."

"I know, but I have one for you anyway," she insisted. "He's everything you've ever said that you wanted in a husband."

"But I don't want a husband. At least not right now. I'm only twenty-four years old, and I'm not getting married before I'm thirty. My calendar is planned, and there's no room to pencil in a man for a good while. I want to travel and maybe even go back to school—I'm not sure. But for certain, I'm not looking to settle down."

"Tell her, Melvin," Sharon said as if to totally ignore Nicole's speech. "Tell her about Bryan Walker."

"Sharon," Nicole whined.

"Well," Melvin started, "what can I say? Bryan's a cool guy. He's saved, responsible, athletic, and he works with the counseling ministry. He's twenty-six years old, and a lot of the women have their eye on him, according to Pastor Gaines."

"So, what do I want with a playboy?" Nicole asked. "I don't need a man who thinks everybody wants him. I'm sorry. I'm not interested in this Bryan Walker."

"You've got it all wrong, Nicole," Sharon said. "See how you've sized him up already? Bryan's not a playboy at all. He doesn't even pay attention to any of those girls who chase after him. Tell her, Melvin."

"That's true," Melvin agreed as he completed the hookup of Nicole's television. "In the year that we've been attending the church, I've never seen him take out

14

or go after any of the women who chase after him. And before you think it," he continued, "let me say that some of these women look pretty nice too."

"Maybe something's wrong with him," Nicole mumbled.

"See, that's why you're by yourself," Sharon said. "Ain't nothing wrong with him! He's quite the looker. He's a great catch, and you better believe he is all man."

"Hey!" Melvin tossed a pillow at her playfully. "I am in the room, you know."

"But not half the man that you are," she added as she blew a kiss across the room at her husband.

"Oh, stop it." Nicole laughed.

"Seriously," Melvin said. "He says that when the time is right, God will send the right girl his way."

"Well, that's a good way for him to think," Nicole said. "He's waiting on God as he should, so I think you two should stay out of it, Mr. and Mrs. Matchmaker."

"I ain't trying to match make," Melvin defended. "I'm just agreeing with the truth."

"Besides, if he's such a find, he would be taken by now."

"Not if God is keeping him just for you," Sharon pointed out. "It won't hurt to meet him."

"If he's a friend of yours, I'm sure I'll meet him at some point. However, if and when I do, I don't want you trying to bring us together. I mean that. Especially you, Sharon. I'm not interested in any relationship right now. Not with Bryan and not with anyone else. Do I make myself clear?"

Even now, Sharon would throw those words back at Nicole every chance she got. When Nicole did meet Bryan, it changed everything. Her priorities changed completely as her instant attraction to the handsome, brown-eyed

15

bail bondsman and his instant captivation with her took a front-row-center seat.

The courtship blossomed quickly and became serious almost overnight. Nicole loved Chinese food, and eleven months into their relationship, Bryan took her to a Chinese restaurant and reserved one of the private dining rooms. He had arranged for a special band to play her favorite love song. After they had enjoyed their meal, the band played and Bryan looked into her eyes and said, "A lifetime of love, peace, and happiness will be yours if you say yes."

With tears in her eyes, she looked on as Bryan opened a small box that was in his hand.

"Will you?" he asked as the one-and-a-quarter-carat diamond sparkled from its casing.

"Will I, what?" Nicole whispered knowingly as tears streamed down her face.

"Spend a lifetime of love, peace, and happiness with me."

"You want to marry me?" She knew they loved each other, but what about her calendar? Marriage was still more than five years away.

"I want to marry you more than anything else I've wanted in a long time," he said as he looked deep into her tear-filled eyes. "Will you marry me?"

"Yes," she mouthed silently as her voice escaped her. He understood, and she watched and trembled as he slipped the ring on her finger.

The waiters, waitresses, and even the kitchen help came out to applaud and congratulate them as Nicole silently fell into his arms and wept uncontrollably. Bryan fought back his own tears as he held her close and whispered, "I love you," over and over again in her ear.

From their first meeting to the day of their wedding

was a short fifteen months. She and her new husband shared a lingering kiss at the altar after being pronounced husband and wife.

"Go on, girl!" someone yelled from the audience as the couple still embraced. "We ain't mad at you!"

The remark even brought laughter from the newlyweds as they released one another and walked from the church linked hand in hand, dipping their heads to dodge the rice that was being thrown from well-wishers before being whisked away in a beautifully adorned horse-drawn carriage.

They didn't even make it to their own reception. Being brought up in the church all of her life, and accepting Christ as a young teenager, Nicole had never been sexually intimate with a man. The wedding night brought fear as well as excitement to her. Though Bryan couldn't share that same testimony of virginity, he understood and made sure that the night was as enjoyable for her as he knew it would be for him.

Five years later, their intimacy was as passionate and fulfilling as it had been that night in their honeymoon suite. Nicole awoke and brushed her neatly weaved braids away from her face as she watched her king, as she liked to refer to him, lying asleep beside her. The breakfast that they had only nibbled on a couple hours earlier was now cold, still on the tray.

"I love you," she whispered as she kissed his neck gently.

She smiled as he let out a soft moan. She quietly eased from under the covers and out of the bed. Wrapping herself in Bryan's vacated robe and stepping into his bedroom slippers, she picked up the tray from the nightstand and took it to the kitchen to clean up. The time was passing quickly. It was 1:00 in the afternoon.

She quickly rushed to pick up the ringing phone so that it wouldn't wake up her Bryan.

"Hello?"

"Hi, Nicole."

"Hi, Sharon."

"I didn't want anything in particular; I was just calling."

"Are you still at the church?" Nicole asked.

"No. We finished up an hour ago."

"So everything is set for tomorrow?"

"Sure is, and we finished it without your help. See, we can do something without you!"

"I never said you all were stupid, Sharon."

"I know, girl. I'm just teasing. I really could have used your help arranging the greenery, but I think it looks pretty good."

"I'm sure you did fine."

"So did you enjoy your day off?" Sharon asked.

"Yeah," Nicole said after a slight chuckle.

"See?" Sharon said. "I told Melvin y'all were over there being bad. I just knew you were. I could hear vibes in Bryan's voice when he asked me to take over because you needed to sleep in. I knew he had ulterior motives."

"Girl, stop." Nicole laughed heartily at Sharon's antics.

"I guess I'm one to talk, huh?" Sharon laughed with her. "I'm the one with two babies under the age of two years old," she said, referring to her sons, Michael, age twenty months, and Benjamin, who had just turned six months old.

"Yeah," Nicole said soberly.

"I'm sorry, Nicole." Sharon realized she'd struck a sore spot in her friend.

Nicole wanted so desperately to give Bryan a child. He never complained or even mentioned the desire to have children, but Nicole knew that he did. She would watch him play with Michael and Benjamin, and he was so good with them. He'd be a great father, but so far they had been unable to conceive.

As a teenager Nicole's doctor had informed her mother that Nicole's having a child wasn't totally impossible, but it was highly improbable. Nicole had told Bryan this prior to their getting married, and he had said that he would be totally satisfied just being her husband.

He had proven his words to be true over and over again, but sometimes Nicole would find herself praying for the child that she knew they both wanted. Every now and then she'd even dream of having a son with eyes like his or a daughter with a smile just like Bryan's.

"It's okay, Sharon," she assured her friend with a sigh. "As long as Bryan and I don't have any, your boys will have more Christmas gifts than they can handle."

"Don't I know it?" Sharon said as she thought of the recently passed holiday. "But I'd trade a scarce Christmas any day if you'd have that baby that you want."

"Thanks." Nicole smiled.

"Change the subject?" Sharon offered.

"Yes," Nicole agreed.

"So, what are you wearing tomorrow?" her friend asked.

"Oh." Nicole perked up. "Bryan bought me a royal blue silk dress a couple of weeks ago. I'm going to wear that. I think all the honorees are wearing black and white. Bryan's wearing a black suit."

"Sounds good," Sharon said. "Listen, I have to go. I have a hair appointment in an hour. I'm going to get a French roll. I wish I had braids like you. I'd give anything to be able to just get up and go. Are you going to pin them up or anything for the service?"

"Bryan likes them just hanging down," Nicole said as she ran her hands through the small braids that hung just below her shoulders.

"Then wear them down, girl. Do it like your man wants it."

"That's the plan." Nicole laughed.

"Remember this?" Sharon asked as she mimicked Nicole's soft-spoken voice. "'I am not interested in a relationship right now. Not with Bryan and not with anyone else. Do I make myself clear?'"

"Okay, already." Nicole laughed. "Give it a rest. It's been five years now. Am I ever going to outlive that one statement?"

"Not if I can help it," Sharon said. "See you at church tomorrow."

"Okay," Nicole said. "And thanks for handling the work at church today."

"Don't mention it."

CHAPTER TWO

Bryan wrapped his towel around his waist as he stepped out of the shower. The water's temperature had been so hot that the mirrors were steamed. A romantic dinner for two prepared by the love of his life and the night of passion that followed had resulted in a very restful sleep. He opened the bathroom window and allowed the cool Florida breeze to clear the mist from the room as he prepared to touch up his neatly trimmed mustache and beard.

"Good morning." He smiled sheepishly, admiring his wife's body as she made her way to the shower.

"Good morning," she replied as she wrapped her arms around him from behind and kissed his shoulder.

"Sleep well?" he asked as her touch sent ripples through his body.

"Very," she said.

His five-feet-eleven-inch frame topped hers by five inches as he began shaving carefully. Through the slowly clearing mirror, he watched her hand as it slowly caressed his chest and wiped away the lingering water in the process.

"Don't start nothing, and it won't be nothing," he warned.

"You'd just better be glad we've got church this morning," she responded as she stepped into the stall and turned on the water.

He continued to smile as Nicole sang softly in the shower. He loved to hear her sing. She wasn't the world's greatest singer, but singing meant that she was happy, and her happiness was important to him.

He remembered her telling him stories of her childhood. She grew up in a Christian home, but being the oldest child in a family of six children had its drawbacks. She was the only girl, with five younger brothers. When Bryan took the drive to Orlando with her to meet her family six weeks into their courtship, he met her parents, Otis and Deborah Wilson. They were a pleasant couple, but Nicole had already warned him that her family wasn't exactly a close-knit one.

It seemed that the reverend and his wife spent so much time at church functions and local and national meetings that the children were sometimes left to look out for themselves. Nicole found herself having to play mother to her siblings as her parents traveled and did God's work. It was as though her childhood was taken away from her. She told him that she never held it against them. She knew they meant well and did the best that they knew how with raising them.

Nicole took him to the school that she and her siblings walked to every day because their mother couldn't drive and their father was generally too busy preparing his next sermon or doing something church related to take them. It wasn't far. It was less than a half-mile walk, but for small children, it had been no easy task.

Her family didn't have much money, but Mrs. Wilson was blessed with a talent to sew, and she made most of the children's clothes. As busy as she was with her husband and the church, she somehow found the time to teach her only daughter how to sew as well. It was time with her mother that Nicole cherished. Rev. Wilson spent more time with his sons than with his daughter. He wasn't big on extracurricular activities, but he would take his sons fishing with him whenever he had a free Saturday.

Nicole and her brothers grew up in a small home with only three bedrooms. She shared her bedroom with two of her brothers, so she never had the privacy that little girls liked. She tried to keep the room clean, but her brothers would step out of their clothes and leave them in the middle of the floor. Most days, from the time she was thirteen, she was responsible for cooking dinner. All of her parents' time away from home was well intentioned, but it put so much distance between them and their children.

Sometimes, Bryan worried when Nicole would work on church projects as much as she did with the preparation for todays' program. He worried that perhaps some of her mother's tendencies had rubbed off on her unaware. He vowed that she would never have to work as hard as her mother and he would never burden her with church issues, although he was very active in the church himself.

As much as possible, he tried to share household chores with her as well. He felt that she had done her share of keeping house as a child. Life with him would be as stress free as he could possibly make it, yet he wouldn't stand in the way of the things that she wanted to do.

By the time Nicole exited the shower, stepped out into the bedroom wrapped in a towel, and pulled the shower cap from her head, Bryan had already put on his suit pants and was finishing with pressing his shirt.

"Is there anything you want me to iron for you?" he offered.

"No, thanks." She smiled. "The dress I'm wearing doesn't need pressing," she concluded as she disappeared into the closet.

"I was beginning to think you didn't really care for that dress," Bryan said as she walked out with the royal blue dress in her hand.

"I was just waiting for an occasion special enough to wear it," she assured him. "I love this dress."

"When I saw it," Bryan said as he began putting on his shirt, "I knew it was you. I thought the fit was so perfect for you."

"Looks even better on," Nicole said excitedly.

"Whoa," Bryan said with raised eyebrows, "my wife is going to be the best-dressed lady in the place!"

"Answer the phone, silly," Nicole said as she playfully pushed him away.

"Hello?"

"Hey." It was Melvin. "Just wanted to remind you to bring your black and gray paisley tie so I can wear it today."

"I didn't forget. It's already in the car," Bryan said. "Why are you dressing in black and white, anyway? You're just trying to be like me, aren't you?" He laughed.

"Hey, I may not be one of the ones being honored today, but I'll be dog if I let the brothers who are out-dress me."

"I heard that." Bryan laughed. "Well, we're on our way out as soon as my bride gets ready."

"We'll see you there," Melvin said.

"All right."

"I'm ready in five minutes," Nicole told him as she disappeared into the restroom after putting on her shoes.

"I have your purse, camera, and Bible," Bryan called. "I'll meet you in the car."

"Okay."

Unlike Melvin and Sharon, who lived less than a mile from the church, it was a twenty-minute drive for Bryan and Nicole. They arrived shortly before the start of the service and mingled briefly with other members before finding their seats.

"Sorry, Brother Walker," a middle-aged usher said with a shake of her head as she approached the chatting couple. "I know you want to sit with your sweetheart today, but you've got to sit up front with the other honorees."

"Up front?" Bryan grimaced.

"That's right," she said, "See the chairs up there that Pastor Gaines had us move to the side? That's where you have to sit. Now, if you like, I can find a closer seat for Sister Walker to sit near the front. Brother and Sister Gibbs are sitting somewhere up there. I can sit you with them if you want me to."

"Thanks." Nicole smiled, "I'd appreciate that."

Hand in hand, the couple followed the usher as she escorted them to the front. She spotted Sharon and Melvin and directed Nicole to sit with them. Bryan was escorted to the reserved seating near the pulpit. He waved at Nicole from his seat after he greeted the others and sat down. In their five years of marriage, they'd always sat side by side. Bryan felt awkward.

The services started at 10:30 sharp, as scheduled. The devotional and praise service was always quite spirited.

The choir would join in and assist the praise leaders, and the congregation's participation was always excellent. As he stood and clapped to the beat of the music, Bryan periodically glanced toward his wife and admired her in her new dress singing and holding Benjamin.

Bryan knew her heart's desire. He knew that she wanted a child. This was one of those things that he couldn't do anything about. It was something he couldn't fix, and sometimes it saddened him. He really did find total fulfillment in being her husband and sharing a life with her, but a child would bring him as much joy as it would her. However, he never wanted her to feel that she was in any way inadequate, so he never brought up the issue of childbearing.

Midway through the praise service, Pastor Gaines walked in dressed in a black and white ministerial robe. Bryan smiled. Charles Gaines was not only his pastor and mentor but also his uncle. He credited his Uncle Charles with saving his life. Bryan didn't talk much about his past, but he had been quite the rambunctious problem child growing up in Chicago.

His father was a truck driver and was rarely at home. His mother worked as a hotel maid to keep food on the table. The two were never married, but his father would drop by periodically for a free meal and to share his mother's bed. Although Bryan didn't see him much, he knew his father well and was unconsciously turning out just like him. He even looked like him.

Garrett Walker was a tall, handsome man with distinct facial features. His jawline was strong, his skin smooth and caramel in color, and his eyes a piercing brown. He had soft, rich-black hair that he locked and let grow long until he could pull it into a ponytail in the back. The ladies loved him, and he had the girlfriends and babies to prove it.

The last time Bryan saw his father was when he stopped in for what had become one of his every-now-and-then visits. Bryan was fourteen. His parents had a big fight that day because Teresa, his mother, found out that Garrett had another baby on the way by yet another girlfriend. Teresa wanted desperately to feel special, but it was a lost cause. The fact was that she meant very little to the man she loved. After screaming at each other for what seemed like hours, Teresa put him out and told him to never come back. He gratefully obeyed.

As little time as Bryan spent with his father anyway, it still angered him that his mother would insist upon his leaving permanently. He actually looked forward to seeing his father whenever he decided to stop by. Unknown to him, when Teresa put Garrett out, she really didn't want or expect him to leave, let alone never return. She hoped he would beg her to allow him to stay. She had already planned to accept him back, but he didn't even ask. He left, and neither she nor Bryan ever heard from him again.

Bryan rebelled. He began disrespecting his mother's orders and wishes. He would neither come straight home from school nor do his chores. He began hanging out with the wrong crowd, which led him down a declining path of trouble.

To be accepted in a gang, he lost his virginity at age fifteen to a girl he barely knew. She was actually one of the gangbanger's sisters. At night, he and his new friends would walk the streets, getting into trouble, stealing from people's mailboxes or turning over garbage cans and letting dogs loose from their chains. He dropped out of school in his junior year and got arrested for breaking into his former science teacher's house to steal a computer.

It was the last straw for Teresa. The teacher graciously dropped the charges only after Teresa promised to
send her son away for help. It was then that she contacted her half-brother in Jacksonville, Charles Gaines. He
and his wife, Maggie, personally flew out and picked up
their nephew and brought him to live with them. First,
they got him back in school and gave him a strict schedule to follow daily.

School and church weren't optional. He tried their
patience, but they had more tolerance than he could ever
have imagined. It was that persistence combined with a
lot of tough love that encouraged him to not only finish
high school but also attend Florida A&M University in
Tallahassee, and graduate with a degree in business management.

It always tickled him when he thought of how both
he and Nicole were enrolled in separate colleges in the
same city for at least two years, yet their paths never
crossed. Timing was everything. It showed how God's
timing puts things perfectly into place.

Bryan enjoyed college and kept his grades up. He
lived on campus and was no longer under the strict
scrutiny of his church-going uncle and aunt. Like a lot of
young men on campus, he chased the girls. It wasn't until he went back to Jacksonville to spend the summer
months between his freshman and sophmore years that
his life was completely changed. It was then that he
found Christ.

In finding Christ, he found a new role model to pattern his life after. He had much respect for his uncle and
his aunt, but his uncle in particular. He didn't give up on
his sister's only child. It was mainly because of Charles
Gaines that the church was honoring Bryan today.

The praise and worship ended, and Pastor Gaines

stood in the pulpit to deliver the sermon. He was such a great teacher and preacher. He could stand flat-footed and teach a lesson verse by verse and break it down so that even the children could understand. He could also take Scripture and arouse the crowd as the organ music played in the background.

Today was the latter example. Bryan loved it when his uncle preached. In his opinion, no other preacher could hold a candle to him when he was at his best. It seemed that musicians and ushers were never going to get a rest, as every time there was a calming, Pastor Gaines would say two or three more words that would get the "fire" ignited again.

When the excitement finally did subside, the services moved forward. Following the offering, the honorees' names were announced and the ceremony began. Pastor Gaines, one by one, called the name of the ministry that each honoree represented. There were five women and three men being honored, and the pastor had glowing words to say about each of them and their accomplishments through the years. Each honoree was given an opportunity to make remarks after accepting their plaques and certificates.

As he finally made his way to the Counseling Ministry and turned to look at Bryan, who stood as instructed in front of his seat, Pastor Gaines turned into Uncle Charles and wiped tears as he spoke of his nephew. Many of the members didn't know Bryan's story, and gasps were followed by thunderous applause as his life became an open book before them.

Tears broke from both the men as they shared a warm and lengthy embrace when Bryan walked to the pulpit to receive his award. After several moments of silence to give the congregation time to settle down and to regain his own composure, Bryan took a deep, shaky breath as he looked out into the congregation and smiled.

"This is such an honor," he began slowly. "All of the glory belongs to God for this moment, for truly He has done great things in my life. He's brought me a long way, and I am so grateful. I know that the life that I was leading was only going to lead me to destruction, but because of Christ and because of Uncle Charles and Aunt Maggie, I am alive, I am well, and I am here."

After giving the applause time to die down, he continued. "I feel like I'm at the Academy Awards," he said as laughter from the congregation followed. "I first want to thank God for allowing His Son to die for me. I thank Him for being so forgiving and loving. Thank you, as I've said many times before, to my pastor and his wife and for my mother, who didn't know it at the time, but she allowed God to speak to her to send me here.

"I'm thankful to all of you, the members here for counting me worthy not only of your votes for this honor, but also of your trust as you share with me in counseling sessions. Your confidence means a lot to me, and it will never be taken for granted or misused. To Melvin and Sharon, who moved here more than seven years ago and became my best friends, thank you for being who you are. There's never a dull moment with the two of you.

"And last but not least," he began as the sound of Nicole's name was spoken verbally followed by laughter from several of the members. "That's right," he continued with a smile, "my bride, my love, my gift, Nicole." He looked directly at her as she sat, still holding Benjamin.

There was a momentary pause while he seemed to gather his thoughts and fight the threat of tears once more. When he finally spoke, no one expected what they heard.

"I need you, you need me, I love you, I need you to survive, stand with me, agree with me, I love you, I need you to survive. You are important to me; I need you to survive." Bryan shocked Nicole by singing the words to her favorite song by gospel artist Hezekiah Walker.

Tears streamed from Nicole's eyes as he winked at her at the conclusion of his song and walked back to his seat to a standing ovation. No one cared that his voice didn't sound like Luther Vandross. The emotions felt from his song even brought tears to others that listened and were now applauding.

"See, man, " Melvin said as he greeted Bryan along with several others of the brothers of the church following dismissal, "you ain't right."

"What?" Bryan said.

"Now we gonna have to go home and buy our wives stuff," Melvin explained.

"I know," one of the others chimed in. "After that pulpit serenade, if we don't go out and do something special, we'll be in the doghouse."

"That's what I'm saying," another brother spoke. "I can just prepare myself right now," he continued, "because I already know that all I'm going to hear on the ride home is 'see how Brother Walker sung that song to his wife.'"

"Y'all need to stop." Bryan laughed.

"I'm for real, man," Melvin said. "Ain't that right, Pastor Gaines?" he asked as the pastor joined them on the floor of the sanctuary.

"What's that?" he asked as he greeted them with handshakes.

"Your nephew, here," Melvin pointed. "Because of

31

him, are we or aren't we going to have to do something for our wives now that at least halfway measures up to what he did today?"

"Oh, I've already called Crawford Jewelers at the mall during announcements and had them put a necklace on hold that Sister Gaines was looking at a couple of weeks ago. I figure, after—forgive the pun—Bryan's song, today is the perfect time to buy it," the pastor said to the laughter of his listeners.

"Aw, Uncle Charles." Bryan laughed as they embraced briefly.

"You're laughing," Pastor Gaines said, "but I'm serious. The mall closes early on Sunday, so I have to run. I'll see you all next Sunday," he concluded as he disappeared through the crowd, shaking hands quickly as the men continued to laugh.

"You guys want to join us for dinner this afternoon?" Melvin offered as he and Bryan made their way through the crowd. "Me and Sharon are going to Red Lobster for the seafood buffet."

"Sounds good to me." Bryan nodded. "We were going to eat out somewhere anyway."

"Cool," Melvin said as Nicole joined them on the front lawn and grabbed her husband by the arm.

Before Bryan could speak, she wrapped her arms around his neck and kissed him sweetly, drawing a deafening silence from the people directly around them.

"I love you," she said.

A brief moment of silence followed as Bryan caught his breath and recovered from the pleasant surprise.

"Rain check?" he asked as he turned to Melvin.

"Yeah," Melvin said slowly as he nodded in agreement, "rain check."

CHAPTER THREE

Business at the day care was booming. The child care facility that Nicole and Sharon co-owned had the capacity to house 140 children on a daily basis. Right now, enrollment was up to 129, the most they'd ever had. Many of the children enrolled were members of Christ Center of Hope, so the parents trusted the friends to see that their children were properly cared for as they worked.

Although they employed over thirty on-site care-givers, cooks, van drivers, and office employees, Nicole and Sharon found themselves spending much of their days at the center making sure that things were done carefully and according to state code.

The center opened its doors at 6:00 every morning. At 8:00 each morning, prior to eating breakfast, all of the children and all of the staff would gather on the backyard playground and hold hands. A volunteer among the staff would lead the prayer, and the children would anxiously wait for the moment when they could all say "amen" together.

"Well, it's the third of the month, and once again God has allowed us to pay all of our bills on time," Sharon announced as Nicole walked into the office holding one of the babies from the infant area.

"Thank you, Jesus," Nicole said with a raised hand.

"Amen to that," Sharon agreed as she smiled at the smiling baby.

"Melvin asked me last week if we gave opening up a second center any thought," Nicole said.

"I guess he wants to know if our minds are in sync, because he asked me the same thing."

"Really?" Nicole asked. "What did you say?"

"I told him that we've thought about it several times, but we weren't ready to make that move yet."

"Oh, good. I told him almost the exact same thing," Nicole said. "Day care is a lot of hard work."

"Yes, it is," Sharon agreed, "and good workers aren't easy to find either."

"You know, I was just looking over our staff changes over the past five years that we've been open," Nicole added. "Do you know that we've fired sixteen workers?"

"I know. And that's not counting the ones who just come and go. I think when people come here, they see this as easy money, but taking the care and safety of other children into your own hands is tough."

"That's true." Nicole nodded.

"But," Sharon continued, "I do believe that God has blessed us with a pretty stable staff now. No turnover in the past year."

"Has it been that long?"

"Yes, it has," Sharon answered. "I think the difference is that all but four of our employees are saved."

"I agree," Nicole said. "That could change if we reach our capacity, though," she continued. "We'll have to hire at least two more."

"All we'll still have to do is trust God to allow us to pay them and pay our monthly bills," Sharon pointed out.

"I told you before," Nicole said as she rocked the baby who was falling asleep in her arms, "I found out that we pay quite well here. Day care providers don't pay their employees much money around here, and the benefits, if they have any, are horrible. We offer an entire benefits package. That's another reason our workers are hanging in. The economy isn't what it used to be, and finding a job these days isn't as easy as it was just a couple of years ago. People are appreciating good jobs now."

"Nicole," Sharon said slowly as she changed the subject entirely, "please don't get offended or upset when I say this, okay?"

"I'll try," Nicole said apprehensively, noting her friend's change in demeanor.

"Melvin and I have discussed this since Benny was born, and I just want to run the idea by you. You can take it to Bryan if you want to, but I wouldn't feel comfortable talking to him about it. Melvin doesn't think either of you will go for it, but if you do, he's willing to go along."

"My God, Sharon," Nicole said as she watched her get up and close the office door. "What are you talking about? Is something wrong?"

"No," Sharon said. "Not really. I just see how you interact with my sons and babies like this one, and I can't help but want you to have your own. You would be such a wonderful mother."

"I want to have my own too, Sharon, but if God doesn't perform some kind of miracle, I won't. It's been hard, but I'm coming to accept that there's a great possibility that Bryan and I will never have our own children. I'm just grateful that the knowledge of that came to light before we got married and that it hasn't affected our marriage."

"I know." Sharon smiled. "That's a blessing. You have a wonderful husband."

"I know."

"I'm glad you're coming to terms with this, Nicole, but I was thinking that maybe you don't have to. Maybe there's an option that you haven't looked into yet."

"Adoption?" Nicole cut her off. "I've thought about that. I even brought it up to Bryan a couple of years ago. He said that we could discuss it again if it ever became a burning issue with either of us, but he didn't want me considering it because I thought he wanted it. Once I found out that he wasn't feeling a void, I backed away. I was willing to wait and see if it happened naturally."

"But it hasn't," Sharon said.

"You don't have to tell me that, Sharon. I know it hasn't."

"But maybe there's another way, adoption aside."

"What do you mean?"

"Artificial insemination."

"There's no problem with Bryan's sperm, but my eggs won't take fertilization. I don't ovulate properly. The doctor spoke to me about in vitro fertilization, but even with that she said the probability of me getting pregnant is very slim."

"But the probability of me getting pregnant," Sharon said, "is close to 100 percent. Melvin and I bat a thousand every time I don't use birth control."

"What are you suggesting?"

"I'm suggesting that you and Bryan allow the doctors to impregnate me with his sperm, and I'll carry the baby for you. I could be a surrogate mother."

"Sharon . . ."

"All you guys would have to pay are the doctor and hospital bills, and you know Melvin and I can be trusted. We wouldn't change our minds and want to keep the child. This would be *your* baby. Totally *yours*. Oh, God, Nicole, please don't cry," Sharon said as her friend burst into tears. "I'm sorry. I didn't mean any harm. I just want you to have a baby so badly because I know it's what you want. I should have listened to Melvin and kept this to myself, but I just thought that maybe we could help you make this one wish come true. I'm sorry, Nicole. I'm sorry."

"No, no," Nicole said through her tears. "I'm not mad. I just love you so much for this. It's just so sweet. I never expected this from you."

"You're not mad?"

"No," Nicole said as she cradled the sleeping baby close to her chest and wiped her tears with the tissue that Sharon handed her.

"Promise?"

"Oh, girl, come here." Nicole laughed as she hugged her friend close, being careful of the child in her arms.

"So, you want to give this a try?" Sharon asked as she released her.

"No." Nicole sighed as she wiped her lingering tears. "Thank you so much for the offer. I can't tell you how much I appreciate your selflessness, and maybe it's my own pride and stupidity, but I want to know the joy of carrying Bryan's baby myself."

"That's not stupid," Sharon assured her. "That's totally understandable. I'm just glad you're not angry."

"Not a chance." Nicole smiled. "Bryan's going to flip when I tell him this."

"Maybe you shouldn't, I don't want to risk him getting upset."

"Are you kidding?" Nicole laughed. "Bryan already thinks you're the best friend a girl can have. This will just floor him."

"Really?"

"Yes, really."

"Well, since I couldn't tempt you with breakfast, can I at least treat you to lunch?"

"You didn't offer to take me to breakfast."

"I offered you my fertile eggs, and you turned them down," Sharon explained. "Get it? Breakfast? Eggs?"

"Oh, that is so lame."

"It's funny, and you know it."

"Okay, it's funny. But it's still lame."

"Let me take little Charlene here back to the baby room and check on the progress of the children's lunch. I'll be right back," Sharon said as she took the baby from Nicole.

"Thanks, Sharon," Nicole said as she watched her disappear from the office.

Nicole walked around the desk and filed away some records that she had pulled earlier in the day when checking the children in. She could hear the sounds of the teachers saying grace with the different classes as she picked up the telephone and dialed.

"Walker's Bonding," Carol Adams, Bryan's secretary, answered.

"Good afternoon, Carol."

"Well, good afternoon to you too, Mrs. Walker," she said. Carol was a delightful Haitian woman in her mid-fifties. "Haven't spoken to you in a while."

"I know. How's business?"

"Oh, it's skipping along as usual," she answered in her heavy accent. "Like Mr. Walker says, dere's always somebody somewhere needing to get out of jail."

"I suppose." Nicole laughed. "Is Bryan there?"

"No, ma'am," she said. "Mr. Gibbs came by a while ago and de two of them left together. I tink dey went to lunch."

"Oh, good. Okay. I'll just speak with him later."

"No message?"

"No. I may call him back later, but you don't even have to mention that I called. I didn't want anything important."

"Okay, den. It was nice to hear from you."

"Nice talking to you, too, Carol," Nicole said as Sharon joined her in the office. "You have a nice day."

"Same to you, Mrs. Walker. Good-bye."

"Bye."

"Bryan's secretary?" Sharon asked.

"Yeah. I was going to chat with him for a second, but he wasn't in. Carol said that he and Melvin went to lunch together."

"Maybe we'll run into them," Sharon suggested as the two of them headed toward the exit door.

"Thanks for inviting me to lunch," Melvin said as he finished off his second glass of sweetened tea.

"Always a pleasure." Bryan smiled. "I think it was my turn anyway. You treated last time."

"Well, you know it's very seldom that the two of us can get away to take a lunch break on the same day."

"I know. I started to call Nicole to see if she wanted to get together, but the two of us can always get away. You and I, on the other hand, rarely can."

"It's mostly my fault," Melvin said. "I'm the one who's always at some construction site somewhere. I'm not complaining, though. I thank God for the work. Sometimes it just seems never-ending."

"Speaking of never-ending work," Bryan said, "I have two counseling sessions tonight, and I need to call Nicole before the end of the work day and let her know."

"Did they suddenly come up?"

"Actually, the 7:00 session has been scheduled for the past two weeks. The 8:30 one got scheduled at 10:00 this morning. It's an emergency intervention that Mother Peek wants me to have with her grandson."

"Trouble?"

"That's my assumption, but I don't know the details yet."

"You deserved that award, man. You are really good. The people seem to seek you out when it comes to trouble with their teenaged relatives. Especially the boys."

"I know. I guess my past prepared me for it."

"Yeah, and since Pastor Gaines talked about your past at the service a couple of weeks ago, I guess everybody understands now why you're so good at what you do."

"I suppose," Bryan agreed.

"How do you do it?" Melvin asked. "I mean, I know you won't discuss details of any of your sessions with anyone other than Pastor Gaines, and I respect that. But tell me how you get those rebellious kids to open up and talk to you. Is it hard?"

"My sessions are an hour long," Bryan said. "There's hardly ever enough time in one session to get to the root of the problem, but generally within that hour I can get even the most stubborn kid to loosen up."

"But how? I know you don't threaten them, but do

you like tell them horror stories of how they'll end up in jail or dead? What do you do to shake them up?"

"Naw, man." Bryan shook his head. "They already know the dismal end their lifestyles can lead to. In most cases, they don't think they'll ever get caught or killed, and if they do, they don't care. There's always a deeper reason why these kids act out like they do. Most times, they're not bad guys; they're just misguided and easily influenced by other people.

"Like I said before," he continued, "we have a whole hour together without interruption. I don't let them out before that hour is up, so it's up to them. We can stand there and stare at one another silently for sixty minutes, or they can answer my questions. They always opt to answer. My stare can get intense. It's hard to look into these eyes that my father gave me for very long. They become intimidating after a while."

"So they just give up on being stubborn after a while?"

"I don't like to call it giving up," Bryan explained further. "I call it giving in. Not necessarily to me, but to the cause. They know that all I want for them is what is best, and most times they really do want to be helped. They don't really want to be troublemakers; they just don't know any other way to express themselves and the anger or hurt that they feel inside. With some of them, I'll do something as simple as ask a question and toss them a football. Every time I ask a question that they feel comfortable answering, they catch the ball and answer."

"And if they don't feel comfortable?"

"Then they let the ball hit the floor and kick it back to me."

"That works?"

"Perhaps not all in one session, but by the time our scheduled sessions are ending, we're tossing the ball back and forth and even laughing about some of the questions and answers."

"So you use different methods with different kids."

"Exactly. No two methods are exactly the same, but there is one thing I never do in any of the sessions."

"What's that?"

"I never let them answer a question with a question. When I ask a question and if they catch the ball or move the king on the chessboard or hit the punching bag, they have to answer. That's the rule, and I explain it ahead of time. If they don't want to answer the question, they don't make a move. But I never let them answer the question with a question. It never accomplishes anything, and it gives them a feeling of control in a situation of which they are not and should not feel in charge."

"Sounds like a good rule."

"Hey." Bryan shrugged. "It works. When I found that it worked and worked almost every time, I figured it was a good rule to stick with."

"Okay," Melvin began. "How about you and I have a heart-to-heart mini-counseling session right now?"

"The two of us?"

"Nothing official. Just an honest talk between brothers," Melvin said.

"Okay." Bryan leaned forward on both elbows. "I'm all ears."

"Well, it's not me, necessarily. It's you. I want to turn the tables. I need you to open up to me about something."

"Oh," Bryan said. "Okay. What about?"

"You and Nicole."

"What about us?"

"Well, the two of you seem to have it so together all the time. You seem like the perfect pair, and frankly I hope so, because Sharon and I pat ourselves on the back all the time for introducing the two of you."

"I never knew love could be so deep and so beautiful until I met Nicole."

"That's good to hear." Melvin smiled broadly. "Sharon and I will continue our back-patting with renewed purpose."

"As well you should," Bryan said as he drank a sip of water.

"Be honest with me, man. You never talk about this, but does it ever bother you that the two of you can't have children?"

"Where did that come from?"

"No, no." Melvin held up his hand. "See, I'm asking the questions. You can't come back with a question. That's the rule, and you're the one who invented it. Does it ever bother you that you can't have children?" he repeated.

"That's good." Bryan smiled.

"I know," Melvin agreed. "I should join the Counseling Ministry."

"I wouldn't go that far," Bryan said, "but that was good."

"So," Melvin said as Bryan caught the crumpled napkin that he tossed across the table. "Does it?"

"Honestly," Bryan began, "no, it doesn't *bother* me that we can't have children. Do I want to have children with Nicole? Absolutely. I'd love to have babies with her, but only with her. I don't really want to go through adoption, but I will if she insists, and I'll love that child as my own, but it's not my preference. Would I be perfectly happy living a life with her without children? Yes, I would.

"When I married Nicole, I knew the possibility of us having children was remote. All of my adult life I've wanted children. I think that because of the lack of love I got from my father, I wanted children to love and prove myself to be different than him. But when I met her, she became more than enough to satisfy my need to love and be loved."

"That's deep, man. You really do have something special with her."

"Yes, I do."

"So you wouldn't consider anything artificial or surgical in order to conceive?"

"Frankly, Melvin, I'd probably try anything within reason that Nicole wanted to try if it would make her happy, but no, it wouldn't be my choice. We both want a child, but if it doesn't happen naturally, she's certainly enough for me, and I'd like to think that I'm enough for her and that she wouldn't take it to that level."

"Enough said," Melvin said as he caught the napkin that Bryan tossed back to him.

"Will that be all for you, or can I get you something else?" the waitress asked as she approached their table.

"That will be it, Becky," Bryan said as he handed her the bill and enough cash to cover it and her tip. "Thank you."

"Thank *you.*" She smiled as she walked away.

"How is it," Melvin said as they both stood to leave, "that we eat at the same restaurants, and your stomach looks like that and mine looks like this?" He patted his stomach, which was beginning to hang over his belt.

"Because I just ate a turkey sandwich on wheat with no mayo and a side of fresh baby carrots and fresh fruit," Bryan explained as they walked toward the door. "You, on the other hand, just ate two pieces of fried chicken, home-style mashed potatoes, macaroni and cheese, and a biscuit with enough butter to swim in."

"Well, let's not forget the babies," Melvin pointed out.

"The babies?"

"Yeah," Melvin said, "Mike and Benny."

"What about them?"

"Well, you know I wasn't like this before I had Benny."

"Oh, you're kidding," Bryan said as he burst into laughter.

"No, really. The weight really does get harder to lose after every baby," he said as Bryan continued to laugh.

CHAPTER FOUR

Bryan was satisfied with his counseling sessions for the evening. He felt that he had made headway even with young Todd Peek. His problem wasn't totally solved by any definition, but using the dartboard and getting Todd to agree to answer a question whenever Bryan hit a bull's-eye worked perfectly. Poor Todd didn't have a clue that Bryan was an expert when it came to throwing darts.

"All done for the night?"

"Uncle Charles," Bryan said as his uncle's voice startled him.

"I'm sorry, Bryan. I didn't mean to alarm you."

"I was kind of deep in thought at the moment, that's all. Come on in."

"I was just stopping by to see if everything was okay," Pastor Gaines said. "You know I always like to stop by, especially after an emergency intervention to see if you need any backup."

"Please, sit down." Bryan smiled as he motioned toward a chair across from his desk. "You know I can always use your wisdom."

"There's no knowledge like the knowledge that comes with experience, son. That's one you have a slight upper hand on."

"Todd reminds me so much of myself," Bryan said. "He has so much potential in him, but he feels misplaced and unloved. He's playing tough, but inside he just wants to feel loved."

"Perhaps living with his grandmother is a step in the right direction," Pastor Gaines suggested.

"Oh, it's definitely a step in the right direction, but he hasn't come to that realization yet. All he knows is that his mother sent him to live with his aunt, and now his aunt has sent him to live with his grandmother. Uncle Charles, I know what it feels like to think nobody wants you. That's all he can see right now."

"Can he see yet how blessed he is to have access to a counselor like you?"

"You know what I found out about him tonight?" Bryan asked as he smiled at his uncle's compliment. "I found out that he was originally scheduled to see Brother Lovett. He heard you speak on my history during the ceremony a couple of weeks ago, and he asked Mother Peek to switch him over to me."

"He requested you?"

"Yes. That means a lot to me. He didn't tell me that. Mother Peek did. I don't think he wanted me to know. I'm sure he doesn't want me realizing that he already trusted me before he walked through my doors. I played along. We enjoyed a nice game of darts in the process."

"Have I told you lately how proud I am of you?"

"I know you are, Uncle Charles." Bryan smiled. "But

you're not nearly as proud of me as I am of you. I watch you stand in the pulpit every Sunday and teach us the Word of God. If other ministers were as dedicated and passionate as you, a lot of churches would be stronger."

"Thank you, Bryan. Maybe your counseling ministry will lead you to the pulpit one day."

"Now I do remember my negative response when you first approached me concerning what you believed was a call on my life to counsel. As it turned out, you were right, and it is a ministry that I thoroughly enjoy and thank God for. However," Bryan continued, "I think I can honestly say without a doubt that this is where my ministry ends. The pulpit is not my place."

"Perhaps you're right. Only God knows for certain."

"Well, it's late," Bryan said as he checked his watch. "My bride awaits."

"Ah, the fair Lady Nicole."

"Indeed."

"God has certainly shown you favor, Bryan."

"Yes, He has," Bryan agreed. "I'm grateful. I couldn't have asked for a better wife, who I never want to take for granted."

"That's good, son, because marriages are certainly under attack, as evidenced by how many couples I counsel on a regular basis."

"Nicole and I try to cover all of the bases in our relationship by not allowing any unforgiveness to fester or anything else to go unaddressed. Now, I *really* want to go home and hold my wife in my arms forever and never let her go. Thanks, Uncle Charles. Good night. I'll see you on Sunday, if not before."

"Good night, son."

The house was dark as he walked inside. He disarmed

the alarm and immediately armed it again once he closed the door behind him. The flickering of a single candle glowed from the dining room. He walked back and rechecked the door he had just closed and all the other entrance doors to be sure that they were all securely locked.

Walking slowly and quietly into the bedroom, he breathed a sigh of relief as he saw Nicole lying, resting peacefully. Getting a closer look with only the light of nearly burned-out candles that glowed from the bathroom, he noticed the gold silk gown that she wore. There was water in the tub, but the suds from the bubble bath had almost disappeared.

"You were waiting for me," he whispered with a smile as he thought of the romantic atmosphere that she had set for him.

He knelt silently by her side of the bed and gently held her hand as he prayed softly.

"Dear God, thank You for my many blessings, and forgive me if I don't thank You as often as I should. I know that You know that I am grateful and I cherish the home, the life, and the love that You have given me, but I want to tell You anyway. Help me to keep a watchful eye, a listening, ear and a prayerful heart always. Please give us the strength to stand and fight together. These things I ask in Your name, amen."

"Nicole," he called softly. She didn't respond, nor did she stir from her position.

He kissed her forehead, and she sat up to greet him and asked if anything was wrong.

"How did your sessions go tonight?"

"The sessions went well, I think. I had a talk with Uncle Charles tonight, and I guess the things we discussed were still on my mind," he said as he stood to re-

50

move his shirt and tie.

"Go on," Nicole urged as he sat on the side of the bed and removed his shoes before resting his face in his hands.

"The subject of our marriage came up, and I told him about the wonderful life you and I share together and how much I love you."

"I love you too, sweetie." Nicole smiled.

"I know you do, baby. There's no doubt in my mind that you love me, and I know you don't doubt my love for you."

"So, what was said that made you concerned?"

"Uncle Charles reminded me of the favor God has shown me and encouraged me to be prayerful."

"That's good, honey," Nicole said. "I'm glad we don't take the serenity of our marriage for granted."

"I know," Bryan said as he took her hand in his. "I can't explain the feeling that overcame me as I walked in the house. I thought about my conversation with Uncle Charles the entire ride home. I saw you lying here and looking beautiful in this gown, and I saw the candles and the water in the bathtub and realized that you had been planning a special evening with me. I'd hate to think that I take our happiness for granted, yet I can't imagine anything happening that could possibly come between us."

"Neither can I," Nicole admitted.

"Is there anything that could possibly tear you away from me?" Bryan asked, as he looked Nicole directly in the eyes. "Is there anything in the world that could possibly be stronger than your love for me?"

"Bryan, I can honestly say that I can't think of anything that could change my love for you. There are things that you could do that could make me unhappy enough to leave, but I think I'd still love you."

"What would make you unhappy enough to leave me?"

51

"Infidelity . . ."

"That would never happen. I could never be unfaithful to you. I love you too much, and the price would be too high to pay."

"I know you wouldn't, baby."

"What else?"

"Abuse."

"I'd never lay a hand on you. I'd never hurt you physically, spiritually, emotionally, or verbally."

"I know."

"What else?"

"I don't know," Nicole said. "I can't think of another reason that I'd leave, and I really can't think of any reason that I'd lose my love for you."

"Sweetheart, if you leave me it would be just like losing your love for me in my eyes. Every day of my life, I need to be able to see, hear, and touch you. I can't do that if you're not with me."

"I know, baby. You're my king. You know that. I don't know what I'd do if you changed and became someone else. I'd be devastated. I'd never want to leave you. I'd only do it if I had to."

"Then you'll never leave me, because I'll never give you a reason. I can do without a lot of things in my life. I don't need a lot of money. I don't need fame. I don't even need children, but, baby, I need you. You're not an option. Even a king is nothing without his queen."

"Thank you, Bryan." Nicole smiled as she touched his face and kissed his lips. "It's funny you should mention children," she continued after a brief silence. "Sharon and I talked about that same subject at work this afternoon."

"Really?" Bryan raised his eyebrows. "That's funny. Melvin and I did the same thing during lunch today. What did Sharon say?"

"What did Melvin say?" Nicole asked with curiosity.

"You first," Bryan insisted.

"The shock nearly floored me," Nicole said. "She made an offer that was actually incredible."

"She offered to give us one of the boys?" Bryan asked in surprise.

"No." Nicole laughed. "Not quite that incredible. But get this. She offered to carry a child for us."

"Say what?"

"Yes. She said that since it could possibly be unsuccessful for me to be pregnant, she would donate the egg and carry the baby and give him or her to us after giving birth."

"She said that? She was serious?"

"Yes. She and Melvin had apparently discussed it, and he agreed, but told her that he didn't think we'd go for it."

"So that's what he was hinting toward today when he asked me if I'd go for anything artificial."

"What did you tell him?" Nicole asked.

"I told him that I'd only do it if you insisted and it made you happy. Artificial insemination isn't my choice or my desire, and I told him that. I'd only do something like that for you."

"You'd do it for me?" Nicole asked.

"Yes," he answered after a moment of hesitation. "Why? Did you tell Sharon that you wanted to try that?"

"No," she said to Bryan's obvious relief. "I thanked her because I think the offer was incredibly selfless."

"I agree. Sharon is some kind of friend."

"I told her you'd say that if I told you about this. She was worried that you'd be angry."

"Not at all. How could I be angered by such a selfless offer?"

53

"That's what I told her."

"However," Bryan said, "I sure am glad that you turned it down. Don't get me wrong—a child would be wonderful but only if we make it together. If we're unable to conceive the old-fashioned way, then I'd be satisfied to think that it wasn't God's will for us to have children."

"You're one of a kind, you know that?" Nicole said as she wrapped her arms around him and pulled him close.

"I'm sorry I missed our bubble bath," Bryan said.

"Me too," Nicole said as she looked toward the bathroom. "I ran the water at 10:00. It was steaming at the time. I figured you'd be home by 10:30 at the latest, with your last session ending at 9:30. That would give it thirty minutes to cool down a little."

"My session with Todd ran a little late. I ended up finishing with him around 10:15, but stayed longer talking with Uncle Charles."

"I can run you some fresh water if you like," Nicole offered.

"No, I'll just shower."

"Are you hungry?"

"Starved." Bryan laughed as he rubbed his stomach and stood up. "It's so late now, though. I'll probably just grab a sandwich and some juice or something. Don't worry yourself. Just go on back to sleep. I'll take care of it."

The hot shower did little to clear Bryan's head, but it felt good. He couldn't help but wonder why this situation weighed so heavily on his heart. Surely he couldn't have been so naive to believe that he and Nicole would never face problems in their marriage. After all, they'd faced them before.

There was the time when he donated her old wooden jewelry box to a secondhand store and bought her a brand-new jewelry box with a dancing ballerina that sprang into motion behind lovely music whenever the lid was lifted. He proudly presented her with it when she came home from work one day less than a year into their marriage. She loved the box until she found out that he had gotten rid of the old one. He'd never forget the look of horror on her face.

The old jewelry box was just about the only gift her father had ever given her. He'd made it himself and given it to her for Christmas when she was ten years old. It was old, but she cherished it and planned one day to varnish it and give it to her daughter, if she ever had one. "How could you give it away as though it had no value?" she'd asked.

He had spent two days getting the box back, which he had thought was junk. Someone had already purchased the box by the time he got back to the store. With the help of the reluctant store manager, to whom he eventually had to pay $100 to get him to pull the cash receipt and give him the buyer's address, he finally located the buyer. If that weren't enough, the buyer charged him another $50 to get it back. According to the receipt, the box had been purchased from the shop for $5.00.

The lesson came with a cost, but the smile on Nicole's face when he returned it to her was more than enough to compensate for the payout.

They had experienced other disagreements in their five-year marriage, but nothing that even came close to tearing them apart. They had never slept in different beds or stormed out of the house during an argument or even slammed doors. Every disagreement had always been settled before they went to bed at night.

CHAPTER FIVE

As the days and weeks passed, life returned to normal in the Walker household. Pastor Gaines's words were never forgotten, but neither Bryan nor Nicole chose to dwell on the likelihood of trouble in their marriage.

Bryan was making headway in his sessions with Todd, but they still had some things to work through together. His grandmother reported to Bryan that Todd had enrolled back in school after his third session with him. Session four was to be their final one.

"How does it feel to be back in school?" Bryan asked with his foot propped on the stool beside his desk.

"It's okay." Todd shrugged.

"Do you like your teachers?"

"What's there to like? They're teachers. I guess they're okay. I can't really say that I like them, but they're okay."

"Other kids treating you all right?" Bryan asked the question he really wanted to know the answer to. "I mean the guys that you used to hang out with. Are they pressuring you in any way?"

"Naaa. Not really. They don't really have nothing to do with me anymore. I've been what you old folks call blackballed."

"Old folks?" Bryan laughed.

"I don't mean that in a bad way. At least not where you're concerned, Brother Walker. You're still cool. That's the way I want to be when I get old."

"Thanks." Bryan laughed again. "I think," he continued. "So, the boys that used to be your friends don't bother you; they just don't acknowledge you anymore. Is that what you're saying?"

"Uh-huh." Todd nodded.

"How does that make you feel?"

"How do you think it makes me feel?"

"That's a question. Remember the rule?"

"Yeah."

"How does the rejection from your former crowd make you feel?"

"I have to be honest, Brother Walker. Sometimes it makes me want to apologize to them for leaving the group."

"But you do realize that you are better off not being a part of them, right?"

"Yeah, I know, but it's hard, man. I mean, I miss my friends. You know. People that I can hang out with."

"Are there no students at the school who stay out of trouble that you can become friends with?"

"Most of them remember me as a troublemaker and don't trust me to do no better, so they stay away from me. I guess the teachers like you better when the kids you hang out with have never given them problems and stuff."

"Several of the kids who attend the church here go to your school, don't they?"

"I go to a big school. They probably do go there, but I don't see much of them. I see a couple every now and then. This is a big church. I don't know the kids that go here all that well."

"Are you telling me that you have no friends now?"

"I have a couple of girlfriends, but no close hang-out buddies."

"A *couple* of girlfriends?" Bryan repeated slowly. "Are you talking girlfriends as in girls who are your friends or girlfriends as in girls that you are dating?"

"Well, I ain't really dating them 'cause Grandma won't let me, but they're my girls. So, yeah, they're my girls that I kick it with."

"Why do you need more than one?"

"All I have is time. Since I don't have no buddies, I have all this free time, and girls still like me whether I'm a part of the in-crowd or not."

"It's amazing how much you think like I did when I was your age." Bryan smiled as he shook his head slowly. "Todd," he continued, "our goal here is to convince you to see your potential. There is so much greatness and promise inside of you. You told me a couple of weeks ago that you loved baseball and once dreamed of being the next Hank Aaron. Do you still have that dream?"

"Yeah, but what does that have to do with girls? Ballplayers can get girls easy."

"Remember in our first meeting when I talked to you about the importance of Christ in your life?"

"Yeah."

"Christ should be our foundation in all that we do. Whatever we strive to become should begin with a strong belief and faith in Christ. I want you to be a good student, but I want you to be that with Christ. If you want to play professional ball, do it. But do it with a deep abiding love for Jesus. Only what we do for Christ is going to last, Todd.

"Getting you to break away from the crowd that kept you in trouble was only a part of what I had hoped we could accomplish. Replacing the guys with a bunch of girls will just lead you to a whole new set of problems. Friends of either sex can't fill the emptiness that you are experiencing. You're feeling empty because you need Christ."

"Now you sound like Grandma," Todd said. "I understand that I need to accept Jesus in order to get to heaven, but I'm not ready to do that right now. I want to have some fun first. Once I get all caught up in church and stuff, I can't have any more fun. Not only will the guys not like me, but the girls won't either. I don't want to be a nerd right now. Let me get out of school first. Then I'll do it."

"Whoever told you that you can't be a Christian and have fun? Who said girls don't like Christian guys?"

"They don't. Not the pretty girls, anyway."

"Do you think Sister Walker is pretty?" Bryan asked.

"Man, you are good," Todd said with a short laugh after a moment of silence. "Does the church pay you for these sessions? They should. Do they?"

"That's a question," Bryan said, trying not to show the delight he felt at Todd's compliment.

"Everybody thinks Sister Walker is pretty," Todd said, almost shyly. "She's the bomb, but like I said earlier, you're a cool guy. I guess that's why she likes you."

"When I was your age," Bryan said with a smile, "I was convinced by my crew that the more girlfriends I had, the more of a man I was. I've had more girlfriends than I can count. Honestly, most of them meant little or nothing to me. They were just trophies to prove what a man I was. Being promiscuous like that can come back to haunt you. Then you'll have added troubles."

"I ain't trying to prove to nobody that I'm a man." Todd shrugged. "I ain't got to. I *am* a man and the honeys know it. That's why they like me."

"Todd, you're barely fifteen years old. You're not a man in any sense of the word."

"Yes, I am," he quickly defended. "Grandma was in that house all by herself before I moved in. Now, I'm the man of the house. Ain't no other man there."

"Do you have a job, Todd?"

"No, but . . ."

"Do you pay any of your grandmother's bills?"

"What for?"

"That was a question, not an answer."

"Okay, no. But it's her house. She was there before I got there."

"Do you use the electricity?"

"Yeah, but . . ."

"The water?"

"Yeah."

"The telephone?"

"Uh-huh."

"Are you eating the food?"

"Yeah."

"Do you offer to help buy groceries?"

"Okay." Todd threw up his arms. "I get your point. But she's got to feel safer with me in the house with her. That's got to count for something."

"Todd, before a couple of weeks ago you were never at home. When you moved in with your grandmother, you didn't bring her a sense of security. You were worrying her half to death. She sat up all night wondering where you were and praying that you weren't getting into any trouble or being locked up. That's not what real men do, son."

"I don't mean to worry her." Todd's voice broke.

"I know you don't, Todd. But that's what you're doing when you get involved with the wrong crowd and in the wrong activities, whether it is with other boys or girls that you call girlfriends."

"Well, what am I supposed to do?" he asked as tears began streaming from his eyes. "I know that's a question, but I need to know. What am I supposed to do? Sit around the house with Grandma and watch the cooking channel or news or preaching shows all day? I'm sorry, Bryan, I mean, Brother Walker . . ."

"Bryan is fine," Bryan told him as he handed him one of his handkerchiefs.

"I'm sorry," he repeated as he continued, "but if that's what being saved is all about, I know I'm not ready. I can't just sit around the house during the day and go to church on Sundays. I don't mean to be a problem. I know nobody don't want me, but them passing me around like a hand-me-down pair of shoes ain't going to make me no better. First it was Mama giving me to Aunt Felicia. Then she didn't want me, so she gave me back to Mama, who gave me to Grandma. I'm just waiting to see who Grandma is going to give me to. We're running out of family members. I guess next I'll be put in some juvenile home. I know it's coming. I'm just waiting to see."

"Todd," Bryan said once Todd seemed to be finished speaking, "your grandmother isn't giving up on you that easily. She loves you. I'm sure your mother and your aunt love you too. They just didn't have a clue as to where your head was or what to do about your behavior."

"They didn't try too hard either," Todd mumbled as

he wiped his face. "All I ever heard was 'You ain't going to be no good. You're just like your sorry daddy.' There must have been something good about him," he concluded. "The women liked him, and she was one of them. She had me, didn't she?"

"You know," Bryan leaned forward, "I see so much of me in you, Todd. It's almost frightening, yet it lets me know that there is so much hope for you. Sometimes I have sessions with some of the guys here and I can feel where they're coming from with their problems, but I can't say that I've experienced what they have. You, on the other hand, are *just* like I was at your age. I can honestly say that I know what you're feeling.

"I felt the same way when my mama passed me to Pastor Gaines. I didn't want to come and live with my uncle. I didn't even know him all that well. I *hated* home, I hated school, I hated my daddy, and quite frankly, I hated my mama. I hated the world, Todd, because I felt like everybody owed me something, but nobody was paying up. Like your father, my father abandoned me. I haven't seen him since I was younger than you are. The part that hurt me the most is that I knew that there were times that he was right there in the same state and probably the same city with me, but he never stopped by.

"In my opinion, everybody was out to hurt me, so I set out to hurt everybody right back. I quit school just because I knew my mother wanted me to go. I stayed out in the streets and hung out with the wrong people because, as far as I was concerned, she didn't want me around. The girls made me feel like a man. My daddy used to always brag about how many girls he had. I set out to be just like him. I too was always reminded of how much I looked like my daddy and how I was going to turn out like my daddy.

"I felt like my whole family was screwed up. I grew up in the house with my mama all alone. I had no siblings there with me, but my daddy talked about how I had at least six brothers and sisters scattered here and there. *That* was one thing about my daddy that I never set out to accomplish. I messed around and had my share of girls and women, but having babies was never on my agenda.

"The older I got, the worse I got. I started smoking and even started committing crimes. When I got picked up for breaking and entering, it was the last straw. That's when I ended up here with Uncle Charles and Aunt Maggie. Just like you were doing with Mother Peek, I was trying to wear them down. I was just sitting back, waiting for the day when they'd send me back to Mama or somewhere else. Man, was I wrong. It was hard, but they stuck with me. I hated them, but they loved me regardless.

"I got back in school. It wasn't optional with Uncle Charles. He'd run late for work every morning because he refused to trust me to catch the school bus. I didn't deserve his trust. I had abused it way too often. He'd take me to school and walk me to my classroom. When he didn't have to work, sometimes he'd stay at school all day. It was tough, but after a while I got tired of being picked on by the other kids because my uncle was always at the school checking to see if I actually went and stayed all day.

"I straightened up so he'd trust me to be where I was supposed to. He embarrassed me into responsibility. After a while, going to school wasn't good enough. I had to make good grades. I figured if I didn't, he was probably going to embarrass me somehow, so I studied and made good grades. Soon, I built a sense of pride in myself for making those grades. I was proving everybody wrong who ever said I couldn't do it.

"Then after high school there was college. That brought on a whole new set of problems. I went away to college. When I moved from Jacksonville to Tallahassee, I was out from under the watchful eye of Uncle Charles, but he had proven to me by then that he cared. When I left for school, he told me that he believed in me and that he was praying for me and that he loved me. That meant everything to me.

"I still got into stuff that was wrong, but every time I did, I felt guilty. I'd even find myself praying and asking God for forgiveness. That was new for me. God was making a change in me, and I didn't even know it. It was the beginning of a new life for me. That summer when I came back here to wait for fall quarter to begin, I gave my life to Christ.

"I went through a lot to get to this point, Todd, but now I know that I was *never* alone. Even when it felt like it back on those Chicago streets, I was never alone. God was with me all the time.

"And you know what? I didn't miss any of it. God gave me new friends. There were really good people at school all along. I just didn't see them because I was looking in all the wrong places. Sure, my old friends didn't find me fun to hang out with anymore, but they respected me. My life wasn't boring at all. I had different interests, and I pursued them.

"I said all of that to say this: You are not alone. Somebody loves you. Your grandmother loves you. I love you. Salvation isn't about taking away from your life. It's about adding to your life. You don't have to feel as though you're in prison and can't do anything when you're saved. Salvation sets you free. Nobody is trying to tell you that you can't have friends. You'll just have a different set of friends, that's all. Salvation doesn't mean girls won't like you. They will, and when you're ready and old enough, God will give you the perfect girl."

"So, I could end up with a fly honey like Sister Walker." Todd smiled slightly.

"They don't fly any higher, and honey doesn't come any sweeter," Bryan said.

"Wow," Todd said. "You really do know what I'm feeling."

"I do."

"Well," he said, "I can't make no promises right now, but I'll give it some thought. I ain't never quite heard it broke down like that before. You know what I'm saying? I mean, you almost make being saved sound kind of cool."

"It's the coolest."

"Can I ask a question?"

"I guess I can make an exception." Bryan smiled. "What is it?"

"How do you feel about your father now? I mean, really. You never see him. He ain't never really been there for you. How do you feel about him now after all this time?"

"It's been so many years that sometimes I forget I have one," Bryan admitted. "I can honestly say that I no longer hate him, but I can't say that I see him as my true father anymore. Uncle Charles has been my father in every sense of the word for about fifteen years now.

"However, I love Garrett Walker with the love of Christ. If nothing else, he's partially responsible for my being here, and I'm glad for that. I had to learn to forgive and move on. That's what I did, but it took a while, and it took Christ in my life to get me to that point."

"Do you ever want to see him again?"

"If I don't, I don't know that I'll feel any sense of genuine loss," Bryan said. "To be quite frank, I feel like I see him every time I look in the mirror. I may no longer act like my father, but I definitely look like him. From what I remember, he was a dashingly handsome man," he added with a laugh as Todd laughed with him.

"Sometimes I get the feeling that I'll run into him again," Bryan said. "I don't know how I'll react, whether I'll be overwhelmingly touched or standoffish, but that's something I'll deal with if the situation arises. The important thing is that I forgave him just like Christ forgave me."

"Like I said," Todd replied, "I can't promise you nothing, but I'll give it some serious thought."

"Good enough," Bryan said as the two stood.

"I guess I took you overtime again tonight. I know Sister Walker will be mad with me."

"No." Bryan shook his head. "Sister Walker understands. Besides, it'll be all worth it if you make the right decisions for your life."

"So this is it, huh?"

"What?" Bryan asked.

"Our last meeting."

"Officially, yes," Bryan told him. "But I'm here for you, and I want you to know that. You have my number and Mother Peek knows where I live. If you ever need to talk about anything, you get in touch with me. I mean that. It doesn't matter the hour of the day or night. I'm here."

"You're pretty cool," Todd said as Bryan pulled him in for a quick embrace.

"For an old dude?" Bryan laughed.

"Yeah." Todd laughed with him. "For an old dude."

CHAPTER SIX

O kay," Sharon said as she burst into Nicole's office at the day care with a handful of pamphlets. "I've done it. I have found the perfect vacation spot for us this year."

"You did?" Nicole brightened as she began looking through the information that her friend handed her.

For the past three years, the Walkers and the Gibbses had enjoyed summer vacations together. They generally went every June, and each year they chose somewhere that they had never been before. The first year, the girls planned a trip to Mexico. The trip was enjoyable but rushed. They could only stay four days because of the unseasonable rain that lingered. Last year, the guys planned a cruise in the Bahamas. It was nearly disastrous for Sharon, as she was four months pregnant and terribly seasick.

"Yes," Sharon answered. "We said that we didn't want to go out of Florida this year so that we could stay longer, right? Well, there it is. We can enjoy a fun-filled week in Destin, Florida, at Family Tides Resorts."

"This looks good, Sharon."

"I know, and it's reasonable. We can go and rent just one of the homes there on the beach. Just that one house right there"—Sharon pointed—"has five bedrooms and four and a half baths. It has three floors. We could all stay there and still have our own living quarters."

"Private heated pool," Nicole read aloud, "deck space, gulf views, entertainment room with TV, VCR, pool table, exercise equipment . . ."

"And the third floor has its own kitchenette and balcony," Sharon added. "On the bottom floor, there's even a spacious play room. That would make things way more comfortable for us if I have to take the kids again this year. The first year was okay, but I was pregnant with Michael so I couldn't really have fun like I wanted. Last year, the trip to the Bahamas was way too much, and with me being pregnant again and having Michael too, I really couldn't enjoy myself at all. I killed everybody else's spirit too. This year, the boys are bigger, I'm not pregnant, and we can have a really good time."

"Sounds perfect to me." Nicole placed the information back on the desk. "I'll run it by Bryan. Did Melvin like it?"

"Yeah. He said we may even like it better than Mexico. He thinks we'll be able to relax more, and since none of us has ever been there before, there'll still be enough sites to keep us curious and interested."

"I agree."

"Good. That's three votes, and if *you* like it, I know Bryan will. He just wants to keep his bride happy."

"Yeah." Nicole laughed. "He's just a sweet guy. He's so attentive, and he has such a big heart. Not just with me. He's really been taking up a lot of time with Todd lately."

"I thought his sessions were over."

"They are, but Todd comes by the house if he needs help with homework or just needs to get away from Mother Peek for a minute or two. I watched them through the kitchen window as they were having batting practice in the backyard a couple of days ago. I think he's definitely won Todd over."

"Was Melvin there too? It seems like he mentioned something like that to me the other day."

"Yeah, he was there trying to teach Michael how to hold a bat." Nicole laughed. "It was quite entertaining. No matter how he tried, Mike would just drop the bat to the ground and walk away with it dragging behind him as though he were pulling a wagon or something."

"Michael is still a month shy of being two. He isn't strong enough to hold a bat yet."

"They weren't using a real bat, silly. It was that little red plastic bat that we bought him for Christmas."

"Well," Sharon said, "I guess it's never too early to teach him. Maybe he'll be a ballplayer one day."

"I don't know, but I think Todd has real potential. He was hitting balls left and right. He had Bryan and Melvin running all over the yard."

"My husband was running?" Sharon laughed. "Oh, yeah. There is definitely some good coming out of this. I haven't seen Melvin run since the Mexico vacation when he was flying that kite on the beach. We both have set goals to slim down before Destin, which is a little more than two months away, so maybe he's getting his exercise in now."

"Maybe," Nicole said.

"Speaking of which," Sharon continued, "I'm going

to walk the track during lunch today. You want to come?"

"Not today," Nicole said. "Catch me next time. How often are you going to go?"

"I figured three times a week is good. I probably will go Mondays, Wednesdays, and Fridays."

"Good. I'll go with you Friday."

"Okay." Sharon smiled. "So then," she returned to her prior thought, "you're smiling because of the fun Bryan's been having during the day and not the fun the two of you have been having during the night," she teased.

"You are so silly." Nicole pushed her playfully. "Actually, it's one of those rare months. We haven't been able to have that kind of fun for the last couple of days."

"You're having a cycle this month?"

"Yeah. It should be ending today or tomorrow. Actually this is two in a row."

"Well, that's good," Sharon said. "At least for you, it is. I dread monthly cycles, but for you, it's a good thing."

"It's a good thing for you too, girl," Nicole reminded her. "Without it, we'd have two less students at this day care."

"Yeah," Sharon agreed, "you're right. They definitely keep me busy, but God knows I don't know what I'd do without those boys. Have you ever had two in a row before?" she asked.

"No," Nicole said. "The closest I've had to two in a row was last year, when I had one and then missed the next month, but had another the month after that. This is a first. Generally, if I have three or four a year, I'm doing well. It kind of worried me. I went to the doctor the day before yesterday on my lunch break. That's why I couldn't join you for lunch."

"You went to the doctor and didn't tell me? What did you go for?"

"Well, the bleeding was slightly heavier than normal, and just the fact that it was two in a row made me think something was wrong. I guess I went for peace of mind."

"You thought something was wrong and you didn't tell me? I can't believe you, Nicole."

"I'm sorry, Sharon, but there was no need to get you upset if I didn't have to."

"Well, you're telling me now and getting me upset, so what's the difference?"

"The difference is," Nicole explained, "that everything turned out to be okay, so I can tell you and you can know that there's nothing to be upset about."

"No, I'm still upset," Sharon said. "I mean, I'm glad nothing is wrong, but I'm upset because you waited until today to tell me. Would you have told me if something was wrong?"

"Of course, I would have."

"Are you sure?"

"Yes."

"Well, I still don't like the fact that you didn't tell me before going. Did you tell Bryan?"

"Yes, I told Bryan. He told me that nothing was wrong, but I went anyway. I know," Nicole said. "I should have told you. I'm sorry."

"It's okay, I guess," Sharon replied. "But don't let it happen again."

"Yes, Mother."

"I mean it," Sharon pointed her finger.

"Okay," Nicole said.

"So, your doctor said everything was okay?"

"Yeah. Dr. Sims said that it was actually a good thing. The last time I went to her for my regular physical six months ago, she put me on low-grade birth control pills. She said she wanted to see if they would regulate my ovulations. Until now, they didn't seem to be working. Now she thinks maybe they might be beginning to take effect."

"What does that mean?" Sharon asked.

"Well, it could mean that my chances of getting pregnant would get better, or it could mean nothing at all, basically. I just have to keep my appointments and see how it progresses."

"Is it making you anxious at all?"

"No," Nicole said, "and that's a first for me. For the past three years, I've been sweating over having a baby with Bryan. We both want one, and I know that, but for some reason, after my last talk with him and your offer to carry the baby for me, I realized that some things were more important.

"I have good friends like you and Melvin and a storybook romance with my husband. Some women have several babies and can't testify to having experienced real friendship or true love in their lives. So I'm learning to be content and enjoy the life that God has blessed me with."

"Amen to that," Sharon agreed. "So," she continued after a silent moment, "you take this information to Bryan and see what he thinks. Then you or I can make the arrangements and get things all set up."

"I'll do that," Nicole said as she slid the information in her tote bag.

"Notice I said that you and I would make the arrangements. Not the two of them. Who plans a cruise when one of the participants is four months pregnant? Men!" she concluded with a disgusted look on her face.

"I know." Nicole sighed with a smile. "What would

we ever do without them?"

"Oh, Lord." Sharon waved her wrist as she walked from the room. "I forgot who I was talking to."

Nicole laughed as she picked up the ringing telephone.

"Heaven's Angels. How may I help you?"

"Well, hello, heaven's angel," Bryan said. "How are you?"

"Hey, sweetie." Nicole smiled. "I'm okay. How are you?"

"I'm fine. I left the house this morning without being able to chat with you since I left so early. Are you feeling better today?"

"Nicole, . . ." Sharon burst into the office before noticing that she was on the phone. "Oh, never mind," she said as she noted the glow on her friend's face. "Tell Bryan I said hello," she said as she disappeared once more.

"Was that Sharon?" Bryan asked.

"Yeah." Nicole laughed. "She says hello. She's crazy."

"That she is," he agreed. "So, you never answered my question. Is today a better day for you than yesterday?"

"Yeah," Nicole said. "It's really a good day now that I've heard from you."

"Oh yeah?" Bryan beamed. "What do you say about us making it a great day?" he offered in a flirtatious tone.

"Bryan, what do you have in mind?" Nicole laughed.

"I'm talking about lunch."

"Right," she said.

"I can pick you up in ten minutes."

"I'll be waiting."

"Bye," he said.

Nicole was still laughing as she hung up the phone. Sharon reentered with now nine-month-old Benjamin in her arms.

"Is the coast clear?" she asked.

"Yes," Nicole said. "Hi, Benny Bear," she said in her baby voice as Benjamin smiled.

"I decided to take him with me to the tracks. Greta just finished feeding him in the infant room, so I won't have to worry about him getting cranky during my exercise routine."

"It's such a nice day out today, too," Nicole added. "He'll enjoy the sunshine. He'll probably fall asleep in the stroller, especially if he has just eaten."

"Too bad he can't walk too." Sharon laughed. "He needs to get rid of some of this weight."

"He is a big one," Nicole agreed as she gently pinched his thigh.

"Say, 'I'm just gonna be beefy like my daddy,'" Sharon said as she kissed him.

"He certainly looks just like him." Nicole laughed. "You all have one apiece. Michael looks like you and Benjamin looks like Melvin."

"It must be true," Sharon said. "Everybody says it."

"Oh, it's true," Nicole reiterated.

"So, are you just going to stay here for lunch and finish up that paperwork that the state sent?"

"No. Actually, Bryan just invited me to lunch. He should be here any minute."

"Where are you going?"

"He didn't say."

"Hello, lovely ladies," Bryan said as he walked in on the friends.

"Hello," Sharon said as he kissed her on the cheek.

"Okay, what did I just miss?" he asked as he looked

suspiciously at the two of them before walking over to hug his wife.

"Nothing." Sharon laughed. "You two enjoy your meal and think of me and my lunch that consists of a tuna sandwich, an apple, and water as you stuff your little skinny faces with delicious greasy stuff."

"We will," Nicole said as Sharon threw her a grimace.

"Don't walk too long out in this hot sun," Bryan said.

"I don't plan to," Sharon said. "But if pushing Benny doesn't get the weight off of me fast, I don't know what else will."

"Bye." Bryan and Nicole waved as she drove away.

Seeing that Bryan had the top down on his Chrysler convertible, Nicole pulled her braids back in a ponytail. They drove the short distance to Bennigan's. The restaurant served delicious seafood cuisine but, as usual, was crowded during the lunch hour.

"Do we have a reservation?"

"No," Bryan said, "but there's that manager who likes you. We'll get a seat."

"What makes you think that?" Nicole asked.

"Hello there, Mr. and Mrs. Walker." The manager met them as they walked in. "I haven't seen the two of you in a while."

"Hi." They shook his hand.

"Lunch for two today?" he asked.

"Yes," Bryan said. "Nicole here was just talking the other day about how long it had been since we'd been here."

"Well, you do offer the best food and the best service." Nicole smiled back as she kicked Bryan's ankle slightly.

"You all look crowded here this afternoon," Bryan said. "I guess we chose a bad day not to make a reservation."

"Oh, don't you worry," he said as he scanned the crowd quickly. "I'm sure I have something for you. I'll be back in a minute," he said as he walked briskly away.

"You are so bad." Nicole laughed.

"Well, you did mention this restaurant a couple of weeks ago—Shhh!" Bryan said as he saw the manager returning.

"If you don't mind sitting out on the patio, we have a nice table for you."

"The patio is perfect," Bryan said. "It would be a shame to let such good weather go to waste."

"I agree," he said as he led them to their table and pulled the chair out for Nicole.

"Thank you," she said.

"The pleasure is mine," he said as he handed them the menus. "Your server will be here shortly."

"Thank you," Bryan said. "You're the man, DeWayne," he remarked as the manager walked away with a satisfied smile.

The service at Bennigan's was always prompt and thorough. Within a few minutes of being seated, they had placed their orders with the waiter and had been served.

"So how are things at the center today?" Bryan asked as he cracked open a crab leg.

"It's been good. Business is good."

"That's a blessing," he said.

"I know," Nicole agreed. "How's Carol and the bonding business today?"

"Carol is fine, and of course, there's always somebody needing to get out of jail, so the business is good, too," he said.

"That's good. Carol's a good secretary, isn't she?"

"Yes, she is, and she thinks you're," he said as he switched to an imitated Haitian accent, "de prettiest ting she's ever seen."

"Did she say that?" Nicole smiled.

"Yes, she did."

"See, I knew I liked her."

"I'm going to miss her next week. She goes on vacation."

"So what are you going to do in her absence?"

"Get this," he said. "I'm going to let Todd fill in for her."

"Todd?" Nicole asked in surprise. "Fill in for Carol?"

"Yeah." Bryan nodded. "He'll just be answering the telephone and taking messages, mostly," he explained. "He told me that he can type, but that remains to be seen."

"So you've told him already."

"Yes. I told him earlier today. I was really just sort of kidding, but he says he wants to do it, and Mother Peek gave her okay."

"That's nice of you to let him do that, but what about school?"

"Oh. Next week is spring break. He'll be out for the week. Mother Peek thought this would be a great way to give him something to do, and Todd thinks it's a great way to get him out of the house for much of the day. He and his grandmother are getting along fine now. I think he just gets his fill of being around an older woman all day long."

"So he thinks the two of you are about the same age? Does he know you're thirty-one years old?" Nicole laughed.

"Oh, yeah. He knows how old I am. Actually, he thinks I'm old, but he also thinks I'm cool, so I guess that's the only thing that sets me apart from his seventy-year-old grandmother. Not that she's thirty-nine years my senior, but that I'm cool and she's not."

"I see." Nicole laughed again. "Oh." She sobered quickly. "Speaking of vacations, look at these brochures that Sharon gave me today."

"Destin, Florida?" he said as he wiped his hands on his napkin and looked over the information that she pulled from her purse.

"Yes. What do you think?"

"A house almost right there on the beach," he remarked as he read the information. "This is a big, nice house. We only need one of these, right?"

"Yeah," Nicole said as she continued eating her salmon salad. "It has five bedrooms and four and a half baths."

"Are they bringing the kids along?"

"I think so."

"Prices look reasonable, especially being split between the two families," he continued thinking aloud. "The beach is beautiful too."

"I know."

"Is it booked already?"

"No. We were waiting for your opinion. You're the last to see the information."

"Oh," Bryan said. "Do you like it?"

"Yes. It looks like the perfect vacation spot. It's not out of our state, but it's a place we've never been for any length of time. It looks like a great place to go and relax, and there's plenty of space."

"Sounds like a winner to me. The time is getting close. We'd better get it booked."

"Great," she said as his cellular phone rang. "I'll tell her to set it all up."

"Excuse me, sweetheart," he said as he answered his telephone. "Hello?"

"Bryan," his uncle responded.

"Hey, Uncle Charles."

"Can you get away?"

"Uh, sure, I suppose," he said hesitantly. "What do you need?"

"You. I need you to come to my office at the church."

"What's the matter, Uncle Charles?"

"We'll talk when you get here, son. Is it possible that you can bring Nicole with you?"

"She's right here with me having lunch. I'll ask her. Uncle Charles . . ." he began.

"I'll see you shortly, Bryan. Thanks."

"Is something wrong?" Nicole asked as he ended the call.

"I don't know," Bryan said slowly. "Uncle Charles wants to see both of us in his office. It sounds urgent, but he didn't go into any details."

"Did he sound upset?" Nicole asked as Bryan took the money for the meal out of his wallet.

"Not upset," he said, "just different, almost sad. I hope nothing's wrong with Aunt Maggie."

"I hope not either," Nicole said as they gathered their things and left the money on the table. "I'll call Sharon from the car to let her know I'll be late coming back and to tell her to book the beach house."

CHAPTER SEVEN

U ncle Charles." Bryan greeted him with a quick
embrace where he waited for them on the front
steps of the church.

"Hi, Bryan. Hi, Nicole," he said as he kissed her
cheek.

"What's the matter?" Bryan asked as he noted the
somber look on his face.

"Come with me," he said as they took the outside
route to his office. "Have a seat," he said, motioning to
the chairs.

Nicole felt butterflies in her stomach. She couldn't remember the last time she'd felt so nervous. She held
Bryan's hand as his uncle rounded his desk and sat down
quietly. They waited for him to speak.

"I had a phone call and a visit today," he started
slowly.

"From whom?" Bryan asked.

Pastor Gaines's lengthy silence was disturbing them.

"Uncle Charles?" Bryan urged.

"I don't know how to say this, son," he admitted. "And now I'm wondering if I should have spoken to you alone and let you talk to your wife later."

"It's okay, Uncle Charles," Bryan said. "You can say it in front of Nicole. We have no secrets. Is something wrong with Aunt Maggie?"

"No."

"Have you heard something from my mother? Is she all right?"

"It's nothing like that, son. Your mother is fine."

"Pastor Gaines," Nicole said, "can you please just tell us? You're scaring me."

"I'm sorry, sweetheart. I'm not trying to. I guess I was just so unprepared for this. I wasn't prepared for any of it. Not the phone call and certainly not what I saw during the visit."

"Phone call from whom, Uncle Charles?" Bryan asked again. "Visit from whom?"

"Someone from your past, son."

"Who?" Bryan asked.

"A woman," he said.

Nicole closed her eyes and swallowed. Bryan felt her hand as it began trembling inside his grasp.

"What woman?" he asked.

"Does the name Tricia Smart mean anything to you?"

"Who?" he asked. "No. I don't know a Tricia Smart."

"Think back to your freshman year at FAMU."

"I don't know a Tricia Smart," he repeated. "What about her?"

"She's here. She's in the sanctuary right now."

"Why?"

"She says the two of you were an item back then."

"It's possible that I met her," Bryan admitted. "I can't

84

totally deny that possibility. We couldn't have been much of an item, though. I don't know her, and I don't remember her. The name doesn't even ring a bell."

"You do have a history," Pastor Gaines said.

"Yes, I do," he said, as Nicole remained quiet, holding her breath, waiting for the axe to fall. "As I said," Bryan continued, "it's possible. However, that was a long time ago. What is she doing here now?"

"She has a child," Pastor Gaines said softly. "Your child."

"Oh, God," Nicole said as tears flooded her eyes. "Oh, God," she repeated as she covered her face with both hands.

"Baby," Bryan said as she cried uncontrollably, "don't cry. Please don't cry."

"I'm sorry," Pastor Gaines said sadly.

"Uncle Charles, this can't be true," Bryan said as Nicole wept in his arms. "I was a freshman, what, thirteen years ago?"

"He's twelve," his uncle informed him. "The timing adds up."

Bryan sat quietly, blinking back his own emotions as he held his wife's trembling body close to his.

"I'm going to give the two of you a few minutes. I'll be back shortly, and then I'll bring Ms. Smart in to explain her reasons for being here." Pastor Gaines left the room slowly and closed the door behind him.

"I'm sorry." It was all Bryan could think to say.

Nicole cried until it felt as though there were no tears left. It was like some kind of nightmare. She wanted to wake up and find out that none of it was true, but she knew better.

"I can't believe this," she finally whispered as she pulled away.

"I know," he said. "Neither can I. I don't even know a Tricia Smart."

"I thought you said that you always used protection."

"I did."

"Apparently not, Bryan. You have a child!" She began crying again.

"Nicole . . ."

"Oh, my God," she whispered through her tears. "You had a baby with another woman."

"Nicole, please don't cry. You know I can't stand to see you cry."

"Well, I'm sorry, Bryan," she snapped as she pulled away from him. "I'm sorry that I'm not laughing all over the place right now, but I just found out that another woman gave my husband, perhaps in one night, what I haven't been able to give him in five years."

"Nicole . . ."

"I'm sorry," she said. "I know this was well before me, but I'm just having a hard time with this. I can't find any good in this, and frankly, I'm not looking for any. All I know is that there's another woman on the other side of that door who you shared at least one night with, and now, for some reason, she's coming back into your life."

"I understand that, sweetheart. You don't owe me any apologies. I just don't know what to say right now."

"How am I supposed to deal with this, Bryan? How am I supposed to deal with a former lover becoming a part of your life again?"

"She's not going to become a part of my life."

"It can't be helped. She has your kid. She's always going to be a part of your life."

"Wait a minute," Bryan suddenly said. "What if she's

lying? Maybe it's not my child. Maybe she just wants it to be my child."

"Why would she do that?" Nicole asked.

"I don't know," Bryan admitted, "but it's a possibility. Maybe I can ask her some questions. Maybe she'll get stuff mixed up."

"Maybe you're right." Nicole gained hope. "Actually, a simple paternity test would solve the whole mystery."

"Bryan," Pastor Gaines said as he peeked in the door.

"Come on in," Bryan said.

"Are you ready for me to bring in Ms. Smart?" he asked as he closed the door behind him.

"Are you ready?" Bryan asked Nicole.

"I don't know," she said as she sat back in her chair. "I guess so."

"I'll bring her in," the pastor said as Bryan sat quietly next to his wife and took a deep breath.

The door opened again after a few moments, and Pastor Gaines returned with Bryan's visitor. Tricia Smart was a tall, very thin, leggy woman with a short, natural hairdo. She was fairly attractive but, because of an overbite, showed a lot of gum when she spoke. Even with a face-to-face look at her, Bryan still had no remembrance of the woman who stood quietly before them.

"This is Ms. Tricia Smart," Pastor Gaines began. "Ms. Smart, this is Nicole Walker, and this is—"

"I know who he is," she said sharply as she sat in the chair that Pastor Gaines directed her toward.

"That's funny," Bryan said, "because even after hearing your name and seeing your face, I haven't the slightest clue who you are."

"You liar," she snapped.

"Okay," Pastor Gaines said as he took his seat. "We

are not here to argue. Thirteen years is a long time, Ms. Smart. Bryan could very well have forgotten who you are. Perhaps there's something you'd like to say to refresh his memory."

"Freshman year," she began, speaking with much attitude. "Frat party in Grady Hall. Do you remember that?"

"Yes," Bryan admitted.

"Do you remember the big dance? There was dancing practically all night. Do you remember?"

"Yes."

"And do you remember drinking?"

"Yes."

"Do you remember the bedrooms?"

"Yes," Bryan said as Nicole turned her head and looked away.

"Remember using one of those bedrooms?"

"No," Bryan said quickly. "I don't remember using one of those bedrooms."

"Maybe you drank too much that night," Tricia suggested.

"I couldn't have drunk so much that I don't remember taking you to bed. I don't even know you. Why would I sleep with you?"

"Did you know all the girls you slept with back then, Bryan?" she asked.

"As a matter of fact, I did," Bryan said. "I may not have loved them, but I knew who they were. I didn't sleep with strangers."

"Are you calling me a liar?" she asked as she leaned forward.

"This is getting us nowhere fast," Pastor Gaines interrupted. "Now, when you called me last night, Ms. Smart, I told you that before coming here, you needed to calm down."

"Calm down?" she said as she stood. "I have cared for my son by myself all of his life, and you want me to be calm when I finally find his deadbeat dad, who wants to catch a case of amnesia?"

"Excuse me?" Bryan's voice level rose. "You're getting close to crossing the line. I'm not anybody's deadbeat father."

"Oh, yeah?" she asked. "I have a twelve-year-old son that proves differently."

"In all fairness, Ms. Smart," Pastor Gaines interrupted again as Nicole got up and walked toward the window to stare at nothing in particular, "he is just finding out about the child. It's not as though he's known all along."

"Funny how he *conveniently* moved away and made a new home and got an unpublished number. I think he knew."

"Wait a minute," Nicole said as she turned from the window. "Bryan went to Florida A&M University for four years. If this happened in your freshman year, why are we just hearing about it? He graduated from FAMU. He was there three years after the party for the new frat brothers. He lived on the same campus with an accessible published number during that time. Why wasn't he contacted then?"

"This doesn't even concern you," Tricia snapped.

"*Now,*" Bryan said as he stood, "you have crossed the line."

"I agree," Pastor Gaines said.

"This is about my son and his son," Tricia said emphatically. "It has nothing to do with her, and I won't be questioned by her."

"This is my husband," Nicole said, fighting tears once more. "Don't tell me that this doesn't concern me."

"Well, this was before you, sweetheart," Tricia snapped back. "In other words, you ain't the only one to have had a piece of him, and in this situation, I had him first."

"That's *enough!*" Bryan said angrily.

"Okay, let's calm down here," Pastor Gaines said.

"She's not going to talk to my wife like that," Bryan continued. "You will *not* speak to her like that." He turned to Tricia. "Now, *that* I will not tolerate," he concluded.

"Calm down, I said," Pastor Gaines repeated harshly. "Now, I agreed to allow us to meet here today," he told Tricia, "but I will end it right now if you can't settle down and stop ruffling everybody's feathers. Yes, you have some real issues here, but I will not have God's house turned into some kind of battlefield. That goes for all of you. Now return to your seats."

Pastor Gaines drank a sip of water as he watched them slowly return to their chairs. Their body languages spoke volumes. Tricia was a feisty one and reeked of trouble. Bryan sat staring at the floor and slowly shaking his head in utter disbelief. But it was Nicole who concerned the pastor the most. The generally happy woman, who almost always found a reason to constantly touch her husband lovingly, seemed to find it hard to even look at him right now as she stared at the wall, continuously fighting tears.

"Now," Pastor Gaines finally spoke, "it is understandably apparent that we have a serious situation here, but it won't be settled like this. You may not want to answer to Nicole, Ms. Smart, but she has raised a valid point. You and Bryan both attended FAMU. How or why is it that you never approached him about this throughout your pregnancy or even after the baby was born in the years that you were there together?"

"I did not attend FAMU," she said. "I was invited to the party by a friend. I didn't really know anything about Bryan except his name and that he was popular. All the girls were trying to get with him that night. I guess you can say I won. We danced and drank together, and we ended up going to one of the bedrooms and having sex. Afterwards, we danced some more, and I left with my friends before the party was over."

"Does this spark any memories with you, Bryan?" his uncle asked.

"None," Bryan remarked, "and I remember the party well. I danced with a lot of girls, but I do not remember having had sex with anyone that night. I admit, I fooled around with a lot of girls back then, but aside from this lady, I think I remember every one of them that I actually slept with. Names may escape me, but I remember faces well."

"Ms. Smart," Pastor Gaines said, "why did you never tell Bryan about the child? Even if you didn't attend the school with him, you had affiliations and connections to him. Why didn't you tell him thirteen years ago?"

"Because I was threatened."

"What?" Bryan sat straight up.

"By whom?" Pastor Gaines raised his hand to silence Bryan.

"By his fraternity brothers," she said. "Word got back to them by way of my so-called friend that I was pregnant by Bryan. The next thing I knew, four or five of his brothers stopped by for a visit and threatened to kill my baby and me if I told. They didn't want their brother's name dragged in the mud. They even offered to pay for an abortion. I turned it down, but I promised not to disclose to anyone else who the father of my baby was."

"I don't believe this," Bryan mumbled.

"What? You still think I'm lying?"

"What were their names?"

"What?"

"The guys who visited you. What were their names?" Bryan repeated.

"I don't know their names. I didn't know them. They were your friends. You tell me what their names were. You probably sent them."

"What?" Bryan leaned forward. "You think I had something to do with them coming to your house?"

"Yes, I do. I know how frat brothers stick together and watch each other's back."

"Stop it." Pastor Gaines held up his hand. "At this point in the game it doesn't matter who sent them or why. It's done. For the record, let me say that I believe my nephew when he says he didn't know about this."

"Why doesn't that surprise me?" Tricia said with a short laugh.

"But as I said," Pastor Gaines continued without response to her last remark, "that's in the past. We have to look at what's going to happen from this point on. Today officially marks the first day that Bryan has known about the child. Nothing that may or may not have happened before today can be proven true or untrue. So, let's start with today. Why have you now come forth after all these years to tell him about the child?"

"Because I am tired, that's why," she said. "For twelve years I have taken care of our child all alone. I've fed and clothed him. I've taken care of him when he was sick. My social life was practically destroyed because I had a child and could not afford a babysitter so I could go out and have fun. I couldn't date, like he could.

"Look." She pointed at Nicole. "He even found a wife

and settled down. Do you know how hard it is to find a good man, let alone a good husband, when you've got a kid? I'm tired. I weighed all the issues. I knew he was married. I knew he was in the church. I waited a year after finding out where he was to try and contact him. I knew all this would probably cause problems for him, but it ain't been easy for me all these years. It's time for him to take some of the responsibility. I didn't get this kid by myself, and I shouldn't have to take care of him by myself."

The silence following Tricia's speech seemed endless. Tears continued flowing silently from Nicole's eyes. Bryan looked at her. He wanted to touch her hand or hold her close and comfort her, but he knew that it wasn't what she wanted at the moment. Tricia sat seemingly cold-hearted and emotionless as she stared at the distraught couple who sat across from her.

"Bryan," Pastor Gaines spoke softly, "you have a responsibility, whether you want it or not. You can't be held accountable for the time that you were unaware of this child, but now that you know, you can't turn away."

"I'd like a paternity test," he responded.

"A *paternity* test!" Tricia said in an insulted voice.

"Bryan," Pastor Gaines said again, "under normal circumstances, I'd agree. However, I've seen this child. He's in the playroom with your Aunt Maggie. If you insist on a test, we can certainly arrange to have that done, but let me say, personally, I don't think it's necessary."

Silence fell across the room once more.

"Maggie," Pastor Gaines called through an intercom system, "bring in the child."

Shortly afterwards, the door to the pastor's office opened, and Maggie Gaines walked in with a strikingly handsome boy.

"Hello again, Gerald," Pastor Gaines said.

"Hi." The boy smiled slightly as his eyes turned toward the carpet.

It was Nicole's worst fear come true. He was the mirror image of Bryan. He was the child she dreamed of—the child with his father's eyes and his father's smile. He even shared the same dimple in his chin. It was more than she could stand. She ran into the office's restroom and locked herself inside where she could cry privately. Unable to hold back his emotions, Bryan buried his tearful face in his hands.

"Take him back out," Pastor Gaines told his wife.

It was obvious to Bryan that a paternity test would only prove this woman right.

The compassionate pastor was fighting his own tears as they could hear Nicole's weeping through the bathroom door.

He turned to Tricia. "Please allow this to end today's meeting. I don't feel that anything else can be accomplished today. There's too much emotion involved right now. Give us all a couple of days. I have your number. I promise to contact you within forty-eight hours. We need time for healing of the initial hurt right now before we can go on."

"*Twenty-four* hours," she stressed as she picked up her purse. "That's all the time I can afford to give you. It's already been way too long," she said as she headed toward the door. "I hope child support arrangements can be settled without a lawyer," she added before walking out and closing the door.

Pastor Gaines watched in silence as Bryan walked slowly to the bathroom and leaned against the door helplessly.

"Baby," he called softly. "Please open the door. Please, baby," he begged.

The only response heard from Nicole was her continuous sobbing. Pastor Gaines quietly picked up the phone and dialed Melvin's number.

"Hello?" Melvin answered.

"Brother Gibbs," Pastor Gaines said, "I know you're at work, but I need you and your wife. I need both of you at the church immediately. Can you come?"

"Give me a minute to pick her up," Melvin said without hesitation. "We'll be there shortly."

"Sweetheart, please," Bryan continued to call through the closed door. "I'm sorry. I'm so sorry. Please open the door."

"Son," Pastor Gaines said quietly as he walked over and placed his hand on his nephew's shoulder, "let her cry; she just needs some time."

"Oh, God, Uncle Charles," Bryan said, weeping. "What have I done? I don't know what I'll do if I lose Nicole. Have I destroyed my family?"

"Don't hand the victory over just yet, son," he said as he led him to the nearest chair. "You have not destroyed your family. The peace and tranquility are certainly being put to the test, but this doesn't have to lead to destruction. She's hurt, yes, and the wounds are deep, but love is a mighty weapon, and that's one form of artillery that I know you and Nicole don't run short on. And even more than that, you have God on your side."

"I don't even know her," Bryan said, referring to Tricia.

"Unfortunately, son, you don't have to know her or remember her. I think your affiliation with her is undeniable. But I will follow through on your wishes to get a test done."

"I don't know what else to do," Bryan said.

"You're not alone," Pastor Gaines assured him. "We're

all here for you every step of the way. We'll figure it out together."

Pastor Gaines sat with his nephew's hands in his in silence for several minutes. In his heart, he prayed that God would restore Bryan's faith and help him to find inner peace and strength.

"Brother and Sister Gibbs are here," Maggie interrupted as she peeked in the door, holding Benjamin.

"Thank you," her husband responded. "Let them in."

Melvin and Sharon rushed in, holding hands and looking worried.

"What's the matter?" Melvin asked as he saw his best friend sitting in a chair with his face once again buried in his hands.

"Listen." Pastor Gaines spoke softly as he pulled the concerned couple aside. "I don't have time to go into detail as I need to right now. I need your immediate help and intervention, so I need you to listen carefully to what I'm saying without passing judgment. Can you do that?"

"Of course," Melvin said as Sharon nodded in agreement.

"I called Bryan and Nicole here earlier this afternoon because they had a visitor. A young lady from Bryan's past contacted me, and I arranged for them to meet here in my office. She was quite irate and compassionless as she spoke to them concerning the fact that she and Bryan had a baby together twelve years ago."

"She said *what?*" Sharon asked in disbelief.

"The validity of her claim is somewhat in question due to her attitude, but she brought the child with her. I think that seeing the child who is a dead ringer for Bryan is what disturbed Nicole the most."

"Oh, God," Melvin said softly.

"They could have a long hard road ahead," Pastor

Gaines continued, "and they are going to need our prayers and support. I called you because you are their best friends, and they need you. This girl is, frankly, quite heartless, and she could be a real thorn in their marriage from here on out. She has the upper hand with this child, and she knows it. Reminding Nicole that she had her husband first, I think, is only the tip of the iceberg of what she's capable of saying to hurt her."

"What?" Sharon said. "Where is she?" she asked as she looked around the room.

"Nicole has locked herself in the restroom and won't come out right now."

"No," Sharon said. "I mean the girl. Where's the girl?"

"Sister Gibbs," Pastor Gaines said impatiently, "if you can't keep a level head, you won't be of any help in this situation. I've witnessed enough disarray for one afternoon. I don't need you ready for a fight. I need you to be the spiritual strength that Nicole doesn't have right now. Are you up for this challenge?"

"Yes." Sharon took a deep breath. "I can do this. I'm sorry."

"Thank you," Pastor Gaines said. "Melvin, your brother needs you."

Pastor Gaines watched as Sharon walked to the bathroom door, patting Bryan's back as she passed him. Melvin pulled Bryan to his feet and hugged him tightly before leading him into the sanctuary, away from listening range of the women. Overwhelmed, Pastor Gaines left the office as well and went into the conference room of the church where he could once again become Uncle Charles and release the emotional tears that he had been holding without being seen or heard.

Just then Pastor Gaines's wife walked up and embraced him.

"Honey, please go and see about Nicole," Pastor Gaines said.

Aunt Maggie found Nicole still in the bathroom. She lifted Nicole's head, looked her in her red, tear-filled eyes, and said, "Baby, I know you feel as if you've been hit by a Mack truck, but before you make any rash decisions, know that we'll get through this. We are standing with you and Bryan, and we will not let you give in or give up."

"Yes, ma'am, thank you," Nicole said through a flood of tears.

CHAPTER EIGHT

"N icole, you have to eat," Sharon said as she brought her a bowl of soup. Nicole sat crumpled on the living room floor of the Gibbs's home.

It had taken a while, but Sharon had finally gotten her distraught friend to open the bathroom door in their pastor's office. They spoke for a short time at the church, and then Sharon convinced her to come home and spend the night with her.

Bryan had initially protested, but Sharon succeeded in convincing him that, for the moment, it was for the best. Melvin agreed to spend the night at the Walker home with Bryan. The separation hit Bryan hard. He was in tears at the time Sharon and Nicole left church.

Now, hours later, Nicole had barely moved from the spot where she had sat when Sharon let her in the house. The rain that had begun to fall just seemed like the appropriate end to a day that had been overcast with adversity.

"Nicole." Sharon sat next to her on the floor. "Please eat something. I fixed your favorite. Here's a bowl of tomato soup seasoned with lots of pepper."

"I'm not hungry," Nicole mumbled.

Sharon set the bowl aside as she took a deep breath and searched for the right words to say. She had never seen Nicole like this before, and it was becoming increasingly hard not to show her own emotion.

"Talk to me, Nicole. Tell me what's on your heart. I know you're hurting, but it's not good to hold it all inside. We've always been able to share anything. Don't shut me out now. Please talk to me."

"I guess this is it." Nicole's voice trembled as she finally spoke after a long silence.

"This is what?" Sharon asked as she handed her a tissue from her coffee table.

"This is the storm that Bryan and I feared was coming."

"Oh," Sharon said. "Well, maybe it is a storm, Nicole, but you don't have to let it become a hurricane. You and Bryan can get through this."

"How?" Nicole asked.

"Women marry men who have other children all the time. It's not unusual to have a stepchild."

"It's not that easy, Sharon. I feel like I don't even know Bryan anymore."

"Why, Nicole?" Sharon asked. "It's not as though you didn't know about his promiscuity before you married him."

"I didn't know it resulted in a child," Nicole said.

"Neither did he," Sharon defended. "Nicole, Bryan didn't lie to you, cheat on you, or even hide this child from you. You can't let this turn into bitterness against him. He learned about his son the same time you did."

"His son," Nicole desolately repeated her friend's words.

"Well, that will be determined after the test. Nicole," Sharon said, supportively stroking her friend's braids away from her face, "I know that another woman possibly having had a child with your husband when you can't at the present time is really hurting you on the inside. I can only imagine what it feels like."

"It's not fair, Sharon," Nicole said while wiping new tears. "He doesn't love her. She doesn't love him, but they get to share one of God's greatest gifts together. I used to pray so hard for a child with Bryan. I knew that the possibility of our having a child together was small, but I'd been taught all of my life that God answered prayers and performed miracles."

"And He does," Sharon interjected. "Don't let this make you doubt God's abilities."

"I don't," Nicole said. "I know God can perform miracles. I've heard testimonies of people's marriages being healed after blatant and repeated adultery. I'm not doubtful of God's ability to perform miracles. It just hurts too much right now. I had come to a state of contentment where my barrenness was concerned," Nicole continued. "Bryan had convinced me that he felt totally complete in our marriage, even without children. I had stopped worrying and watching and buying home pregnancy tests every other month. We were happy just being in love, Sharon. Now . . . "

"You can't let this ruin your happiness, Nicole. It'll take some time, but you'll get used to the fact that there's a child in the mix of things now. This child doesn't have to mean the end of your marriage. You can't let that happen."

"You know," Nicole said. "I don't think it's the boy

that worries me the most. I think his mother is going to make it her business to make life as difficult as possible for Bryan and me. I think she's going to use this child to wreak havoc in our lives."

"That might be true." Sharon shrugged. "From what you and Pastor Gaines have said about her, I wouldn't put it past her to use him like that. But that's just why you and Bryan have to band together. If her agenda includes plans to plant seeds of discord in your marriage, you have to counteract by praying and having a strong determination to stick by your husband and fight for your marriage.

"Yes, you are a victim, and you are hurting here," she continued, "but so is Bryan. He's been blindsided with this just like you. Don't you know he's scared, too? He has to be afraid of what effect this is going to have on his life. Especially his life with you, Nicole. I could see it in his eyes when we left them at the church tonight. He's scared to death of losing you."

"You think so?" Nicole asked.

"I know so. Girl, I know this is hard. It would be a hard pill for me to swallow, too, but you've got to get yourself together so that you can help him to hold himself together."

"I don't know if I can, Sharon. I've never really had drama like this in my life. I honestly don't know if I can handle it."

"Well, I do," Sharon said. "You sound like you're thinking of leaving Bryan, and I know you don't want to do that. I know that because as much as you are hurting right now, I know you still love that man."

"I do." Nicole nodded tearfully. "I do love him. I love him with all my heart. I can hardly bear to think of life without him. I just don't know if I have the strength to be able to handle another woman's presence in his life. Another woman who had his baby. How am I supposed to receive her? Am I supposed to make her feel like family or make his son feel like he's welcome in my life? What am I supposed to do?"

"Yes and no," Sharon said. "Yes, you are supposed to make that boy feel welcome in your life. He's going to be a part of Bryan's life, and that makes him a part of yours. None of this is his fault. You don't make him feel like a stepchild or an outsider. When you find out if he's Bryan's son, God will give you the grace to accept him as a part of your life.

"Now as far as Ms. Thing is concerned," Sharon said, "Lord, forgive me if I'm wrong, but I don't think you have to receive her as a part of your life. I don't even think she wants that. I think you have to accept the fact that she shared something with your husband some years ago that produced a child, and because of that, she will always be there. But receive her into your life? I don't think that's necessary. Deal with her only as it pertains to the boy—again, *if* it's his son."

"I don't want to talk about this anymore," Nicole said.

"Fine by me," Sharon agreed. "You want to watch something on television or listen to some music? I have that new Men of Standard CD that you said you wanted to get."

"No." Nicole shook her head. "I think I'm starting to get a little hungry now. Can I have that soup?"

"Sure." Sharon smiled. "Let me reheat it. After you eat, we'll get a good night's sleep, and then we'll face the new day with a new attitude. How is that?"

"Okay," Nicole said softly as she began wondering what Bryan was doing at the moment.

What Bryan was doing was standing at his window in his bathrobe, watching the rain as it fell under the dark night skies. The light from the muted television was the only light in the living room where he and Melvin had been talking and praying for the past several hours.

"Do you want some more coffee?" Melvin asked as he headed to the kitchen.

"No, thanks," Bryan responded as he turned away from the window and walked slowly to the couch.

"I guess I need to stop drinking it, too," Melvin called from the kitchen. "All this caffeine is going to keep me up until it's time to go to work tomorrow."

"She's not even my type," Bryan abruptly said as Melvin joined him on the couch. "Not only do I not remember her, but she's not even the type of girl I went for back then."

"Well, if you were drunk, maybe you would have," Melvin offered.

"I would have had to be," Bryan said.

"Is she ugly or something?" Melvin wondered out loud.

"It's not that," Bryan explained. "She looks okay, I guess, but she's skinny. I never went for skinny girls."

"Nicole's small."

"Yes, but Nicole is fine, too. This Tricia girl is just skinny. She's just straight up and down. You know?"

"Stringy?" Melvin asked.

"Yeah. I've never liked skinny girls. And she's tall."

"Like I said," Melvin replied, "a few drinks and anything looks good to you. Don't beat yourself up over it, Bryan. It happened in your past."

"Yeah, but it's threatening my future."

"Bryan, the test may prove differently. Nicole's going to be okay, man. All this just caught her off guard. That's all."

"I've never seen her cry like that." Bryan shook his head sadly. "As a child, I used to see my mama cry all the time because of stuff my father had done. I promised Nicole a lifetime of happiness, and now this."

"You didn't plan it, Bryan. You didn't see it coming. It's just one of those things from your past that came back to haunt you. You and Nicole will get through this."

"We've never slept apart before," Bryan said. "At least not due to any disagreement. The only time we've ever slept apart was when one of us was away visiting our parents or something."

"Well, I can't attest to that. Sharon and me have certainly slept apart due to arguments. I mean, it's never lasted more than one night, but we've experienced it before."

"I miss her so much."

"Bryan, you're talking like Nicole's dead. She's not."

"No, but I am," Bryan said. "I'm dead without her."

"You're not *without* her."

"That's how it feels, Melvin. What if she doesn't come home? What if she decides that this is too much confusion for her to deal with? This Tricia lady basically threatened to drag me through the courts when she left the office today. She was already talking child support. Nicole's not going to want to have to deal with her."

"Maybe she won't have to," Melvin said. "This girl doesn't live in Jacksonville, does she?"

"I don't know where she lives. I'm guessing she's still in Tallahassee. What if the test proves that I'm the father?"

"Well, you can get a middleman, so to speak. In fact, I'll do it. I can be the person to pick . . . what's the kid's name?"

"Gerald."

"I'll be the one to pick Gerald up and take him back

home after his visits with you and Nicole. You can make her a generous child support offer that she'll agree to—if the test results are positive; and no lawyers or courts will have to be involved. Just sign an affidavit with the agreed-upon amount and have it notarized. Both of you can have a copy of it, and it'll be a binding agreement. The only time you'll have to deal with the court is if you don't pay, and we know that won't happen."

"You make it sound so easy," Bryan said.

"I know. And it may not be that easy," Melvin admitted. "But at least when you meet with her again tomorrow afternoon, you'll have a plan set and an offer ready to hand to her. Pastor Gaines is a notary. He can make it legal and binding. It'll show Tricia that you mean business, and you want to do this in an amicable manner."

"You're right," Bryan agreed. "That sounds good. I'll draw up the agreement tomorrow morning and see if she'll consent to it. It's worth a try."

"I hear he looks like you," Melvin said cautiously after a brief silence.

"Does he ever. That's why I don't think we need to take a paternity test. I have pictures of myself at his age, and he is the spitting image of me at the age of twelve and thirteen. I couldn't deny him if I wanted to. When I saw his eyes, I knew I had lost that battle."

"I don't think you've lost the war, and you're not going to. There are too many of us fighting with you. Man, are you sure you don't want to take the test?"

"I don't know what I want to do, Melvin. I appreciate everything you've done to help," Bryan said.

"You'd better get some sleep, man," Melvin said as he drank the rest of his tea. "You have a full day ahead of you tomorrow."

"I know."

"You think Nicole is going to go to the meeting with you tomorrow afternoon?" Melvin asked.

"I wouldn't even ask her to." Bryan shook his head. "This has been hard enough for her. She probably wouldn't come anyway, but I wouldn't add insult to her injury by asking her to endure another meeting with Tricia there. I got into this by myself, and I'll bear the burden of dealing with her by myself."

"So let's get a plan together," Melvin said as he grabbed a writing pad from the bookshelf in the corner and retrieved a pen from his pocket. "Well, we know that she's going to make monetary demands, and you can decide how much you're willing to shell out in child support without contesting. But with her making those demands, you can make a few of your own. If you're going to financially support your child, you can also have some rights to him, which I think you should take advantage of."

"You mean visitation?" Bryan asked.

"Yes." Melvin nodded. "Now, I know this is going to take some getting used to with both you and Nicole, but you have to keep in mind that regardless of what the situation at hand may be, he is your son, and you now have a responsibility as a man and as a Christian to care for him."

"I know," Bryan agreed. "I was thinking about that earlier. You know, the visitations and all. It's Nicole I'm concerned with. Gerald's spending time with me and around her is going to be a constant reminder of my past and of what she and I can't have."

"But there's no way she could possibly genuinely respect you if you chose the option of not spending time with him. She'd see you as less than a man, and you'd feel less than one too."

"No, I wouldn't want to abandon him. My father did

that to me, and I know what it feels like to know that your father is somewhere near but not taking the time to see you. I would want some visitation, but all of my time with him must be unsupervised. I don't want his mother anywhere near me and certainly not near Nicole."

"Okay." Melvin wrote on the sheet of paper. "Unsupervised visitation," he said aloud. "I'm also going to put on here that the kid will be picked up and brought back home by me. Now, you'll probably need an alternate in case I can't do it."

"What about Sharon?" Bryan suggested.

"Are you kidding?" Melvin said with a short laugh. "You'd better not put Sharon too close to that girl. She's not too happy at all with the way Nicole is hurting, and I think my wife is capable of letting Tricia know that. No, you have to think of someone other than her."

"Okay, put Uncle Charles on there. I'm sure he'll do it if I need him to."

"Much better choice," Melvin said as he wrote it down. "Now," he continued, "how often do you want visitations?"

"Oh gosh, I can't even think about that right now. I think I need to speak with Nicole first."

"Maybe," Melvin said. "But I think you can put a tentative number on here right now, just to show that you mean business and that you have good intentions where the kid is concerned."

"Okay." Bryan sighed as he got up and walked toward the window again. The rain had slowed, but he could still hear the water as it hit the leaves on the trees in his front yard.

"One weekend out of the month?" Melvin suggested.

"Every other weekend," Bryan said. "You can pick him up for me on Friday evenings and return him on

Sunday evenings. Two weekends out of the month should be sufficient."

"Sounds sensible to me," Melvin said as he scribbled on the paper again. "This is a good start. At least you won't go into the meeting without your minimal expectations on paper."

"Thanks, Melvin."

"Glad to help," Melvin said. "Now," he said, "I propose that we take a few minutes to pray together and prepare to face tomorrow with fresh minds and a renewed sense of strength and faith."

"Yes," Bryan agreed.

"I may not be able to be in that meeting with you, Pastor Gaines, and this lady tomorrow," Melvin continued, "but you can rest assured that my thoughts and prayers will be with you. I believe that things will work out."

The friends stood and joined hands. Bryan gladly agreed to let Melvin lead the prayer. It did his heart good to hear his friend not only pray for him but for Nicole as well, asking God for renewed stability and trust in their marriage. Bryan felt an overwhelming sense of peace when Melvin asked the Lord to meet his best friend at the meeting and let him know that he wasn't facing the battle alone. He ended the prayer by including a prayer for Gerald and his mother, something that Bryan inwardly admitted that he might not have thought to do.

"Thank you," Bryan said as they embraced following the prayer.

"Get some rest, my friend," Melvin said as Bryan stretched his body across the sofa.

"I'll try," he responded.

"You're sleeping out here?" Melvin asked as he prepared to go into the guest bedroom.

"Yeah," Bryan said. "I'll move back in the bedroom when Nicole comes home."

"Good night," Melvin said as he walked away with an understanding smile.

"Good night."

CHAPTER NINE

The following morning brought clear skies and sunshine to Jacksonville. Bryan woke up to find a note from Melvin that he had left for work but could take time to come by the house if he needed him. Bryan smiled as he thought of how blessed he was to have a friend like Melvin.

It was 10:00. He picked up the telephone and dialed with the hopes of hearing Nicole's voice.

"Heaven's Angels." It was Sharon. "How may I assist you?"

"Hi, Sharon."

"Bryan," she responded in surprise. "Hi. How are you?"

"Well, since it couldn't have gotten much worse," he said, "I suppose I'm doing better today."

"Are you, really?" she asked with concern.

"Yes. Actually, I am. I was hoping to hear my wife's voice this morning, though."

"I'm sorry, Bryan. She's not here. She didn't feel up to coming to work this morning."

"Oh." He was disappointed. "How is she, Sharon?"

"She's better," Sharon said. "It took her a while to get to sleep last night. We were up way past midnight."

"Us too," Bryan said. "I think it was after 1:00 in the morning when Melvin left me and went to bed."

"What time did you get to sleep?" Sharon asked.

"I'm not sure. I think it was around 2:30. I just woke up a few minutes ago."

"Nicole was still asleep when I left this morning. She had such a time getting to sleep that I thought it was best not to wake her. I'm sure she would have found it hard to go back if I had."

"Yeah," Bryan said. "Have you spoken to her since you've been at work today? I mean, do you know whether or not she's awake now?"

"No, I haven't," Sharon said. "Why?"

"I was thinking of calling her. I know I'm probably the last person she wants to hear from right now, but I want so badly to hear her voice. I miss her so much."

"I know you do, Bryan. I can't really comment on that. I mean, I don't know if she wants to hear from you or not, but I can tell you truthfully that she misses you too."

"Did she say that?"

"Certain words, between friends, don't have to be spoken," Sharon said. "I know she misses you, and I know her love for you hasn't changed. She's just hurting right now, and you have to understand that."

"I do," Bryan said. "I just miss her," he restated.

"I just remembered," Sharon said. "I turned off my ringer and I turned down the volume of my answering machine last night when Nicole and I were talking. I wanted to make sure we weren't interrupted."

"So she wouldn't hear me if I tried to call her anyway, huh?" Bryan asked in disappointment.

"I'm sorry," Sharon said. "I guess it's possible that she may have turned them back on. She knew I had adjusted them."

"Maybe it's for the best," Bryan concluded.

"What time is your meeting today?"

"I'm not sure yet. I'm waiting to hear from Uncle Charles."

"Are you ready?" Sharon asked.

"Ready?" Bryan said. "No. Prepared? Not yet, but I plan to be."

"You know I'm praying for you, right?" Sharon asked.

"I know, and I appreciate it. Nicole and I have always said that you and Melvin were true friends. Not that you hadn't proved it before, but last night sealed it. I'm glad you could be there for her, and I know Melvin's presence and listening ears helped me immensely."

"The two of you would have done the same for us." Sharon smiled. "There's no doubt about it. Melvin and I have had plenty of disagreements over the years, and you and Nicole have been right there to help us through them."

"That's true," Bryan agreed. "But it still means the world that you were there for us."

"You're welcome."

"Well," Bryan said, sighing, "I have some paperwork to prepare before today's meeting."

"Okay," Sharon said.

"Sharon?"

"Yes?"

"What are the chances that my wife will come home tonight?"

"I wish I could answer that, Bryan. I don't know. I

just think that you should prepare to give her whatever time she needs. She'll come home when she's ready."

"I suppose you're right," Bryan said solemnly. "When you see her, will you tell her that I love her?"

"I will," Sharon promised.

As soon as Bryan ended his call with Sharon and walked into his study to turn on the computer, the phone rang.

"Please let this be Nicole," he prayed softly as he picked up the phone and took a deep breath. "Hello?" He tried not to sound anxious.

"Bryan. How are you?" Pastor Gaines asked.

"I could be better, Uncle Charles," Bryan answered, "but I'm blessed."

"Well, you sound better than you did last night," Pastor Gaines said.

"I am," Bryan said.

"I certainly don't want to bring your spirits down," his uncle continued, "but I'm calling to set a time for today's meeting."

"Actually, that doesn't bring my spirits down, Uncle Charles. I'm ready to get this over with. When do you want me there?"

"I just got off the phone with Ms. Smart," he said. "She is going to meet us here at 3:00 this afternoon. That's just a few hours away. I hope that works for you, because I'm ready to get this settled as well."

"Three o'clock is fine, Uncle Charles. I'm preparing some notes to bring along with me. What are the chances that this is going to be a civilized meeting?"

"Son, I am going to pray before this meeting starts. I suggest you do the same. One thing is certain. The only way for this meeting to have any hope of proceeding in an orderly manner is for those of us who know the Lord to act as though we know Him. Do you understand what I'm saying?"

"Yes sir."

"Is Nicole coming with you?" Pastor Gaines asked. "I think it would be good if she did."

"No, she's not," Bryan said.

"Is she still not ready to face the issue at hand?"

"I don't know, Uncle Charles. I haven't seen Nicole since she and Sharon left the church last night."

"What?" he said in surprise. "Why not? Where is she?"

"She spent the night with Sharon," he said.

"I didn't know that," Pastor Gaines said. "I didn't know you spent the night alone. I would have invited you to come and stay with me and your aunt."

"Thank you, Uncle Charles," Bryan said, "but I didn't spend the night alone. Melvin stayed here with me. Nicole needed some time away from me, I guess."

"I see. When is she coming home?"

"I'm not sure. Like I said, I haven't spoken to her."

"But you will, right?" Pastor Gaines asked.

"Yes, eventually," Bryan said. "I tried to call her at the day care this morning, but Sharon said that she didn't go to work today. I was going to call her at Sharon's house, but according to Sharon, the ringer is turned off and the answering machine is turned down, so she wouldn't hear it ringing anyway."

"So when are you going to speak with her?"

"I was thinking that maybe I'd stop by the house after the meeting. Sharon thinks I should give her the space she needs. I don't want to be selfish, but I miss my wife. I just want to know that she's okay."

"Why don't we take it one step at a time?" the pastor advised. "Let's concentrate on the meeting first. I think it would show a sign of strength if Nicole was with you, but I understand her not wanting to be here. So, let's go ahead with the meeting, and then you can decide what you want to do afterwards. We'll talk it over together."

"Thank you."

"You're welcome, son. I'll see you later this afternoon. I love you."

"I love you too, Uncle Charles," Bryan said as he hung up the phone.

He went to the kitchen and prepared two slices of toast and grabbed a bowl of sliced peaches from the refrigerator before returning to his office and sitting in front of the computer screen. He looked over the notes that Melvin had jotted down the night before and began slowly typing the paperwork. His typing skills were almost nonexistent, and he knew it would take a while.

The phone interrupted his hunt-and-peck session with the computer keyboard. Once again, he hoped to hear Nicole's voice from the other end.

"Hello?"

"Hi, Brother Walker. It's Mother Peek. How are you?"

"I'm doing okay. How are you?" He hoped his disappointment couldn't be heard in his voice.

"I'm doing fine. Are you sure you're okay?" she asked. "I called your office, and your secretary told me that you wasn't going to be coming in today. I figured you wasn't feeling too good. Are you coming down with a bug? My great nephew, Ralph, picked up some old virus early this week. Monday, I believe," she continued. "You met him a couple of Sundays ago. Remember? He came to church with me. He's the one that has that godforsaken pierced ring in his nose. He just needs saving. Anyway, his mama said he's got that old bug that's been going around. She said he's been spending half the day sitting on the toilet stool. Is that what you got too, baby?"

"No ma'am." Bryan smiled slightly. "I took the day off to take care of a little business."

"Oh, well, that's good," she said. "I'm sorry to bother you on your day off, but can you go to the school and pick up my Todd?"

"What's going on with Todd?" Bryan sat up straight.

"Oh, he ain't in no trouble or nothing like that," she eased Bryan's mind. "Englewood High is letting out early today because they done had three bomb threats called in already this morning. I guess they're just tired of emptying out the classrooms and calling in the police, so they're letting the kids go home for the day. I would go and get him, but I let my niece use my car to take my great-nephew to the doctor. I just told you about him. He got that old bug that's going around, you know," she continued. "Anyhow, Todd didn't know that I didn't have my car, and he didn't bother to catch the bus."

"I understand, Mother Peek." Bryan ended her babbling. "I'll go and get him."

"Now, you know he's gonna want to come to your place instead of coming here, and that's fine with me if you got time for him to be there without disturbing your work that you're doing there. It's up to you."

"Okay," Bryan said. "We'll see."

"Thank you so much, Brother Walker," she said. "You've just been such a blessing to me and that boy. If there's anything . . . anything at all that I can do for you, you just let me know."

"You're welcome, Mother Peek," he said. "As a matter of fact, there is something that you can do for me today while you're at home."

"What's that?"

"Pray for me. I need your prayers, and that's what you can give me today. I'd appreciate it."

"I sure will, baby."

"Thank you," Bryan said as he hung up the phone and quickly changed his clothes before leaving.

The drive to Englewood High took him about fifteen minutes. Bryan blew the horn as he pulled into the parking area, and Todd beamed at the sight of him. He grabbed his backpack that lay by his feet and ran across the lot to the silver convertible.

"Hey, Bryan," he said as he got inside. "I didn't know you were coming."

"Your grandmother called me," Bryan said as he drove out of the parking lot.

"You're not working today?" Todd asked as he noted the casual clothes that his mentor wore.

"No. I have some things to take care of today, so I didn't go in."

"Great. Can I come to your house?"

"I don't know if that's a good idea today, Todd. I have some paperwork to type, and then I have a meeting at 3:00."

"I promise I won't get in the way," he pleaded. "You won't even know I'm there. I promise. Please?" he continued. "I just don't want to go home yet."

"Okay," Bryan reluctantly gave in.

"Thanks." Todd smiled.

"Help yourself to whatever is in the fridge," Bryan said as they walked into the house.

"Thanks," Todd said as he looked around and put his backpack on the floor. "You slept on the sofa or something?" he asked after noticing the pillow and covers that were still crumpled there.

"Yeah," Bryan said as he placed his keys on the coffee table.

"Why?" Todd asked.

"That's not your concern, Todd."

"Sorry," Todd said as he went into the kitchen, washed his hands, and began preparing a sandwich.

Bryan returned to his office and to his computer as he bit into a slice of his toast that had now gotten cold. He began typing once more.

"I can type that if you'd like me to," Todd said from the doorway as he ate his peanut butter and jelly sandwich.

"Any other time I'd probably let you," Bryan said. "God knows I'm not doing a good job at it. But I can't let you do this."

"Is it confidential?"

"Yes."

"Oh," he said as he looked over the books on the bookshelf of Bryan's office.

"You want to watch television or something?" Bryan asked.

"Not really," Todd answered. "Why? Am I bothering you?"

"I just need to get this work done, and it's going to take me long enough with total silence. The sound of your footsteps as you walk around isn't helping."

"Sorry," he mumbled as he disappeared and headed back toward the living room.

Bryan stared at the computer screen in silence. He had only typed eight words. It was now noon. The meeting was three hours away, and he realized that his short patience with Todd was a result of his anticipation of the rest of his day. He covered his face and took a deep breath.

"Catch," Todd said as he threw the baseball he kept in his backpack to Bryan.

Bryan's quick reflexes allowed him to catch the ball just in time.

"So, what's the matter?" Todd asked as he stood in the doorway.

"What makes you think something is the matter?" Bryan said.

"You can't answer a question with a question," Todd said. "You caught the ball. What's the matter?"

Bryan looked at the fifteen-year-old kid as he stood in his doorway waiting for an answer. It was amazing how much he had grown mentally over the past couple of months.

"I can't talk to you about this, Todd. This is an adult problem, and I don't think it would be wise to share it with you."

"That's how I used to think about you," Todd said as he sat in a chair near the door. "You used to be trying to get me to talk to you and to make me see that you could help, and all I could see was that you were old and there was no way you could relate to what I was going through. You proved me wrong. But I never would have known that if I didn't give you a chance."

"This is different, Todd. I knew I could help you because I knew I could relate. I had gone through much of what you were experiencing. My age was actually a plus in that situation. You can't relate to what I'm dealing with right now. Your age proves that. In this situation, your age is actually a minus."

"I still want to help," Todd said.

"I appreciate that, Todd," Bryan said. "I really do. But I'm just not ready for the world to know about this yet. I mean, everybody will find out eventually, but I'd rather they found out from me."

"I'm not asking you to tell the world, Bryan. I'm asking you to tell me."

"Todd . . ."

"Okay," Todd said. "Yes, I'm just a teenager, but what could it hurt? Apparently it's not helping for you to keep it to yourself. Come on. You need to talk, and I'm willing to listen. I'm not about to put your business in the streets. You didn't do that to me. Man, I trusted you with all my junk," Todd said. "All I'm asking is for you to trust me with yours."

"I have a son," Bryan suddenly said.

"What?"

"You still want to hear about my junk?" Bryan asked.

"Yes." Todd took a deep breath and sat up straight. "How come you hadn't said nothing about him before?"

"Because I didn't know. I just found out about him yesterday."

"You got a girl pregnant? I mean, I ain't trying to judge, 'cause you didn't judge me, and I know Christians make mistakes. Grandma says that all the time, but I guess I had just put you in a different place than most other people."

"No, Todd. I didn't make a mistake. I mean, I did," he explained, "but not as a Christian. This happened years ago when I was in college. The kid is almost thirteen years old."

"How come you're just finding out about a twelve-year-old?"

"Because his mother and I never really dated. Fact is, I don't even remember her. But apparently I spent a few senseless minutes with her, and it resulted in a child. She never told me before yesterday."

121

"Naw, Bryan." Todd shook his head in suspicion. "I'd get one of them paternity tests if I was you. I mean, that just don't sound right."

"I thought the same thing until I met the child," Bryan said. "He's definitely mine."

"What? He looks like you?"

"He doesn't just look like me, Todd. He *is* me when I was his age."

"Oh," Todd said quietly. "What are you going to do?"

"Well, I am meeting with Pastor Gaines and the child's mother at 3:00 this afternoon. I'm hopeful that we can settle child support and child visitation issues at this meeting."

"So you want to take care of him?"

"He's my child, Todd," Bryan explained. "It's my duty to take care of him. He didn't ask to be here."

"His mama should have taken birth control," Todd said. "If she didn't take birth control, then she was asking for trouble. She should have been more responsible than that."

"*We* should have been more responsible, Todd," Bryan stressed. "Neither one of us ever should have been in that situation to begin with, but since we were, it was both of our responsibilities to be responsible. We both played with fire and got burned."

"I guess so," Todd said slowly.

"So have I lost your respect now?" Bryan asked as he looked at his young friend. "Do you see me any differently now?"

"No," Todd said. "I've got a whole lot of respect for you. I don't know a lot of people my age, including me, who would step up and take responsibility for a child that they didn't plan to have, no matter how much like him the kid looked. I mean, if I had hit it with some girl and she got pregnant, I don't know what I'd do."

"It's all a part of being a man," Bryan explained, "and being a Christian. If I weren't a Christian, I don't know how I'd handle it either. I'm doing the right thing."

"I wish my daddy thought like you," Todd mumbled.

"I wish my daddy did too." Bryan smiled slightly.

"So is that why you slept on the sofa?" Todd asked. "Did Sister Walker, I mean, Ms. Nicole put you out of the bedroom last night?"

"No. Ms. Nicole stayed with a friend last night, and I just didn't want to sleep in our room alone."

"Is she mad at you? Are you getting a divorce?"

"She was upset with the situation," Bryan said, "not necessarily mad at me. Honestly, I can't really say how she felt because we haven't spoken since the meeting that we had with Pastor Gaines and the child's mother yesterday afternoon. She was upset, so I agreed to give her some time to herself. As far as a divorce is concerned, no, we're not getting a divorce."

"I'm glad." Todd sighed in relief. "If there are two people in the world who are perfect for each other, it's you and Ms. Nicole. Grandma says that all the time, and I agree."

"So do I," Bryan said with a smile. "I hope I haven't overwhelmed you with this information," he said.

"No. I'm cool." Todd shrugged. "I'm glad you told me."

"Can I trust you to keep it to yourself for now?"

"Sure." Todd smiled at the faith that Bryan showed in him. "Am I the only one who knows besides Pastor Gaines?"

"Not exactly," Bryan said. "Brother and Sister Gibbs and, of course, Sister Gaines know as well."

"So what's your son's name?"

"Gerald."

"Are you and Ms. Nicole going to keep him?"

"Occasionally, hopefully," Bryan said. "That's the purpose of this paperwork that I need to finish in time for the meeting."

"Is it a lot of paperwork?"

"No. I'm just a very slow typist."

"You want me to type it for you?" Todd restated his previous offer.

"Sure." Bryan smiled appreciatively. "I'm going to go and make some fresh toast for myself, and I'll be back."

It only took a few minutes, but by the time Bryan returned, Todd was printing out the information that he had typed.

"Are you finished?" Bryan asked in surprise.

"Got you right here," Todd said proudly as he handed the sheet of paper to Bryan, who quickly read over it.

"That's perfect, Todd. Thanks. Print me out about five more copies, and I'm going to finish what has now become my lunch, before getting dressed. You're still available to work with me at the bonding company next week, right?"

"Yes." Todd smiled.

"Okay," Bryan said as he disappeared to get prepared for the biggest meeting of his life.

CHAPTER TEN

Before heading to the church for his meeting, Bryan had two things to do. First, he did something that he had desired to do all day. He picked up the telephone and dialed the number to Melvin and Sharon's home. As expected, since the ringer was turned off, the answering machine picked up. He listened to Melvin's message and waited for the beep.

"Hello," he began slowly. "This message is for Nicole, and I hope that somehow you get to hear it. Baby, I miss you so much. I know you need your space right now, and I respect that, but it doesn't stop me from missing you like crazy. I just wanted you to know that. I'm on my way to meet with Uncle Charles and Tricia right now. The meeting was set for 3:00, and I want to be on time so I won't give any reasons for extra drama.

"I know you won't be there, and I thoroughly understand that. But if you get this message, I'm asking you to say a prayer for me. It feels as though I'm going in a lion's den all alone. But I know that God is with me. I wish you were too. I just wish I could hold you right now and take away the hurt that my past has brought to my life with you. You don't deserve this, and I wish I could turn back the hands of time, but I can't. It's done now, and all I can do is step up to the plate and take responsibility for my actions. I know you need time, but I hope you'll come home soon. I need you with me. You and our marriage mean everything to me, and I'll do anything necessary and within God's will to hold it together. Don't give up on us, baby. Please, don't. I love you. I love you very much. Hope to see you soon. Bye."

He was fighting tears as he hung up the phone, but he held it together as he rushed to leave the house. Second, he had to take Todd home. Todd loved riding in the convertible with the top down. He assured Bryan that he'd keep their conversation to himself, and he even surprised Bryan by saying that he would be praying for him. It was a good feeling.

As he pulled up to the church, he was relieved that Tricia hadn't beaten him there. He knew she'd be arriving soon, so he grabbed his briefcase and hurried up the stairs. His Aunt Maggie met him in the sanctuary and greeted him warmly before leading him to the office where his uncle was waiting. They shared a quick but warm embrace before Pastor Gaines took his hands and began praying quietly.

"Heavenly Father," he began, "we come before You asking that You be with us as we face and take on this task that has been set before us. We ask that You arm us with increased strength of mind and ability to exhibit temperance throughout this meeting. Show us when to speak and what to say. God, we ask that You anoint these walls and cover us under Your wings.

"In closing, Lord," he continued, "we ask that You travel to North Lee Street and give healing to Nicole's broken heart. Give her comfort in her time of distress. Let the strong love that I know that You have placed in her heart for her husband become the guiding map in how she handles this situation from this point on. We release it right now and give it over to You, for we know that You are able to do what we cannot. We will give You the glory as You give us the victory. In Your name, we ask these things. Amen."

"Amen," Bryan said as he wiped a lone tear that fell from his eye.

"Ms. Smart is here," Sister Gaines said as she opened the door wide enough to peek inside.

"Send her in," Pastor Gaines said as Bryan took a deep breath and sat in his assigned chair.

Tricia walked in and immediatly gave Bryan a cold stare before sitting in the seat that Sister Gaines escorted her to.

"Good afternoon," Pastor Gaines said.

"Good afternoon," she responded.

"I'm going to try to do as little talking as possible in today's meeting," the pastor said as he took the seat at the head of the table where Bryan and Tricia sat. "My main purpose is to keep order and hopefully to witness and notarize the written agreement between both of you concerning your son's well-being and future. Do you have a list of wishes that you'd like to see met today, Ms. Smart?"

"I don't have a written list," she said, "but I do know what I feel is fair, and I hope Bryan will agree. Like I said yesterday, I would like to settle this without a lawyer."

"So would we," Pastor Gaines said as Bryan shifted his feet. "What is it that you think is fair?"

"Well, since I have raised him for twelve years on my

own, I think that he should pay back child support."

"Ms. Smart," Pastor Gaines interrupted, "even a court would not make him pay back child support. If you had told him about the child before and he had just refused to help out, it would be one thing. But the fact that you actually withheld the information from him frees him from having to pay back child support."

"I didn't withhold anything from him," she defended. "I was threatened."

"I'm not refuting that," he said. "However, since you say that you do not know the names of the persons who allegedly issued the threats, that claim can't be proven. We have to start this process as though young Gerald was born yesterday. That's the day you told Bryan."

"I don't agree with that. You say he didn't know. I say he did."

"Ms. Smart," Pastor Gaines said, "let's make a small compromise. Let's start somewhere else first, and we'll come back to monetary issues. Okay?"

"No," she said impatiently. "I think child support payments should be the first thing that we cover," she said. "Any decent man ought to feel some responsibility for the fact that his only child has gone without while he has lived the good life."

"How do you know what kind of life I've lived?" Bryan asked impatiently.

"I know about your business and your nice house and new car," she said. "Your son has lived in a two bedroom apartment in the projects all of his life. I work as a waitress. I can't afford all the stuff that he needs. I've done my best for twelve and a half years. Don't you feel any responsibility here?"

"Excuse me," Sister Gaines interrupted, opening the door.

"Yes, Maggie?" Pastor Gaines said.

"Nicole is here," she said.

"Send her in," Pastor Gaines said as Bryan slowly stood.

"I'm sorry I'm late," Nicole said with a smile as she walked in, "but I had some business to take care of before coming."

She looked refreshed and quite lovely in her black and white business suit. Her braids hung just the way her husband liked them, and her makeup was light, fresh, and flawless. Bryan's heart fluttered as her eyes met his briefly. He fought the urge to take her in his arms and feel her lips against his.

"How is everybody?" she asked as she smiled at the pastor and their guest.

"Fine," Pastor Gaines said with a look of approval. "Please join us."

"I thought this meeting was just between the parents," Tricia said.

"But I am a parent." Nicole smiled as she sat in the chair next to Bryan. "You see," she continued, "Gerald is Bryan's son. Therefore he is my son as well. I think it is very important that he feels that when he visits us, he not only has a father, but a mother."

"I'm his mother," Tricia emphasized.

"Oh, I agree," Nicole continued with the same smile as Bryan and Pastor Gaines looked on in pleasant surprise. "However, now he's been blessed with two mothers. You are definitely his mom, and I would never try to tell him otherwise. But as his stepmother, I will choose to treat him with the same love and respect that I would treat a child that I had given birth to. I don't think I should treat him any other way."

"I agree," Pastor Gaines said as he smiled. "I'm glad

you could make it, Nicole. I think it's important that you be here."

"So do I," Nicole agreed. "Did I miss anything?" she asked as Bryan slowly placed his hand on top of hers.

"Actually, we were just getting into the subject of child support, but we've been unable to see eye to eye so far. We are still in discussion. Ms. Smart," he continued, "shall we begin again?"

"I've already made my wishes known," she said. "I haven't changed my mind. I believe that back child support is in order."

"Bryan." Pastor Gaines turned to his nephew. "You did bring a list with you, am I right?"

"Yes, I did," he began as he slid the paperwork from his briefcase. "However, I didn't have the chance to go over it with Nicole."

"I'm sure it's okay," Nicole said.

"You sure?" he asked.

"Yes."

"Well," he began again. "I do believe that child support is in order, but not back support. I think you will find what I have proposed to be acceptable."

"That remains to be seen," Tricia remarked.

"Let's listen to what he has to say," Pastor Gaines said.

"Thank you," Bryan said before proceeding. "I have taken into consideration the fact that I am, as you've stated, the owner of a successful business. In spite of that, however, I also have a home and a wife to take care of as well. I've considered my income and my responsibilities, and I believe that $500 per month is more than generous."

"Seven hundred," Tricia said.

"No," Bryan said. "This is not an auction."

"Ms. Smart, your child is twelve years old," Pastor Gaines said. "I don't think a court of law would give you any more than that. I think it's munificent."

"I don't know what munificent means," she said, "but I think he can pay more. Not only is he a business owner, but so is she." She pointed toward Nicole.

"Nicole's income isn't a factor in this settlement," Bryan defended.

"Okay," Pastor Gaines said, and he began writing. "Your demand of $700 per month in child support has not been met. However, you will receive $500 a month. What else do you have there, son?" he asked Bryan.

"Since I am paying child support, we would also like for Gerald to spend some time with us. I was thinking that two weekends out of the month would be fair."

"And some time over the summer when he's out of school," Nicole added.

"The summer months?" Tricia didn't exactly know what to think of this generosity. It had caught her totally by surprise.

"This year we're going to spend a week on the beach in Destin, and I'm sure Gerald would love to go along."

"Tricia?" Pastor Gaines prompted with a smile.

"I, uh—" she started. "I guess that's okay."

"Now we're making progress," Pastor Gaines said as he continued to make notes. "Anything else, Bryan?" he asked.

"Just one thing concerning his visits," Bryan said. "I want every visit to be unsupervised."

"No," she said without hesitation.

"Yes," Bryan said.

"He doesn't know you," Tricia said.

"He will get to know me," Bryan said. "I have a friend who is willing to pick him up from your home on Friday evenings and return him on Sunday evenings. All of our visits with him will be here in Jacksonville and unsupervised by you."

Tricia looked toward Nicole as though looking for her to jump in and sway Bryan differently.

"I agree as well," Pastor Gaines said.

"Fine," Tricia gave in. "But there will be no brain-washing from either of you. If I find out that either of you are feeding him negative stuff concerning me, I will take back the unsupervised visits. I mean that. I want that put in the agreement." She turned to Pastor Gaines. "I want it put in there that the unsupervised visits will be revoked if they start to try and turn him against me."

"Why would we do that?" Bryan asked.

"I will add it in," Pastor Gaines assured her. "Anything further, Bryan?"

"No sir," Bryan said as he sat.

"Is there anything that you wish to add, Ms. Smart?" Pastor Gaines asked.

"No," she said quietly, seemingly lost for words.

"Good," he said as he pressed the call button to ask his wife to come in. "Can you please get this typed up and print it out on my letterhead? I need to get everyone to sign it before I notarize it."

"I'll be back shortly," Sister Gaines said with a smile.

"Well," Pastor Gaines said with a satisfied smile as he clasped his hands together on top of the table. "I just want to commend each of you for the way you conduct-ed yourselves in this meeting. Thank you for your coop-eration and for your flexibility where there could have been disorder." He looked directly at Nicole. "Thank you," he concluded.

The room was quiet for several minutes.

"So, where is Gerald?" Pastor Gaines asked, break-ing the silence.

"He should be at home by now," Tricia said without

much expression. "His school dismisses as 2:45."

"I see," he continued. "Will we be seeing him this week? I guess I didn't get clarification on when visitations were to begin."

"It's up to her," Bryan said as he looked briefly toward Tricia.

"I have a name," Tricia said as she glared across the table at Bryan.

Nicole swallowed hard to hold her tongue. She could see the tightness in Bryan's jaws as she glanced at him.

"Ms. Smart," Pastor Gaines jumped in. "Do you wish for Gerald to begin his weekend visits this week?"

"No," she said. "I have to prepare him. I haven't told him about any visitation plans yet. It's been over twelve years. I think he may need a few days to get used to the idea that his father is finally going to take some responsibility for him."

"I'm sure that will make the transition easier," Pastor Gaines concluded.

Tricia responded by pursing her lips and turning her head away from them. The door, opened and Sister Gaines walked in.

Bryan thought about the fact that putting his visit off by a week would mean that the child would be spending Easter Sunday away from his mother and with strangers. He didn't have a problem with that, but he wondered if Tricia even gave that any thought. He might be in an Easter program at their church.

Church? The thought almost made Bryan laugh in spite of himself. *I'll bet this woman has never been to church herself, let alone taken her child. Easter is probably just another Sunday to her.*

He decided not to bring up the issue. Gerald would probably be better off with him on that day anyway.

"Here it is," Sister Gaines said as she walked into the room with the completed agreement in her hand and handed it to her husband.

"Thank you," he responded and quickly looked it over before passing it around for each of them to see and sign.

After each of them had signed, Sister Gaines quickly made copies for each of them to have. Pastor Gaines explained that the original would be placed on file and could be obtained by either party should the other party renege on the agreement that they had promised to uphold.

"She is quite bitter," Pastor Gaines remarked after Tricia quickly left without speaking to either Bryan or Nicole. "Overall," he continued, "you all handled yourselves well, and I know that it wasn't easy. Especially you, Nicole. I'm proud of the class and strength that you displayed."

"Thank you." Nicole smiled.

"No," Bryan said quietly as he faced her. "Thank you."

"You're welcome," she said, almost shuddering as she looked briefly into his handsome brown eyes. "Well, I have to be going," she continued, stepping away from her husband and gathered her purse and belongings.

"Where are you going?" Bryan asked.

"I have some business to take care of," she said as she began walking away.

"Wait," he said. He walked over to stand with her at the door. "Will you be home tonight?" he asked as he touched her arm.

"No," she shook her head slowly, without looking up at him. "Not tonight."

Bryan wanted to ask, even beg her to come home with him, but he thought of Sharon's words. She was right. He had to respect the time that she needed. She had come to the meeting with him, and that meant something to him. It told him that she still cared. He was grateful.

"Okay," he said after a moment of thought. "I understand."

"Do you?" she asked as she finally looked into his eyes once more.

For a moment, Bryan thought he saw a familiar look of passion and desire in her eyes. It took him by surprise. But when she turned away and put her purse over her shoulder, he assumed that what he saw was only wishful thinking.

"Yes," he answered.

"I don't think you do," she said as she opened the door and turned away.

"Nicole," he said as he touched her shoulder.

"I'll call you later," she said as she pulled away and left.

Bryan stood in the doorway silently as he watched her walk through the church's sanctuary and out of the front doors.

"That is some kind of girl that you married," his uncle said as he walked up behind him and placed his hand on Bryan's shoulder.

"I know." Bryan smiled faintly.

"Things will work out, son." Pastor Gaines tried to encourage Bryan as he saw the sadness in his eyes.

"I love her so much, Uncle Charles," Bryan said. "That house is so empty without her there."

"Have patience, son. The best things in life are worth waiting for."

"I'll wait if I have to," Bryan said. "I just don't want to have to."

CHAPTER ELEVEN

B ryan stepped out of his shower and began drying off. He had showered so long that the water was no longer hot. He purposely didn't prepare his mind for the possibility of spending another night without Nicole. He had hoped and prayed that she would return before nightfall. It was now 8:30, and it was evident that she wasn't coming home.

Melvin had offered once again to keep his friend company, but Bryan had graciously refused the offer. He was thankful for Melvin and Sharon's undying support, but right now he just wanted to be with his wife. He needed to find a way to dissolve the pain in her heart and hear her laugh again.

Bryan slipped on his pajamas and stared at his empty bed. It was still just as it was when Nicole made it up before leaving for work yesterday morning. Walking to the side of the bed, he picked up the phone and dialed. He was about to hang up after several rings, but someone finally picked up.

"Hello?" It was Sharon.

"Hi."

"Bryan?"

"Yeah," Bryan said. "How is everybody?"

"We're doing fine," she said. "How are you? I guess you're feeling better now, huh?" she added with a smile.

"Huh?" Bryan was confused by the cheer in her voice, but then again, why should everyone be sad because of his plight. "Oh," he continued. "Yeah, I'm feeling better that the meeting is over and it went well, considering how badly it could have been."

"That's what I heard," Sharon said. "Nicole said that you all had actually come to an agreement that the kid's mother accepted."

"Yeah, we did," Bryan said. "Can I speak to her?"

"Who?" Sharon asked.

"Nicole."

"Nicole's not here, Bryan." Sharon sounded bewildered.

"What do you mean she's not there?"

"I mean, she's not here. I thought she was with you."

"What made you think that she was with me?" Bryan asked.

"Because she's not here," Sharon answered. "I just figured she was with you. She wasn't here when I got home from work today. She left me a note concerning how the meeting went, but I haven't seen her."

"Is her stuff gone?" Bryan asked, trying not to panic.

"She didn't really have any stuff over here. I let her wear one of my nightshirts last night, so all she had were the clothes that she wore here after we left the meeting at the church yesterday."

"Where could she be?" Bryan thought aloud.

"Melvin," Sharon called as she continued to hold the phone.

"Yes?" Melvin answered from their living room where he was getting the kids ready for bed.

"You haven't heard from Nicole today, have you?"

"No," he answered. "Is that Bryan? Nicole's not at home?"

"Yes, this is Bryan, and no, she's not there with him," Sharon said as she turned her attention back to Bryan. "You want me to call her mother?"

"No," Bryan said. "If she's not there then that will just get her all upset. If she was there, I probably would have heard from her daddy by now."

"Where did she go after the meeting?" Melvin whispered over Sharon's shoulder as he joined her in their bedroom.

"Where did she go after the meeting?" Sharon asked.

"I don't know," Bryan said as he took deep breaths and paced the floor as he spoke. "She just said that she had business to take care of. She didn't say what kind of business."

"It's not like her to go somewhere and not tell anybody," Sharon said. "Even if she didn't want to tell you, I think she would tell me."

"Hold on," Bryan said. His phone beeped as a call was trying to get through.

"Okay," Sharon said.

"Hello?" Bryan answered the second line after a moment to calm himself.

"Hi."

Bryan was so relieved at the sound of Nicole's voice that it almost overwhelmed him. The sweet sound of her soft voice forced him to sit on the side of the bed as the weight of worry that was lifted from him made him physically weak.

"Nicole."

"Hi," she repeated.

"Hold on for just a second, baby," he said. "Please don't hang up. Give me fifteen seconds."

"Okay," she said.

He quickly switched back over to Sharon.

"Sharon," he said, "it's Nicole on the other line. I'm sorry I worried you guys. I'll talk to you later."

"Tell her . . ." she began.

"No," Bryan said. "You tell her. I have too much to say to her to remember your stuff too. I have to go now."

"Okay," Sharon said with a laugh. "Bye."

"Nicole?" He switched back over.

"Yes?"

"I'm so glad to hear your voice," he said. "I was so worried."

"Why were you worried?"

"I didn't know where you were. I thought you were still at Melvin's house, but when I called, Sharon said she hadn't seen you all day. I didn't know where you were."

"I'm a big girl, Bryan," Nicole said.

"I know. I'm sorry."

"It's okay."

"No, it's not okay," Bryan said. "I'm sorry. I'm sorry about everything. I never meant to hurt you. I never meant to make you cry, and God knows I never thought I could possibly do anything to make you not want to come home to me at the end of the day. I know you need time and space from me, but I was so hoping that you'd come home tonight."

"I told you that I wouldn't be there."

"I know," Bryan sighed heavily. "I know," he repeated. "I spent some much-needed quality time with God in prayer earlier this evening. I felt a sense of peace and tranquility afterwards. I guess I was hoping that it was a sign that you would change your mind and come home. Baby, I miss you so much."

"I miss you too, Bryan," Nicole said as tears filled her eyes.

"I'll do anything," Bryan's voice dropped to a whisper. "Whatever you want me to do, I'll do it. I want to make it right. I love you, Nicole, and I know you love me. Let's work through this together."

"You have a son, Bryan." Nicole began crying softly.

"I know."

"I keep trying to stop this pain I feel in my heart," she continued. "I know you didn't mean to hurt me, but it hurts, Bryan. It hurts so much."

"I know, baby."

"You're right," Nicole said through sniffles, "I do love you. That's why this hurts so deeply. I love you so very much, but I can't stop the aching."

Although it pained him to hear her cry, hearing her express her love for him somehow soothed his heart and gave him renewed comfort.

"Then let me try," he pleaded softly. "Let me try and stop the hurt. Please, Nicole. Just tell me what you want me to do. I'll do anything."

"Hold me," she whispered back after a moment of earsplitting silence.

"Oh, baby," he said. "I want to, but you have to come home to me."

"No," she said.

"Nicole . . ." he started.

"You come to me," she added.

Her tearful words and the soft and sultry sound of her voice stirred a yearning inside of Bryan that he hadn't experienced in a long time. He stood beside the bed where he once sat.

"Where are you?" he finally asked.

"On Baymeadows Road," she replied.

"Where?" he tried to maintain calm as he fished for more information.

"Embassy Suites Hotel," she said. "Room 219."

Embassy Suites was the three-star hotel where the two had spent their wedding night. It was an upscale inn with 277 spacious suites. Bryan remembered reserving the honeymoon suite there five years ago.

"Give me twenty minutes," he said as he abruptly hung up the phone.

Bryan didn't even bother to change from the pajamas that he had put on. He grabbed an overnight bag and shoved a pair of jeans, a T-shirt, and a fresh pair of underwear inside. Going into the restroom, he grabbed his toothbrush, toothpaste, and deodorant. After slipping on his bedroom shoes and grabbing a pair of gym shoes from the closet, he headed out the door that led to their garage.

In less than fifteen minutes, he was pulling into a parking space at Embassy Suites and bounding up a flight of stairs to find Room 219. As he neared the door, he approached cautiously. He felt uncommonly nervous as he knocked softly on the door.

"Hi," Nicole said as she opened the door.

"Hi," Bryan said. Despite the tears that were still visible in her eyes, she looked beautiful in her purple satin nightgown as she stepped aside to let him in.

He never took his eyes off of her as he watched her lock the door while he placed his bag on the floor near the bed.

"Remember this hotel?" she asked as she stood with

her back against the door and looking around the room.

"Yes," he answered as he walked toward her slowly.

"You wore your pajamas here," she said as the tension mounted with each step he took in her direction.

"I was already dressed for bed when you called," he said.

"You could have taken them off. I wasn't going anywhere."

"I told twenty ten minutes," he said as he now stood directly in front of her. "Besides," he continued, "I figured I'd just take them off once I got here."

Before she could respond, Bryan slipped his arm around her waist and pulled her body to his. The kiss that started out softly turned deep and passionate as he picked her up and carried her to the king-sized bed.

"I have so much I want to say to you," he whispered. He looked into her dark, watery eyes as she lay underneath him. "There is so much that I need to say to you," he continued through the kisses he placed strategically on her face and body. "But right now, those words are apparently buried so deeply inside me that I can't seem to find them. A thousand words couldn't truly explain what I'm feeling for you right now, Nicole," he said. "Not even a thousand words," he repeated.

"It's okay," Nicole said breathlessly as she helped him remove his clothing. "You can just show me."

"Thank you," he whispered as he gave in to his passions and created a night of intensity that compared only to the first night they'd spent there together years earlier.

There didn't seem to be enough hours in the night for the lovers to express how much each of them meant to each other, how much they missed each other. Finally drained, the two collapsed into each other's arms, where they lay together quietly for several minutes.

Nicole lay on his chest, and Bryan held her close, as though he were protecting her. He softly kissed her forehead, wiping beads of sweat in the process. Bryan wanted to thank her for supporting him at the meeting, but didn't want to chance bringing up the touchy subject for fear that it would dampen the mood.

"She's not going to make this easy for us, you know." Nicole finally broke the silence, as though she was reading his mind.

"I know," Bryan said as he tightened his arms around her body.

"It may take some time," she continued, "but I'm sure I can get used to the idea of you having a child. I can accept that. But I don't know if I can deal with her."

"You don't have to deal with her," Bryan said.

"How can you be sure?" Nicole asked as she sat up and looked at her husband in concern. "She doesn't strike me as the nicest person. I think she'll see that we have to deal with her in some way or another."

"Then I'll deal with her in that situation," Bryan said. "You won't have to. You're not responsible for this predicament that we're in, and I don't want you suffering any more than you have already. I mean that."

"You always have tried to protect me from anything that remotely smelled like trouble," Nicole said after she had planted a kiss on the side of his neck.

"I don't know if I'm protecting you or protecting her." Bryan chuckled. "You handled her pretty well in that office today."

"You think so?" Nicole smiled.

"Baby, she didn't have a chance." Bryan laughed again. "You caught her totally off guard. You caught me and Uncle Charles off guard, too."

"I expected her to get angry with me," Nicole said.

"I think she wanted to," Bryan said, "but she couldn't. It was obvious that God had a hand in it all, but the fact is, she didn't stand a chance against you."

"Really?" Nicole smiled, enjoying her husband's bragging on her actions.

"Sweetie, when you walked in there in your business suit, looking a combination of classy and sexy, it was one thing," he said. "We volunteered to spend some time over the summer with Gerald, as well as two weekends out of each month. It blew her away. It had to blow her away. It blew me away. Baby, I was so proud of you. I know it wasn't easy."

"No, it wasn't," Nicole admitted, "but when I listened to your message at Sharon's house, I had to come. I meant every word of what I said. In a way, we do owe him. You may not have known of his existence until now, but that's not his fault. Maybe Tricia was threatened. Who knows? The point is that this child is a part of you, which makes him a part of me. That is a hard pill for me to swallow. It still hasn't totally digested yet, but at least I've swallowed it. It's no longer in my mouth leaving a bad taste."

"I love you," Bryan whispered, interrupting her speech.

"I love you too."

"I missed you so much last night," he continued. "I couldn't even sleep in our bed without you there. I've never been that scared and lonely in my life."

"I'm sorry," Nicole said as she touched his face with her hand. "Maybe I handled it the wrong way. I just didn't know what else to do."

"I'm not asking for an apology," Bryan said. "I don't deserve an apology. I understood your anger."

"I was never angry with you, sweetheart," Nicole said to his surprise. "I was hurting so badly inside that if

I had a choice I would have opted to die instead of face the facts. It's been five years," she continued. "You've been a wonderful husband, and our life together, by my standards, has been almost perfect. There's only one thing that I desire that our marriage hasn't given us."

"A baby," Bryan interjected.

"Yes," she said. "A baby. I had come to accept that. You told me that you felt complete in our marriage, and that eventually became enough for me. Then the nightmare began."

"If I had cared anything at all about this woman, I think I could forgive myself a lot easier," Bryan said as he held Nicole close to him. "I guess this is one of the ultimate prices to pay for sin. To have something as wonderful as a child with a woman that doesn't even begin to jog any memories."

"You still don't remember her?"

"Not at all. It's as embarrassing as it is pathetic. I guess my drinking and partying got way out of hand that night." Bryan continued after a silent moment. "When I gave my life to Christ twelve years ago, I set all of these attainable goals for my life. I began to see myself with a much brighter and purposeful future. Nowhere in there did I ever dream that I'd become responsible for the well-being of a twelve-year-old child."

"Have you decided how you're going to tell everybody about him?"

"Well," Bryan said, "at first, I was worried about that. I kept wondering how I was going to face people, especially church people, after finding out about Gerald. At first, I figured I'd make a public announcement to the entire congregation on a Sunday morning. Then I thought that maybe I'd just tell my closest friends and leave everybody else out."

"So what did you decide?" Nicole asked.

"Funny thing is," he said, almost as though he didn't hear her question, "I chose the most unlikely person to tell about it first."

"Who was that?"

"Todd."

"Todd?" Nicole was surprised that he would tell someone so young about such a thing.

"Yes," Bryan said. "I think our Todd showed a lot of maturity this afternoon when I talked to him."

"What made you tell him?"

"I had to pick him up from school today due to a bomb threat. Mother Peek asked me to. He came and spent some time with me at the house when I was getting my paperwork together for the meeting with Tricia. He could tell that I was troubled, and I felt amazingly comfortable with sharing my situation with him."

"Did he take it okay?" Nicole asked, worried. "I mean, he just finished his counseling with you. He looked up to you. Something like this could set him back."

"He took it with amazing calm." Bryan smiled as he thought about it. "I think it may have helped him in the long run. My situation proved to him what his life could have ended up being like had he continued down the road that he was traveling. Having a bunch of girls hanging around you all the time has a way of making a boy feel like a man. But what Todd now sees is that it can also lead you into a situation that you would pay any amount to change if it were possible."

"But you can't change it," Nicole said.

"Not with all the money in the world," Bryan said.

"I wonder who he's already told."

"Nobody," Bryan said.

"Do you really believe that?"

"Yes, I do," he said. "I asked him not to tell anyone, and he promised that he wouldn't. I believe him. He's earned the right to be trusted."

"Okay." Nicole nodded. "So how are you going to tell everyone else?" she asked.

"I'm not going to," Bryan said. "I've decided that it's not everyone's business. They will find out eventually, and if they ask me, I will tell them what I want them to know. It's bound to come up, because every single weekend that he spends with us, he'll attend church. Our worshipers aren't stupid. He's twelve years old. They'll know he was before you. They already know that I led a pretty wild life at one time. I'll let them put two and two together. It's not like I'm trying to hide it. When they see him, they'll know."

"He looks just like you," Nicole said with a heavy sigh.

"I know," Bryan said as he kissed her forehead. "That bothers you, doesn't it?"

"Yes, it does," she confessed, "but I think I'm going to be okay."

Bryan smiled as he touched her face with his hand. "Do you think I'm handling this properly?" he asked her. "Do you think I should make a public announcement?"

"I think you should handle this however you feel comfortable," Nicole said. "You're right. It's not necessarily everybody's business. Most of the members don't even know us on a close, personal level, and those who do will understand. It was something, as you said, that happened a long time ago. I'm sure we all did things in our sinful days that we regret. I will support you in whatever decision you make."

"Thank you," he whispered as he hugged her.

"Are you scared?" Nicole asked.

"Yes, I am," Bryan admitted. "But I am confident that with a little work and patience, things will work out. Especially now that I know you have my back."

"Everything is going to be okay," she said. "You're going to be a good father. I'm sure of it."

"I just wish . . ." he began.

"Shhh." Nicole placed her fingers over her husband lips.

"I'm sorry," he apologized.

"Don't be," she said. "I wish the same thing, but neither of us can make that wish come true. We'll just make an effort to make Gerald feel comfortable with us. The fact is," she said hesitantly, "he is our child."

"I love you so much, Nicole Aaliyah Walker," Bryan said as he kissed her warmly and pulled her closer to him.

"I guess we should get some sleep," she said as she glanced at the clock on the stand by the bed. "It would be a waste of money if we didn't get to sleep in the room that I paid for."

"Are you sleepy?" Bryan asked.

"No," Nicole whispered, familiar with the look that she saw in his eyes.

"Today is Thursday. There's only one more work day in the week," he said. "I say we take tomorrow off and use that time to sleep in as late as we want."

"So what do you suggest we do with the rest of tonight?" she asked knowingly.

"I have a couple of ideas I'd like to run by you," he said, and his lips covered hers once more.

Chapter Twelve

Melvin and Sharon smiled as Bryan and Nicole edged past them, hand in hand, to their seats in Sunday's service. After spending the last two days and three nights in virtual solitary confinement, they had rejoined the rest of the world, beginning with Sunday morning worship.

As painful as it had been for Nicole to come to the realization and to accept the fact that the man she loved shared a child with another woman, she felt closer to him than ever. She knew where his heart was, and that was comforting to her otherwise wounded spirit.

She listened to the sermon from Pastor Gaines as she held Benjamin in her arms. The message served as additional comfort, as her pastor spoke on the strength of love and its almost endless boundaries. Nicole smiled as she listened. Love had been the commanding force in the Walker household for the past two days. When she and Bryan weren't making it, they were discussing it. They understood that if they were to keep a strong and happy marriage, their love for each other would have to pass the toughest test that had been set before them since they began their life together.

Following the service, they mingled among the other members as normal. It became very clear to Nicole that Todd had obviously kept his word. Even his grandmother showed no signs of any knowledge of the happenings of the past few days.

"I was so glad to see you guys walk in together," Sharon remarked as she hugged her best friend. "I was worried there for a little while."

"So was I," Nicole admitted.

"But you're okay?" Sharon asked.

"Yeah, we're fine. We just needed some time just to ourselves to talk everything out and make a plan for the future that includes Gerald. It did us both good to speak our hearts and our feelings and then for the other to listen and understand what we felt and where we were coming from."

"So you were able to find a middle ground and work everything out?" Sharon asked, still worried. "I mean," she continued, "everything is really okay?"

"Yes," Nicole said with a short laugh.

"Oh boy," Sharon said as she shook her head. "I know that look. You really did work everything out, didn't you? And I have the feeling that it wasn't all talk."

"You are so silly." Nicole laughed.

"No," Sharon said. "What I am," she continued, "is so right."

"You remember when you told me a couple of years ago that big disagreements were almost fun in your marriage, because you knew that there was going to be a time to make up in the future?"

"Yeah," Sharon said. "Making up is the best part."

"Well, I guess for the first time in my marriage, I experienced that. It really was incredible."

"See?" Sharon smiled.

"But," Nicole stressed, "I don't want to have to go through another ordeal like that. I admit, making up was nice, but I'll think of some other way to keep that kind of passion in my marriage."

"As if your marriage needs any more passion." Sharon laughed as she took her reaching son out of Nicole's arms.

"Whew!" Nicole sighed. "Now that's a load off."

"You leave my baby alone." Sharon laughed.

"Hello, ladies," Bryan said as he joined the women.

"Hi," they responded.

"Hi, Todd," Nicole said as she kissed the cheek of the teenager who had become an almost constant shadow to her husband.

"Hi, Ms. Nicole," he said, blushing.

"Well, now," Sharon said in mocked jealousy. "Can I get a kiss too?"

"Yes, ma'am." Todd beamed as he gave her his other cheek to smooch.

"How's school?" Nicole asked.

"It's fine."

"I overheard one of the kids that go to your school talking about report cards," Bryan said. "I hear you will be getting it on Monday following spring break."

"Yeah," he said.

"How well do you think you did this semester?" Bryan asked him.

"I think I did okay. Better than last time, anyway."

"Good to hear," Bryan said as he patted Todd's shoulder. "You're definitely capable."

"Okay, ladies and gentlemen," Melvin said as he walked up to the group with little Michael in tow. "Our loving pastor and his wife have asked to keep the kids for the afternoon. That gives the Mrs. and me some rare free time. I say let's take advantage of it. Who's up for Mexican today? I have a taste for enchiladas that just won't wait."

"Sounds good," Bryan said. "Is that okay with you, baby?" he asked Nicole.

"Mexican is fine."

"This totally cancels out all the dieting that we did last week," Sharon scolded Melvin.

"You don't need to diet, Sharon," Melvin said. "You look good just like you are."

"Thank you, sweetie pie," Sharon smiled as she hugged him.

"Do you want us to ask your grandmother if you can come along, Todd?"

"I wish I could go, Ms. Nicole," Todd said. "But grandma said that my mama is supposed to be coming to visit us this evening."

"Well, that's good," Bryan said.

"I guess so." Todd shrugged with an unhappy grimace.

"What's the matter, Todd?" Bryan asked as he pulled him aside. "Don't you want to see your mother?"

"I guess," he said. "I just don't want her to take me back with her."

"Who says she's going to take you back?"

"Nobody," he admitted. "I just can't help but think that Grandma might tell her that I'm doing better now, and she'll want to take me back home."

"But you used to say that you wanted to go back."

"I know," he said, "but that was before I started liking it here. That was before I got to know you."

"Come on." Bryan smiled as he led Todd in the direction of his grandmother's car.

Mother Peek was standing in the parking lot near her old station wagon, testifying of God's goodness to a fellow member of the church.

"Child, I'm telling you," she was saying with a raised right hand, "the God I serve is what?" she asked and then immediately answered. "A mighty God. Yes he is."

"Amen," the sister agreed.

"And right here is the proof in the puddin'," she said, pointing toward Todd as he and Bryan joined them.

"How are you, Mother Peek?" Bryan asked, hugging her warmly and greeting the other woman, who then turned and walked away.

"Oh, I'm fine, sugar," she said.

"That's good," Bryan said. "I just wanted to check up on Todd. How's he doing around the house now?"

"Oh, he's doing much better, Brother Walker. He still don't like to clean his room, but that's nothing compared to the trouble I used to have."

"No talking back?" Bryan asked.

"No talking back. No cutting classes. No sneaking out at night. Todd's like a different boy now, and I owe that all to you and the good Lord," she said.

"That's good to hear," Bryan said with a smile. "I hear he's getting a visit from his mother today."

"Yeah," Mother Peek said. "She said she'd be here around 4:00 this afternoon. I told her that he was doing good, and I guess she had to come and see the miracle for herself. Just like old Doubting Thomas in the Good Book." She laughed.

"She's not coming to get him, is she?" He asked the question that worried his young friend.

155

"Not as I know of," Mother Peek said. She looked as though the thought had never crossed her mind prior to his asking. "He ain't ready to go back yet, is he?" she asked.

"Personally, I think he needs to stay longer," Bryan said. "He's made a lot of progress, but I don't think he's quite confident enough to fly. He still needs to be under our wings for a little longer."

"I don't know if Sheila was planning on taking him back or not, but I sure will let her know that he's still getting spiritual counseling and therapy."

"I'd appreciate that, Mother Peek," Bryan said as Todd smiled in relief. "If Sheila needs to talk to me, she can call me at home or on my cell. Todd has the numbers."

"Thank you, sugar," Mother Peek said as she hugged him. "You've been such a blessing to this boy. One of these days, God's gonna bless you with a child of your own. You and Sister Walker are going to be some good parents one day."

"Thank you." Bryan tried to smile as he and Todd exchanged glances.

"Well, we better get on to the house and get ready for that daughter of mine," she concluded.

"All right." Bryan waved as he walked away. "Be good, Todd."

"I will," Todd said, smiling as he got into the car.

After leaving Michael and Benjamin with Pastor Gaines and his wife, the two couples made their way to a nearby Mexican restaurant and settled down at the table where they had been escorted. While waiting for their orders, they munched on the chips and salsa that they were given as appetizers.

"It's been a while since we've all eaten together," Bryan remarked.

"Well, we're not the ones always asking for rain checks," Melvin said, and they all shared a laugh.

"Well, I would apologize," Bryan said, "but I'd just be perpetrating a fraud."

"We're just glad that the two of you are back together," Sharon said.

"You make it sound like we'd split up," Nicole said.

"You were in one place, and he was in another," Sharon pointed out. "You weren't on vacation. You were in the same city. You were sleeping in one house in one bed, and he was sleeping in another house in another bed," she continued.

"No," Melvin corrected. "He slept on the sofa. He couldn't even sleep in the bed without her."

"And all the streaming tears," Sharon said.

"And the flying snot," Melvin added.

"Sounds pretty close to a split up to me," Sharon concluded.

"It was pretty pitiful." Melvin laughed.

"You've made your point," Bryan said.

"We were only separated for a day," Nicole said.

"It felt like forever," Bryan said softly, and he kissed the back of her hand.

"For me too," Nicole said as she looked back at him and smiled lovingly.

"Hold up," Melvin said as he gave the time-out signal. "Hold up," he repeated. "We ain't rain-checking this meal, do you two understand me? So you just need to cool it down right now. I'm getting my enchiladas, and both of you are going to sit here and enjoy your meals as I enjoy mine. Are we clear?"

"You need to calm down." Bryan laughed. "Your wife is the one who brought up the subject."

"Yeah," Sharon said, "but I didn't mean for it to turn

into something steamy."

Their meals finally arrived, and the conversation changed as they discussed business plans for the week ahead. With the school year nearing an end, the enrollment at Heaven's Angels was slowly increasing. During the summer months, beginning in the month of June, they kept school-aged children up to the age of twelve. Sharon announced that in the two days Nicole had been absent from the center, although the end of the school year was still several weeks away, parents had been completing applications and paying enrollment fees to hold available spots for their children.

"Seems like God gave all of us the right lines of business to go into," Melvin said. "Every time we turn around, new businesses are going up or new houses need to be built. Construction is in demand."

"Babies are certainly born every day of the year," Nicole added.

"And as I always say," Bryan said, "somebody is always needing money to get out of jail." He laughed as the others chimed in to complete his sentence with him.

"So," Melvin said as they continued to eat and talk. "Do you have the kid's address so I'll know where to pick him up on Friday?"

An unexpected silence blanketed the table. Sharon elbowed her husband's side.

"Ouch," he said. "I'm sorry," he added after a moment of silence.

"It's okay," Bryan said. "We'll discuss that later."

"All right," Melvin nodded.

"No," Nicole said. "It's all right. You can talk about it now."

"No, Nicole," Sharon said. "It can wait. Melvin just wasn't thinking. You know he ain't the brightest child that his mama had."

"Hey!" Melvin said as the others laughed.

"No, really," Nicole said. "I want you to talk about it now. Everybody can't walk on eggshells around me when it comes to Gerald. He's a part of my life now. I'm fine. Please," she urged. "Go on."

"Okay," Bryan said after a brief silence. "Yes, I do have the address, but I'm not sure of the directions for how to get there."

"Is she still in Tallahassee?" Nicole asked to everyone's surprise.

"Yes, she is," Bryan answered.

"Well, I'm sure I can find her house," Melvin said.

"You could always map it out on the computer," Sharon offered.

"I'll get the actual address to you at some point this week," Bryan said.

"I'll be getting off of work at 3:00 on Friday. I want to get there and back before too late."

"That's good," Bryan said cautiously as he glanced at his wife.

"I have an idea," Nicole told Sharon after a brief silence.

"What?"

"Instead of going to the track and walking during lunch this week, how about you go with me to the mall instead?"

"The mall?" Sharon asked in confusion.

"Yeah," Nicole said. "We can walk around the mall while I shop for some things. I mean, Bryan and I have never had a child in the house, so there's really nothing there that would interest Gerald."

"So you want to go shopping for Gerald?" Sharon asked slowly as Melvin and Bryan exchanged glances.

"Yeah. I mean, we need to change one of the guest rooms into his room. We can change the comforter and curtains into Spiderman or whatever is the popular thing now. Maybe we can even put a desk in there in case he has to bring homework here to work on some weekends."

"An excuse not to exercise and to go shopping? Well, let me see," Sharon said in exaggerated thought.

"Okay now," Melvin said as he drank the last of his soda, "you'll be risking the chance of me being finer than you on the beach in Destin."

"I don't think one week is enough time to do that, sweetie," Sharon said as she rubbed his stomach. "Shopping it is," she told Nicole.

"Do you think she realizes that she's allowing him to be away from home on Easter Sunday?" Nicole asked.

"I actually thought about that," Bryan said. "They probably don't have any church plans, so it's probably no big deal for him to be away."

"On the positive side," Melvin said, "I think that's a good day for him to come to the services at our church. He'll get to take part in the Easter egg hunt, and he'll get a goody bag to take."

"I think he may even enjoy it," Nicole agreed.

The couples finished their meals, said their good-byes, and headed their separate ways. The ride to the Walker home was relaxing but quieter than normal. After arriving home, Nicole sat on the edge of the bed and removed her shoes.

"Is everything okay?" she asked Bryan as she noted his unusual quietness.

"Everything is fine." He smiled as he sat beside her. "I just keep thinking of how blessed I am to have you."

"You think so?" she asked with a smile.

"Yes, I do," Bryan said, taking her hands in his. "I

just want you to know that I don't expect you to go out of your way. I mean, I know you're in support of me and Gerald, but you don't have to go out of your way."

"I know," she said. "I want to do this. I mean, I've always wanted to fix up a baby room. I guess this is the next best thing."

"You're incredible, you know that? I know this ordeal has been tough on me, but it's probably been even tougher on you. You could have made this much more punishing for me, but you're not. I love you for that. Every woman wouldn't have triumphed as you have."

"It would be stupid of me to punish you for this. Even when I was away, it wasn't to punish you."

"I know," Bryan said.

"I'm proud of the way you've stepped up to the plate," Nicole continued. "I admit that in my perfect world, there wouldn't be a plate for you to step up to, but in reality there is, and you have. I wouldn't expect any less from you, and had you given less, I would have been disappointed.

"Yes, this has been hard for me, and it still is to a degree, but I know that what you are doing is the right thing. I know that what both of us are doing is the right thing. That boy needs us, whether he knows it or not. He needs a Christian balance in his life that I'm sure he's not getting right now.

"I have to try and look at this through his child's eyes. He's probably going to be scared and apprehensive enough as it is. He may even be bitter. We're the adults here. It would be childish, not to mention stupid, of me to make this transition in his life any more difficult than it's already going to be. I'm sure he's been fed negative stuff about you and me. I think it's important that he feels comfortable and loved in this house. He's not to blame for any of this, and he shouldn't be treated as though he is."

Bryan couldn't respond verbally. All that he could do was pull Nicole to him and hold her close. Once again, words to express what he felt in his heart escaped him, so he kissed the top of her head and closed his eyes in silent thankful prayer.

CHAPTER THIRTEEN

As the workweek neared its end, Nicole found herself struggling with a level of nervousness that she hadn't experienced since the day of her wedding. Each day, she and Sharon spent their lunch breaks shopping the nearby mall, finding items to use as decoration in the room that Gerald would be sleeping in.

With Bryan's approval, she decided to use the Fat Albert theme for the bedding and curtains. The heroes were saved for the video collection that included Batman, Superman, Spiderman, and The Incredible Hulk. A bookshelf was purchased to house the videos and reading materials that she bought. After she shelled out $400 for an X box and video games, Sharon convinced her that she had done enough.

Bryan and Melvin did their share to help ready the room by adding a new coat of paint to the walls and putting together the bookshelf that Nicole had purchased. He tried not to show it, but Nicole knew that Bryan was nervous as the day of Gerald's visit approached.

When Friday finally arrived, Nicole thought of what her weekend would be like as she looked over the business's books in her office. Concentrating on the numbers in front of her eyes was difficult, as her mind seemed to process a thousand thoughts at once. Sharon's entrance went unnoticed as she stared at the open book and tapped the desk with the eraser of her pencil.

"You look nervous." Sharon broke her trance.

"Oh," Nicole said. "I didn't see you come in."

"Are you nervous?" Sharon asked as she sat across from her friend.

"I think frightened is a better word," Nicole admitted.

"You're scared?" Sharon was surprised.

"Oh, God, yes," she answered.

"But you've been so calm about this all week long. I mean, we've been shopping and decorating all week."

"I know," Nicole said as she stood and exhaled heavily. "All week I've been preparing myself for this day. Gerald will be here in a few hours, and every day I've been talking to myself and facing the reality of it all. Now I'm so jittery and jumpy at the thought of his visit."

"What are you scared about?"

"I don't know. I guess I'm just not sure what to expect. I have so many 'what ifs' going on in my head. You know. Like what if he likes Bryan but doesn't like me? What if he's a rebellious kid and won't behave properly in our home? What if he runs away? What if he goes back home and tells his mother negative things about his experience with us?"

"Slow it down, girl," Sharon said. "Everything is going to be all right. You can't go into this expecting the worst. I'm sure there will be a period of adjustment for all parties involved, but you have to try and keep positive expectations."

"I'm trying to, Sharon. I really am."

"Well, try a little harder. The last thing you want is for Bryan to pick up on your apprehension. He's counting on your strength," Sharon said as a familiar figure stood in the open doorway.

"Hi," Bryan said as he slowly entered.

"Hi," both friends responded after silent glances at one another.

"Can we have a minute alone?" Bryan quietly asked Sharon.

Realizing that Bryan had overheard her conversation with Nicole, Sharon gave her friend an apologetic smile before closing the office door and leaving her alone with her husband. Bryan sat in the chair that Sharon had vacated and motioned for Nicole to sit in the empty seat beside him. He took her hands in his and kissed the back of them before speaking.

"I could get a hotel room and keep him away from the house if that will make things easier for you."

"No, baby," Nicole said. "I don't want you to do that."

"I don't want you to feel forced into anything here," he said.

"I don't feel forced, Bryan. I don't feel forced at all. That's not what I was saying."

"What then?"

"I'm scared."

"Scared?"

"Yes. Aren't you? I mean, we're about to take on the responsibility of helping to raise a child. Not just a child, but your child, Bryan. Your almost teenaged son. Doesn't that scare you just a little bit?"

"It terrifies me," Bryan said.

"So you are scared."

"Yes, I am," he admitted again. "Today's the day. As ready as I've been planning to be for today, I'm not."

"That's the same way I'm feeling," Nicole said. "I'm not saying that I don't want him in our house or in my life. I do. He's family. I'm just saying that I'm afraid of something that I've never experienced before."

"Fear of the unknown," Bryan added.

"Yes."

"I've always known that you were a strong woman," Bryan said, "but over the past week and a half, you've proven to be stronger than I ever gave you credit for. I have no doubt that you will get through this just fine."

"And you?" Nicole asked.

"I'll be fine too." He smiled. "I think what both of us are feeling is perfectly normal. At least, that's what Uncle Charles has convinced me of. We'll both be fine," he concluded and a knock on the door interrupted their discussion.

After a brief conversation with one of the caregivers, the couple was once again left to themselves. The time they spent talking eased their concerns about Gerald's arrival.

"Are you headed home right now?" Nicole asked.

"I had just left Melvin's job before I stopped by. He should be on the highway headed toward Tallahassee right now. He said he should be at our house no later than 9:00 tonight. I'm going to head home early, but not right now," he explained. "I need to go back to the office and pick up Todd at 5:00 and take him home before going home myself."

"He did well this week, huh?" Nicole asked.

"Todd actually did a great job. Now, since we're sure

his mother has no immediate plans to take him back from Mother Peek, I've promised him an internship, of a sort, this summer. He's going to be helping me out whenever needed."

"You're so good with him." Nicole smiled proudly. "I'm sure you'll have the same kind of impact on Gerald."

"Speaking of which," he said as he stood and pulled her to a standing position with him, "I need to get going. After we close the office, I'm going to take Todd to that Christian bookstore on Cascade Avenue. He wants to use a portion of his paycheck to purchase a Bible. I think I'll pick up one for Gerald while we're there."

"Okay," Nicole said, kissing him briefly. "I'll see you at home later, then."

"What time are you leaving today?" he asked.

"I'm hoping to be out of here by 5:00. I'm sure I'll beat you home. I'll just get started on dinner. Anything you have a taste for in particular?"

"Yes," Bryan said with a sheepish grin, "but we'll discuss that later."

"You are so bad." Nicole laughed as she hugged him close.

"What?" he asked as he dropped the seductive tone. "I was talking about fried chicken. What are you talking about?"

"You were not!" Nicole said as she playfully pushed him toward the door.

"Told you to keep your mind out of the gutter." He laughed as she walked with him out of her office and through the front exit.

The two stood together, face-to-face, as Bryan leaned against the door of his convertible that was parked in the front lot. Nicole laid her head against his chest and took in the alluring fragrance of his cologne.

"We're going to get through this, baby," he whispered.

"I know," she quickly agreed.

"Well," he said, "let *me* get going so I can get back to work."

"You still have to drive back to the office and take Todd home, right?"

"Yeah. Hey, it's close enough to 5:00," he said. "Why don't you let me take you home first?" The look in his brown eyes was a familiar one.

"I have my car," Nicole laughed again as Sharon walked out and joined them.

"What are you two doing out here?" Sharon asked.

"Nothing," Nicole said. "Bryan was just leaving."

"We could come back for your car," he said without acknowledging Sharon's presence.

"No." Nicole laughed as she pushed him away. "Now go on and get your work done. I have to stop and pick up a few things for dinner on the way home anyway."

"Does the recipe call for you to pick up candles or oils or anything like that?" Bryan asked.

"Oh, Lord." Sharon rolled her eyes as she shook her head.

"You know I'm all about satisfying my man's appetite," Nicole said as she kissed him one last time.

"Oh yeah?" Bryan smiled.

"Third person in listening range," Sharon announced.

"I'm talking about that fried chicken that you said you wanted earlier," Nicole said as she stepped away from him. "What are you talking about?"

"That's cold," Bryan said as he put his sunglasses on.

"See you at home later," she said, laughing as she waved at him.

"Stop torturing that man, girl." Sharon laughed.

"He loves it," Nicole said.

"So you're headed home?" Sharon asked as the two of them walked back into the center.

"As soon as I finish up with this filing," Nicole said as she began putting the remaining files in the drawer.

"So did the two of you talk about it?" Sharon asked. "I mean, the way you feel about tonight?"

"Yeah. Bryan's just as afraid and uncertain as I am. We're just going to have to face it together. I feel better about it after talking to him."

"That's good," Sharon said.

"Well," Nicole said as she locked up her desk and file drawers, "remember us in your prayers while you're out."

"Of course we will," Sharon said. "The two of you will do just fine."

After checking Gerald's room for the fourth time to be sure that everything was situated perfectly, Nicole began preparations for dinner. She had just laid out all of her ingredients when she heard the house alarm beep. Bryan had arrived. She heard his slow footsteps as he headed first to their bedroom to take off his watch. It was always the first thing he did when he got home from work.

"Hi," he said as he entered the kitchen and kissed her cheek.

"Hi," she responded before he disappeared.

Nicole knew that Bryan was going to go and check on the same room that she had checked and rechecked. The hourly chime on the clock hinted that the time of Gerald's arrival was getting closer. It was 7:00. She heard Bryan coming back down the stairs as the phone rang.

Nicole's secret recipe for fried chicken had earned her the blue ribbon for three consecutive years at Christ Center of Hope's annual cookout. She mixed her marinade ingredients, laid the chicken in the juices, and placed the pan in the refrigerator.

"Melvin said that they will be here in about an hour and a half," Bryan said as he rejoined her in the kitchen.

"Did everything go smoothly with him picking Gerald up?" Nicole asked as she washed her hands in the kitchen sink.

"I got the feeling that something went on that he didn't want to discuss in front of the boy. He said that he'd fill me in on everything when they got here."

"He's making good time," Nicole said as she took a deep breath.

"Yeah," Bryan said as he reached into an upper cabinet and retrieved a pot that he knew Nicole would need for the macaroni.

"Thank you," she said.

"Do you need my help with anything?"

"No, sweetheart," she said. "You go ahead and change into something more comfortable and do whatever it is that you may need to do. I'll take care of dinner."

After giving her a quick peck on the cheek, Bryan left her alone to finish dinner. Her stomach seemed to be a cage of butterflies as Nicole continued preparing the first meal that they would share with her husband's son. She knew that it was only a matter of time before the anxiety she felt on the inside would show on her face, and she didn't want Bryan to see it.

She continued with her preparations as she heard the shower water begin to run. For a brief moment she had thoughts of joining her husband in the hot water. Reality took over quickly, though, as she thought of all that she had to do.

The smell of oven-baked macaroni and cheese began

to fill the kitchen as she began flowering and frying her marinated chicken. By 8:15 she was turning off the oven and rubbing pats of butter across the top of her golden brown dinner rolls. Dinner was complete and none too soon. By the time she had cleaned up the dishes and set the table, she could hear Melvin's car driving up into the driveway.

"They're here," Bryan said as he peeked through the living room curtain.

"I know." Nicole walked by his side and hugged him tightly. "Are you ready?" she asked.

"I don't think I can ask for extra time." He tried to smile as the doorbell rang.

"Hey, there," Melvin said as he stepped into the house with Gerald following closely behind.

"Hey," Bryan said before turning to look at the handsome boy. "Hi, Gerald," he said as he extended his hand.

"Hey," Gerald said, shaking his hand without looking the strange man directly in the face.

"This is my wife, Nicole."

"Hi." Nicole shook his hand as well.

"Hey." He smiled slightly.

"Let me show you to your room so you can put your bags away," Nicole offered as she led him up the stairs.

"Man, that boy looks so much like you it ain't funny," Melvin said as soon as he knew Gerald couldn't hear.

"I told you," Bryan said.

"Yes, you did," Melvin said, "and you weren't lying."

"I know you need to go," Bryan said. "Thanks for doing this for me. Did everything go all right?"

"Man, what in the world attracted you to that

chick?" Melvin asked. "I mean, I'm not talking physically. She's an okay-looking lady and all, but she's got about as much personality as sour grapes."

"I don't know what I saw in her," Bryan said. "I don't even remember seeing her. But in her defense," he continued, "I think she's just bitter. She took care of him for a long time by herself. Did you give her the money order?"

"Yeah. She didn't even bother to thank me for bringing it to her. She just looked at it and said, 'It's about time.' I'm telling you, man. She's quite a handful."

"Well, thanks for picking him up for me," Bryan said as Nicole and Gerald made their way back down the steps.

"We picked a winner." Nicole smiled. "He loves Fat Albert. He likes the FUBU gear that has the Fat Albert gang on them."

"Do you have any of that gear?" Bryan asked.

"No." He shrugged.

"I see," Bryan said.

"I'm going to get out of here," Melvin said. "Thanks again," Bryan said as Melvin left.

"Are you hungry?" Nicole asked Gerald as he stood quietly looking at his empty hands.

He shook his head no.

"Did you already eat before coming?" she asked.

"Uh-huh."

"You like ice cream?" she tried again.

"Yeah," he nodded.

"Just help yourself to as much as you'd like, okay?"

The family sat down and held hands as Bryan gave thanks for the food. Gerald obediently joined hands with them, but it was apparent that he wasn't used to the ritual. Although he claimed not to be hungry, he ate heartily.

Conversation was minimal. It was clear that Gerald did-n't feel comfortable enough for much chatter. After eating his ice cream, he took his bath and chose to go to bed instead of sitting up late.

Bryan and Nicole cleaned up the kitchen together. While Nicole prepared for her bath, Bryan walked up to the boy's bedroom and turned on the light. Gerald turned over in the bed to face the tall man as he entered his room.

"Are you comfortable?" Bryan asked.

"Yeah," Gerald responded.

"Did you say your prayers?"

His silence was enough for Bryan to know that he hadn't. It was yet another spiritual practice that he wasn't accustomed to.

"Come on." Bryan smiled as he patted the boy's back and knelt beside his bed. "Let's pray."

Gerald hesitated for a moment but crawled out of the bed and knelt beside his new father.

"When we pray," Bryan explained quietly, "we thank God for all the things that He has done for us through-out the day, and then we ask Him for the things that we need Him to do for our lives and our futures. Do you understand that?"

"Yeah."

"Good." Bryan smiled as he proceeded to lead the brief, simple prayer.

After he had finished, he covered the boy's body with the new sheets that Nicole had bought for him, said good night, turned out the lights, and joined Nicole, who was just climbing into bed.

"How is he?" Nicole asked.

"He's okay," Bryan said. "We said our prayers to-gether. I think praying is new for him."

"I picked that up too," Nicole agreed.

"He appears to be a little uncomfortable right now," Bryan admitted, "but that's understandable."

"Absolutely."

"You were great, by the way, Mrs. Walker."

"Was I, really?" Nicole smiled.

"Yes." Bryan slid closer to her in the bed. "The way you got him to eat was the work of a pro. I guess motherly instincts do come naturally."

"I guess so," Nicole said as he kissed her cheek.

"So did you get any of that ice cream?" Bryan asked.

"No," Nicole said as she buried her head in his chest. "I was thinking that maybe we could have a different kind of dessert."

"I like the way you think," Bryan said as he wrapped his arms around her and kissed her forehead.

"What?" she pulled away. "I was talking about cheesecake. What are you talking about?"

"Oh, I got your cheesecake," Bryan said as he pulled the covers over both their heads and slid her giggling body under his.

CHAPTER FOURTEEN

Nicole,

I have a counseling session at the church this morning from 7–8 AM. I'm sorry that I forgot to mention it to you earlier. I hope you're okay with being there with Gerald alone for a few minutes. I checked on him at 6:00, just before I began writing this note. He was sleeping peacefully. If you need me for anything at all, page me. My phone will be off during the meeting, as usual. I should be home by 8:30 if all goes well. I love you.

P.S. Thanks for last night. You were great with Gerald . . . and with me. Your fried chicken may have received the blue ribbon, but it's your cheesecake that gets the gold.

Love, Bryan.

Nicole laughed as she peeled the note off of the bathroom mirror and placed it in the metal box where she kept all of the little notes that Bryan had left her over the years. Returning to the restroom, she proceeded to take her morning shower before heading to the kitchen to prepare breakfast.

"Can I call my mama?"

Gerald's voice startled her as she stirred the pot of grits. Just that quickly, she had forgotten that there was another person in the house. He stood in his pajamas waiting for her answer.

"Of course, sweetheart," she said using the dishcloth to wipe the grits that she had splashed onto the stove top when she jolted at the sound of the child's voice. "The cordless phone is by the couch."

Feeling flushed with embarrassment, Nicole continued with breakfast, taking two extra eggs out of the refrigerator for her forgotten stepson. She was just preparing to pour the beaten eggs into the skillet when Gerald walked back in with the phone in his hand.

"My mama wants to speak to you," he said.

"She does?" Nicole asked in surprise.

"Yeah," he said.

After wiping her hands on a dish towel, she turned off the stove where the skillet was warming and placed the bowl of eggs in the refrigerator.

"Thanks." She smiled. "Why don't you go upstairs and get dressed? Breakfast will be ready in a few minutes."

"Okay," he said.

"Hello?" Nicole spoke cautiously.

"Where is Bryan?" Tricia asked.

The harsh tone of her voice caught Nicole unprepared. It almost frightened her. Looking around the dividing wall that separated the kitchen from the living room, she noticed that Gerald had already gone back upstairs.

"Excuse me?" she asked.

"Where is Bryan?" Tricia asked again, enunciating each word slowly as though Nicole was stupid.

"He's not here." Nicole tried to remain civil. "Is there something I can help you with?"

"I know he's not there," she said as though insulted. "I'm not stupid. Gerald told me he wasn't there. I didn't ask you whether or not he was there. I asked you where he was."

"He's at the church," Nicole said after a deep breath to calm her nerves.

"I did not send our son there for him to dump him off on you," she blurted. "You ain't his babysitter, and you ain't his mama. I should have known he'd pull some mess like this. You ain't got the sense enough to make him take care of his own child!"

"He did not dump Gerald on me." Nicole felt her rationality fade as she walked into her bedroom and closed the door. "He had an early morning meeting at the church. He'll be home shortly."

"Yeah, yeah. Tell me anything, okay?" she snapped back. "I should have known better than to think he really had any intention of being a father to Gerald. It ain't just about paying out money, you know," she continued. "Y'all think y'all can just dish out your little money to me and don't have to treat my son right. Well, that ain't the way it goes."

"You listen to me," Nicole said angrily, trying to keep her voice at a sensible level. "Don't you dare imply that Bryan isn't taking responsibility for his son."

"If he was taking responsibility for him he'd be there right now," she interrupted. "You think I've been able to run the streets all these years? No. I had a son to raise, and everywhere I went he had to go. I ain't had nobody to dump him off on while I did stuff that I wanted to do."

"Why do you keep insinuating . . ."

"Don't be throwing around your big words with me, sister," Tricia interrupted again. "I may not have the education that you have, but I ain't no dummy. As a matter of fact, I'm smart enough to know when somebody is making a fool out of me, but I see you ain't. You can't even see that he's using you as a nanny for his son 'cause he don't want to take care of him. You think 'cause he married you that makes you something special? You think I'm some kind of trash 'cause I let him get me pregnant?"

"What?"

"Well, one thing is for sure," she continued. "He might've married you, but I see he treats you like a tramp just like the rest of the women he's been with. He ain't got no wife. You're just his live-in tramp."

"Let me tell you something." Nicole raised her voice as she lost control of the anger she had been trying to keep on a leash. She didn't even notice that Bryan had entered the room. "Don't you ever," she continued as she fought tears, "ever call me a tramp! I am Bryan's wife. He's not using me for any reason. I'm here with Gerald because I want to be. He's not just Bryan's responsibility. He's my responsibility as well."

"He is not your—" Tricia began.

"No." Nicole cut her off. "Let me finish. You have said quite enough. For Gerald's sake, I'm going to remain as urbane with you as possible, but I will not tolerate being belittled by you."

"Let me make something very clear to you," Bryan said furiously to Tricia after abruptly taking the phone from Nicole. "Don't you ever disrespect my wife. You don't call her a tramp. You don't call her anything. Don't ever let her name come out of your mouth again. Don't even pray for her. Do I make myself clear? You have no right to talk to her that way, and I will not put up with it. Not for one minute."

"Ain't nobody disrespecting your precious wife. This is all your fault anyway. I'm just calling it like I see it," Tricia said. "How are you gonna just leave the house and leave Gerald with her? He's supposed to be spending time with you. You're supposed to be getting to know him. How are you gonna get to know him while you running the streets and leaving him home with her? He ain't her child."

"My visits with Gerald are unsupervised," Bryan reminded her as he watched Nicole go into the restroom and close the door. "It's not your place to check up on my whereabouts when he's in my custody. I don't answer to you. Gerald is being well taken care of by both me and Nicole."

"You're supposed to—"she began.

"I have spent enough of my God-given breath on you. This conversation has already taken three minutes out of my life that I can't get back and use to do something worthwhile. I don't owe you any explanations. I don't tell you how to take care of him when he's there," Bryan continued as he raised his voice above hers, "and you're not going to tell us how to take care of him when he's here."

With that said, he hung up the phone without giving her a chance to respond. He blew out a lungful of breath as he tried to calm the seething anger that he felt inside before approaching the door of the restroom.

Nicole stood over the sink, splashing cool water over her face. Bryan handed her the face towel as she felt

179

around the counter for it. She looked at him through the bathroom mirror.

"You think he heard me?" she finally spoke. "I didn't mean to raise my voice."

Bryan looked back at her reflection and laughed softly. All that she had just gone through with Tricia and her biggest worry was whether or not Gerald had overheard the argument.

"I don't think so," he said as he pulled her close to him and hugged her.

"He asked to call her," she said. "I thought I was doing the right thing by letting him call her, but when she found out you weren't here, she just went mad. I tried not to lose my temper, but she just kept pushing."

"Sweetheart," Bryan said as he lifted her chin so that she could look him straight in his eyes, "you don't owe me any explanation, and you certainly have no reason to feel guilty. You didn't do anything wrong."

"But I had promised myself that I wouldn't stoop to her level. I promised I wouldn't let her get under my skin."

"You didn't do anything wrong," he repeated. "Nobody expects you not to defend yourself or your integrity," he said as the phone rang.

"What if that's her?" Nicole asked sounding worried.

"Unless Melvin gave her our number," Bryan said as he headed for the cordless phone that he had left on the bed, "she has no idea how to reach us at home."

Nicole walked over and looked at the caller ID box on the nightstand as Bryan answered the phone. The phone call was coming from Mother Peek's home.

"Hey, Todd," she heard Bryan say as she walked out of the room and back into the kitchen.

The grits were still warm, but she turned the eye of

the stove back on and added a little water to heat them up a little more. Her mind was filled with thoughts as she retrieved the previously beaten eggs from the refrigerator to pour them into the skillet that was heating next to the pot of grits.

What could ever have attracted Bryan to such a cruel-hearted person? she thought. *I'm sure that she's bitter for the hardships that she apparently endured as a result of having to raise Gerald on her own, but why the hatred and anger? She can't really believe that Bryan knew about his fraternity brothers' threat. Even if she'd thought it were true initially, she had to know better after meeting with him again.*

Could she be so angry because of Bryan's failed recollection of her? Maybe she thought that she had meant more to him than that. But how could she? They had only met that same night that they slept together. She couldn't really believe that he had loved her.

"A penny for your thoughts." Bryan's voice snapped her train of thought.

"Can you set the table for me?" she asked.

"Sure," he said as he proceeded to take the plates from the cabinet.

"I was just thinking about the phone call and the depth of the animosity in Tricia's voice. I was trying to make sense of it all."

"You're always analyzing," Bryan said as he placed the plates on the table and then pulled the glasses from the dishwasher. "There are some things that just can't be figured out. I mean, what more does she want from me?" he asked while looking around the corner to be sure Gerald wasn't in listening range.

"I wish you could remember her," Nicole said.

"Why?"

"So you could explain to me what attracted you. I mean, I'm not insulting her at all. She's not an unattractive girl, but she's just not the type of girl I would think you'd be attracted to. You know what I mean?" she continued. "You've always told me that you were attracted to women who were four or five inches shorter than you. She has to be every bit as tall as you. You like women with shapely legs and arms," Nicole continued, finding herself becoming angry at the thought of it all. "She's just kind of long and lean. Her legs and arms are skinny. She's flat chested. She has no hips, and aside from all of that she has no personality. At what point in your life were you ever that undemanding and desperate?"

Bryan stood quietly staring at the last glass that he held in his hand as he listened. It sounded harsh, but he knew that in spite of the fact that anger drove a portion of her speech, Nicole was right. He had made a horrible mistake when he had let himself get involved with Tricia Smart, and he wasn't the only one suffering the consequences.

"I'm sorry," Nicole apologized quietly as she walked up to him and took the glass from his hand. "I'm sorry," she repeated while wrapping her arms around his waist and hugging him tightly.

"It's okay," he whispered. "That's what I want from you. I want you to tell me what you're feeling. Don't keep it bottled up. I want to know where your head is about this whole thing at all times. It hurts," he admitted, "but I need you to be open with me."

"She spoke to me like I was some kind of animal," Nicole said. "I just keep thinking that, because of one mistake, we're going to have to deal with a lifetime of this kind of aggravation."

"I know it's hard, baby," Bryan said. "I'm sorry

about the phone call. I'm trying to do everything I can to make it as stress free for you as I can. Just promise me that you won't leave me again. I can deal with this, but I couldn't deal with that."

"I'm not going to leave you, Bryan," she assured him. "I just need to be a little more patient, I guess."

"You don't have to be more patient," Bryan told her. "You're doing great with Gerald, and he's the only one who matters here. You don't owe Tricia your patience or anything else," he concluded as the doorbell rang.

"Are you expecting company?"

"Oh, yeah," Bryan said as he pointed towards the breakfast table. "I set four places. I told Todd he could come over this morning. That's okay, right?" he asked as he walked towards the front door.

"Sure," Nicole said as she looked at the eggs, hoping she had scrambled enough for the four of them.

"Hi, Ms. Nicole," he said as he walked into the kitchen. "It smells good in here."

"Thank you, Todd." Nicole smiled.

"Come on and let's get washed up for breakfast," Bryan told him. "We'll go to the upstairs restroom. That way you can meet Gerald."

"Cool," Todd said as they disappeared.

"You have got to keep it together, Nicole," she thought out loud once they had left. "You can't let her get to you like that."

She set the bowls of food out on the table and had just put the orange juice out when the three men joined her. Gerald seemed to feel a little more comfortable with Todd being there. The four of them sat down and joined hands for grace.

Breakfast went better than expected. Nicole briefly forgot about her episode with Tricia and concentrated on the conversation around the table. Todd's presence was a definite help. He announced that he had been chosen to play on the high school's baseball team for the upcoming year. Not only would he get his chance at bat, but he would also serve as a backup pitcher. Bryan was visibly proud. All of their hard work and practice had paid off.

"You like baseball, Gerald?" Todd asked as they were finishing their meal and clearing the table.

"Yeah."

"You want to go outside and hit some balls?"

"Okay," Gerald said.

"Can we, Bryan?" Todd asked.

"Sure, we can." Bryan smiled.

"Not right now, though," Nicole added. "You just ate. Give it at least a half hour for your food to settle some."

"Gerald," Bryan said, "why don't you take Todd to your room and show him your video games and X box."

"You got an X box?" Todd's eyes widened with excitement.

"Yeah." Gerald seemed flattered that his new toy impressed this older kid.

"Can we play some games?"

"Okay," Gerald said as he led the way to the upstairs bedroom.

"Thanks for breakfast, sweetheart," Bryan said as he placed his glass in the sink.

"You're welcome." Nicole smiled. "I'll get the dishes. You go ahead and play with the kids."

"They have to wait awhile anyway." Bryan shrugged as he rolled up his sleeves to run fresh dishwater.

Nicole washed and Bryan rinsed the dishes in silence for several moments. Nicole felt blessed. Bryan was so

184

unlike most men that she knew. Even men who were considered good husbands didn't go the extra mile to help around the house as Bryan did. When she told Sharon about how Bryan would help cook and clean, her best friend told her to count her blessings. Even Melvin didn't lift a hand to do any housework. Nicole smiled just thinking about it.

"A penny for your thoughts," Bryan said as he noticed the smile on her face.

"You still owe me a penny from the last time," she teased.

"Put it on my tab," Bryan said. "My credit is good."

"I was just thinking about how great you are," Nicole said.

"In what way?" Bryan smiled.

"How you're so good around the house."

"Are we talking the kitchen or the bedroom?" he asked with a sly grin.

"Both," Nicole said as she handed him the last pot.

"Well," he said as he dried his hands on the dish towel. "I figure the more practice I get, the better I get."

"Are we talking the kitchen or the bedroom?" she laughed as she welcomed his embrace.

"Both," he said as he kissed her tenderly.

"Minor in the house," Todd said as he entered the kitchen and covered his eyes. "Minor in the house."

"You're supposed to be upstairs," Bryan said as he tossed the dish towel at him.

"I know." Todd laughed. "I just forgot my watch," he said as he retrieved it from the countertop.

"Who's winning the game?" Nicole asked.

"I won the first one, but I let him win the second one," Todd whispered.

"Good for you," Bryan said.

"He's a pretty nice kid," Todd said. "He's kind of quiet, but he's starting to talk to me a little bit now."

"We appreciate your helping to bring him out of his shell," Bryan told him.

"It beats sitting at home watching television by myself on a Saturday." Todd shrugged. "He looks so much like you that it's scary," Todd added. "He can look at you and know exactly what he's going to look like when he's forty or fifty."

"I am not forty or fifty," Bryan said as Nicole laughed.

"Oops," Todd said as he turned to walk away. "My bad."

"You have really turned that boy's life around," Nicole said as they walked into the bedroom.

"He has come a long way," Bryan admitted. "He just needed some positive guidance."

"You think you can do the same for Gerald?" Nicole asked.

"I'm going to give it my best shot. It will certainly be a challenge. He's different. He's not around me constantly like Todd is. Plus, I don't know what kinds of things he's been or is still being exposed to. I hope I can help. He doesn't seem to be a bad kid at all, just a little closed in."

"I noticed," Nicole said as she sat on edge of the bed. "I think we can start by trying to get him to say something other than 'yeah' and 'okay.'"

"I know," Bryan laughed. "I just want to be a good father," he continued. "I don't want him to disrespect me because of what he may have heard about me over the years. I want him to see me as a positive role model in his life. I don't want him to see me the way I see my father."

"You know, Bryan, seeing you playing and hanging

out with the boys reminds me of my brothers and how they wished our dad would've spent more time with them. You are incredible, Mr. Walker. There's not a chance of Gerald seeing you like you saw your father," Nicole said. and she kissed him softly on the neck, causing him to moan softly.

"Now, you know that's my spot," he mumbled. "And you know I have to go outside and practice with the boys. Why are you messing with me like that?"

"Because I like messing with you," she answered.

"You know, I know your spot too," he said as he began nibbling and kissing her earlobe.

"Bryan," Todd called from the living room. "We're ready to go!"

Bryan laughed as Nicole let out a disappointed whimper.

"Okay, I'll meet you outside," he called back. "Take the bats and balls from the closet."

"Okay," Todd answered.

"You owe me one," Nicole said just before he kissed her.

"Like I said," he said as he backed away, "put it on my tab. My credit is good."

CHAPTER FIFTEEN

Nicole felt as though all eyes were on Bryan and her as they walked into church on Easter Sunday morning with Gerald. They looked good, as usual. Bryan wore an olive green double-breasted suit that matched the black and olive dress that Nicole wore as they walked down the aisle, making their way to their regular seats.

She knew the double takes they were receiving were due to the handsome Bryan look-alike boy that walked between them. Gerald looked particularly sharp in the new black suit that Bryan had purchased for him after they played ball in the backyard.

"My God," Sharon whispered in Nicole's ear once they were seated. "He *does* look like Bryan."

Nicole smiled and nodded. It was impossible not to agree. Almost everything about Gerald resembled Bryan. It wasn't just that he looked so much like him. He also talked like him and walked like him. When Nicole was trimming his hair the night before, she even noticed that he had ears like his father.

Bryan handed Gerald his new Bible. It was obvious that this new setting and such a large crowd of unfamiliar faces were making him quite uncomfortable. He took the Bible and clutched it between both hands. Noticing his uneasiness, Bryan patted him supportively on his leg.

The service was ready to begin. As the music started, Todd squeezed through the aisle and took the empty seat beside Gerald. The nervous boy's smile indicated that he found some relief in having his new friend sit next to him.

The Easter production went over well. The youth department performed their own rendition of the Easter story. When they finished, the congregation gave a standing ovation. Gerald seemed to enjoy watching the children wrapped in sheets play their biblical parts. Pastor Gaines followed the production with a stirring sermon on Jesus' gift of life to the world.

Inwardly, Nicole was hopeful that Bryan would be ready to leave promptly following the service. She had tried to prepare herself for the questions that she was sure they would be asked, but now that the time had come, she wasn't nearly as ready as she initially thought she would be. She worried as to how she would handle being bombarded with inquiries concerning Gerald.

As the benediction was given and the assembly began to mingle and disperse, Bryan led Gerald and her toward the front of the church so that they could greet their pastor as normal. Nicole could feel the burning into her skin from the eyes that followed them as they maneuvered through the crowd.

"Bryan." Pastor Gaines smiled as he saw his favorite nephew approaching.

"Hey, Uncle Charles," Bryan said as the two men embraced.

"Nicole," Pastor Gaines said, "you're as lovely as ever."

"Thank you." She blushed as she hugged him as well.

"Come on over here," the pastor said as he reached for Gerald. "We're not strangers. We're family. How are you doing?"

"Okay," Gerald said as he was pulled into a hug.

"Are you enjoying your stay this weekend?"

"Yeah." He nodded.

"Well, the next time he's here," Pastor Gaines told Bryan, "you all have to come over and let me and your aunt cook dinner for you."

"Sounds good," Bryan said.

"Well, hurry and let him get out there and hunt those eggs before the others find them all," Pastor Gaines said.

Nicole held Gerald's hand as they walked toward the exit of the church. She suddenly felt a need to protect him from whatever awaited them on the outside. It was a beautiful Sunday afternoon, and the Florida breeze felt good as it danced across the front lawn of Christ Center of Hope. To Nicole's relief, no one made a big issue of Gerald's presence.

"Brother and Sister Walker," Mother Peek called as they neared their car.

"Hey, Gerald," Todd said. "Take off your jacket. I'll race you. We've got to work on your speed for running around the bases."

"Let him hunt some eggs, Todd," Mother Peek instructed. "Don't run around so long until you miss all the eggs."

Gerald handed Bryan his suit jacket, and the two boys jolted across the lawn and toward the parking lot.

191

"Soon as I seen that boy, I knew he was your brother," Mother Peek said as she watched the two boys in the distance. "How old is he? He's younger than my Todd, ain't he?"

"He'll be thirteen in a couple of months," Bryan said. "He's a couple of years younger."

"Well, either both of you look like your mama, or both of you look like your daddy, 'cause both of you look just like each other."

Nicole took a deep breath as Bryan prepared to speak.

"He's not my brother, Mother Peek."

"There ain't no way that that boy ain't your brother. You gonna try and convince me that the two of you just happen to look alike?"

Bryan lowered his voice. "He's my son."

It took a moment to sink in, but she was finally able to speak. She looked at Bryan and then at Nicole, as though she still wasn't sure that Bryan wasn't just pulling her leg.

"Oh," she finally said. "Well, I guess you ain't never too old to learn something new every day," she said. "I didn't know you had a son. Does Todd know? He's never mentioned it to me."

"Yes, Todd knows," Bryan told her. "I asked him not to tell anyone."

"Baby, I understand you wanting to keep some of the things in your past under wraps, but we was all sinners at one time or another and did stuff that we ain't proud of. But I ain't sure it's right to keep your child a secret. He might get the feeling that you 'shamed of him. You don't want that."

"It wasn't like that, Mother Peek," Nicole tried to explain.

"I wasn't trying to keep Gerald a secret," Bryan said as he placed his arm around his wife's waist in appreciation of her support. "I just found out about him a couple of weeks ago. His mother just made his existence known to me."

"I would ask you if you was sure he was yours, but I guess that would be a dumb question," she said. "You okay with all of this, baby?" she asked Nicole.

"Yes, ma'am." Nicole smiled. "I'm okay."

"Well, then," she said as the boys raced back toward them, holding eggs in both hands and laughing, "I reckon that's all that matters."

"You run pretty good," Todd complimented Gerald. "Maybe you should go for track instead of baseball."

"I might," Gerald panted.

"Two new words," Nicole said to Bryan, and he laughed.

"Hey, guys," Melvin said as he and Sharon approached with their children. "You all up for some barbecue?"

"I just kind of want to eat and relax today," Bryan said. "I don't feel like fighting the restaurant crowd."

"Us either," Sharon said. "Melvin's going to fire up the grill and barbecue out on the deck."

"That sounds good." Nicole looked at Bryan.

"Count us in," Bryan agreed.

"Do you all want to come, Mother Peek? Pastor and Sister Gaines will be there."

"Thank you, son," she said, "but you know I have this old ache in my lower back that comes from time to time. I think it's brought on 'cause I got bad feet, and when I stand up on them too long it flares up that aching right here in my back," she continued. "I think I'll just go home and put my feet up while I listen to Sunday service on the radio. Oooh, they have a preacher that sho' can preach! Do y'all ever listen to it?"

"No, ma'am," Melvin said as the others shook their heads along with him.

"You ought to tune in sometime," she said. "The Lord just blesses my soul through that station. Y'all go on and enjoy yourselves. I would come, but I got this pain in my lower back, and I need to elevate my feet. Y'all just keep us in your prayers."

"Yes, ma'am," Melvin said as the others nodded their heads along with him.

"Can I come, Brother Gibbs?" Todd pleaded softly as his grandmother turned to walk toward the car. "Please?"

"We're going to take Todd with us if that's okay, Mother," Melvin called to her. "I mean, unless you need him to do something around the house for you."

"Oh, yeah, it's all right," she said. "Take him on with y'all. The onlyest one I need is Jesus. Todd's a good boy, but he can't take this pain out my back. Y'all take him on with y'all. You'll bring him home, won't you, Brother Walker?"

"Yes, ma'am," Bryan said.

"That's a fine son you got there," she said as she headed on to her car.

"Thank you."

"See you later, Grandma," Todd called.

"All right," she told him. "Y'all take a switch to him if he misbehaves," she called as she drove away.

Bryan drove his family home first for them to change out of their dress clothes and to begin getting Gerald's things together so he'd be prepared to head back to Talla-hassee with Melvin following dinner. Todd helped him gather his things. All the items that Bryan and Nicole had bought him were to remain at their house so that he'd have them every time he visited.

The cookout was relaxing and enjoyable. What started out as batting practice ended up being a competitive game of baseball, pitting the men against the women. To be fair, since there were more males than females, Todd agreed to pitch for both teams, and Gerald was the shortstop for each team. The women's team, consisting of Nicole, Sharon, and Sister Gaines, lost miserably to the men's team of Bryan, Melvin, and Pastor Gaines, but they enjoyed the competition.

Nicole wasn't the only one who felt a sense of sadness when it was time for Gerald to leave. Melvin wanted to get on the road before it was too late so that he could get back home at a reasonable time. Even Gerald seemed a bit disappointed when Melvin announced that it was time for him to prepare to go home.

"It was good having you with us in church today," Pastor Gaines told Gerald as he followed Bryan and Nicole to their car.

"Yes," Sister Gaines agreed. "You have to promise us that you'll come back again."

"Okay," Gerald said, and he and Todd climbed into the backseat.

"You did real good, girl," Sharon commented in Nicole's ear.

"Thanks," Nicole smiled as she kissed Michael and Benjamin before getting in the car. "I'll see you at work tomorrow," she told Sharon as they backed out of the driveway.

"Okay."

"I'll be over in about an hour," Melvin called, and Bryan nodded and drove away.

Gerald got a much-needed bath before putting on fresh clothes for the trip ahead. Todd volunteered to help him straighten his room before leaving.

"Give us a minute," Bryan told Todd when he met them at the bedroom door, as he and Gerald were getting ready to head back downstairs.

"Okay," he said, and he left them alone.

"Thank you for spending the weekend with us," Bryan said as he sat on the edge of Gerald's bed. "I hope you enjoyed it as much as we did."

Gerald stood at the bedroom door with his suitcase in his hand and smiled slightly as he nodded in silence.

"Come here," Bryan said quietly as he patted the space beside him on the bed. "Sit here for a minute."

Gerald placed his luggage on the floor and obediently sat beside him.

"This is new for all of us," he began. "I know you're not 100 percent comfortable with me and Ms. Nicole right now, but I need for you to know that you can come to us and talk to us about anything, okay?"

"Okay."

"You don't have to feel out of place in our home," Bryan continued. "This is your home too. I know it's going to take some time. We've missed a lot of years of each other's lives. We're not going to make up for it in one weekend, but I want you to know that I want to try. I think we've had a good start this weekend, and I want to grow from this point. Is that all right with you?"

"Yeah," he nodded as he looked at his own lap.

"Say yes," Bryan said.

"Yeah," Gerald repeated.

"No," Bryan said and gently lifted the boy's chin to look into the mirror image of his own brown eyes. "Say yes," he said slowly.

"Yes," Gerald said.

"Good." Bryan smiled. "Now, doesn't that sound better?"

Gerald nodded yes as his eyes returned to his lap.

"I want you to take this." Bryan handed him a business card. "Don't lose it. It has my work, pager, and cell number on here. If you ever need to reach me for any reason, you can find me at one of these numbers."

Gerald quietly got up and put the card in the front pocket of his suitcase.

"When you get back home," Bryan said as he stood and reached into his pocket and retrieved his wallet, "I want you to give this to Mr. Gibbs to help him with putting gas in his car, okay?"

"Okay," Gerald said as he took the money and put it in his pocket.

"And remember to thank him for picking you up and taking you back home, okay?"

"Okay."

"And this," he said as he handed him some extra money, "is for you to stop and get something to eat in case you get hungry on the way. It's a two-and-a-half-hour drive. The barbecue will probably wear off before you get home. Whatever money is left over, put it in your bank and save it for whenever you want to buy something else."

"Okay."

"Say, thank you," Bryan instructed.

"Thank you," Gerald said.

"You're welcome." Bryan smiled as he rubbed his head affectionately. "Don't worry," he continued. "We'll work on it a little at a time.

"Gerald, let's pray before you go," Bryan said, taking Gerald's hand.

"Father God, we thank and praise You for this time that we've spent together, for the joy and the laughter we've shared. We trust You to work out any difficulties that may arise. Protect Melvin and Gerald as they travel and keep us all in Your loving care. In Jesus' name, amen."

Melvin had arrived and was waiting at the door as the two finally came down and joined the others. They all embraced Gerald and said their good-byes. Melvin volunteered to take Todd home on his way out. Bryan and Nicole stood in the doorway and waved as the car drove away.

It was around 9:30 when they got the call from Melvin that Gerald had arrived home safely. According to Melvin, Tricia's mood wasn't much better than when he had picked Gerald up two nights earlier. This time, she accused Bryan of not wanting to spend any time with his child. Nicole shook her head in disgust as she listened to their conversation.

"You're kidding," Bryan said as Melvin told him of his most recent encounter with Tricia.

"Nope," Melvin said. "She said that's the reason why you had me picking him up and taking him home, because you didn't want to spend any more time with him than you had to."

"She knows that she's the reason I have a third party picking him up," Bryan said. "It's she that I don't want to have to spend any time around. I don't want to have to deal with her attitude."

"I wanted to tell her that, but it just wouldn't have been right to say something like that in front of Gerald," Melvin said.

"Gerald was there when she said I didn't want to spend any time with him?"

"Oh, yeah," Melvin said. "He heard every word."

"What was she thinking?" Bryan thought out loud. "How did Gerald react?"

"He didn't really," Melvin said. "At least not in a way that was noticeable. I got the feeling that she feeds him bad stuff about you all the time. I also got the feeling that given a choice he'd rather have spent a few more days with you. He didn't seem excited about being back at home.

"One thing's for sure," Melvin continued. "You've certainly got your work cut out for you. This woman has no intentions of making this an easy transition for either one of you."

"Well, thanks for taking him home for me," Bryan said. "I appreciate it."

"Glad to help," Melvin said. "Oh, by the way, I told Gerald to keep the gas money.

"The way you're sacrificing your time going to pick him up . . ." Bryan replied.

"Man, please. I want to help, Bryan. That's a few dollars that Gerald can have in his pocket."

"All right, all right," Bryan said.

"Be safe, man. I'll talk to you tomorrow."

"Okay."

"We didn't expect this to be easy," Nicole told him as he hung up the telephone.

"I know, baby," Bryan said as he watched her thumb through their video collection.

"You want to watch a movie?" she asked.

"Sure. But make it a comedy or something. I need a laugh to erase thoughts of Tricia out of my mind."

Bryan sighed. "I guess that was an improper statement, but I felt like I had . . . I mean, we had made some progress with him this weekend. Now, I feel like her sole agenda is going to be to destroy the seed of trust that we planted in him before it can grow."

"I don't doubt that," Nicole said as she left the movies alone and joined him on the sofa, "and believe me, I understand your frustrations, but we agreed that we wouldn't let her break us down. Remember?"

"I remember," Bryan said.

"And I need you to be strong," Nicole said. "You're my king. I'm only as strong as you are. You know she easily gets under my skin. I need you to have enough strength for both of us."

Bryan smiled. It had been a while since he had heard her refer to him as her king. He loved that analogy, and she knew it.

"You're right," he said as he cupped her face in his hands. "I'll be your king if you'll be my queen. I'll be your strength and protection for as long as you want me to be. You know I'd never let her hurt you."

"I know," Nicole said, and he sealed his promise with a kiss.

After getting ready for bed, the two sat up late into the night snuggling together on the sofa, laughing and enjoying a bag of popcorn as they watched their favorite comedy for the fifth time.

The weekend that they both had been anxious and unsure of was finally over. Despite Tricia's ongoing attempts to ruin their credibility, they were pleased with the way things turned out.

CHAPTER SIXTEEN

"So, how does it feel to have the house back to your-selves?" Sharon asked as she and Nicole began eating their grilled chicken salads at a local restaurant that specialized in soups, salads, and sandwiches.

"I have to admit that it's nice to be able to veg out. You know, snuggle up and relax on the floor and watch movies or play poker like we did last night. Enough about me already—how much weight have you lost so far?" Nicole asked.

"Can you tell I've lost weight?" Sharon brightened.

"Yes, I can."

"That's why you're my best friend," Sharon said. "It's only been six pounds, but I'm proud of every one of them."

"That's pretty good," Nicole encouraged her. "Six pounds in less than three weeks is a good start."

"Yeah," Sharon said. "Six down and nineteen to go. I'd have to lose weight at a faster rate to be where I want to be by the time we go on vacation."

"I guess the time is approaching fast," Nicole agreed. "What is it now? Six weeks away?"

"Something like that," Sharon said. "At this rate, I'll still have seven pounds to go when it's time to hit the beach."

"That still would have been a great accomplishment," Nicole said supportively.

"I guess." Sharon shrugged. "I'm going to wait until the week of the trip before I buy my swimsuits though. That way, I'll get something that fits perfectly."

"Of course," Nicole said. "You owe yourself that reward."

"You have yours already?"

"No," Nicole answered. "I told Bryan that he could pick mine out for me. I'm going to buy his, and he's going to buy mine."

"You're letting Bryan pick out your swimsuit. Girl, you're liable to end up with a thong bikini." Sharon laughed.

"He'd better not." Nicole laughed with her.

"Well, Melvin went and bought the boys some swim trunks last week. They're the cutest little shorts."

"I guess Bryan will buy Gerald's things."

"Oh, he's coming along?" Sharon asked in surprise.

"Yeah. I thought you knew. I'm sorry. I guess we forgot to tell you guys. That's not a problem is it?"

"Of course not," Sharon said. "It just hadn't crossed my mind that his mother would let him go."

"It was a part of the original agreement that we all signed off on. He's spending some of the summer with us."

"That brings me back to my original question," Sharon said. "Are you glad he's gone?"

"Actually, I really miss him," Nicole said.

"Really?"

"Funny, huh?" Nicole laughed. "I think he kind of grew on both of us last weekend. I enjoyed having him. I know Bryan did too."

"That's good. I knew you could handle it. I don't know any other couple with a love stronger than yours and Bryan's. If any couple could endure something this big, you could."

"You know," Nicole said, "I always knew that Bryan and I had something special. From the first time we met it was special. This whole thing with Gerald scared me at first. I thought it was the beginning of the end of Bryan and me. Instead, it possibly may have made our love stronger. Working together to overcome something so devastating has really shown me how wonderfully sturdy our marriage really is."

"And just think," Sharon reminded her, "you almost missed out because you weren't interested in a relationship. 'Not with Bryan,'" she began mimicking Nicole's famous pre-Bryan speech, "'nor with anyone else, for that matter. Do I make myself clear?'"

"You know what?" Nicole laughed with her. "It's amazing how you can remember every detail of that five-year-old conversation, but this morning you couldn't remember where you put your stapler five minutes after you laid it down."

"I just like messing with you, girl," Sharon said. "I'm glad things turned out the way they did. God had to have a hand in it, 'cause when this thing about Gerald first hit the fan, I have to admit I was scared too."

"You know what I was thinking the other day?" Nicole sipped her water. "I had prayed so long for a child. Maybe he's it."

"Gerald?"

"Yeah. I mean, it certainly wasn't what I was asking for, but maybe in some way God answered that prayer. Maybe my giving birth wasn't in His will for my life. Maybe Gerald is the child I've always wanted."

"That's deep," Sharon said. "I never would have thought of it that way. To me, that's kind of like saying it wasn't God's will to give Bryan a child with his wife, but it was His will to give him one with some girl who he didn't care anything about. That doesn't sound right to me."

"When you say it like that, I agree," Nicole said. "It wasn't as though it was God's will for him to have a child outside of marriage, but he had to reap what he sowed. But because he also turned his life over to Christ, God blessed him with a wife who would support him. And because that wife wouldn't be able to have a child of her own, He made it so she would be able to accept the son born previously and care for him like her own."

"So it's like taking a negative," Sharon said, "and making a positive out of it."

"Right," Nicole said.

"And Bryan still has to pay for the sin he committed," Sharon continued, "but the price isn't as high as it would have been had he not, first of all, come to Christ, and secondly, chosen you for his bride."

"Exactly." Nicole smiled.

"You really are amazing," Sharon smiled at her friend. "I guess when God says He'll put no more on us that we can bear, He means it. I don't know if I could be that open-minded about the whole thing."

"Sure you could," Nicole said. "It's a matter of putting everything in perspective. If Bryan had been unfaithful and this was a three- or four-year-old kid, things would be very different. I wouldn't be able to support him or accept his child as my own."

"What about Gerald's mom? Are you trying to accept her as well?"

"No," Nicole admitted. "I don't see why I should have to even try. I respect her as his mother, but that's where my loyalty ends. She's hostile, she's vindictive, and she's bent on making everything with Gerald as difficult as possible. I only hope she doesn't succeed in her plans."

"Good always defeats evil in the end," Sharon said, and she popped a plum tomato into her mouth.

"Telling our parents was hard," Nicole said.

"Oh, yeah," Sharon said. "You said you all were going to tell them on Tuesday. That was two days ago. You didn't say anything else about it. Is that a sign that they didn't take it well?"

"Well, we waited until last night to call them. Bryan's mother pretty much had a carefree attitude. It was like it was no big deal to her. She told him to bring him the next time he visits Chicago. She told him that she was glad he was taking responsibility and not being like Garrett. Of course," Nicole continued, "she didn't call his daddy Garrett. She called him a few other choice names that I don't care to repeat."

"I can imagine." Sharon laughed. "What about Rev. and Mrs. Wilson?"

"Well, my parents were shocked at first. Then my mama, bless her heart, said the dumbest thing. It really should have hurt my feelings, but I knew that she didn't really mean any harm by it."

"What did she say?"

"She said, 'Well, you know, in the Bible, Sarah couldn't have any babies with Abraham, so she gave him a concubine to have a baby with.' Now really, Sharon," Nicole said, "what kind of thing was that to say to her infertile daughter? She made it sound like Bryan had just gone out and had a kid, and that I had given him permission."

"Yeah, that was kind of thoughtless," Sharon agreed.

"I know," Nicole said. "Daddy just wanted to know if I was okay. He said if I was willing to forgive Bryan, so were they. Again, as though Bryan had cheated on me. Anyway, they went on to tell me to pray for my 'hard-headed brothers' who were 'yet running from the Lord.'"

"Well, at least the most important people in both your lives now know, and they heard it from you and nowhere else."

"Yeah," Nicole said. "I guess everybody else in our lives, including the church people, will find out over time. We're not giving any big announcements or anything."

"One thing about news and the church," Sharon said, "it gets around real fast."

Sharon was right. By Sunday morning, it seemed that everyone knew the identity of the child whom Nicole and Bryan had brought to church with them the previous Sunday. Through the process of elimination, they figured that Mother Peek was the one who got the ball rolling.

She didn't mean any harm, they were sure, but all it would take was for her to mention it to one of the other old mothers in the church, and the spark would spread like a wildfire. No one seemed to take it negatively or treat Bryan any differently because of this new knowledge. For Nicole, it was almost a relief to have it out in the open.

As usual, the service was enjoyable. Pastor Gaines gave a surprise announcement that the following Sunday would be set aside for the youth of the church. He wanted the young members of the church to lead the praise service and to serve as ushers. He instructed the youth choir director to have the youth choir ready to sing.

"It's time for our young people to be about God's business," he said from the pulpit as the service was ending.

"Amen," the crowd agreed.

"I've already spoken with Minister Wright," he said, referring to the youth pastor. "He's going to be our speaker, and if any of you young people have something special that you want to do in next Sunday's service, let Sister Wright know, and she and her husband will see to it that your name gets on the program. We ain't turning none of you away," he said. "The devil sure ain't turning you away. He doesn't think you're too young to serve him, and God doesn't think you're too young to serve him either."

"Amen!" the crowd answered with enthusiasm.

When the service ended, it was as though Christ Center of Hope had never had a youth service before. There was excited chatter all around about how the service would be carried out. Many of the young people lined up to put their names on the program, while others shied away from the idea.

Nicole had left at work some vacation brochures that she had planned on looking over that night, so she asked Sharon to stop by the center with her for a quick moment.

Sharon put Benjamin, who had fallen asleep during the ride, in one of the baby beds in the infant area and put the safety gate up in the doorway so that Michael could play inside the room without getting into anything dangerous or hurting himself.

"Looks like everything is set for tomorrow," Sharon said as Nicole turned out the lights in her office and prepared to leave.

"The ladies did a good job of sanitizing the toys. Did you notice?" Nicole said.

"Yes, I did." Sharon smiled. "Are you going to get that message off of your voice mail?" She pointed to the blinking light on Nicole's phone.

Nicole reached for the brochures on her desk.

"I'm sure it could have waited," Nicole said, but pressed the button to hear the message on her speakerphone anyway.

The two women stood in disbelief while the message played. For three minutes, they listened to Tricia angrily swear and curse at Nicole for cutting Gerald's hair. She told Nicole in no uncertain terms that she had no right to alter anything about her son.

"I am trying to be civil with you," Tricia's message continued, "but I think you're just trying to mess with me. If you don't like the way I keep my child's hair, then that's tough," she continued. "You keep your hands off of him. He did not want his hair cut, and you ain't had no right cutting it. He wants to grow braids. Now, because of you, we got to start all over again. Thanks for nothing!" she said before hanging up the phone.

"She's got some nerve!" Sharon said as Nicole sank into a nearby chair. "Who does she think she is? Where did she get this number from?"

"Oh, God," Nicole whispered with a heavy sigh.

"And what does she mean by suggesting that you're trying to get her unraveled? She's the one who's been messing with you," Sharon continued angrily. "What's her phone number? I'll call her. She just don't know who she's fooling with. I ain't been saved all my life," Sharon said as she paced the floor. "There are certain things in life that once you learn how to do them, you never forget," she continued. "Like riding a bicycle or driving a car or knocking somebody's teeth out. Girl, I'm from the 'hood, and I used to have to fight to survive. Girls used to pay me and my sisters to beat up other girls who messed with them. You just say the word, Nicole. I'll beat the fool out of this one for free."

"Gerald's been back at home for a week," Nicole said. It seemed as though she hadn't even heard Sharon's raging speech. "Why is she just calling about it now?"

"I don't care if you cut it yesterday," Sharon said emphatically. "She has no right calling your place of business or anywhere else for that matter, talking all that junk! I'm going to call her back. What's her phone number? Lord, guide my tongue," she added as she looked toward the ceiling.

"I don't have her number, Sharon, and even if I did, I wouldn't give it to you. Especially with you being so upset."

"Aren't you?" Sharon asked.

"Yes, but for different reasons. I'm angry because she's making it seem as though I have a personal vendetta with her. I don't. I mean, maybe I should have gotten her permission to cut his hair. I didn't even cut it, really. I just trimmed it into a fade. He didn't have nearly enough hair to catch into braids. Gerald never gave any indication that he didn't want it cut. As a matter of fact, I asked him if he wanted me to shape his hair, and he said he did."

"Even if you did cut it against his will, Nicole," Sharon said, "there's a right way to handle it. She didn't have to call here with her foul mouth and leave that mes-

209

sage on your phone. Why didn't she call Bryan's job and talk to him like that? Because she knew better, that's why. She's just trying to break you down because she knows this situation with Gerald has already been stressful to you."

"I am trying so hard, Sharon." Nicole's voice quivered as tears began rolling down her cheeks. "I really am. I don't have a problem with Gerald, and I'd never do anything to hurt him. If he had told me that he didn't want me to shape his hair, I never would have. I'm not looking for trouble. I'm trying. I really am."

As Nicole sobbed and spoke, Sharon had picked up the phone and quickly dialed.

"Hello?" Bryan answered his cell phone.

"It's Sharon. Where are you?"

"At church going over some things with Pastor Gaines. I have about fifteen minutes left in my session. Why?"

"Cut it short," Sharon said. "Your wife needs you at the day care now."

"No, Sharon," Nicole pleaded as Sharon immediately hung up the phone.

"Too late," Sharon said.

"Why did you do that?" Nicole raised her voice. "I don't need Bryan knowing about this."

"Why not? He has a right."

"I'm trying to keep peace here, Sharon. I don't need to upset Bryan. I can handle this."

"Look at you, Nicole. You can't handle this. Look at you," Sharon repeated. "You're crying. You may want to be able to handle this, but you can't."

"This is between Tricia and me."

"Nicole, I'm sorry if my calling Bryan upsets you, but I'm not sorry that I called him. He needs to know."

"Isn't that my place, Sharon? Isn't it my responsibility to tell him and not yours? You're always butting in! This wasn't your business!"

"If I thought there was a chance that you'd tell him, Nicole, then maybe I would have stayed out of it. But you weren't going to tell him, and you know it."

"So what?" Nicole said. "If I didn't tell him, then he didn't need to know. That's the point I'm making. You were out of line. This doesn't concern you."

"You're my best friend," Sharon continued. "You're hurting over this situation. When you're hurt, I'm hurt. That makes it my business."

"God, you just don't get it," Nicole said through new tears. "You're the one who told me that Bryan didn't need to see me breaking down and that he needed my strength. This isn't strength, Sharon. If he sees me like this, he won't see strength. It'll look like I can't handle this, and I can."

"You can handle it *with* Bryan," Sharon said, "but not without him. He has a right to know. So maybe I do butt in, and maybe I crossed the line, but you're my friend, and she's hurting you, and I don't like it. The choices are simple. Either you can let Bryan know what's going on here or I will. I mean that. I'm going to tell him about the call if you don't."

Nicole sat in angry tears for several minutes as they waited for the inevitable.

The screeching of brakes, slamming of a car door, and banging on the front door signaled Bryan's arrival. Sharon rushed to the door to open it while Nicole tried desperately and unsuccessfully to wipe her face and appear that she hadn't been crying.

"What's wrong?" Bryan asked.

"She's right here." Sharon pointed to the office.

211

"And just in case she doesn't tell you, there's a message on the phone that you need to listen to," she concluded as she walked toward the infant room to check on her children.

Bryan closed the door behind him. He stood in silence for a few moments and looked at Nicole as she stared at the Kleenex in her hand. He knew from Sharon's tone that the message was from Tricia. He walked slowly to the machine and pressed the button for the message to replay.

To Nicole, the message sounded even worse the second time around. Bryan folded his arms and closed his eyes as he listened. There were several minutes of silence after the message finished playing.

From his side profile, Nicole knew he was trying to restrain the anger inside of him. She could see the tightening of his jaws and the coldness in his eyes as he stared at the painting on the wall. He quietly reached in his pocket and retrieved his wallet and pulled out a slip of paper.

"No, Bryan," Nicole said as she stood.

As though she hadn't spoken a word, he slowly dialed what she knew was Tricia's number. She could only hear one end of the conversation, but she knew that Gerald answered the telephone. Bryan spoke with him briefly and then asked to speak with Tricia.

"Bryan," Nicole whispered in a pleading tone.

"I know Gerald is in the house," Bryan said as Tricia got on the phone; "therefore I'm going to make this brief. As a matter of fact, don't even talk—just listen. I want you to lose Nicole's phone number right now. Don't you ever call her again. Do you understand me? Whatever you need to say from here on out you say it to me. Gerald has the numbers where I can be reached, and I'm sure you're aware of that.

"I consider myself to be a very patient man, Tricia, but my wife is where I draw the line. I said, don't talk," he said, apparently stopping her from interrupting. "My wife is where I draw the line," he repeated. "She is bending over backwards to make Gerald's visits with us comfortable and enjoyable for him. Because she trimmed his hair was definitely no reason for you to call and curse her out the way you did. I will not have it.

"Our allegiance is to Gerald and not you. Your voice need never to be heard by Nicole. You have no reason to deal with her. If you have a problem, you deal with me. Gerald will be well taken care of when he's with us. I don't know what your agenda is, but I do know that you're lashing out at Nicole because you want to upset me. Well, let me tell you—you've succeeded. I'm very upset. It's taking every bit of God that I have in me not to totally lose my head here and say some things that I know I'll regret later.

"But listen to this warning carefully," he continued through clenched teeth. "You have crossed the line. This is the second time. The next time you cross it, you'll have to deal with me. And make no mistake, Tricia, you don't want to deal with me. I promise you. You don't want that."

That said, he hung up the phone and slammed his elbow into the filing cabinet behind him before he blew out a lung full of breath in an attempt to calm himself.

Nicole had never heard him speak so harshly to anyone before. She wondered how much more of Tricia he could handle. It was a scary thought, knowing that their dealings with her had just begun.

His face softened as he looked at her, still standing quietly and holding the tissue in her hand. He walked around the desk and pulled her close to him and squeezed her tightly.

"I'm sorry," he whispered. "I know you're tired of hearing that, but I am. I'm sorry."

Nicole didn't respond. She knew he was doing all he could to protect her, but it was becoming a tougher battle than either one of them had ever imagined.

CHAPTER SEVENTEEN

G ood morning," Sharon said as she walked cautiously into Nicole's office on Monday morning.

"Hey," Nicole said, looking up from the paperwork
on her desk.

"Are you still mad at me?" Sharon asked.

"No." Nicole smiled. "I'm sorry for yesterday. I never should have yelled at you like that."

"I was only trying to help."

"I know, Sharon. Let's just forget about it."

"I guess you've erased the message by now," Sharon
said.

"Actually, Bryan forwarded the message to our home
phone last night so that he could keep the message in
case he ever needed it for some kind of evidence."

"What kind of evidence?" Sharon asked.

"I don't know." Nicole sighed as she began filing the
paperwork in the cabinet. "We don't know what this
woman is capable of, so I guess it's best to play it safe."

"Are you afraid of her?"

"I don't think I'm afraid of her," Nicole said. "One thing is for sure, though. She certainly knows how to get to me. I found that out yesterday. That phone call really upset me more than I was willing to admit."

"I know," Sharon said. "I just don't understand why she's so angry with you," she added. "You haven't done anything to her."

"Well, Bryan and I talked about it extensively last night. I mean, at first I didn't even want to discuss it, but he thought I needed to, and he was right. He believes she's really just lashing out at me because she knows that it's a surefire way to get him angry."

"That makes sense." Sharon nodded. "She's really angry with him, but she wants to make sure that she gets to him, so instead of taking out her anger on him directly, she chooses to aim for you. She knows Bryan would rather she irritated him than to upset you. She's hitting below the belt."

"That's his theory," Nicole said.

"And what's yours?"

"I'm not sure. I mean, his explanation certainly makes sense. She seems devious enough to do something like that. But I just wonder if it's more emotional than that."

"What do you mean?"

"Well," Nicole explained, "what if it's not about upsetting me so that she'll upset him? What if it's about inflicting so much mental anguish on me that I just can't handle the situation anymore? What if she wants me to break and just decide that I can't handle a marriage that includes not only an outside child but his complicated mother?"

"You think she wants you to leave Bryan?"

216

"It's crossed my mind," Nicole said.

"So maybe she'll have a chance at getting him." Sharon began seeing Nicole's point.

"I could be wrong," Nicole said, shrugging, "but it's something to consider."

"Did you mention that to Bryan?"

"Yeah. But he said that he couldn't see that as a possible theory because of the fact that the two of them never dated, and there were never any emotional ties."

"That's true," Sharon said. "I mean, he can't even remember her. Why would she even want a man who can't even remember her?"

"Maybe she wants her family to be a real family," Nicole said. "Maybe she feels that if Bryan just gave her a chance, he'd grow to love her. Bryan doesn't agree, and I admit that I can certainly see his point."

"About them never being in love?" Sharon asked.

"That," Nicole said, "and the point he made of how Tricia was aware that her taunting of me was angering him, yet she was continuing to do it."

"And if she was interested in roping him in," Sharon said thoughtfully, "she wouldn't be doing anything that she knew made him angry."

"Exactly."

"Then I go along with Bryan," Sharon concluded.

"Why doesn't that surprise me?"

"Seriously," Sharon said. "His theory makes more sense. I think she's a woman scorned, and she's just full of hatred because her life has been hard as a single mother, and Bryan has been living a pretty comfortable existence and enjoying a marriage for the past five years that most men only dream of. I think she just wants to make him feel some of the stress that she's felt for so long."

"Well, I don't know how much stress he's feeling, but

I know that he was very upset last night. I guess we both were."

"Did you argue?" Sharon's face showed the worry that she felt inside.

"No."

"You didn't go to bed upset last night?" Sharon asked doubtfully.

"No," Nicole repeated.

"Are you telling me the truth, Nicole?"

"Yeah," Nicole said, smiling.

"Oh boy, I know what that smile means." Sharon laughed.

"Well, when Melvin and I are really upset with each other, it usually lasts for a while. If he makes me mad, he knows he'd better not touch me. We need at least a day to let things cool off. Then we can talk business."

"But we weren't upset with each other," Nicole explained. "We were upset about the situation. We can't let Tricia's stupidity turn us against each other. I'm sure she'd love that, but I won't give her the satisfaction."

"So," Sharon said, trying to get a full understanding, "you're saying that both of you were upset about the phone call and the whole Tricia thing, and you were discussing it at length, but as soon as you turned out the lights and hit those satin sheets that you all sleep on every night, you could just put the whole situation behind you."

"Yeah, something like that. We slept peacefully because Bryan had to head to the office early this morning, so he was gone when I got up."

"Good," Sharon said. "So when you got up this morning, did you feel better about the situation, having discussed it?"

"Not really," Nicole admitted. "I mean, I was glad

that we talked it out, but when I got up this morning, I started thinking about all those horrible names she called me, and it made me physically ill. I started wondering if there would be another call waiting when I got in this morning. My stomach started knotting up so much that it felt like I was going to vomit. No one in my life has ever stressed me the way she does."

"Did you have any messages from her this morning?"

"I don't know," Nicole said as she pointed toward her blinking message light. "I haven't listened to my messages yet."

"What?" Sharon stood.

"I'm not in the mood to deal with her this morning, Sharon."

"Fine," Sharon said as she reached for the button. "I'll deal with her. I wish her voice would come over this speaker."

There were four messages on the phone. The ladies listened to each one of them. Nicole breathed just a little easier with each one that played. The last one was Bryan. It was short and sweet.

"I love you, baby," his message said.

Nicole smiled as she pressed the button to end the messages.

"See what you missed by not listening to your messages?" Sharon asked.

"Yeah," Nicole said.

"You can't let her make you paranoid like that, Nicole."

"I know," Nicole agreed. "You're right."

"You're a strong woman, Nicole," Sharon said as she leaned forward. "If anybody can make it through something like this, you can. If you can hold it together long enough to fool her into thinking she can't get to you, I think she'll get tired of trying."

"I wish I could believe that," Nicole said.

"Plus," Sharon added, "you have the advantage of knowing the Lord and a loving husband who would go to the ends of the earth to protect you. I'm not saying it's going to be easy. I'm just saying that you can do it."

"Thanks, Sharon." Nicole smiled.

"Well, I guess we'd better get to work," Sharon said.

"I guess so."

"Are you meeting Bryan for lunch today?"

"We don't have any plans," Nicole said. "But I think I'll pick up something and stop by his office and surprise him."

"Well, I'll be walking the track with Benjamin."

"Good for you." Nicole smiled.

It was almost 1:00 by the time she stopped by a restaurant and ordered a takeout order of Chinese chicken wings and rice and pulled into the parking lot at the bonding company.

"Well, hello dere, Mrs. Walker," Carol greeted her as she walked in the front door. "Sumting in dem bags sure does smell good."

"Hi, Carol," Nicole said as she brought her voice down to a whisper. "It's lunch for my hubby. Is he in?"

"He's in his office." She smiled as she pointed in the office's direction. "He was just saying dat he needed to run out and get sumting to eat. It's been so busy around here today dat he didn't have time to go when Mr. Gibbs invited him earlier."

"Good thing," Nicole said as she walked toward the office door and knocked.

"Come in," Bryan said without looking up from the paperwork on his desk.

"Got a minute for your girl?" Nicole asked.

"Sweetheart!" Bryan smiled widely as she got his attention. "What a nice surprise," he said as he walked around his desk and greeted her with a soft kiss.

"I just thought I'd drop by and share lunch with you since we didn't get to eat breakfast together this morning."

"You must have heard my stomach growling." He laughed. "I was just looking at a lunch menu to see where I wanted to go and grab something."

"Well, I hope you're in the mood for Chinese," she said.

"I am in the mood for whatever you brought with you," he said as he backed away and motioned for her to follow him as he pulled a second chair up to his desk.

"So, what do you have planned for this evening?" Nicole asked after they had said grace for the food that she had divided between them.

"Nothing in particular," he answered. "Actually, this will be the only evening that I'll have free this week. Why? Do you want to do something?"

"It's been a while since we walked the beach," Nicole said. "I was thinking that if you weren't too tired, we could drive out there this evening."

"I'd love to do that." Bryan smiled. "You're right, it has been a while. Are you planning to leave work a little early?"

"The beach is only fifteen miles from our house, Bryan." Nicole laughed. "I'm going to leave a little early, but that's just because I want to fix a little dinner for us to take and eat while we're there."

"On the beach?" Bryan raised his eyebrows.

"Yeah."

"Nice." He smiled in approval. "I know I can't leave early today though," he continued. "It'll be 5:30 by the time I get home. If we can leave by 6:00, we can be there by 6:30 at the latest. We won't have much time before the sun starts to set."

"Perfect," Nicole said. "We can watch it together."

Bryan admired her silently for a few moments.

"What?" she asked as she caught him looking.

"Nothing," he said with a smile while they enjoyed lunch together.

It had been quite some time since Nicole and Bryan had walked the sands at Jacksonville Beach. The drive was short but enjoyable and relaxing as the couple talked and laughed the entire trip. Once there, they found a nice quiet spot and spread their beach towels on the sand and settled down to eat the food that Nicole had packed.

There was still quite a number of people enjoying the water, although the tide was beginning to get a little high. The lifeguards were busy monitoring the children and directing the tourists to safer waters.

"You said that tonight was the only free night you had this week," Nicole said as they shared the sandwiches and fruit that she had prepared. "What all do you have planned?"

"Well, I promised Melvin that I'd take him to the gym with me tomorrow night," he began. "Then on Wednesday night, I have two counseling sessions beginning at 8:00, which means I won't be finished until after 10:00. Thursday, I'm attending a father/son dinner with Todd at his school, and on Friday Gerald will be here around 9:00 or so."

"And you say I stretch myself too thin," Nicole said.

"I know," he said as he drank his Coke. "I didn't realize I was putting so much on for one week until it was too late. I hope you don't mind."

"No, it's fine," Nicole said. "I'm going to take tomorrow off to get my hair done."

"Oh?" Bryan said. "It still looks good to me. Are you getting the braids again? Is that why you're taking the whole day?"

"Yeah," Nicole said. "Everybody keeps telling me that it doesn't need to be done again, but nobody can see or feel my roots like I can. I don't know how women keep them for so long before getting them done over."

"You always look so good," Bryan complimented as he brushed her hair away from her face and tucked it behind her ear.

"You just think that because you're my husband," Nicole said, blushing.

"So what's the excuse for all the other men in the church?"

"What other men?" Nicole asked in surprise.

"All of them," Bryan said. "They're always telling me how beautiful and graceful you are."

"Really?" Nicole was flattered.

"Really," Bryan answered. "I think Todd has a little crush on you."

"He does not," Nicole said, laughing.

"Sure he does," Bryan said. "You can't tell?"

"I always thought he had a little thing for Sharon," Nicole said as she ate the last of her ham sandwich.

"Why would you think that?"

"I don't know. He seems to be more personable with her."

"Yeah, who knows? Maybe he has a slight crush on her," Brian said, laughing.

They sat in silence for several more minutes, watching the activities around them. The crowd was beginning to thin. Nicole leaned her head back against Bryan's chest and dug her toes into the sand in front of her. The gentle breeze felt good. And so did Bryan's touches as he softly caressed her arms.

He broke the silence. "Tired?"

"A little," she admitted.

"Maybe we'd better get up and walk off this food before we both fall asleep."

"Okay," she agreed. She began putting the leftovers back in the cooler while he shook the sand out of the towels and folded them.

They walked back to their parked car and put the items in the trunk before joining hands and beginning the mile-long walk to the pier. They were in no hurry as they stopped along the way and watched seagulls and picked up shells that lay at the edge of the water.

By the time they finally made it to the pier, the beach was almost empty, and the skies were darkening even more. All the souvenir and gift stores that lined the pier were closed. Bryan and Nicole sat on the sand and watched as the sun disappeared completely.

"I should have brought a jacket," Nicole remarked as she wrapped her sundress close around her legs.

"Here," Bryan said, peeling off his shirt and draping it around her shoulders.

"You aren't cold?" Nicole asked, as he was left wearing only a sleeveless T-shirt.

"It's a little breezy, but I'm okay," he said.

He sat directly behind her, put one leg on either side of her, and wrapped his arms around her to keep her warm.

"Better?" he whispered in her ear.

"Much," she said, and a different kind of chill ran through her body as he held her close.

"I love you," he whispered.

"I love you, too."

"I wish . . . " he began and then stopped short of completing his thought.

"What?" Nicole asked.

He sat quietly for several moments.

"What?" she urged.

"That I had waited for you," he finally said.

"What do you mean?"

"I mean I wish I hadn't lived such a rowdy and undisciplined early adult life. I wish I had waited until I found you before becoming intimately involved with a woman. My life would have been so different. And so would yours, I suppose."

"Sweetheart," Nicole said. "Don't get me wrong. I wish you had waited for me, too, but you didn't, and we can't change that. I want you to know that I have no problem whatsoever with Gerald. I think he's actually grown on me in a short time. I think he's grown on you too."

"I know that," Bryan said. "I know you don't have a problem with him, and you're right. He has grown on me. I'm actually looking forward to the weekend with him. I don't mean that. I just mean that I wish I could say that the first time I was with someone sexually, I was in love with that person and sharing a future with that person. I wish I could say that it was magical and special and sacred. You know?"

"I know all too well," she said as she smiled over her shoulder at him. "You were all of that for me."

"You were all that for me too," he said. "Except you weren't my first. I should have waited for you."

"You've always said that you were never in love before me," Nicole said. "I just can't imagine being with

225

someone that I didn't totally love and adore."

"That's the problem. I was never in love, just involved. It meant absolutely nothing. It was just another notch on the bedpost."

"You are such a loving and compassionate person," Nicole said. "It's just so hard to picture you as the person you describe."

"I've come a long way." Bryan sighed. "Sometimes it's hard for me to admit that I was so nonchalant and disconnected from reality at one time. I was pretty stupid back then."

"That's okay," Nicole said. "It's hard for either one of us to see sometimes, but there is a bright side to your story. It all worked together to make you the man you are today. You had to be that in order to be this."

"If I had to go through that period in my life to be at this moment holding you in my arms, then I count it all worth the prize."

"That's so sweet." Nicole blinked back tears.

"You may not have been the first woman I was with," he continued, "but you're the first woman I ever made love to. What I have with you makes me know that what I had with anyone else before was nothing. I'm not ashamed to admit it, baby. I am so sprung. I would kill or be killed for you. I can't imagine living my life without you."

"Aside from my death," Nicole said as she turned and faced him, "you'll never have to live life without me."

"Say it again," he said, cupping her face in his hands and looking deeply into her eyes.

"As long as we both shall live," she said, "we'll live this life together."

Bryan smiled slightly before covering her lips with his and pulling her body in closer.

CHAPTER EIGHTEEN

The only positive point about going to the hair salon, in Nicole's opinion, was the fact that once she got her hair braided, it would be several months before she'd have to go back again. Usually when she got there, she had to wait at least a half hour past her appointment time to be seen. Today, she thought she'd beat the rush by getting her appointment on a less-busy weekday and before 10:00.

She and Bryan had gotten home at 11:00 the night before, but they sat up for another two hours taking the braids out of her head so that she could wash the sand from her hair. She didn't get to bed until very late, but since she didn't have to go to work, it wasn't a problem.

Her day got off to a rough start. Sharon called and awakened her at 8:00 and told her that one of the teachers at the day care had taken a phone call at 6:30 in the morning from Tricia. She didn't leave a message. Once she found out that Nicole wasn't there, she had hung up.

The news put a knot in the pit of Nicole's stomach. She got up with that sickening feeling again. She dragged herself into the restroom after forcing Sharon to promise not to mention the call to Melvin or Bryan. The warm shower seemed to make her feel a little better.

After such an amazing evening and night with her husband, she had to be faced with Tricia first thing in the morning. She determined within herself not to let it bother her, but her body told her that the stress of it all was trying hard to get to her. Not really feeling hungry, she got dressed and went into the kitchen for a glass of orange juice.

Nicole . . . You are such a sleeping beauty. I was tempted to wake you before I left, but after placing such a demanding night on you, I didn't want to be responsible for your not getting enough rest. Thank you for being my every fantasy come true. I know you have a full day ahead of you, so you'd better get started. If you need me for anything, give me a call. Remember that I'll be getting home a little late tonight. I don't expect Melvin to last in the gym past 8:00, so I'll be there soon after that. I love you.

Bryan.

Nicole's smile widened at the thought of their evening as she placed Bryan's note in with her many other notes from him. She loved Bryan so deeply, and she knew he felt the same way about her. Last night was just another example of their love's never growing old or boring.

Her thoughts were still on Bryan as she walked into Renown Crown, a small but busy hair salon on Hickory Road. JaQueeta, Ashley, Rochelle, and Kadeejah ran about the most ghetto salon that Nicole had ever seen.

230

But when it came to weaves and braids, none of the up-scale beauty salons could come close to measuring up.

"Hey, Nicole, girl!" Kadeejah yelled from the back as she washed another client's hair. "Just have a seat in my booth, and me and Queeta will be right there."

Another reason that Nicole liked this shop was because whenever she came in for braids, there were always two girls there to work on her hair at the same time. It cut the time in half of what other salons took with only one girl doing the job. At first, Nicole was skeptical. She didn't understand how two women could braid her hair and the style look as neat and patterned as though it were the work of only one. She still didn't understand it, but they had proven that it could be done.

At Renown Crown, there was always some hot subject of the day. Including Nicole, there were only three customers in the shop, but the chatter was already going strong. Everybody was trying to give Ashley advice on what things not to tolerate from her new boyfriend.

"Girl," JaQueeta said to Ashley as she began combing through Nicole's hair, "a man will run you raggedy if you let him."

"That's right," Rochelle agreed from the other corner of the room. "Like TLC said, 'I don't want no scrub.' I told y'all why I had to kick D-Money to the curb."

D-Money? Nicole thought.

"Uh-huh," Kadeejah said as she put conditioner in her client's hair and placed her under a dryer. "A girl's got to do what a girl's got to do," she said.

"And then," Rochelle said with a smack of her lips, "his lil' new girlfriend gonna come runnin' up in my face a couple of weeks ago, talking 'bout some stuff she heard that I said about her. Girl, if my sister hadn't stopped me I'd-a kicked—"

"All right now," Kadeejah held up one hand. "Y'all respect Nicole up in here."

"Oh, yeah," Rochelle said as she smiled apologetically in Nicole's direction.

Kadeejah was Nicole's primary hairstylist. When she wasn't getting braids and was just getting regular styles, which wasn't often, Kadeejah was the one who did it. She was also the owner of the shop that she took over after her mother died a couple of years ago.

Once she found out that Nicole was a Christian, she instructed her usually loose-lipped stylists that they had to be mindful of Nicole's presence when she was there. Nicole appreciated the respect.

"Anyway," Rochelle continued, "I told her I had better things to do with my breath than waste it talking about her."

"She's just jealous, girl," JaQueeta said.

"Of what?" Rochelle asked. "She got him."

"Yeah," Kadeejah added, "but she know D-Money would go back to you in a hot second if he thought you'd take him back. She just feels threatened."

"Well, she ain't got nothing to worry about," Rochelle said. "I do not want that broke-down, bicycle-riding, no-good, no-job, no-car, no-money loser. Like Toni Braxton said," she added, "he wasn't man enough for me."

"I heard that!" JaQueeta said, and the other listeners joined her in laughter.

"Well, I think Quintin is a pretty nice guy," Ashley said.

"We ain't saying that he ain't nice," JaQueeta said. "We're just saying that you need to watch your back. I ain't found a man yet who won't try and take advantage of you if you let him."

"You need to bring Quintin in here, Ashley, so we

can size a brotha up," Rochelle said.

"I don't know." Ashley shook her head. "Y'all don' run my man away. I don't want to mess this up. He could really be the one. I could fall in love with him."

Nicole tried concentrating on the magazine article she was reading as Kadeejah joined JaQueeta in braiding her hair. The discussion changed periodically as other customers came in and out, but somehow it always found its way back to the topic of men. Ashley's man, in particular. An hour later, they were still on the same subject. Nicole's cell phone interrupted her reading.

"Hello," she answered.

"Hey, baby." It was Bryan.

"Hey," she replied, smiling.

"Have you even made it to the chair yet?"

"Yeah," Nicole said. "They've been braiding for close to an hour now."

"That's good," he said. "Are you hungry?"

"A little," she admitted as the beauticians and clients burst into laughter about something that one of them said.

"It's loud in there," Bryan noted.

"I know," she said, hoping that none of them could hear her. "It always is."

"Did you eat breakfast?" he asked.

"No, I just had some juice. There's a McDonald's next door. I may take a break in an hour and run over there and get something and bring it back."

"McDonald's?" Bryan asked in surprised. "When was the last time you ate from there?"

"That's as good as it gets around here," she said.

"Okay," he said as another round of laughter nearly drowned him out. "I'm going to let you go. Call me if you need me."

"Okay."

"I love you," Bryan said.

"I love you, too."

She didn't care what the babbling beauticians said. There were good men in the world, and she could prove it. As she continued to listen, she understood why Ashley didn't want to bring her boyfriend around her co-workers.

"The way I see it," Kadeejah said, "every man has either cheated in the past, is cheating right now, or is planning to cheat in the future."

"So you don't think that anyone has a faithful boyfriend?" Ashley asked.

"Not if they've been dating for more than two years," Kadeejah said.

"What about a husband?" Ashley asked.

"One year of faithfulness, tops," Rochelle said.

"Why are you shaking your head, Nicole?" Kadeejah asked.

"Was I shaking my head?" Nicole hadn't even noticed her own reaction.

"Yes," Kadeejah and JaQueeta said in unison.

"Well," Nicole said, "I guess it's because I don't agree."

"Thank you." Ashley was relieved to finally get some help.

"How long have you been married, Nicole?" Kadeejah asked.

"Five years."

"And you think your man's been faithful for five years?" Rochelle asked.

"I know he has."

"Well, that's just because you got yourself a church man," Kadeejah said.

"Pah-leeze!" Rochelle butted in. "Church men are the worst. I was hit on by a married preacher once. Church don't mean nothing."

"My reason for believing and knowing doubtlessly that Bryan is faithful to me has nothing to do with church," Nicole said. "All kinds of people go to church. Rochelle is right. Church doesn't mean a thing. It's about the God that's on the inside of you. I believe in the God that I know Bryan has in him. I know he loves me, and I love him. We'd never jeopardize our marriage with something as senseless as an affair. We're too important to each another."

"That is so sweet," Ashley said. "See, that's what I want, right there."

"No," Rochelle said, "that's not sweet. That's being naive. Men prey on women who trust like you do, Nicole."

"Where is your man right now, Nicole?" JaQueeta asked.

"At work."

"How do you know?" she asked.

"I just spoke with him a little while ago. He called to see how far along you all were with my hair."

"Aha!" Rochelle said with a pointed finger. "That's the classic move for a cheating man."

"What?" Ashley asked.

"Classic move," Rochelle reiterated. "He wanted to know how far along we were so he'd know if he had time for a little rendezvous with the other woman before you got home. He's cheating. Like Sunshine Anderson said, I heard it all before."

"That is so sad," Nicole said.

"What?" Rochelle asked.

"That you have been mistreated and beaten down by so many men that you think that they are all liars and cheaters. I'm not going to spend my time defending my husband or his dignity. I know what I know."

"He got a brother?" Kadeejah asked.

"Child, please," Rochelle said, unconvinced. "You know what my perfect man is like? My perfect man is tall, dark, handsome, and got to be sexy."

The beginning of her description drew "oohs" from the salon's listeners.

"He cooks dinner for me," she continued, "gives me massages, sends me flowers for no reason at all, calls me in the middle of the day just to say 'I love you,' works hard, doesn't mind cleaning up around the house or taking care of the kids just to give me a break. He takes me on long drives, long walks on the beach, treats me to candlelight dinners, gives me money if I need it without asking me for it back, washes my car, opens doors for me, brushes my hair, makes me feel safe and secure, and even after a hard day's work, he can come home and make love to me all night long."

Rochelle's neck-rolling speech brought laughter and applause from the others who listened. Her client gave her a high five in agreement.

"So you've met Bryan?" Nicole asked sarcastically.

Her comeback drew even louder applause.

"She got you," Ashley said to Rochelle.

"She's just frontin'," Rochelle said. "Ain't no man all of that."

"Shh!" Kadeejah instructed as a visitor entered.

"Ooo Wee," JaQueeta sang softly over Nicole's head as the salon quieted suddenly.

"I got this," Rochelle said, walking toward the front of the store.

"Now, that's a man," Kadeejah whispered as she looked over her shoulder toward the counter.

Nicole tried to look, but couldn't see from her position.

"Well, he's got the tall, dark, handsome, and sexy," Kadeejah said. "I'll have to give him a try to see if he got the rest."

"He's wearing that suit, now," JaQueeta added.

"Can I help you?" Nicole heard Rochelle asked. Her sassy voice had turned seductive as she flirted shamelessly with the visitor.

"Look at her," Kadeejah said as JaQueeta laughed with her.

"No, thank you," the familiar voice said. "I see who I want."

"Is that Bryan?" Nicole turned, forcing Kadeejah and JaQueeta to turn with her.

"That's Bryan?" Kadeejah asked.

"Hi, ladies," he said as he approached.

"Hi," they said as they stared brazenly.

"Hey, boo," he said softly as he leaned in close and kissed Nicole's lips.

"Hey." She touched the side of his face.

The salon had come to a total silence with the exception of the hair dryers that blew from the back.

"I brought you some lunch," he said and handed her the bag in his hand.

"Chinese?" She smiled. "Oh, sweetie, you didn't have to do that. I told you I'd get something."

"I know," he said. "But I missed you. I just thought it was a good excuse to come by and see you. I wish I could stay longer, but I have to meet a client."

"Well, I'm glad you stopped by," Nicole said. "By the way, this is Kadeejah, and this is JaQueeta."

"Nice meeting you," he said with a quick bow of his head.

"You too," they said.

"You all do such a wonderful job with my wife's hair. I appreciate that."

"You're welcome," they said.

"Oh," Nicole said. "That's Ashley, and you've met Rochelle."

"Yes," he said. "It's a pleasure."

"Hmm," Rochelle moaned as she scoped his physique. "I bet it is."

"Chelle!" Kadeejah scolded in embarrassment as she eyed her harshly.

"Sorry," Rochelle mumbled.

"There's a drink in that bag," he told Nicole without responding to Rochelle's remark. "Be careful not to spill it."

"I won't." She smiled.

"I'll call you later," he said with a touch to her chin.

"Okay. Thanks again for lunch."

"Anytime, sweetheart," he said. He kissed her again and stood straight up to leave. "I should be home no later than 9:00," he said as he began walking away.

"I'll wait up," she called after him.

"Is that an invitation?" he asked as he stopped and turned to face her.

"Maybe," she shrugged flirtatiously.

"Make that 8:30," he said as he turned and walked out.

"See, that's how I want my man to look at me," Ashley said as the others let out a collective sigh as soon as the door closed behind him.

"Girl, why you didn't tell me!" Kadeejah said.

"Tell you what?" Nicole laughed.

"Girl," Kadeejah continued, "if I didn't like you, I'd go after that brotha."

238

"Child, please," Rochelle said. "I like you, a___ I thought I had half a chance, I'd go after him right n___

"You don't," JaQueeta said.

"I know it," Rochelle said as she went back to her customer. "I saw the way he looked at her."

"Where'd you meet him?" Kadeejah asked.

"Here."

"In Jacksonville?" she asked.

"Yes."

"Where?"

"At church."

"That's it," Ashley announced. "I'm going to church every Sunday from now on."

"Amen," Kadeejah agreed.

"He's not from here, though, is he?" JaQueeta asked.

"No," Nicole said as she opened her bag to begin eating her shrimp fried rice. "He's from Chicago."

"That's it," Ashley said. "I'm giving my two-week notice. I'm moving to Chicago."

"Girl, you got yourself a good-looking husband," Kadeejah said. "His eyes are gorgeous."

"Thank you," Nicole said, feeling proud and flattered at how Bryan's presence had moved her beauticians.

"Is he really as good as he looks, Nicole?" Rochelle asked. "I mean, well, you know what I mean," she added.

"Chelle!" Kadeejah said. "That ain't even your business."

"No, it's okay," Nicole said.

"Well, is he?" Rochelle urged.

"Actually, he's incredible," Nicole answered. "Like Whitney Houston said," she continued, "he's all the man I need."

"Hel-lo!" one of the other clients exclaimed as they laughed once more.

239

"That's a good one, girl," Kadeejah said.

"I can believe it," JaQueeta injected. "He looks like he knows his way around."

"Well, I'm going to put this as respectfully as I know how," Rochelle said, and she paused to choose her words carefully. "All I can say is," she continued, "if you can keep a Negro that fine and that good-looking from going after other women like me who would love to have just about fifteen minutes of his time, girl, you must be serving it up."

Even Nicole couldn't help but join the others as they laughed hysterically at Rochelle's remark and her emphatic tone of voice as she stood with her hands on her hips.

"And I mean serving it up on a platinum platter," she added. "Work-it-girl!" she enunciated with a snap of her fingers for each word as her audience continued to laugh.

CHAPTER NINETEEN

To Nicole's relief, there were no other phone calls from Tricia, and when Gerald arrived Friday night, he seemed happy to visit Bryan and Nicole again. When Melvin walked him inside, Gerald gave both of them a quick hug before disappearing to his room to put his things away.

"How'd it go?" Bryan asked Melvin.

"She wasn't even there when I got there this time," he reported. "I was worried at first. Gerald said that he wasn't afraid and that she had to go somewhere."

"He was at home by himself?" Bryan asked.

"Legally, there's nothing wrong with that," Nicole reminded him.

"I know," Bryan said. "He just seems kind of young to be home alone."

"Yeah," Nicole agreed.

"It's not the being at home alone that worried me," Melvin said. "What worried me is that he was sitting outside on the porch with his suitcase."

"What?" Nicole asked.

"What do you mean?" Bryan asked.

"He was sitting on the porch," Melvin said. "It's just like it sounds," he continued.

"I mean, he could get in the house if he needed to, right?" Bryan asked.

"Nope," Melvin said, shaking his head. "He didn't have any keys or anything. I didn't ask how long he'd been out there, but as soon as I picked him up and got on the highway, we had to stop for him to use the restroom."

"I can't believe that she . . . " Bryan stopped as he heard Gerald walking down the stairs.

"Are you hungry?" Nicole asked as she looked up the staircase.

"Yeah," he said. "I mean, yes."

"Good." Bryan smiled as he gave him the thumbs-up signal.

"Why don't you go ahead and get your bath," Nicole said. "I put a fresh towel and cloth in the restroom for you. I ordered a pizza for us. It should be here by the time you're done."

"Okay." He smiled as he turned around and went back to run his bathwater.

"Look," Melvin said, "as I said, I don't know the details. He didn't talk much on the drive in, and when he did, it wasn't about that. I guess the main thing is that he seemed to be okay. He didn't appear to be afraid or anything."

"What time did you get there?" Bryan asked.

"Around 7:00."

"That's too late," Nicole said. "It's getting dark by that time."

"I know," Melvin agreed. "But like I said, I didn't

pry. Quite frankly, I was just happy not to have to deal with her today."

"Thanks, Melvin," Bryan said. "I appreciate this. If you ever get tired of being my taxi service, let me know. I'll understand. Tricia's not the easiest person to deal with, and this is a pretty long trip after working all day."

"It's cool," he assured Bryan. "It gives me a legitimate reason to get off from work a little early, and it's not a problem. As far as Tricia is concerned, if she really becomes a problem, I'll start bringing Sharon along."

"That would make for an interesting breaking story for the 11:00 news," Nicole said, laughing.

"Wouldn't it, though?" Melvin laughed with her. "If you guys want to do anything special this weekend, give me and Sharon a holler," he said as he prepared to leave.

"Okay," Bryan said. "Thanks, Melvin."

Nicole could see the look of concern on Bryan's face as he closed the door.

"Do I ask him about this?" he asked.

"I don't think you'll have peace of mind until you do," Nicole said. "But maybe you should wait until later."

"Maybe," Bryan said.

Nicole returned to the dining room and began setting the table. She heard Bryan go to the door when the door bell rang. The pizza had arrived, and Gerald knew it. He came downstairs as soon as he heard Bryan open the front door.

"I hope you like pepperoni and sausage pizza with extra cheese," Bryan said as he led the eager child into the dining room.

"So how are you doing in school?" Bryan asked after they had settled down and said grace.

"Okay," he said.

"What's okay?" Bryan pressed. "What kind of grades are you getting?"

"Bs," he said.

"All Bs?" Nicole asked.

"I got four Bs and one C," he said.

"That's not bad," Bryan said. "You think you can pull that C up to a B before the end of the school year? You only have a few more weeks."

"I don't know." He shrugged.

"What subject is it in?" Bryan asked.

"Math."

"Oh, well, Ms. Nicole is good with math. She can help you if you want her to."

"I sure can," Nicole agreed. "And if you bring it up to a B, maybe we'll pick up something special for you."

"A baseball and a bat?" he asked.

"Sure," she said, smiling. "We can even throw in a baseball cap and a baseball jersey of your favorite player if you like."

"For real?" he asked as his eyes widened.

"For real," Nicole said as she laughed.

"Okay," he agreed.

Bryan looked at Nicole and smiled appreciatively. They ate in silence for a few minutes.

"Gerald," Nicole said.

"Huh?"

"Say yes," Bryan said.

"Huh?" he asked.

"No," Bryan said with a short laugh. "Don't say huh. When an adult calls you, say, 'Yes?'"

"Oh," Gerald said.

"Let's try it again," Bryan said.

"Okay," he said.

They all sat silently for a few moments.

"Go ahead," Bryan urged.

"She didn't call me," Gerald said.

"I'm sorry." Nicole giggled. "Gerald," she called.

"Yes?"

"Very good, you two," Bryan said as they laughed.

"I'm sorry that I cut your hair the last time you were here," Nicole continued. "I didn't know that you wanted braids. I wish you had told me. I feel really bad about that."

"I don't want no braids," he said with a grimace.

"You don't want braids?" Nicole asked as she and Bryan exchanged glances.

"No."

"You've never wanted braids?" Bryan asked.

"Why y'all asking me that?" he asked with a baffled expression. "I never said I wanted braids."

"No, you didn't," Bryan said as Nicole sat in silence. "We just thought that someone told us that you wanted them."

"Not me," he said. "Some of the boys at my school wear braids, but I think braids are for girls."

"Excuse me," Nicole said as she got up and abruptly left the table.

"Are you ever going to let your hair grow long again?" Gerald asked Bryan.

"Naaa," Bryan said as his mind became preoccupied with Nicole. "I think it's for girls too."

"Me too," Gerald said as he drank his juice.

"I'll be right back," Bryan said.

"Can I get another piece?"

"Help yourself, dude," he said, and he patted him on the back.

Bryan walked into the bathroom attached to their bedroom and found Nicole splashing her face with water.

She looked at him in the mirror as she wiped the water dry with her towel.

"Are you okay?" he asked.

"He never wanted braids, Bryan," Nicole said.

"I know."

"So if she can't find a legitimate reason to hound us and make our bonding with Gerald difficult, she'll just create one? Is that what this is about?"

"Probably," Bryan said. "But it's not working. We are bonding with him. Can't you see it? He's actually sitting and enjoying a meal with us and saying more than the two words that he almost lived by just a few weeks ago."

"Is she ever going to give up?"

"Maybe she already has," he said. "She wasn't there to hassle Melvin when he picked Gerald up tonight, and she hasn't called you anymore. It's a good start."

Nicole was tempted to tell him about the call she'd missed from Tricia just days ago, but decided against it. Bryan was trying to think positively, and she didn't want to ruin that.

"You're right," Nicole said.

"Come on, let's finish dinner. Then we can play a couple of quick games of Uno before sending Gerald to bed for the night."

"I'm not hungry anymore."

"But you haven't even eaten one full slice of the pizza yet," Bryan insisted.

"I know," she said. "I just don't feel well right now. I don't feel like eating anything else. I think I'll just get my shower, and then I'll join the two of you for the card game."

"Don't let this get you down, sweetie," Bryan said as he pulled her in for a hug.

"I'm not," she said. "I'm fine."

"Okay," Bryan said. "Gerald and I will clear the table when we're done. We'll wait on you for the game."

"Okay."

Nicole turned on the hot shower and tried to wash away the thought of being unnecessarily taunted by Tricia.

How cruel and low-down could a person be? she thought. *How can a mother use her innocent child as a tool of aggravation like that? I guess she thought we'd never ask him about it. Otherwise, she would have clued him in on what to say in case we did. Of course, to think of that, she would at least need a functioning brain.*

She turned off the shower and began drying herself with the towel. She sat on the side of the bathtub and buried her face in the towel.

Come on, Nicole. You can't keep letting the very mention of her name turn your stomach like this.

She finally got herself together, put on her pajamas, and joined the guys as they sat on the living room floor watching an old episode of *The Cosby Show*. It was after 11:00.

"Better?" Bryan asked as she sat with them.

"Yeah." She smiled.

Nicole temporarily forgot about her earlier troubles as she got into the game with them. Bryan won the first game easily and started the second game, which turned out to be a little more competitive.

"Gerald," Bryan said as Nicole pondered over which card to put down next.

"Yes?"

"Very good," Bryan said, smiling. Gerald seemed pleased to have his father's approval. "I have a question for you," Bryan continued, "and I would really like an honest answer. Okay?"

"Okay," he said.

Nicole stopped trying to figure out which color to put down next and turned her attention to her husband.

"Mr. Gibbs said that you were at home alone and sitting on the porch when he picked you up tonight. Is that true?"

"Yes."

"Why were you at home alone, and why were you sitting on the steps?"

"Mama had gone to a party with some friends. Her ride came before Mr. Melvin came to pick me up, so she told me to sit out there and wait on him."

"Why couldn't you just wait inside?"

"Mama didn't think I would remember to lock the door, and she didn't want to leave me with a key."

"How long were you out there?"

"Her ride came at 6:00. I think Mr. Melvin got there around seven something."

"You weren't scared?" Bryan asked.

"No," he said. "I've done it before."

Nicole decided on a blue number five to match the yellow number five that Bryan had put down before her. She noticed her husband's uneasiness with Gerald's last answer.

"My turn?" Gerald asked.

"Yes," Nicole said.

"What do you mean you've done it before?" Bryan asked, trying not to appear upset.

"One time I went to a birthday party at my friend's house," he explained, "and when I came home from the party, she wasn't there, so I had to sit outside and wait for her to get home."

"Was that at night?" Bryan asked.

"It was night by the time she got home," he said. "The party was from 2:00 to 5:00."

"What time did she get home?" Bryan asked.

"I don't know." He shrugged and put a card down. "It was dark. Uno," he said.

"How old were you then?" Bryan asked.

"I had just turned twelve. Your turn," he told Bryan.

"Oh," Bryan said as he put a card down.

"You couldn't have changed the colors?" Nicole tried to lighten the mood as she pulled a card from the stack.

"It wouldn't have helped none," Gerald said as he threw his last card on the stack. "I win."

"How about we play one more time and we let Ms. Nicole win?" Bryan said, laughing.

"Okay," Gerald whispered as though Nicole couldn't hear him.

"No, thank you," Nicole teased. "I don't need your charity. I'm just going to go to bed."

"I guess that means bedtime for you too, slugger," Bryan said to Gerald.

"Okay," he said. "Can Todd come over and play video games with me tomorrow?"

"He'll be here," Bryan said.

"Can I have a good-night hug?" Nicole asked.

Gerald smiled as she hugged him and kissed his forehead.

"Go on and brush your teeth," Bryan said. "I'll be up in a minute."

"Okay," Gerald said.

"You look tired," Bryan said as he hugged Nicole.

"I am," she said. "I'm going to turn in."

"Are you sure you're okay?" He looked concerned.

"I'm fine," she said, smiling.

"Okay," he said. "I'll be in as soon as I see to it that he says his prayers and is tucked in."

"Okay," Nicole said as she kissed him and walked away.

Gerald was folding his covers back when Bryan joined him in his room.

"Ready for your prayers?" he asked.

"Yes," Gerald said, and they knelt by his bed.

"You want to pray this time?" Bryan asked.

"No," he said.

"Give it a try," Bryan urged.

"I don't know what to say."

"Just say whatever is on your mind. It doesn't have to be perfect. God hears you."

"God, bless Mama," he began slowly, "and, uh," he hesitated, "Mr. Bryan and Ms. Nicole and Mr. Melvin and Ms. . . . ummm, his wife," he continued. "God bless all my friends at school and Todd and everybody in the whole world. Amen."

"Amen." Bryan smiled. "That was good."

"I forgot her name," Gerald said as they got up.

"Ms. Sharon?"

"Yeah. I mean, yes."

"Are you confused as to what to call me?" Bryan asked as Gerald slid under the covers.

"Yes," Gerald admitted.

"Did your mom give you any suggestions on what to call me?"

"No."

"Why don't you ask her and see what she thinks?"

"I did."

"You asked her?" Bryan was surprised.

"Yes."

"What did she say?"

Gerald's hesitance made Bryan almost wish he hadn't asked the question. It was clear that he didn't want to answer. He almost seemed afraid to.

"It's okay, Gerald," Bryan said. "I can handle it. Tell me."

"She said that I didn't have to call you nothing since you ain't never done nothing for me."

"Is that so?" Bryan tried not to show his disdain for his child's mother.

"Yes," Gerald said. "She told me to tell her if either you or Ms. Nicole ever told me to call you Daddy or Mama. Please don't tell her I told you that," he pleaded.

"I won't," Bryan promised. "I'll tell you what," he added holding his tongue on how he wanted to respond to this new knowledge. "You can just call me Bryan for now. If you want to call me Daddy later, that's fine too, but I'm perfectly comfortable with Bryan. How's that?"

"Okay."

"Gerald," Bryan began as he looked down in the child's innocent face, "I can't control the way your mother feels about me, and I don't think that it's my duty to try. However, what you think of me is very important to me. I need you to know that you can come to me and talk about anything. Don't believe everything you hear. I promise you that I won't lie to you. If you have any questions concerning our relationship, or me, just ask. I mean that. Okay?"

"Okay," Gerald said.

"Now, you get some sleep," he said as he headed for the door. "Good night."

"Good night," Gerald said.

"I love you," Bryan added.

He didn't mind the boy's silence that followed. He knew that they were words that he wasn't used to hearing or saying. It would take a while for him to be able to admit whatever feelings he had for his new father figure.

As he walked back into his bedroom and prepared to shower, Bryan noticed that Nicole was already asleep. He stood and watched in silence for a few moments. Even asleep, she was beautiful.

"I love you too," he whispered.

He quietly showered and prepared for bed. It was after midnight, but Nicole was right—he wasn't going to rest until he spoke with Tricia about Gerald being locked outside. He retrieved her number from his wallet, walked into the living room to get the cordless phone, and dialed.

Either she was asleep or still hadn't gotten home from her party outing. He waited for the beep on her answering machine.

"Tricia," he started, "this is Bryan. First, let me say that everything is fine with Gerald. This is not an urgent call. However, I need to speak with you when you have a minute. I should be available after 8:00 in the morning. Please call me on my cell. You have the number. Bye."

CHAPTER TWENTY

The community where Bryan and Nicole lived had its own park that included swings, slides, a track, picnic tables, open space to play games or have cookouts, and a swimming pool. Melvin, Sharon, and their children joined Bryan, Nicole, Gerald, and Todd for a fun day outdoors.

The weather was beautiful and the sun shone brightly as the grown-ups, the men especially, played about as hard as the children did. Nicole pushed Benjamin in the toddler swing while Sharon pushed Michael. They watched everybody's belongings that lay on the ground in a pile and laughed as their husbands played a little baseball and then a little football with Todd and Gerald.

"Gerald seems to really like spending time with you all," Sharon said while they watched Gerald jump on Bryan's back in a failed attempt to tackle him before he crossed the imaginary goal line.

"I think he does," Nicole said, smiling. "The first time

he came to visit us he was kind of quiet that Friday and Saturday. Then Sunday he started kind of breaking out of his shell, but it was time to go before he really warmed up to us. This visit, he dove right in. I didn't know he could talk so much."

"That's great," Sharon said. "And look at you. He's really grown on you. You may not have given birth, but you're glowing like a real mother."

"Oh, girl, stop." Nicole blushed.

"Girl his mama would flip if she could see you. If she thought her negative attitude would make you dislike Bryan's son, she was wrong."

"Speaking of Tricia. . ." Nicole lowered her voice as though she thought there was a chance that Gerald might hear her. "Guess what Bryan and I found out last night."

"What?"

"She lied about Gerald not wanting to get his hair cut."

"What do you mean?"

"I mean she lied," Nicole said. "When we were eating pizza last night, I apologized to Gerald for trimming his hair. I told him that I didn't know he wanted braids. He told us that he's never wanted braids."

"What?" Sharon said in disbelief. "He actually said that?"

"Yes," Nicole said. "He doesn't even like braids. He thinks they're for girls."

"What did he say when you told him what his mama said?"

"Oh, we didn't tell him. It didn't seem appropriate. There's no need of putting him in the middle of trifling nonsense. I just wasn't prepared for that. Why would she lie like that?"

"I'm beginning to think she's Satan's mistress," Sharon

said. "Melvin told me that Gerald was locked outside the house when he picked him up last night. What kind of mother locks her child out of the house at night to wait on a ride?"

"Isn't that bizarre?" Nicole asked. "When Melvin told us that, it blew us away. Bryan was very angry. He said that he was going to call her, but we both thought it was best that he cooled off first."

"Why does everybody try to cool off when dealing with this moron? That's a part of the problem right there. Somebody just needs to go off on her and act as crazy as she does."

"What would that accomplish, Sharon?" Nicole asked as Bryan's cell phone began ringing from the pile. "That would make us seem just as ignorant as she is. I'm not stooping to her level."

"Something needs to be done," Sharon mumbled.

"Hello?" Nicole answered the phone.

"I'd like to speak to Bryan," the caller said after a brief silence.

"Sure," Nicole said as she began walking the phone across the lawn. "May I ask who's calling?"

"No, you may not. He asked me to call. He's expecting my call. Thank you."

Nicole stopped in her tracks. She suddenly realized that it was Tricia as the tone of the caller's voice became abrasive. She was tempted to press the button to end the call, but decided not. She took a deep breath and continued walking.

"Phone call for me?" Bryan asked as she handed him the phone without explanation. Her silent, stone-faced nod made Bryan realize whom the call was from.

"Come on you two," Melvin told the boys as he caught the look between his friends. "Let's take a break and get some juice from Ms. Sharon."

"What did she say to you?" Bryan whispered as he pressed his hand over the phone so that Tricia couldn't hear him.

"Nothing worth repeating," Nicole said as she turned to walk away.

"No." Bryan stopped her. "You stay with me. I may need you to keep me focused."

Nicole sat on the park bench as he answered the phone.

"Hello," he said.

"You sure did take a long time to answer the phone," she said as though annoyed by the amount of time it took. "Am I disturbing you or something?"

"No. We're at the park with some friends."

"Where's Gerald?"

"He's here too. He's taking a break from a game of football."

"Well, I got your message, and I was just calling to see what you wanted."

"Then I'll get right to it," Bryan said, not wanting to talk to her any longer than he had to. "Melvin told me that Gerald was locked out of the house last night. I was concerned as to why you would leave him outside like that."

"He got there okay, didn't he?" she said.

"Yes."

"Then what's your point?"

"My point is," Bryan said after a deep breath, "I don't think that it's such a good idea to leave a child his age outside by himself like that. Especially during the evening hours."

"Gerald was fine. He knows the neighbors, and he knows the neighborhood. He can take care of himself. He ain't no baby."

"My point exactly," Bryan said. "He's not a baby. He's capable of locking the front door when he leaves the house."

"I ain't leaving my house unlocked while I'm gone," she defended.

"He can have it locked while he's in there and then lock it again when he leaves," Bryan suggested.

"Let me tell you something," she said defiantly. "I don't need you telling me how to handle my stuff. You were the one who told me the last time that he was there that you wasn't going to tell me how to raise him when he's here and for me not to tell you how to raise him when he's there."

"This is different, Tricia," Bryan said. "When he was here, he was with Nicole. He wasn't by himself, and he certainly wasn't locked outside in the dark."

"I would rather that you did lock him outside in the dark," she said.

"Watch yourself," Bryan warned.

"Or what?" she said. "You make me sick. How you gonna sit on your judgment throne and try and tell me how to handle my child? You ain't been around for all these years, and now you think you can just throw your demands around and I'm gonna just come to attention?"

"I'm not making any demands, Tricia. I'm just saying that it's not safe to leave a twelve-year-old kid outside in the dark with no means of getting back into the house if something happened. What if Melvin had car trouble or was delayed for hours? Gerald would have just had to sit there until you got home from your outing."

"Then that would have been on you," she said. "It wouldn't have been my fault. You have to make sure that whoever is coming to pick him up is reliable and has reliable transportation."

"You just don't get it, do you?" Bryan said as Nicole sat next to him shaking her head. "It's just too dangerous to leave him outside like that. What if somebody came along and kidnapped him or something?"

"That's not going to happen," she said, sounding insulted. "You act like I live in some crime 'hood or something. Just 'cause my house ain't in some high-class community with security gates don't mean I live in the slums."

"Okay." Bryan sighed. "I see we aren't going to see eye to eye on this."

"That ain't nothing new," she said.

"Listen," Bryan continued. "All I'm really trying to say is whenever you need to leave early like that, just give me a call, and I'll see to it that he's picked up before you have to leave."

"Yeah, right," she said.

"I'm serious, Tricia," Bryan stressed. "I can have him picked up earlier if necessary. Just let me know."

"Is there anything else?" she asked sarcastically.

"As a matter of fact, there is," Bryan said. "After apologizing to Gerald last night for cutting his hair, we found out that he never wanted braids. Would you care to explain that?"

Bryan's confrontation caught Tricia off guard. She couldn't seem to think fast enough to come up with an answer for Bryan's question.

"He told you that?" she asked in an almost demanding manner.

"Yes, he did," Bryan said. "But don't worry," he added. "We didn't tell him that his mother was the one who lied on him and said that he was upset about the haircut. I don't understand you," Bryan continued. "Nicole and I are trying very hard to establish a relationship with our son, but you seem determined to make sure that doesn't happen. Why?" he asked.

"He just didn't want to tell you that he wanted his hair to grow out, that's all," she lied. "He's been wanting braids for a while now. I don't appreciate you going behind my back and checking with him on stuff I tell you."

"As I said," Bryan said, "we were apologizing for our actions when we found out. I wasn't checking up on you. It never crossed my mind that you were fabricating a story. I assumed that what you said was true."

"Are you calling me a liar?" she asked.

"I don't believe you heard that from me," he said. "But hear this. I'm going to cut his hair again before we go to church tomorrow. If you have a problem with that, I suggest you voice it now."

Nicole watched as he pulled the phone from his ear and handed it back to her.

"I guess she didn't have a problem with it," he said.

"She hung up?" Nicole asked.

"Yeah," he said.

"He's such a sweet little boy," Nicole said. "It's so hard to believe that she's the one who's raised him all this time."

"I think he's been raising himself," Bryan said.

"Well, he's done a pretty good job," she said as she laid her head on his shoulder.

"Are you okay?" Bryan asked.

"It's the strangest thing," Nicole said. "Every time she calls I get this nauseated feeling in my stomach. It's sad to say, but it's true. It's like she's some kind of poison. She literally makes me sick."

"You've had to deal with a lot for the past month and she's been a part of it all. I guess it can't help but take a toll to some degree. I just don't want you getting sick on me. If there's anything I can do to make it easier, let me know."

"I'll be okay," she said as Todd came running over with the football in his hand.

"Hey, Bryan," he said. "You want to play some more?"

"Maybe in a little while," Bryan said. "Will you do me a favor and bring Ms. Nicole a ginger ale from the cooler?"

"Okay," he said as he raced back across the lawn.

"That's son number two, you know." Nicole laughed softly.

"He's a good kid," Bryan said, smiling. "At the dinner at his school the other night, his teachers couldn't say enough about how he's improved in his grades and attitude. I was so proud of him. I think he was proud of himself, too."

"Here, Ms. Nicole," Todd said as he returned with her soda.

"Thanks, Todd. You're so sweet."

"You're welcome." He smiled as he looked down at his shoes.

"Can we go swimming now?" Gerald asked Bryan as he joined Todd.

"Sure," he said. "Make sure that you sign in at the lifeguard station first."

"Cool!" Gerald said as he and Todd dashed toward the swim area.

"See how he couldn't look you in the eye?" Bryan said as Nicole sipped on her soda.

"What?" she said.

"Todd," Bryan clarified. "I told you he had a crush on you. See how bashful he got when you spoke to him?"

"You'd better be careful," Nicole teased. "He may

have befriended you just to get to me."

"I never thought of that," Bryan said, laughing. "I'll watch my back from here on out."

"Is everything okay?" Melvin asked as he and Sharon joined them on the park bench.

"Yeah," Bryan said. "I'd asked Tricia to call about Gerald being left outside last night."

"What was her excuse for that one?" Sharon asked.

"She didn't really have one," Bryan explained. "She doesn't seem to be the brightest bulb on the Christmas tree," he continued. "For the life of me, I don't know what it was I drank the night I was with her, but it must have been some powerful stuff. Nothing about her appeals to me. I don't see how it could have back then either."

"From what I've heard," Melvin said, "back in the day, you had the pick of the litter. Seems to me when you picked her, you just picked litter."

"That's not nice Melvin," Nicole said.

"It may not be nice," Sharon defended, "but it sure is true."

"Maybe you were looking for the motherly type back then," Melvin suggested.

" Tricla's not motherly " Nicole grimaced.

"I don't mean motherly to say that she's a good mother," Melvin clarified. "I'm saying motherly to say that maybe she reminded Bryan of his mother."

"Tricia doesn't look like my mama," Bryan said.

"Her facial features don't," Melvin said, "but her build and her skin complexion are a lot like your mother's. Think about it," he continued. "She's tall, skinny, and dark with short hair. That's just like your mother."

"That's true," Sharon agreed.

"So let me get this right," Bryan said. "You think

that when I went off to college, I missed my mama so much that I decided at this one party to pick a girl who reminded me of my mom? Come on now, man, you can't really think that I thought like that."

"Hey, I'm just trying to help a brotha out," Melvin said. "You were the perfect player in my opinion before I found out about Tricia. I mean, back when you first told me about your past life and your long list of women," he continued with a laugh, "I knew that you covered a lot of ground in such a short time, but I assumed the women were all fly. Now I find out there's a flaw in your record."

"I know!" Bryan laughed.

"Can we talk about something else?" Nicole suddenly said, and she got up and walked away.

"Stupid! Stupid! Stupid!" Sharon said as she hit Melvin's arm with each word.

"Ow!" Melvin said.

"Oh, God," Bryan whispered as he watched Nicole walk across the lawn toward the pool where the boys had gone to swim.

"I'm sorry, man," Melvin said.

"I'm the one who should have known better," Bryan said as he stood to follow her.

"No," Sharon stopped him. "You two have done quite enough already," she concluded as she got up and sat Benjamin in Melvin's lap. "Watch the kids," she instructed. "Think maybe you can do that without saying something stupid?"

The men watched silently as Sharon rushed to catch up with her friend. Nicole had made her way to the pool area and sat on an empty bench, mindlessly watching the children splash in the water.

"Hey," Sharon said as she sat beside her.

"Hey," she responded without looking at her.

"Please don't be mad at Melvin," Sharon said. "You know sometimes his mouth runs faster than his brain. He didn't mean anything by it."

"I'm not mad at Melvin," Nicole said while continuing to stare ahead.

"Well, don't be made at Bryan either," Sharon said. "I mean, I know you think he's perfect all the time, but he's not. He's a man just like Melvin, and you've got to face reality."

"I'm not mad at Bryan either," Nicole said. "I'm not mad at anybody. Anger isn't what I'm feeling, Sharon."

"What, then?" Sharon asked.

"I knew about Bryan's past before I ever married him," Nicole said. "He told me the whole womanizing story on our second date. He said that was when he knew he was in love with me. He had never told anyone the whole story before me. Everybody else found out after me. Even his Uncle Charles only knew bits and pieces at the time. I've never held his past life against him, Sharon. I look at Bryan and I actually understand why all the girls were so crazy about. He's got the whole package, and I can't say that I blame them for going after him. I guess if I was just out there and living the wild life, I probably would have been one in the number."

"But you don't necessarily want to hear about it, right?" Sharon inquired.

"No, I don't," Nicole admitted. "I mean, I can listen to it if it's in the form of testimony of where God brought him from or if it's a counseling tool to help others from making the same mistakes. But I don't want to hear it the way Melvin was describing it. He made it sound like it was a good thing, like it was something to be proud of. I don't want to hear that. You know what I mean?"

"Yes, I do," Sharon said. "It was a very thoughtless thing for him to say."

"It wasn't just him, Sharon. Bryan sat there and agreed to it and laughed. I don't know, maybe it's a man thing," Nicole said, "but I don't see where there's anything funny about using women as some kind of tool to satisfy some stupid manly need of conquest."

"You're right, Nicole," Sharon said. "It was foolish. They both were wrong. I'm not going to make any excuses for them. As far as I'm concerned, they got off easy. I think you should have punched Melvin in the mouth and then kneed Bryan in the groin."

"That would have been kind of harsh, Sharon."

"Humph," Sharon grunted. "Let's just say they'd better be glad it wasn't me, or we might be smelling burning flesh right about now."

"Remind me to always be your friend and never your enemy," Nicole said, laughing.

"Here he comes," Sharon said as she saw Bryan walking toward them.

"Yeah," Nicole said. "I see him."

"What do you want?" Sharon asked as Bryan approached the bench.

"I'd like to talk to my wife, if you don't mind," he said.

"How are you going to talk with all that foot that you have stuck in your mouth?" Sharon asked.

"It's okay, Sharon," Nicole said.

"Fine," Sharon said as she stood to leave. "But if you say anything to upset her more than you already have, I will convince her to withhold the goodies from you for so long until you will think that you're losing your mind."

"What?" Bryan said.

"Oh, don't test me," Sharon said with a pointed finger. "It can be done. Just ask Melvin. And frankly, to punish you wouldn't be that hard. Two days should be just about long enough to send you to the loony bin," she concluded as she walked away.

Nicole nearly shuddered as Bryan sat next to her and brushed her braids away from her face with his hand. She could feel the side of her face turning hot as he stared at her silently as she continued to look away.

"I'm sorry," he finally spoke softly. "It was thoughtless, it was foolish, and it was inconsiderate of both of us, but especially me. I know how it must have sounded," he continued, "but I promise you that it wasn't meant in that way. I know it sounded like I was somehow proud of the way I had misused women back then, but I'm not, and I think you know that."

"Bryan, I'm hurting here," Nicole said as she finally faced him. "Some days are better than others, but not a day goes by that I don't hurt because of your past life."

"I know," Bryan said.

"No, you don't know," Nicole said, holding her hand up to stop his interruption. "Sweetheart, you have no idea," she said. "Don't misunderstand me," she continued. "I care very much for your son, I place no blame on him for any of this, but every time I look at him I see your eyes, your smile, your hair, and your feet. When I cut his hair, I even see your neck and your ears, Bryan. That hurts me.

"I'm not holding anything against you," she said as she wiped a tear from her eyes. "I know this was well before you met me and, most importantly, before you met God. But that doesn't stop it from hurting. To top it all off, I have to deal with her. She's determined not to be civilized. She's making my life miserable, Bryan. I deal with her, but I don't like it. She's rude and she's annoying and she's a liar.

"For the next five or six years, she's going to do everything in her power to make our lives as difficult as she can. I find myself praying all the time because I don't want this sickness that flares up in the pit of my stomach to be hatred for her. She's trying me in a way that I've never been tried before, and I'm afraid that she's going to push the envelope just a little too far and she's going to meet a personality in me that maybe I've not even met yet.

"She's from that same past that you and Melvin can find room to joke about. Maybe I seem strong enough to handle your light chatter about your many women, but I'm not. I need you to know that I'm not strong enough to laugh about it. I mean, I used to, but that was before Tricia. She's beat all the laughter out of me. I'm tired of her lies, her tricks, her harassing calls to my job, her . . . "

"Calls to your job?" Bryan interrupted. "What calls to your job?"

Nicole stopped and quietly wiped more silent tears that streamed down her face.

Bryan slowly cupped her face in his hands and wiped her tears with his thumbs as his sharp brown eyes looked directly into her eyes.

"What calls, Nicole?" he repeated slowly.

"She's called the day care," Nicole said softly.

"She's called since the first time?"

"Yes."

"How many times?" Bryan asked.

"At least once," Nicole said. "We've had some hang-up calls lately as well. I can't prove it, but I know it's her."

"Baby, why didn't you tell me about this before?"

"I'm trying so hard to keep the peace here," she answered. "For Gerald's sake, we have to keep peace."

"Not at this expense," Bryan said. "You are more important to me than anything, Nicole. Keeping the peace between Tricia and me does not come before keeping your peace of mind. Do you understand me?" he asked.

"Yes."

"I'm sorry," Bryan said. "I apologize for me and for Melvin. Charge it to our heads and not to our hearts, sweetie. I wish I could take the whole two-minute conversation back, but I can't. Please forgive me."

"I do," Nicole said.

"Thank you," Bryan said as he kissed her hand. "You want to walk to the pond and feed the ducks?"

"No," Nicole said. "Actually, I'm just going to walk to the house and lie down for a while. I think all this talk of Tricia has challenged my stress level. I have a pounding headache now."

"I'm sorry," Bryan said. "We can all just go on home."

"No," Nicole said as she looked toward the pool and saw Gerald and Todd laughing and swimming. "The boys are having way too much fun. I don't want to spoil it for everybody. I'll be at home when you get there."

"Okay," Bryan said, and they stood and embraced. "Don't worry about dinner," he added. "I'll make sure the boys are fed."

"Thanks," she said as she walked away.

"Is she okay?" Melvin asked as he, Sharon, and the kids joined him.

"I think so," Bryan said.

"Bryan, I can't believe you could be so tactless." Sharon shook her head slowly. "I mean, Melvin I can see. But you?"

"I can hear you, you know," Melvin said.

"I don't need you to beat up on me, Sharon," Bryan said. "I know I was wrong and I've admitted that. I'm kicking myself in the behind already. Cut me a little slack here, okay?"

"We'll watch the kids if you want to go on home," Melvin said.

"I think you should give her a minute, Bryan," Sharon said.

"Hey, Bryan!" Gerald called from the pool. "Come swim with us!"

"I think you're right," Bryan agreed as he walked toward the pool. "If she wants to talk later, she knows I'm available."

CHAPTER TWENTY-ONE

Saturday's rest was just what Nicole needed. She was up early Sunday morning and cooked a full meal for Bryan and the boys. Todd had begged his grandmother to let him spend the night at the Walker home, and she had agreed.

The smell of Nicole's blueberry pancakes served as an alarm clock for Bryan and the boys. She began hearing them stirring around and getting prepared for Sunday morning's service.

"Good morning," Bryan said as he walked into the kitchen wearing a T-shirt and his suit pants.

"Good morning." She smiled back at him as he kissed her.

Yesterday's misunderstanding at the park hadn't been mentioned between the two of them since Nicole left for home. After leaving the park, Bryan took Todd and Gerald to the store to buy Gerald a new outfit for Sunday. He didn't seem to have any dress clothes, and the suit that he had worn on his last trip was at the cleaners. Todd was satisfied with the pair of socks that he got out of the trip.

"It's been a while since you've cooked blueberry pancakes," Bryan observed as he took the plates from the cabinet and began setting the table.

"I know," she responded. "I had a sudden taste for them."

"Did you go to the store this morning?"

"Yes," Nicole said with a laugh. "I didn't have any blueberries. I think between yesterday afternoon and last night, I got too much sleep. I've been awake since 4:00 this morning."

"So what have you been doing since 4:00?" Bryan asked as he set the glasses out. "I know you didn't spend all that time at the grocery store."

"I woke up at 4:00, but I didn't get out of the bed until shortly after 4:30. For half an hour, I just watched you sleep. Then I got up," she continued as Bryan smiled at her last remark, "took a shower, read a few Scriptures, and said my morning prayer. By 6:00, I was in the checkout line at the grocery store with the blueberries, juice, syrup, and milk. I started cooking breakfast at 7:15, and that brings us to now. It's 8:30, and breakfast is waiting for some hungry mouths and empty stomachs."

"And here they come," Bryan said as the laughing boys joined them, still in their pajamas.

"What's that smell?" Gerald asked as they peeked in the kitchen.

"Why aren't you guys dressed?" Bryan asked.

"We didn't want to mess up our church clothes," Todd said.

"What?" Bryan laughed. "You can't eat without making a mess?"

"Did you at least wash your hands and faces?" Nicole asked.

"Yes," they said in unison.

"Why don't you two have a seat on the sofa for a few minutes while Ms. Nicole and I finish getting breakfast on the table?" Bryan suggested.

"Okay," they said, and they disappeared into the living room and began chatting softly, but excitedly.

"What are they up to?" Nicole wondered out loud.

"Who knows," Bryan said with a laugh.

"They get along so well, it's easy to forget that they're almost three years apart."

"I know," Bryan said as he stepped close to her and pulled her close to him.

"Thank you," he whispered.

"For what?"

"For allowing me to make a mistake every now and then without holding it against me forever."

"Even Superman had a human side," Nicole said. "He couldn't be a superhero all the time."

"You know," Bryan said, "being labeled as a superhero puts a lot of pressure on a man. I'm not sure that I know what to do to live up to that."

"Just keep doing what you're doing, baby," she said, and she kissed him warmly. "That's not a new label for you. You've been my superhero for five years now."

"Oh sorry!" Gerald and Todd said as they walked in on the embracing couple.

"What?" Nicole asked as she walked toward them and kissed them both on the cheek.

"Ughhh!" Gerald said as he wiped the kiss off of his cheek.

Todd smiled and blushed as she kissed him.

"Ahhh," Bryan said. "The age difference shows."

"I hope you boys are hungry," Nicole said with a laugh as she motioned for them to sit at the table.

Breakfast was a hit. Nicole only ate two pancakes, but Bryan and the boys made short work of the remaining pancakes and sausages. With church time quickly approaching, they all scampered to get the kitchen cleaned and to get dressed. They made it to their seats with only five minutes to spare.

"Thought you guys weren't going to make it," Sharon remarked as she allowed them to edge by her.

The youth department took charge of the service as Pastor Gaines had instructed. It was refreshing to see them carry out the praise services and to listen to the youth choir minister. The Cradle Choir, as they called the toddler singers, was especially adorable as they sang off-key and rocked out of sync with the music and each other. It was always a pleasure for the adult members to see them involved in the program.

Before the youth minister got up to deliver the message of the day, Pastor Gaines opened the floor to any young members or visitors who weren't on the program but desired to sing or speak. To the congregation's surprise and delight, several of the children volunteered to go up and read Scriptures or sing songs.

No one was more surprised than Nicole and Bryan when Todd abruptly got up and walked to the front of the church with Gerald following close behind. Todd took the microphone from Pastor Gaines's hand and began to speak.

"My name is Toddrick Peek," he began. "When I was thirteen, my mother gave up on me and sent me to live with my aunt because I was doing bad things at home. When I was fourteen, my aunt gave up on me and sent me here to live with my grandmother because I was doing bad things at home. When I turned fifteen, my grandma said she wasn't going to give up on me, and she sent me here to the church to have counseling sessions with Bryan Walker because I was doing bad things at home."

Mother Peek took a handkerchief from her purse and wiped her eyes as the audience applauded, temporarily stopping Todd's speech.

"I just want to say," he continued, "that I'm glad that somebody finally sent me somewhere so I could get some help. Bryan, I mean, Brother Walker," he corrected, "is kind of like a father to me, and Sister Walker is like a mother to me. They let me come to their house, and they take me out and Sister Walker feeds me, and they spend time with me. I just want to tell them thank you."

Bryan and Nicole smiled and clapped along with the rest of the congregation as Todd handed the microphone to a shy Gerald, who held it and stared at the floor in silence for a few moments. Todd nudged him with his elbow as though trying to rush him to speak.

"That's all right, baby," somebody called from the audience. "Take your time."

"My name is Gerald Walker," he started slowly, never taking his eyes from the floor. "I just want to say that I think this is a nice church, and I like coming here."

Nicole looked up at Bryan and smiled as Gerald continued.

"I want to say thank you to my father and stepmother, Bryan and Nicole Walker, for letting me come to stay with them and making me feel at home. I want to thank Ms. Nicole for cooking for me and cutting my hair and buying me an X box," he continued as the crowd chuckled while Nicole fought tears, "and Bryan for buying me clothes and playing ball with me and Todd and praying with me at night and trying to make up for all those years when he didn't know about me. Thank you," he concluded as he handed the microphone back to Pastor Gaines.

Seeming glad to finally have their speeches over with, the boys walked quickly back to their seats. They were surrounded by thunderous applause and warm embraces from both Nicole and Bryan.

After all the youth who desired to take part in the service had their chance, Pastor Gaines took the microphone and led the ovation in appreciation of their courage and willingness to participate.

Minister Wright didn't get a whole lot of opportunities to speak on Sunday mornings. He generally spoke at youth rallies or revivals. He seemed honored to have a chance to speak to the congregation on a Sunday morning.

His sermon was short, but meaningful. After such a lengthy program consisting of songs and tributes from the children, Minister Wright thought it was best not to make the sermon too long and lose people's attention. His message turned into an altar plea. He almost sounded as though he was begging the youth to turn their lives over to Christ. His words were profound and powerful.

Following the message, Pastor Gaines asked all of the members of the congregation under age twenty to gather around the altar for prayer. For the adults, it was a beautiful sight to see the front of the sanctuary crowded with children and teenagers. Some of them seemed genuinely touched by the prayer that was offered by their pastor.

Gerald's leaving for Tallahassee that evening seemed equally as hard on him as it was on Nicole and Bryan.

They had turned down a dinner offer from Melvin and Sharon to take Gerald out to eat and spend some quality time with him. They had kept him as long as they could, but the time had come for him to go home.

He threw his backpack over his shoulder and hugged them both warmly before joining Melvin in the car. He waved as they pulled out onto the street. Nicole watched in silence as Bryan somberly walked into his office and closed the door behind him.

Nicole was almost finished cleaning the kitchen when she finally heard Bryan start the shower. His silence following Gerald's departure spoke volumes. When he finished his shower, she heard him as he settled in the living room and switched the channels with the remote control. She stopped by his side briefly to kiss his forehead on her way to the room to take her own shower.

"Are you okay?" she asked him as she joined him on the sofa afterwards.

"Yeah, sweetie," he said. "I'm fine."

"It's not easy letting him go back home anymore, is it?" she persisted.

"Am I that transparent?" he asked.

"It's been over an hour, and you haven't spoken a word. It's pretty obvious."

"Am I overreacting?"

"Not at all, Bryan. I know that I hate to see him leave. Being that you're his biological father, I can only imagine how his leaving must make you feel."

"It's hard for you to let him go home?" Bryan asked.

"You sound surprised," Nicole remarked.

"I guess I am to a certain degree," Bryan admitted. "I mean, I knew you had accepted him as a part of your life as well as mine, but I think I misjudged just how close you felt to him."

"He's very easy to fall in love with." Nicole smiled. "I guess that's a trait that he definitely got from his daddy."

"Maybe so," Bryan replied, blushing. "It's only been a few weeks, but I think I just might be getting the hang of this fatherhood thing."

Nicole's silence following his words made Bryan wish he could take it back.

"I'm sorry," he said as he touched her arm. "I didn't mean that in a disrespectful way."

"No." Nicole shook her head. "I know how you meant it. It's okay. I think you're a wonderful father. I can't pretend that I didn't wish the circumstances of his existence were different, but I also can't pretend that I wish he didn't exist. I'm glad he's a part of our lives, too."

"You mean that?" Bryan asked.

"Yes. I honestly do. He's a wonderful child. He just needs more stability and guidance. You give that to him."

"So do you," Bryan interjected.

"We give him that," Nicole corrected herself.

"I just wish he had more time with us so that we could continue to give him that," Bryan said. "All of this back-and-forth living might be okay for now, but I wonder how it will affect him in the future."

"I have an idea," Nicole suddenly said after a short silence between them.

"What?"

"Why don't you see if Tricia will let you keep him for a while?"

"What do you mean?"

"Well, she's always fussing about how she's had to give up so much of her life while raising him alone and how it's about time that you did something, right? Well, let's do something. Let's let her know that we're willing to take him in with us for a while."

"Are you serious?" Bryan sat up straight.

"Yes."

"And you think Tricia will agree to it?"

"Why not? I'm not talking about trying to take parental rights or even permanent custody from her. I'm just talking about turning the responsibilities for a while. We'll keep him here full-time, and she can take him every other weekend. That way, we'll get to spend more time with him like we want to, and she'll get to have a break from around-the-clock responsibility for him."

"What about school?"

"We could start the arrangement after the school year ends. There are only a few weeks left in this school term anyway. When Gerald comes for the summer, we could start the arrangement then."

"Wow," Bryan said as he stood from the sofa and rubbed his chin with his hand. "You do realize that this would be a major change for us, right? I mean, having him here all the time will be a whole lot different than having him here a few days a month."

"I know. But think of the benefits. You'll have more time to be the kind of father that I know you want to be," she began enumerating. "He'll have more positive role models as well as positive reinforcement. We can really get him involved with the youth department at the church. You could help him with his baseball and track dreams and maybe get him on one of the middle school's teams next year. And on the selfish side," she concluded, "I could get a more realistic feeling of what it's like to be the mother of your child."

"You know what?" Bryan said as he pulled her to a standing position. "You are unbelievable. Absolutely unbelievable," he continued. "Sometimes I look at you and listen to you and I wonder what in the world I ever did to deserve a woman like you."

"Really?" It was all Nicole could think to say, looking into his soul-burning eyes as he held her close.

"Our lives have been turned upside down and inside out over the past couple of months. It had the potential of blowing a hole in this love nest that we've created. It was shaky for a while, but it could have been disastrous. Gerald's reality could have been the end of us, but instead you've taken it and made it into a way to bring us even closer together. Baby, I don't know how it's even possible, but I promise you, I love you more right now than I did just two minutes ago."

Nicole opened her mouth to respond, but found it impossible to do so as Bryan's lips covered hers with such passion that she had to wrap her arms around his neck just to keep her legs from crumpling beneath her.

He swept her off of her feet and continued to kiss her as he carried her into the bedroom and laid her gently on the fresh linen that graced their bed. Her white-laced nightgown blended right in with the white satin sheets on the bed. Bryan peeled his robe from his body and joined her on the bed, brushing her braids away from her face as his lips found hers once more.

"Your phone," Nicole mumbled as his cell phone began ringing from the nightstand.

"Let it ring," he said.

"It could be Melvin," she reminded him.

"Okay," he whispered as he reluctantly released her and picked up the phone.

"Hello," he said.

"Where's Gerald?" It was Tricia.

"What do you mean, where is he?" Bryan said, trying not to sound annoyed. "He's on his way to Tallahassee.

Melvin is bringing him as usual."

"Well, last time he was home by now!"

"There's no reason to yell, Tricia," Bryan said as he watched Nicole slide off of the bed and go into the bathroom. "They left later than last time."

"Ain't you the one who told me that if I wasn't going to be at home when y'all came to get him to let you know? Well, I guess it was too much for you to pick up the phone and call me to let me know that your friend would be late bringing him home this week, huh?"

"I'm sorry," Bryan said. "I didn't know I was on a time schedule. I will call next time."

"You are so selfish," she continued. "You want everything done your way. I had a date tonight. I could have stayed out later or at least invited him in for a beer or something. I think the least you could have done was call me to let me know."

"I said I was sorry, Tricia. I will call next time."

"Did you send a money order?" she asked.

"What?"

"Did you send a money order with Gerald?"

"A money order for what?"

"Don't act stupid, Bryan." She smacked her lips. "A money order for child support."

"Tricia, I sent a money order the last time Gerald came. It's not time for me to send another until the next time he comes."

"Well, don't think I'm going to forget. I'll take your sorry, two-timing—"

"Now you just hold on a minute," Bryan said as he stood from the bed angrily and raised his voice. "You just wait one minute. I don't know who you think you're talking to, but I am not sorry, nor am I a two-timer. I am being a father to my son, and, although she's not obligated to, Nicole is being a good mother to him."

"Nicole ain't never gonna be Gerald's mother," she said through her teeth.

"When he's here, she is," Bryan said. "And as far as two-timing goes, I have allegiance to one woman and one woman only, and I would never cheat on her, so don't you call me a two-timer."

"Oh, you can settle down and be faithful to her, but you couldn't do that for me, could you? You couldn't make it work for us like that, could you?"

"What?" Bryan said as Nicole finally came out of the restroom and slipped under the covers with her back turned to him.

"What do you mean 'us'?" he asked. "There never was an 'us,' Tricia, and you know that. The only thing that you and I shared was one careless night that, aside from Gerald, I'll regret the rest of my life."

"You ain't got no respect for the mother of your only child, do you?" she asked. "How you gonna talk to me like I was just a conquest for you?"

"Listen." Bryan tried to calm himself. "This conversation isn't accomplishing a thing. You called because you were concerned about Gerald's whereabouts. Well, he's fine. They should be there shortly."

"And I'm supposed to be stupid enough to let you just bail out of the conversation like that?" Tricia said. "You might not have married me, but it's pretty clear to me that I'm about the only girl you ever known who wasn't stupid and didn't just let you treat her any kind of way. That's probably why you didn't marry me. You wanted some trick you could walk all over. That's why you married that thang that you got there with you now."

Tricia's verbal abuse of Nicole was taking Bryan's

anger to a boiling point. He was nearly trembling as he tried to control his seething anger. His response caused Nicole to sit up in the bed.

"I have warned you," he said quietly through clenched teeth, "not to disrespect my wife. But you continuously do so, and I've just about had it. I don't need to defend her honor, because it speaks for itself. However, from now on, when and if you ever degrade her again, our conversation is immediately over. I will not tolerate it for one second. Your problem is with me and not with her. Now is there anything else that you'd like to know concerning Gerald before I end this call?"

"Let me tell you what your lil' stankin' wife can do for me," she began.

Nicole winced as Bryan suddenly pressed the button to disconnect the call and then threw the phone against the bedroom wall, shattering it into pieces. She watched him in silence as he stood quietly with his eyes closed and his fists clenched tightly.

Slipping on a pair of blue jeans and a shirt, he slowly walked to the dresser and picked up his keys before walking to her side of the bed and kissing her forehead.

"I'm sorry," he apologized quietly. "I didn't mean to scare you."

Nicole saw water in his eyes as he spoke. She knew that anger was the cause of most of it.

"Where are you going?" Nicole whispered.

"I don't know," he answered softly. "I just need to go for a ride and clear my head."

"Don't go, sweetheart," she pleaded. "Let's just get some sleep. You'll feel better about it in the morning."

"I can't," he said, and he stepped away. "I can't sleep right now. I just need some fresh air. Don't wait up for me."

Nicole watched him slip on a pair of shoes before walking from the room and quietly closing the door. She heard the garage door open and close as he pulled away in the car. Suddenly she didn't feel well. She lay on her pillow and cried herself to sleep.

Chapter Twenty-Two

So what you're basically saying," Sharon said as she and Nicole shared lunch together, "is that things aren't getting any better."

"Sharon, I have never seen Bryan that upset in the entire five-plus years that we've been married."

"And you say you don't know what she said to him?"

"Well, all I could hear was his end of the conversation. I know at the height of his anger she had apparently said something negative about me."

"That'll do it every time," Sharon interjected.

"But there's more," Nicole continued. "He was already mad by the time she started on me. He was telling her that they were never a couple and that he hadn't cheated on her."

"What?"

"Yeah. It was like she was accusing him of being unfaithful to her by marrying me."

"Not that she ever really had any credibility with me," Sharon said, "but whatever microscopic respect that I may have had for her is now gone."

"I guess she still believes that Bryan knew about Gerald's existence. I thought that possibly she had been convinced otherwise by now, but I was wrong."

"Why would you think she was convinced otherwise?" Sharon asked. "It's not like she's dealing with a full deck."

"It just seems like she'd take note of how much we care about Gerald and how much he enjoys his time with his father and me, and she'd know that Bryan would not have intentionally abandoned his son."

"You're thinking like a sane woman, Nicole. You have to think like last year's leftover fruitcake to know what goes on in Tricia's half-baked head. She's not ever going to see anything positive in what you and Bryan do. The fact that Gerald actually likes you guys is undoubtedly burning her up on the inside.

"Believe me," she continued, "if she thinks it will make you happy, she's not going to do it, say it, or go along with it. Her purpose was never to bring Gerald and his father together. It was to distract and destroy Bryan's life. She's been harboring a lot of anger over the past thirteen years, and she wants to pass as much of it along to Bryan as she can. Face it, Nicole. She doesn't like Bryan, she doesn't like you, and quite frankly, she probably doesn't like Gerald a whole lot either. He reminds her of all the bad stuff in her life."

"None of this is Gerald's fault," Nicole said. "He didn't ask her to fool around with Bryan, and he certainly didn't have a choice on whether she'd end up pregnant or not. Why would she blame him?"

"Again, Nicole, you're thinking like a sane woman."

"Well, if Gerald is a problem for her, she can give him to Bryan and me. We'll take him."

"Would you?" Sharon seemed surprised.

"Yes, I would. Bryan and I discussed it at length last night not long before she called."

"You're thinking of going after custody?"

"No," Nicole explained. "We weren't talking about going after custody. We just talked about giving Tricia a break. I thought it might be a good idea to offer to keep Gerald with us for a while."

"How long?"

"For as long as she'd allow him to stay. We discussed him staying with us starting in the summer and then throughout his seventh grade school year. Instead of visiting us every other weekend, he'd visit her."

"It's a good idea, Nicole, but believe me, she's not going to go for it."

"Why not?" Nicole asked. "She's always saying that she's had to care for him and alter her life for the past twelve years. Why wouldn't she let us take on the full-time responsibilities for a while so she can have more free time?"

"Because it's what you want to do," Sharon said as she drank her water. "If she still believed that the two of you didn't want anything to do with Gerald, she would probably push for that. But because she now knows that you actually like him and he likes you, she's not going to go along with that."

"That's insane."

"So is she."

"Sharon . . ."

"Nicole, listen to me. She's not going to do it. Ask her. It's the only way that you'll be convinced. I guarantee you that when and if you and Bryan discuss the idea with her she's going to shoot it out of the air."

"Can you have a little faith here?" Nicole asked.

"It's reality, Nicole. I know God is able to do anything, but I think even He needs to have a person with a little bit of sense to work with, and you know Tricia ain't got none. I don't mean to be Doubting Thomas here, but you need to prepare to be disappointed on this one."

Nicole sighed and resumed eating her sandwich in silence. She wanted to believe differently, but Sharon was probably right. She couldn't imagine Tricia agreeing with anything concerning Gerald that would make Bryan and her happy even if she had to sacrifice her own happiness in the process of hindering theirs.

"How was Bryan this morning?" Sharon broke Nicole's thought.

"I don't know," Nicole admitted. "After I fell asleep last night, I only woke up once, and that was when Melvin called to say that he and Gerald had made it to Tallahassee safely. I went right back to sleep afterwards. I didn't hear Bryan when he came in last night, and he was already gone this morning when I got up."

"You haven't called him or anything?"

"Well, he left a note for me on the bathroom mirror this morning and said he was leaving early and had some things to take care of. I called his office this morning, but Carol said that he had left for a counseling session at the church. I didn't even know he had one scheduled. And of course, I couldn't call him on his cell, because he destroyed that last night."

"Do you want to stop by Bryan's office on the way back to the center?" Sharon offered.

"No," Nicole said. "He was really angry last night. He may just need some time. I don't want to interfere with that. He knows where to reach me whenever he wants to talk about it."

Nicole didn't know it, but Bryan's counseling session wasn't for him to counsel, but for him to be counseled. He sat in the chair across from Pastor Gaines's desk and stared at the Ziploc bag in his hands that held the broken cell phone that he had smashed the night before.

"Thanks, Aunt Maggie," he said as his aunt handed him a glass of water after setting one glass on her husband's desk.

"You're welcome, baby," she said, patting his back and then leaving them alone.

Pastor Gaines continued their discussion. "So, how is Nicole doing today?"

"I haven't spoken with her yet," Bryan said. "I left her a note this morning. I left the house at 5:00 and went to the gym to lift some weights and to hit the punching bag for a while. I only stopped by the office for about a half hour this morning, and I've been out ever since."

"You know she's probably worried about you."

"I know, Uncle Charles. She's just had to deal with so much already surrounding my involvement with Tricia. I just don't want to drag her in and burden her any more than I already have."

"She's your wife, Bryan. It's your duty to share with her."

"The whole sordid mess is making her physically ill, Uncle Charles," Bryan blurted. "How am I supposed to handle that? Huh? Am I supposed to keep making her face issues that she had nothing to do with, knowing that she's just going to get sick?"

"I wasn't aware that she'd been ill," Pastor Gaines said in concern. "How long has this been going on?"

"Off and on for the past several weeks," Bryan said as he stood and paced the floor slowly. "Tricia's been harassing her at her job, cursing her out, lying to her, and calling her all of these godforsaken names. Even when she doesn't speak to Tricia directly, the mention of her name seems toxic to Nicole's system. I can't say I blame her. She makes me sick too, but this whole thing is my fault. It's my mistake. I'll deal with the consequences, but not Nicole. I won't let my bad choices continue to hurt her."

"It's just stress related," Pastor Gaines said.

"I know it is. But it's stress related to me. God, Uncle Charles!" Bryan said as he turned and stared out of the office window. "I love that woman. I live for her, and God knows I'd die for her. I can't stand the thought of knowing that I'm in some way the cause of her health not being what it should be. I know hate is a strong word, not to mention a sin, but I have never come closer to hating a person than I am right now where Tricia is concerned."

"Calm down, son," Pastor Gaines said. "You're right. It is a strong word, and it is a sin. We must love everyone, however evil they may seem to be. That's not to say that you have to love her as you love your friends or your family. But you must love her with the love of God. No more than that is required, but no less than that is acceptable in God's sight."

"Then you pray for me, Uncle Charles," Bryan said, "because I'm not there. I love my son, but I can't honestly say the same for his mother. She's purposely trying to destroy the best thing that ever happened to me, and I have a real problem with that."

"I understand how you feel, Bryan. Believe me, I do. I understand and I can see the depth of your love for Nicole, and I can see the same of her love for you. You'll make it through this. And when it's all over, your love will be stronger and deeper than ever."

Pastor Gaines chuckled softly after a few moments of silence.

"Please share the humorous side of this with me," Bryan said. "I could really use a laugh right now, but nothing about this is remotely funny in my opinion."

"I'm not laughing at the humor of this situation, Bryan. I'm laughing at the amazement of it all."

"Amazement?" Bryan asked.

"Yes," his uncle said as he stood and walked around his desk and stood next to Bryan. "I remember you when you were in high school and in your freshman college year," he continued. "I remember talking to you about your rambunctious lifestyle when you first came to stay with Maggie and me. I remember you saying that you weren't ever going to fall in love and get married. You just wanted to explore all life had to offer and have as much fun as you could while you could. You remember that?"

"Yeah," Bryan said softly.

"The amazement of it all is that it only took two beings to change your whole outlook on life and love. It took God, and it took Nicole. You went from being sporadic to being sprung." He laughed. "It's amazing, and it's beautiful."

"The old me seems like a lifetime ago," Bryan said.

"The old you is a lifetime ago," Pastor Gaines said. "When you accepted Christ, you became a new creature. The old things passed, and all things became new. We all have things in our pasts that we aren't proud of, son. And in one way or another, we have to pay for those things even after we've been forgiven and have moved on. Some prices are higher than others, but we all have to pay.

"Our trials come to make us strong, Bryan. If you can pass the test, you'll come out on top in the end. This is causing you to pray more and appreciate those things in life that God has blessed you with even more than you had before. In your eyes, even the value of your most priceless jewel is getting higher every day."

"Nicole?" Bryan asked knowingly.

"Nicole," Pastor Gaines said.

"So what am I supposed to do?" Bryan asked. "How am I supposed to handle this without losing it and doing something extreme?"

"If you were conducting one of your counseling sessions right now, what would you advise someone in your situation to do?" Pastor Gaines asked.

"That's a hard question to answer."

"I know," Pastor Gaines agreed. "But that's the way you have to envision this situation. You have to detach yourself and see yourself on the outside looking in. It's hard to think reasonably when you're the one feeling the actual pain. Give it a try," he urged. "If Todd or one of the other young men or women in the congregation came to you and wanted to know what to do about someone who was blatantly trying to push them over the edge, what would you tell them?"

Bryan slowly walked back to his chair and drank a few swallows of his water as he contemplated his answer.

"I'd probably tell them to seek God's guidance," Bryan finally said. "I'd tell them to pray and be obedient to God. He may not move swiftly, but because we know He does not fall short of His promises, it's a guarantee that He'll be there, and He will reward us for our patience and trust in Him."

"And that," Pastor Gaines said as he looked at Bryan

from the window where he stood, "is the reason that you are such a successful counselor."

Bryan sat quietly for a few minutes and thought on the words that he had just spoken. He was going to need nothing shy of a miracle to be able to take his own advice, and he knew it.

"Would you two care for any more water or anything else?" Maggie said as she peeked in the door.

"Bryan?" Pastor Gaines offered.

"No, thanks, Aunt Maggie," Bryan said as he stood and handed her his empty glass. "That was good," he said.

"Anytime, sweetheart." She smiled back at him.

"Thanks, Uncle Charles," Bryan said as he headed toward the door.

"Are we done?" Pastor Gaines asked.

"Yes sir," Bryan said. "I may need you again later, but I'm good to go for now."

"You always know where to find me."

"Yes sir."

"Oh—," His uncle held up a hand to stop him.

"Yes?"

"Teresa called me about 6:00 this morning and asked about you."

"Mama?"

"Yeah. She said she hadn't heard from you since you called to tell her about Gerald."

"It's not like we have a regular calling schedule," Bryan said. "Prior to my calling her about Gerald I hadn't spoken to her in months. I send her a check every month, and I know she's grateful, but she never bothers to even call and say thank you. We just don't have that type of relationship, I guess."

"You should talk to your mother more often, Bryan," his aunt interjected.

"Why?" Bryan asked. "Is something wrong?"

"No," she said. "She's your mother. I know the two of you have had your differences, but she's still your mother, and she really does care about you. Sometimes I think she just has trouble showing it.

"She said that she tried to call you at home this morning but didn't get an answer. She said she was going to try you at work later, but you probably weren't there if she did. I got the feeling that she wanted to speak to you about something. You should call her."

"I'll call her tonight," Bryan promised. "Right now, I have a cell phone to replace and a woman to see."

"Take care, son," Pastor Gaines said as he and his wife walked him to the door.

Purchasing a new phone took longer than Bryan had expected. By the time he got back to his office, it was closing time, and Carol was packing her things together to leave.

"Calling it a day?" Bryan asked.

"Yes." She smiled. "Mr. Tolbert called again. He's ready to get his son outta jail. He'll call again tomorrow."

"Okay," Bryan said as he took the written message from her hand.

"A lady called here dat said she was your mama," she said. "I don't know if she really was or not, 'cause I've never heard you talk much about your mama, but dat's what she said. She didn't leave a message. Just said she'd try you again later."

"Thanks." He took the slip from her hand.

"Todd called," she continued. "He says he needs to talk to you sometime today if it's possible."

"Did he seem upset or anything?" Bryan asked while taking the written message from her hand.

"No, not upset," she said. "A bit anxious, maybe. He did ask dat I be sure to give you da message."

"Okay."

"Mrs. Walker has called for you two times," she handed him the last written message. "She seemed a bit worried. Is everyting okay?"

"Yes, Carol. Everything is fine. I'll talk to her."

"She said dat she was leaving work at 4:00. I guess she's home by now."

"Thanks, Carol," Bryan said as she threw her purse over her shoulder and put the other messages back on her desk. "Are those for me too?" he asked.

"Yes, but dey can wait. I gave you da today stuff. Dis stuff can wait until tomorrow."

"Okay, boss." Bryan smiled. "You enjoy the rest of your evening."

"Tank you," Carol said, laughing. "You do da same. I'll see you in da morning."

Bryan locked the door behind her and went into his office. He thumbed through the paperwork on his desk and picked up the phone to call Nicole, but decided to call Todd instead.

"Hellooooo," Mother Peek sang as she answered the phone.

"Hi, Mother Peek," Bryan said. "How are you this afternoon?"

"Oh, I'm doing okay, sugar," she said. "I got a little ache in my hip though. You know that old place where that doctor took the knife to me some years ago. I guess that means it's gonna rain. You know, when rain is coming," she continued, "that old hip of mine just go to aching and aching. It just keeps on aching until the rain is over. That's the one problem with letting them old doctors cut into you. It fixes one thing and messes up another, but God is still good anyhow."

"Yes, ma'am," Bryan said.

"How's that beautiful wife of yours?" she asked.

"Nicole is doing fine. I'm on my way home to her in a couple of minutes, but I wanted to speak with Todd if he's there."

"Oh, yeah," she said. "He's here. He's just finishing up with his homework, I believe. Hold on just a minute."

Bryan chuckled softly as he waited for Todd. Mother Peek was such a sweet woman. But in his opinion, she acted even older than she was. If he didn't know her, he'd probably guess that she was in her eighties instead of seventy.

"Hello?"

"Hi, Todd."

"Hi, Bryan."

"Ms. Carol told me that you called me today and wanted to talk to me. Is right now a good time?"

"Yes, but not here." He brought his voice to a whisper. "Can you come and pick me up?"

"Is it that serious?"

"It's something I should have told you already, but I haven't and I need to. Yes, it's kind of serious."

Bryan thought of the fact that Nicole was at home and maybe worried about him. He hadn't spoken to her all day long, and that was extremely unlike him. He needed to spend some time with her, but it was obvious that Todd needed him, too.

"Give me thirty minutes," he told Todd. "I'll be over."

He quickly dialed home after hanging up with Todd. It was obvious that Nicole had been concerned. She answered the phone on the first ring.

"Hey, baby," he said.

"Bryan." She sounded relieved. "Where are you?"

"I'm sorry, sweetheart," he apologized. "I'm at the office. I've been so busy today, but that's no excuse. I should have taken the time to call you earlier. How are you?"

"Never mind me," she said. "How are you?"

Bryan smiled at her selflessness.

"I'm much better. Now, how are you?"

"I'm okay. Much better now that I've heard from you. Are you on your way home?"

"Not immediately, unless you need me," Bryan said. "Something is going on with Todd, and he's asked me to pick him up so we can talk."

"No, I'm fine," Nicole, said. "You go ahead. I'll be here when you get home."

"Are you sure?" Bryan asked. "You're okay?"

"Yes."

"Would you like me to bring you something home for dinner?" he offered.

"No," Nicole said. "Just you."

Her answer caught Bryan off guard. He took a deep breath and regained composure.

"I'll be there shortly," he said smiling.

"I'll be waiting."

"Oh, Todd." He sighed as he hung up the phone. "This had better be good."

CHAPTER TWENTY-THREE

Todd was waiting for Bryan on the front porch as he pulled into the gravel driveway. He didn't even wait for him to shut off the engine. He ran down the steps and jumped into the car with him.

"Where's Mother Peek?" Bryan asked.

"She's taking a bath."

"Does she know you're leaving with me?"

"Yes."

"Are you sure, Todd?"

"I told her," he assured Bryan. "She told me to make sure the door was locked when I left. If you want to go in there and let her know we're leaving, you can," Todd continued. "But I've walked in on her before, and believe me, it ain't pretty."

"Okay," Bryan said, laughing as he drove away. "I'll take your word for it. Where are we going?"

"It doesn't matter." Todd shrugged. "Just somewhere where we can kick it for a minute."

They drove for several minutes with only the music from the car's radio to prevent utter silence.

"You're not about to tell me that you want my wife, are you?" Bryan joked as he pulled into the lot of one of the nearby parks.

Todd laughed. "Naaa. But make a note of that for five years from now. It may come up again."

"I'll do that." Bryan laughed.

They got out of the car and walked to one of the empty park benches and sat. The clouds were beginning to show signs of rain. Mother Peek was right.

"You said you had something to tell me that you should have told me already. What is it?"

"I promised that I wouldn't tell you, but I think you should know."

"You promised who? Mother Peek?"

"No."

"Who?"

"I don't want to make nobody mad at me, Bryan," Todd said. "So you have to promise that you won't get mad and punish him."

"Punish who?"

"Do you promise?" Todd asked.

"It's hard for me to make a promise about something that I haven't a clue concerning, Todd. Who would say something so terrible about me that I'd actually want to punish him?"

"It's not something terrible about you. It's just something that you probably didn't know that he knew. I don't know if I'm telling you this for you or for me. I guess I need an explanation, too."

"Okay," Bryan said. "Let's start over. Why don't you tell me what it is that you need an explanation for, and I promise you that I'll give you an honest explanation?"

"And you promise not to get mad at him?"

"You know I don't make promises that I'm not sure I can keep. That's a hard one for me to make. I don't know who 'he' is and I don't know that I won't get angry. But I can promise you that I won't try and punish him. Is that good enough?"

"I guess." Todd sighed.

"Now," Bryan said. "Who is 'he,' and why are you so worried about how I may react to what he said?"

"It's Gerald," he said softly.

"Gerald?" Bryan sat up straight. "Gerald said something negative about me?"

"No. Not really," Todd said, covering his face with both hands.

"It's okay," Bryan said. "I'm going to be quiet and let you talk. Just tell me. Explain it the best you know how. But give it to me straight."

"Gerald really likes you. He really does, Bryan. I ain't making that up. He told me that he really liked you and Ms. Nicole. He's glad that he gets to come and stay with you guys."

Bryan smiled at the knowledge that Gerald had actually told someone that he liked them.

"He don't want to do nothing to make you not want him around, so that's why he's never told you about this."

"About what?"

"He knows that you knew, Bryan."

"Knew what?" Bryan tried to remain patient through Todd's puzzle of an explanation.

"He knows that you didn't just find out about him when his mama told you back in March. He knows that you knew before then, but he's willing to forgive you and just take it from here. But I need to know why you lied about it."

"Todd, what are you talking about?" Bryan said. "I didn't know about Gerald before his mother told me. I didn't have a clue about him before the meeting that day with her."

"He remembers you, Bryan," Todd insisted. "He says he was really small, and the last time he saw you he was about four years old. But he still remembers. He still has a Lakers jersey that you bought him back then."

"This doesn't make sense, Todd. Why would he tell you that?"

"We were talking when I spent the night with y'all. When we were getting together the stuff we were going to say at the youth service he told me. He said that he can't remember much about you, but he remembers you coming to his birthday party when he turned four. He said that's when you gave him the jersey. That's the last time he can remember seeing you, but he says that you may have come by even after that. He just can't remember it because he was so little."

Bryan sat in shock as he listened to Todd relay Gerald's memory to him. He shook his head in disbelief. It was so hard for him to imagine his son making up such a story, but he knew that he'd never spent any time around him or Tricia during those years.

"Why didn't you just tell the truth, Bryan?" Todd asked. "Why didn't you just say that you made the mistake of abandoning your kid back then, but now you had matured and were stepping up to what you knew was the right thing to do? I could have understood that. I'm sure Ms. Nicole could have understood that, too. You've always told me that the truth is the right way to go. Why did you lie?"

"Todd, you listen to me," Bryan said as he faced the disappointed boy. "I didn't know about Gerald. I don't know what he's remembering or whom he's remembering, but I never attended a birthday party for him. And if he thought I knew about him, why did he say in church last Sunday that I didn't know? Remember his speech?"

"Yeah, I remember. He said it because he likes you, Bryan. He wants you to think that he actually believes you. He's willing to go along with it if it means he gets his dad back."

"This isn't making sense." Bryan stood and stared at the trees in the distance. "Maybe someone came to his party and gave him a jersey, but it wasn't me. I don't even like the Lakers. I never have. I'm from Chicago. In college, I was a Bulls fan. I never would have purchased a Lakers jersey."

"Maybe I shouldn't have said anything." Todd shook his head.

"No," Bryan said. "I'm glad you told me, and I'm not angry with Gerald. He apparently believes that I gave him that shirt. I don't know why, though. Maybe his mother told him that, and he's just kind of grown up believing it."

"But he said he remembers you giving it to him," Todd insisted.

"You still think I'm lying, don't you?" Bryan asked as he sat by him again.

"Well, somebody is," Todd said. "He just seemed to be so sure. I don't know why he'd say he remembered you if he didn't."

"Is there a reason for you to believe that I'd say it wasn't me if it was?" Bryan asked.

"No," he mumbled. "I guess not."

"Todd, I had no more to lose by saying that I knew about Gerald than to say that I didn't know about him. Either way, my involvement with his mother was prior to my marriage to Ms. Nicole, and when I met my wife my life became an open book. I told her all the details of my sordid past. Telling her I had a kid would have been just another detail in my already horrific background with women.

"I wanted her to know everything about me because she deserved to make a choice based on honesty. She deserved to know what kind of man she would possibly marry. I wasn't trying to hide anything from her. I didn't want her to want me *without* knowing about my entire history. I wanted her to want me *in spite of* knowing about my entire history. I wouldn't lie to her like that, and I didn't lie to you. I did not know about Gerald's existence until a couple of months ago, and that's the bare-naked, honest-to-God truth."

"So, Gerald lied?"

"I'm not saying that he lied," Bryan said. "I'm saying that he is in some way confused. Even Tricia never said that I'd met or spent any time with him. If I had been coming by her house to see the two of them, believe me, she would have been more than happy to make that point. I don't know what Gerald is talking about, but I will find out."

"No, Bryan." Todd held up both hands. "You can't go to him with this. He'll hate me. I promised him that I wouldn't tell you."

"I'm sorry, Todd. I have to. My son thinks I'm a liar. I can't let him think that. I won't indict you in any way, but I have to talk to him. I need him to believe me. I need you to believe me, too. Do you?"

"Bryan, I ain't never known you to lie to me." Todd shook his head slowly.

"And I'm not going to start now," Bryan said. "Do you believe me?" he repeated.

"Yes," Todd said after a deep sigh.

"Do you really?" Bryan asked.

"Yes," he answered with more confidence. "Yes, I believe you."

"Good," Bryan said, and he embraced his young friend. "Now, I'm going to get to the bottom of this," he continued, "and I think I can do it without you losing Gerald as a friend."

It was after 7:00 by the time Bryan made it home. An unfamiliar pickup truck parked in his driveway made it impossible for him to get into his garage. He parked beside the curb, grabbed from the passenger seat the store-bought flowers that he had purchased for Nicole, and headed for his front door.

"Bryan," Nicole said as she stepped onto the front door step and closed the door behind her.

"Hey, baby," he said as he kissed her softly. "Whose truck is that?"

"You have a visitor," she said nervously.

"Who?" he asked curiously, noting the almost fearful look in her eyes. "Is Tricia in there?" he asked.

"No, no," Nicole calmed him. "It's not Tricia. I would have never let her in. But I don't know if you'll be any happier to see this visitor. I just think you should at least give him a chance."

"Him?"

"It's your father."

"Garrett?" Bryan asked in disbelief. "Garrett Walker is in there?"

"Yes."

"Why? What does he want? What's he doing here, and how did he know where I lived?"

"I can't answer any of that, Bryan. He's only been here for about ten minutes, and I didn't think it was my place to ask any of those questions. This may be a once-in-a-lifetime chance to talk to him, Bryan. I think you should take advantage of it. He's in there. Why don't you go in and ask him all the questions that you want?"

Bryan stood in silence for several more minutes. He looked at the front door as though he expected it to open itself. Finally, he handed Nicole the flowers.

"Thank you," she said, and she stepped aside for him to lead the way.

Bryan had always wondered how he would react if he ever saw Garrett Walker again. In his late teen and early adulthood years, he had grown to hate him for walking out on him and his mother and leaving them to fend for themselves. After getting his own life together and learning to forgive the man who made him a single-parent child, he had just basically put him in the back of his mind as a distant memory and settled on the fact that he'd probably never see him again.

Nicole prayed silently and nervously as she and Bryan walked into the living room together.

The sight of his son all grown up rendered Garrett visibly shaken. He stood slowly as Bryan entered and almost seemed afraid to speak as Bryan looked at him without emotion.

"Bryan," he finally managed to say. "It's been a long time."

"What do you want?" Bryan asked suspiciously. "How did you know where to find me?"

Bryan had already had a difficult night, and now this. Nicole hoped that this conversation didn't end like the other.

"I don't want anything from you," he said. "I just wanted to see you."

"You just wanted to see me?" Bryan asked. "I haven't

seen you in sixteen or seventeen years. What? You all of a sudden started missing me yesterday and decided to stop by today to see how I was getting along? Is that it?"

"No, Bryan. I didn't start missing you yesterday. Like you just said, it's been nearly seventeen years. I started missing you a long time ago."

"Forgive me if I don't believe that, but you've had a funny way of showing it."

"I know you're angry with me, son, and I understand that."

"Son?" Bryan laughed angrily. "So I'm your son now?"

"Sweetheart," Nicole interrupted as she stood in front of him and touched his face. "Please try not to get upset."

"Baby, it's too late for that," Bryan said.

"It's okay," Garrett told her. "He has every right to be mad at me. Let him speak his piece."

"Why don't you two have a seat?" Nicole asked. "Would you like something to drink?"

"No, thank you," they both said as Bryan reluctantly took the seat across from his father. Nicole went into the kitchen to place her flowers in a vase of water.

"What do you want?" Bryan repeated.

"I told you, Bryan. I don't want anything from you. I just wanted to see you."

"How did you know where I lived?"

"I've always known where you lived."

"How?"

"Bryan," Garrett said, "I know you don't want to believe a word that I say, and I can't fault you for that. But just because I haven't been around doesn't mean I haven't cared about you. I've known everywhere you've been since the day your mama told me not to come back."

"And you were all too happy to fulfill that command, weren't you?" Bryan challenged. "You were just looking for a reason to run. Mama said get out, and you did just that. You couldn't have cared less about what happened to us from then on, could you? You just moved on to your next girlfriend."

"Yes, I left and I moved on. My relationship with your mother wasn't going to work, and I'm not blaming her for that. I made my share of mistakes, but I was a proud man. I wasn't about to beg her to stay with me or to let me stay with her. It wasn't the first time she had asked me to leave, so, as far as I was concerned, she didn't need me around."

"What about me?" Bryan blurted as Nicole returned and sat next to him on the arm of the recliner. "Did it ever occur to you that I needed you? I was a kid who needed his father, however few times he bothered to come around. This wasn't just about you and Mama. How selfish could both of you get? Did you even once consider my feelings? Did I mean anything to you? I could have been dead as far as you cared."

"I've known where you've been every step of the way," Garrett reiterated. "I lost knowledge of your whereabouts for about a four-week span when your mama first sent you to live with her brother. But since then, I've known where you were and how you've been."

"Yeah, right," Bryan said in blatant disbelief.

"I swear to you," he said. "I knew. I've been right here in this city, and I've seen you from a distance. I knew I was no longer welcome in your life after the way I disappeared, so I didn't try to get close to you, but I've seen you. I know about your business downtown. When you started getting established, I didn't want you thinking I was after your money or anything else, but I've been here. I never forgot about you."

"I'm not the little boy who you used to tell anything to and he'd believe it," Bryan said. "I'm not that naive kid anymore. It took me a long time to accept the fact that my father was a liar, but I did, and you can't convince me otherwise seventeen years later."

"I was at your high school graduation," Garrett said as he pulled photos from his sport coat jacket and tossed them on the table in front of Bryan. "And your college graduation," he continued, near tears, as Bryan scanned the photos in astonishment.

"I was even at your wedding. See? That's right. I saw you get married. I heard you say 'I do' to this woman. I wanted to congratulate you afterwards, but I didn't want to chance messing up your day, so I sat in the back and tried to blend in with everybody else. It's true that I haven't been the kind of father that you deserved, but don't you dare say I couldn't care less as to whether you were dead or alive. You were my firstborn. I cared then, and I care now," he concluded.

Nicole looked at Bryan. She didn't know from his expression whether he was still angry or not. He just seemed shocked to hear the things that his father had just said and to see the pictures that proved them true.

"I'm your firstborn?" Bryan finally asked quietly.

"Yeah," his father answered as he wiped his eyes. "But you knew that."

"Actually, no, I didn't," Bryan said.

"Well, you are," he said.

"How would you really know?"

"I know," Garrett assured him. "I think that's why I tried harder with Teresa than with any of the others. She gave me my first child. After the others started coming, I just lost interest in trying to be a real father."

"How many others are there?" Bryan asked. "Do you even know?"

"There are nine of you in all," he said. "I can't say that I know where all of the rest of them are right now, but I promise you that I've always known where you were."

"I'm sorry," Bryan said softly. "I never should have called you a liar."

"Thank you," Garrett said. "I've never done anything to deserve an apology from you."

"So," Bryan said after several moments of silence. "All these years and you've known where I was and you never came around. Why now?"

He shrugged. "I don't know. I think it's the fact that I'm getting older and finally using the little brains that I have left. I was talking to Geneva a few weeks ago, and she said that I needed to make my peace with you. Lately, my separation from you has begun haunting me. I think I just needed to apologize for being such a horrible father."

"Geneva? Is she the flavor of the month?"

"Geneva is my wife."

"Wife?" Bryan asked.

"Yes, wife," Garrett said. "We got married seven years ago."

"I'm sorry," Bryan apologized again. "I didn't mean to disrespect her. You being married just never occurred to me."

"I know it's hard to believe that I ever got to the point of settling down. I played the field for a long time. I wasn't even looking to settle down when I met Geneva, but when I met her, I knew she was the one. You have to meet her sometime. She's heard a lot about you."

Bryan's hard-lined face had softened now as he talked

and listened to his father. The years had been surprisingly good to him. As loosely as he had lived, he still looked good. He still looked the same as Bryan remembered, except he no longer had locks in his hair and he was beginning to gray. He still wore his hair pulled back into a ponytail, but it wasn't nearly as long as it had been when it was locked.

"Where do you live now?" Bryan asked as Nicole walked into the kitchen and returned with a glass of apple juice for each of them.

"Thank you." Garrett smiled. Bryan had definitely gotten his eyes and smile from his father.

"I've lived so many different places," he began. "I moved back home to L.A. when I first retired from driving trucks. I lived in Nashville, Tennessee, for a few months, and then I tried Dallas, Texas. I had driven through all these places when I was delivering, and they all seemed like nice places, but I didn't really care for living there. I lived in Tallahassee for a little while, and then I finally moved to Orlando. That's where I live right now."

"I went to college in Tallahassee," Bryan said.

"FAMU," Garrett said as he pointed to the photo of Bryan's graduation. "I know."

"Do any of my eight brothers and sisters belong to you and your wife?"

"No," Garrett said. "I had a vasectomy about ten years ago. That was before I met Geneva and decided to settle down. She had two children from a previous marriage, so we're raising two teenaged daughters."

"I see," Bryan said.

"Tell me about you," Garrett said, as though not wanting the smooth conversation to end. "Other than what I know about you, what else can you tell me? Do you and Nicole have any children?"

"No," Bryan said. "She is helping me raise a son that I have from a previous relationship."

"You have a son?"

"Yes. He's twelve now. Almost thirteen."

"I'd love to meet him sometime if that's possible."

"He comes every other weekend," Bryan explained. "He just went home yesterday, so it'll be another two weeks before he's back."

"So I'm a grandfather."

"I suppose so," Bryan said. "I'm sure there are others that you just don't know about."

"Possibly," Garrett admitted.

"So why is it that you kept tabs on me and not on the others?" Bryan asked.

"Like I said, you are my firstborn. We had something special at one time. With you, I stayed around much longer than I did with the others. When I'd hook up with a new girl, you were the child I would talk to them about. I remember being so proud when you pledged Omega. I remember sitting up and telling my girlfriend about that. You were the child I talked about, because you were really the only one I'd spent enough time with to really get to know."

"That's sad." Bryan shook his head.

"I know," his father agreed. "I'm hoping that I can eventually catch up with all of my children. I would guess that the last child I fathered is about your son's age. He should be about thirteen by now. It's sad that I've drifted so far from all of you. I'm glad that you're doing right by your son."

"I had my days of living the wild life too," Bryan told him.

"I guess you were a lot more careful than I was,"

Garrett said.

"I guess," Bryan said, "but not as careful as I thought, or else I wouldn't have the one child that I have. I love my son, but he wasn't planned. I'm trying to be a good father. It's a learning process, but I'm trying."

"He's a very good father," Nicole corrected him.

"Having you has really helped me to be what I am," Bryan told her.

"That's great." Garrett smiled at them. "The two of you look really good together. And happy. I'm glad."

"Would you like to stay for dinner?" Nicole offered after a silent moment. "You don't mind, do you?" she asked Bryan.

"No," Bryan said. "I don't mind."

"I've grilled some Alaskan salmon, and there's spinach and mashed potatoes. Can you be tempted to stay?"

"Thank you, sweetheart," Garrett said with a smile, "but I can't stay. I really wish I could, but Geneva is a bit under the weather, and I promised her that I'd be home before midnight. I'm already running behind schedule."

"Maybe when you come back this way again you can bring her and the girls with you, and you could all stay for dinner," Bryan said.

His offer obviously pleased Garrett, as his smile widened, showing a gold tooth on the side of his mouth.

"Thank you," Garrett said as he stood. "I'd really like that."

"Here's my business card," Bryan said. "Just give us a couple of days' notice of when you're going to be here so we can make preparations."

"And here is mine," Garrett responded, retrieving a card from his wallet and giving it to Bryan.

"G&G Lawn Service?" Bryan read aloud.

"Yeah." Garrett laughed as he stood. "The wife and I

got into lawn and gardening after I quit driving the big rigs. Eric, Vivica's boyfriend, helps out. Vivica is our seventeen-year-old. Angela is fifteen. She doesn't have a boyfriend yet. We won't let them date until they're sixteen."

"I see," Bryan said as he put the card in his pocket.

"Can I use this number if I just want to call you sometime?" his father asked as they walked him to the door.

"If you want," Bryan said.

"It sure was a pleasure to finally meet you," Garrett said as he kissed the back of Nicole's hand. "You are as beautiful a bride now as you were at your wedding."

"Thank you," Nicole said, blushing uncontrollably. "It was nice meeting you as well."

"Son," he said, turning to Bryan, "thank you for sharing a little of your time with me. And thanks for not treating me the way I deserve to be treated. I really appreciate it. I know I can't make it all better in one day, but I hope this can be a fresh start for us."

"It's kind of late for you to try to be my father," Bryan said.

"Then let me try and be your friend," Garrett said as brown eyes met brown eyes.

"We'll talk," Bryan said as he hesitantly accepted his father's embrace.

Nicole and Bryan watched as Garrett got into his truck and drove away. Bryan walked back to the sofa and slowly sank onto it. Nicole stood for a moment before finally joining him.

"He's quite a charmer, isn't he?" she said.

"Always has been. Thus the nine children."

"Well, you know they say that a man can tell what a woman will look like in her later years by looking at her mother. If the same holds true for men and their fathers, you're going to be turning heads for several years to come."

"I'll take that as a compliment and try not to get jealous because you think my father is a babe magnet."

Nicole laughed. "I didn't say that. He's a nice-looking man though. When you told me that you looked just like him, I don't think I took it to be as true as it is."

"Yeah," Bryan said almost as though he was no longer listening.

"Are you okay?"

"Seventeen years, Nicole," he said softly. "After seventeen years, my father wants to be a part of my life. What do I do?"

"You let him," she said.

"How do I know he can be trusted? How do I know he won't just disappear again? Am I to really believe that there is no ulterior motive to his visit?"

"There's only one way to find out," she said. "Let him prove it. Let him back in your life, Bryan. You've missed him whether you admit it or not. His absence has been a painful thorn in your side for years. You told me a long time ago that if your father ever came back into your life, there would have to be a divine purpose behind it. Give him the chance that he doesn't deserve. Gerald gave you a chance."

"But that's different. I didn't abandon him."

"His mother thinks you did, and while it's clear he doesn't believe it, I'm sure he's heard that you did. But he gave you a chance anyway, and look how rewarding your time with him has been."

"Actually, he does believe I abandoned him."

"What?"

"That's what Todd wanted to speak to me about. Ger-

313

ald told him Saturday night that he remembers me visiting him as a child. He remembers me coming to his fourth birthday party and giving him a jersey."

"You never went to his birthday party."

"I know. It's just all so strange to me. This whole day is strange. It's like one long dream. First, Uncle Charles tells me that my mother called to check on me, then I find out that my son actually believes that I knew about him but pretended like I didn't, and now my father pays a visit."

"Your mom called?" Nicole asked.

"Yeah. I spent much of the afternoon in a counseling session with Uncle Charles. I just needed to vent after last night's call from Tricia. By the way," he broke the thought, "I bought a new phone. The number is the same. Anyway," he continued, "at the end of the session he told me that she called last night and seemed to want to get in contact with me for some reason."

"You think that maybe she knew that your father was going to stop by and wanted to forewarn you?" Nicole suggested.

"I hadn't thought of that," Bryan said. "That could be the case. I'll call her later tonight. Then I'll start working on a plan to speak with Gerald. I don't know that I want to wait two weeks."

"Where would he get the idea that you came to his party? Do you think that maybe Tricia told him that?"

"That's what I thought at first, but Todd says he told him that he remembered the visit. It's apparently the only real memory he thinks he has of me. What I don't understand is why Tricia hasn't corrected him on that one. I mean, she knows I've never spent any time around him. She wouldn't keep something like that a secret. If there had ever been a time when I was actually involved in his life, she would have been more than ready and willing to bring that up."

"That is strange," Nicole agreed. "Maybe it was a dream he had as a child, and it was so vivid that he thinks it actually happened."

"But he still has the jersey."

"Are you going to talk to him about it?"

"I have to, Nicole. I have to get to the basis of his belief. I can't let him go on thinking that I'm lying to him."

"I agree," Nicole said.

Bryan sighed heavily, rubbing his face with his hands and leaning back on the sofa.

"What a day, huh?" Nicole read his mind.

"Yes," he agreed. "And I still have to call Mama. Makes me wonder what other mind-boggling thing can happen before this twenty-four-hour period is over."

"Well, I don't know what you can expect from your mother," Nicole said, flirting with him as she touched his chest and kissed his cheek softly. "But the night is young. The possibilities around here are endless."

"Mmmm," Bryan responded with a smile and raised eyebrows.

CHAPTER TWENTY-FOUR

A visit from Melvin and Bryan just before the lunch hour a few days later took both Sharon and Nicole by surprise.

"Well, to what do we owe this double delight?" Sharon asked as she kissed her husband.

"Can't a couple of good-looking brothers come and take their best girls out for lunch every now and then?" Melvin asked.

"You get no quarrels from me," Sharon said.

"Are you feeling better?" Bryan asked Nicole.

"Yeah," Nicole said as she hugged him.

"It's all those hang-up calls that she has on her voice-mail every day," Sharon said. "I declare, if I had just one hour alone with that scrawny little coward, I could teach her a thing or two."

"Is she still calling?" Bryan asked.

"We don't know that it's her," Nicole said. "They're just hang-up calls."

"*You* may not know it's her," Sharon said, "but *I* do. I just wish I could prove it. It's just so stupid and juvenile. If you're going to be a bully, be a bold one. I wish she would step up in here and try to start some mess."

"She's not worth going to jail for, Sharon," Nicole said.

"Sometimes I wonder," Bryan said.

"Bryan," Nicole warned.

"I'm sorry, baby," he said, "but you already know how I feel. I'm trying to respect her as the mother of my child, but she makes it darn near impossible."

"I know," Nicole said with a sympathetic smile.

"I used to be so jealous of guys like you when I was in high school," Melvin told Bryan. "You know, the guys who all the girls loved. I wanted so badly to be a ladies' man. I was never real popular in that way, but now I see that even being unpopular has its benefits."

"You live and you learn," Bryan agreed.

"Speaking of which," Sharon suddenly said as she walked behind Nicole's desk and pressed the intercom button.

"What's wrong?" Nicole asked.

"Good afternoon, teachers," Sharon said. "Mrs. Walker and I are about to leave for lunch with our husbands. However, we would appreciate your staying in your classes and monitoring your students as is stated in the Day Care Handbook, Article Four, Section Two," she continued as the others laughed.

"Thank you for your cooperation and adherence to my request," Sharon concluded. "Enjoy your lunch and the rest of your day."

"It's official," Bryan told Melvin as they headed toward the door to leave. "As of today, your wife has finally lost her mind."

"You're gonna let him get away with talking about me like that without saying something?" Sharon asked as she smacked Melvin's arm.

"My bad," Melvin said rubbing his arm. "I'll have you know," he said, facing Bryan as they stood outside, "that my wife lost her mind way before today. Don't you dare shortchange her!"

"You are so silly!" Nicole laughed.

"Ouch!" Melvin said as Sharon hit him again.

"Okay," Nicole said getting into the car while Bryan held the door for her. The four of them decided to take the convertible. It was a good day to drive with the top down. "Where are we going for lunch?"

"Ladies' choice," Melvin said.

"Well, Sharon has been doing very well on her diet, and we shouldn't mess that up. So maybe we'll go to Jason's Deli and have a nice chicken salad or a turkey sandwich or something."

"Fine by me," Bryan said.

"Thank you for watching my back, girlfriend," Sharon said, "but I can speak for myself. I say let's go to Rib Shack."

"Sharon!" Nicole said in surprise.

"Girl, I am so tired of soups, salads, and sandwiches. I've lost some weight, and I want to reward myself. It's just one meal. It won't kill me."

"I agree," Melvin said.

"Makes you feel better about rewarding yourself at least three times a week, every week, at Big Daddy's Pizza, huh, Melvin?" Bryan said.

The four shared a full platter of barbequed chicken and ribs with side orders of fries, corn on the cob, and macaroni and cheese. Conversation was held to a minimum until they were almost finished devouring the feast.

"Yeah, baby," Melvin said as he rubbed his stomach. "The two of us are going to be the finest couple on Destin Beach."

"I'll regret it later," Sharon said, "but right now I am too satisfied to feel guilty."

"I am so looking forward to our vacation," Nicole said. "It's going to feel good to get away for a few days."

"Yes, it will," Bryan agreed.

"Is Gerald still coming along?" Sharon asked.

"Yeah," Nicole answered.

"By the way," Bryan said, "Melvin and I are going to pick up Gerald this weekend."

"Tricia is letting him come on an unscheduled visit?" Sharon asked.

"And she's letting you come along?" Nicole added.

"She doesn't really know," Bryan said.

"You didn't tell her that you were coming?" Nicole asked.

"She doesn't know that either one of us is coming," Melvin clarified.

"She doesn't know we're picking him up," Bryan added.

"What do you mean she doesn't know?" Nicole asked. "I thought we agreed that you'd ask her to allow him to come. How are you going to get him without her knowledge?"

"I called this morning to ask her about him coming, and it turns out that his ailing eighty-year-old great-grandmother is keeping him because Tricia went away on vacation. The old lady can't even get around by herself. She told me that she normally has a nurse to come by and check on her every day at her home, but for eight days she's staying with Gerald, and he's basically her caretaker until his mother comes back home."

"That poor kid." Sharon shook her head. "But for the grace of God, he doesn't have a fighting chance."

"So the great-grandmother said you could come and get him?" Nicole asked.

"Yes," Bryan said. "As a matter of fact, she asked me to come and get him. She said that she really needed to be at her own home because it's equipped for a wheelchair-bound person, and Tricia's home isn't."

"When are you going to get him?" Sharon asked Melvin.

"We're leaving after work tomorrow like I normally do on the weekends that I pick him up."

"When is Tricia coming back home?" Nicole asked. "The last thing we need is for her to come home and find you at her house, Bryan. That won't be pretty."

"She's not due back until Tuesday, according to her grandmother."

"What if she comes back early and finds out that Gerald is here?" Nicole asked, worried. "She's liable to file kidnapping charges."

"It's a chance I'll take. I'm going to have her grandmother sign a permission release for Gerald."

"Is that going to be enough?"

"It's the best I can do, baby," Bryan said, and he placed his hands on hers to calm her. "This lady doesn't know exactly where Tricia went. She thinks it was a cruise but she doesn't know where. She didn't leave a phone number where she could be reached. She's been gone for nearly four days now, and she hasn't called once to check on the boy or his great-grandmother."

"I thought her raising Gerald was supposedly hindering her from having fun," Sharon said. "Seems like she's doing okay to me."

"All I know is that taking care of an elderly dependent

woman is way too much responsibility for a twelve-year-old kid. What if something should happen while she's there with him?" Bryan said.

"You're right," Nicole said. "I just don't want any trouble. I don't know if I can handle it right now."

"I'll take care of it," Bryan said. "While Gerald is here, I don't want you answering any phone calls at the house. I'll get it, and if I'm not there, let the machine get it."

"And I'll answer the calls at work," Sharon said. "And if I'm not there, I'll assign one of the teachers to cover. Don't you even bother reaching for it."

"Everything will be fine." Bryan tried to assure her. "I'm going to leave a note behind for her, because Melvin and I are going to take her grandmother back to her house when we pick Gerald up. I'm also going to leave her the child support payment for the month so I won't have to discuss that with her."

"I wonder if he ever sees a drop of that money," Melvin said.

"Probably not," Bryan said. "I don't really care. Nicole and I will make sure he's taken care of. Let her have the money."

Nicole tried not to worry, but she couldn't help it. Although Bryan suggested that she take advantage of his absence and get to bed early while he and Melvin made the trip to Tallahassee, she couldn't sleep. Instead she found herself sitting up praying and watching the clock, keeping track of when she felt they should be back home.

When Melvin would go alone, he would generally be back by 9:15 or 9:30. When the clock struck the 10:00 hour, Nicole began pacing the floor. Visions of her husband being hauled off to jail began clouding her mind. She reached for the phone to call him, but her fears were calmed when she heard the garage door opening.

322

It was almost 10:15 when Bryan and Gerald finally arrived, and they had made it safely and without incident. Bryan was visibly tired from the long day and the trip. Gerald seemed happy to be returning to their home so soon after leaving. Bryan had stopped and gotten him a fast food meal on the way home, so he took his bath, brushed his teeth, said his prayers with his father, and went on to bed.

Nicole sat under the covers with her back leaning against the headboard and thumbed through Gerald's schoolwork. His grades had improved significantly from what they were when he visited them the first time.

Her attention turned to Bryan as he exited the bathroom after taking his shower. He hesitated briefly as he noticed her watching him. A smile crept across his face, and she turned away quickly as though embarrassed that he had caught her looking.

"This is pretty good work," she said, referring to the homework in a feeble attempt to ease the tension she brought upon herself by watching him.

"I know." Bryan went along knowingly. "He was so eager to show them to me. I want to make copies and keep them on file here."

"That's a good idea," Nicole agreed.

"Were you worried?" he asked Nicole as he sat next to her.

"Huh?"

"About my trip to Tallahassee, I mean. Were you sitting here worrying that something was going to happen?"

"How'd you know?"

"Because I know you," he said.

"I thought you all would be home sooner. When it got past 9:30, I started wondering why you hadn't made it yet."

"Well, we couldn't go there and come right back. We had to take Gerald's grandmother home. Tricia never should have left that old lady to take care of Gerald. It was clear that he was the one doing the babysitting."

"Was it that bad?"

"Yes." Bryan yawned. "Her house isn't fit for an able-bodied person, let alone equipped at all for a woman in a wheelchair."

"What do you mean?"

"I mean she's no neat freak by any stretch of the imagination. The house looks like it hasn't been cleaned in ages. There were clothes thrown everywhere. I made Gerald tidy up his room before we left, and Melvin and I washed the dishes. I didn't touch Tricia's room. The door was open and it looked like the roadrunner and the coyote had been in there, but we weren't about to touch any of her stuff."

"Where was her grandmother sleeping, I wonder?" Nicole said.

"I don't know, and I didn't ask. I asked Gerald why he hadn't tried to clean up while his mother was gone, and he just shrugged his shoulders. Apparently she doesn't make him clean up, and he doesn't volunteer."

"Does she live in a house or an apartment?"

"She lives in a duplex apartment. There are other kids around, but Gerald didn't seem to know any of them too well. They all seemed younger. When we got there, he was so happy to see us. His grandmother had apparently already told him, because he was packed and ready to leave."

"He's such a sweet boy," Nicole said. "I wish it were possible for him to stay with us. The chance was already slim that she would go for it, and after us getting him this weekend without her prior knowledge, I'm sure she won't allow us to keep him full-time now."

"You're probably right," Bryan said. "But I'd do it all over again. That lady certainly needed to be at her own home where she could get the assistance she needed. At Tricia's house there wasn't even a ramp to roll her down to put her in the car. Melvin and I had to pick her up and carry her. On the way home, Gerald told us that he had been living off of leftover pizza and sandwiches since Monday because he doesn't know how to cook, and his great-grandmother couldn't cook from the wheelchair because the stove is set too high."

"Had they at least heard from Tricia?"

Bryan shook his head. "Not a word. That frail old lady thanked Melvin and me over and over again for taking her home and agreeing to keep Gerald for the weekend. The only drawback is that he may have to miss a day or two of school because Tricia isn't due back until Tuesday, and I don't plan to send him home until she gets there. I left her a note and told her to call me."

"This could get really ugly, Bryan."

"I told you that I'm going to take care of everything," he said.

"I know." Nicole sighed. "But I can't pretend that I'm not still worried. I can't help but wonder what she's going to do when she finds out."

"Let me worry about that, sweetheart," he said as he wrapped his arm around her and pulled her close to lie on his chest.

"Did you speak with him about it yet?" she asked.

"No," Bryan said. "I'll talk to him tomorrow."

"Are you afraid of what he might say or how he might react?"

"No," Bryan said. "I just want to make sure the timing is right. I really can't worry about what he might say or how he may act. I just know that I can't go on letting him believe that I'm lying to him. Even if he's willing to live with the lie that he thinks he's being told."

It only took a few minutes for him to drift off to sleep. Nicole felt the rise and fall of his chest as she lay awake for another hour after he had gone to sleep. She wanted to believe that everything would be okay, but the nauseated feeling in the pit of her stomach told her differently.

CHAPTER TWENTY-FIVE

C an Todd come over and play ball with me?" Gerald asked as they sat down to a breakfast of
French toast, eggs, and sausage patties.

"Maybe a little later," Bryan said as he and Nicole
exchanged glances. "Ms. Nicole and I want to spend some
time with you for a little while."

"Are we going to the park?" Gerald asked.

"Maybe when Todd comes over," Bryan said. "We
want to spend some time with you right here."

"Are we going to play Uno?"

"If you want," Bryan said.

"Are we going to let Ms. Nicole win a game this
time?"

"Hey," Nicole said, pointing her fork at him playfully. "I don't need your sympathy. I am very capable of
beating you fair and square."

"Yeah." Gerald laughed.

They ate in silence for a few minutes. The likeness

between Bryan and Gerald almost amazed Nicole at times. They both had big appetites and even held their forks and chewed their food in the same manner.

"I saw your schoolwork," Nicole said. "You're doing really well. I'm proud of you."

"Thanks." He beamed. "Mr. Taylor said that I'm doing real good."

"Is that your teacher?" Nicole asked.

"He's my math teacher."

"How would you like to meet your grandfather?" Bryan suddenly asked.

"Is Garrett coming over?" Nicole asked in surprise.

"Well, I haven't called him yet, but I will. I want to invite him to come to town tomorrow and go to church with us."

"That would be nice." Nicole smiled.

"Is that your daddy?" Gerald asked Nicole.

"He's my father," Bryan said.

"I thought your daddy was dead," Gerald said.

"Why would you think that?" Bryan asked.

"Mama told me," he said.

Bryan and Nicole exchanged glances again.

"When did your mother tell you that?"

"A long time ago," he said.

"Maybe she just thought he was dead because she'd never met him," Nicole offered.

"I guess." Gerald shrugged as he polished off the rest of his orange juice.

"Do you want more?" Nicole asked. She saw the tightening of Bryan's jawline, but he remained quiet.

"I'm too full," Gerald said, rubbing his stomach.

"Why don't you run upstairs and wash your hands and face and get the cards. We'll join you in the living room shortly."

"Okay," he said as he disappeared excitedly.

"Are you okay?" Nicole asked Bryan when they were alone.

"Why would she tell him that my father was dead?" he asked. "She never knew my father. She never really even knew me, for that matter."

"Maybe that was something that she didn't want her son to know," Nicole said as she began clearing the table. "Maybe she didn't want him to know that you were a one-night stand, so she made up stuff so it would seem like the two of you had a meaningful relationship."

"The truth is always better and so much easier," Bryan said as he helped her with the dishes. "She's confusing that boy. I don't like that. She could have just told him that she didn't know his grandfather. That wouldn't have been a lie. But to tell him that the man was dead . . . and now I'm asking him to meet him? That's crazy."

"I'm ready," Gerald called from the living room.

"We'll be there in just a minute," Nicole called.

"I wonder what else she's told him about me and my family," Bryan whispered.

"We may never know," Nicole responded.

"Here," Bryan took the dishcloth out of her hand and handed her a drying towel. "We can get these later. It's time to talk to him."

"Are you ready to do this?"

"Ready or not," Bryan said, "it's time."

"I already dealt them out," Gerald said as they joined him on the living room floor.

"How do we know you didn't cheat?" Nicole asked.

"'Cause I didn't," he said.

"We'll see about that," Bryan said as he looked at him suspiciously.

Gerald laughed. "I didn't!"

The first game went on for about twenty minutes. Nicole had the chance to yell "Uno" twice, but in the end it was Bryan who came out on top.

"See, I told you I didn't cheat," Gerald said.

"Yes, you did," Nicole said as he mixed the cards to deal again.

"Hold on a minute, Gerald," Bryan said, placing his hand on top of Gerald's to stop the shuffling.

"Am I doing it wrong?" Gerald asked.

"No," Bryan said.

Nicole held her breath in anticipation of the impending discussion.

"Let's talk for a minute before the next game," Bryan said.

"About what?"

"About you and me."

"Okay."

"You like me, don't you?" Bryan asked.

"Yeah," he said. "I mean, yes."

"Good." Bryan smiled. "I like you, too. I think you're a pretty cool kid."

"You're cool too," Gerald said. "All my friends at school think you're cool, too."

"Oh yeah?"

"Yeah. I told them how you were teaching me to play ball, and when I wore my new FUBU outfit to school they all said you were the coolest dad around. Now they want to meet you."

"Well, maybe one day I'll stop by your school and say hello."

"Oh, man," Gerald said with wide eyes. "That would be so cool!"

Bryan smiled as he looked at Nicole and shook his head. It was as though he was telling her that he couldn't carry out the conversation that he intended to. He didn't want to risk breaking the boy's spirits. Nicole understood but knew that it was something that he'd regret if he didn't do it now.

"When your daddy or I tell you things, Gerald," she began, "do you believe us?"

"Sure." He shrugged uneasily. "I guess."

"You know we would never lie to you, don't you?" she pressed.

Gerald looked briefly at Bryan and then turned back to Nicole. He bent the cards nervously in his hands and remained silent for a moment. Finally he hunched his shoulders and looked at the cards in his hand.

"Sweetheart," Nicole said as she slid close to him. "We know about your conversation with Todd, and we want to talk about it with you."

Gerald's eyes never left his hands, and his uneasiness was clearly seen. He began breathing heavily as though he was about to cry.

"It's okay, sweetie," Nicole assured him as she placed her hand on his shoulder.

"We're not angry or upset with you, Gerald," Bryan finally spoke. "I just need you to tell me what you told Todd. I need you to tell me what it is that you remember about your birthday party that day."

Gerald let the cards fall from his hand and began wringing his hands together nervously. He swallowed hard but continued staring downward.

"Gerald," Bryan said as he gently placed his hand under the boy's chin. "Look at me."

Silent tears fell down his cheeks as he finally looked up.

"Son, don't cry," Bryan said as Nicole retrieved the Kleenex tissues from the coffee table. "You don't have to be afraid. I promise I'm not mad at you. Remember how I told you on your first night here that you could come to me and talk about anything? Well, that's what I want right now. I want you to talk to me about this. Please?"

He finally spoke. "I just told him that I remembered you coming to the party."

"Do you actually remember that, or is that something that somebody told you?" Nicole asked.

"I remember."

"What else do you remember?" Bryan asked as Nicole looked at him in confusion.

"Nothing," Gerald said, wiping the last of his tears. "I just remember you giving me the basketball shirt."

"And you're sure it was him?" Nicole asked.

"Yes."

"Gerald," Bryan said, "remember when I told you that I didn't know about you until your mother showed up at my church a few months ago?"

"Yes."

"Have you believed all this time that I lied to you?"

Gerald stared silently at his hands once more. Bryan rubbed his own chin with his hand, trying to figure out how to solve the mystery. All he could figure is that someone was at the party, and for some reason Gerald thought it was him.

Nicole tried again. "Sweetie, how do you know it was your dad that was at the party?"

"Because he said that's who he was, and I remember him."

"You remember what he looked like and everything?" Nicole asked.

"Yes."

"And you're sure it was your daddy?"

"Yes," he said. "I remember because everybody at

the party kept saying that I looked just like my daddy. It was you." He turned to Bryan. "I remember."

Bryan sat with his face buried in his hands and shook his head in discouragement.

"I don't care if you want to say that you just found out about me," Gerald continued as he watched Bryan's reaction. "I'm not mad at you, either," he said. "We can pretend like you were never at the party. It doesn't matter anymore."

"Yes, it does matter, Gerald," Bryan said. "It matters that you think I'm pretending that I wasn't there. I'm telling you, son, I wasn't at your party. By the time you were four years old, I had graduated college and was living here. I didn't know about you when you were four and somehow I have to convince you of that."

"But I saw you," Gerald insisted tearfully. "You gave me a Lakers jersey. You still look the same, except you looked a little bit older."

"Older?" Bryan said. "I looked older almost nine years ago than I do now?"

"Maybe not older," Gerald said. "I don't know. Maybe the beard made you look older. I just know you looked the same except you had a beard, and it was before you cut your hair. It was still in long plaits."

"I never had . . . " Bryan began.

"What?" Nicole asked as she saw his eyes widen just before he placed his hands over his mouth.

"Oh my God," he whispered almost frantically, rubbing his hand through his short locks. He blew out a lung full of air.

"Bryan?" Nicole said.

Gerald stared at them silently. He wiped his tears again as he waited to hear whatever Bryan was trying to say.

"Sweetie," Nicole said to Gerald as Bryan stared

speechlessly at the coffee table, "why don't you go up-stairs and watch television for a while? Let me talk to your daddy for a minute alone. Okay?"

"Are you mad at me?" Gerald asked.

"No, sweetie," she said as she kissed his forehead. "We're not mad at you, and we're not mad at Todd either. We don't want you to be mad at Todd for telling us. He was just trying to help. Do you understand that?"

"Yes."

"Okay. Go ahead. Close your bedroom door. We'll come up and talk to you later."

"Okay," Gerald said, and he left the cards on the floor and walked slowly up the stairs.

"Bryan," she said once he was gone. "What's wrong? Do you remember going to the party now?"

He shook his head silently as tears flooded his eyes. The panicky look on his face scared Nicole. She'd never seen him look quite this way before.

"What's wrong?" she asked again as she held his face in her hands. "Talk to me, baby."

"He's not my son," Bryan whispered through his tears.

"What?" Nicole asked. "Bryan, just because he's confused about who he saw or who gave him the gift, it doesn't mean he's not your child. He was four. He was a baby. He's just confused. I don't think paternity is a question here. Look in the mirror. He looks just like you."

"And who do I look like, Nicole?" he asked.

"Your father," she said.

"Exactly," Bryan said. "Gerald looks like me. I look like Garrett. Gerald looks like Garrett. He's not my son. He's Garrett's son. He's not my son," he repeated. "He's my brother."

"Bryan, what are you talking about?" Nicole asked,

near tears. Bryan pulled her to her feet and led her into their bedroom.

"God!" he said. "I don't know how I didn't figure this out before. There were so many signs."

"What signs, Bryan? How are you coming to this conclusion? This is crazy. Why would Tricia say he was your son if he wasn't?"

"Because she's an evil, vindictive, mentally disturbed woman," Bryan said through angry tears.

"Bryan, are you sure?" Nicole asked. "Are you really, really sure?"

"It all makes sense now." Bryan paced the floor. "He looks so much like me because he looks so much like my father. He thought my father was dead because my father's father is dead. He thought I was at his party because my father was at his party. He thinks I had long, plaited hair because my father used to have long hair that he wore in locks that could easily be mistaken for plaits by a four-year-old kid. He got a Lakers jersey for his birthday from his father because my father, who is his father, is from Los Angeles."

"He's not your son?" Nicole asked.

"He's not my son," Bryan said, and he broke into tears.

"How could she do this to us?" Nicole said through her own tears as she tried to comfort Bryan. "How could she do this to him?"

"Remember the phone call last week when she accused me of leaving her for another woman? She accused me of cheating on her and marrying somebody else. It was my father that did that to her."

"She can't think that you're Garrett," Nicole said. "There's no way she has the two of you confused."

"No," Bryan agreed. "I think she knew exactly what

she was doing. She couldn't get back at him, so she went after me."

"Oh my God," Nicole said. "Sharon was right. If this is true, she really is crazy. How do we find out for sure?" she asked.

"I am sure," Bryan said. "It just makes way too much sense."

"You need to have a paternity test. We should have done that from the beginning. How could we have been so stupid?"

"The kid looks just like me," Bryan said. "Just like me," he repeated. "There didn't seem to be a question. I'm sure Tricia was banking on that."

"This is so cruel," Nicole said. "How could a mother do this to her child? How are we going to tell him that you aren't his father?"

"I don't know," Bryan said as he walked toward the phone.

"Please don't call her right now, Bryan."

"I'm not," he said as he thumbed through his Rolodex and dialed.

"Hello?" a female voice answered the phone.

"Hi." Bryan tried to sound calm. "Is Garrett home?"

"Yes," she said. "Just a minute."

"What are you going to do?" Nicole asked.

"Hello?" Garrett said.

"Hi. It's Bryan."

"Hey, son. How are you?"

"Not good."

"What's the matter? Is Nicole all right?"

"Nicole is fine. She's right here standing by me."

"What is it then?"

"I need you to answer one question for me."

"Anything."

"The last girlfriend that you had prior to meeting and marrying Geneva . . . what was her name?"

"Why?" Garrett asked. "Have you crossed paths with her? Stay away from her, son. She's crazy. I had to get a restraining order against her."

"What?"

"Yes," he said. "She's crazy."

"What was her name?" Bryan asked again, closing his eyes and bracing for the answer.

"Tricia Smart," he said.

"Oh, God." Bryan broke into tears once more.

Nicole stood back and cried silently. She could tell from his reaction that his gut feeling was proven true.

"Bryan?" Garrett said. "Bryan, what's wrong? Why are you crying?"

"He's not my son," he said through his tears.

"Who's not your son?"

"My son," Bryan answered. "The son I told you about. He's not mine."

"Son, you're not making sense. What does your son have to do with Tricia?"

"She told me he was my son."

"You had a child with Tricia Smart?" Garrett asked in surprise.

"No," Bryan said. "You did. You had a child with her."

"I know."

"But *I* didn't know," Bryan said. "I didn't know you had a child with her. She told me that he was my child. I've been thinking he was my child. He thinks he's my child. But he's not. He's your child."

"Oh my God," Garrett gasped, finally understanding. "She wouldn't dare."

"What am I going to do?" Bryan asked through a flow of tears.

Garrett realized that Bryan needed him, and it was his chance to really be there for him for the first time in his life.

"Hang up the phone, son," he instructed. "I'm on my way."

Nicole watched in helpless sorrow as Bryan hung up the phone and sank to his knees at the side of the bed, sobbing uncontrollably. She slowly knelt beside him and pulled his head onto her chest and cried with him.

CHAPTER TWENTY-SIX

B y the time Garrett arrived three hours later, word of Bryan's dilemma had already spread to his inner circle of friends. After Nicole finally managed to calm her husband, she had called Sharon and Melvin, who in turn notified their pastor and his wife.

Melvin and Sharon were the first to arrive. On their way over, they picked up Todd. Pastor and Sister Gaines arrived shortly thereafter, and without filling either of the suspicious boys in on any of the details of what was going on, Sister Gaines whisked them off to the park along with Benjamin and Michael to play while the grown-ups faced the problem at hand.

As Nicole went back into the bedroom to check on Bryan, Pastor Gaines, Melvin, and Sharon tried to come up with sensible ideas on how to break the news to Gerald and how to approach Tricia with the new information they had just discovered. They all became silent as the older version of Bryan walked in the front door.

"Wow," Sharon finally whispered.

"Hello," Garrett said as he scanned the unfamiliar faces. "I'm sorry. The door was unlocked. Is Bryan here?"

"Hi," Pastor Gaines walked toward him with an extended hand. "You must be Garrett Walker."

"I am," he responded, shaking his hand.

"I'm Charles Gaines," Pastor Gaines said. "I'm Teresa's brother and Bryan's uncle."

"Thank you," Garrett said, and he unexpectedly pulled the preacher into a firm embrace. "Thank you for doing for my son what I didn't."

"It was a pleasure," Pastor Gaines said once he was released. "It was quite a challenge," he added, "but the finished product made it well worth our time, efforts, and prayers."

"Is he here?" Garrett asked again.

"He's in the bedroom," Pastor Gaines said, pointing toward the closed door.

"Yes?" Nicole responded to the knock at their door as she handed Bryan a glass of water and two aspirin.

"It's Garrett."

Nicole looked at Bryan as he sat emotionless on the side of the bed. She welcomed Garrett's embrace as she opened the door for him.

"I'll be out here if either of you needs me," Nicole said, and she left the two men alone.

Garrett watched silently while Bryan took the medicine and set the half-empty glass of water on his nightstand. After a moment he took the liberty of sitting next to him on the firm mattress.

"How are you feeling?"

"I don't know." Bryan shook his head slowly. "I keep thinking that I'm going to wake up, but I don't."

"I didn't even know that you knew Tricia," Garrett

said, "let alone dated her."

"I never dated her."

"Well, you know what I mean," Garrett said.

"I never did that either," Bryan said.

"You must have," Garrett reasoned. "You thought he was your child."

"Because she told me that he was."

"But if you'd never been with her, you would have known it wasn't possible."

"It's not that simple," Bryan said, rubbing his temples with his fingers. "It's a long story."

"I got no place to go," Garrett said.

For the next several minutes, Bryan told his father the whole sordid story of how he came to believe that the child was his. By the time he was finished, Garrett, too, was amazed at the lengths that she went to in order to concoct the very believable story.

"She had all the facts," Bryan concluded his story. "Right up to the Omega party and all. The timing of it all was almost perfect."

"I was in Tallahassee at the time of your party," Garrett said. "I was the one who told her about the party and where it was held. I told her that you had passed your pledging and were accepted. I was bragging and saying how proud I was of you. In a million years I never would have thought that she'd use that to get back at me."

"She let me get attached to that boy," Bryan said as he punched the pillow on the bed. "What am I going to do now? How am I supposed to tell him that I'm not his father?"

"It's going to be hard, son," Garrett replied.

"Hard?" Bryan interrupted. "I love that kid, and he loves me. It's going to be harder than hard."

"You can still love him," Garrett said. "He's your brother. He still needs your love. You're not going to lose him."

"But I'll lose my son," Bryan said. "He was just about my only chance to have a child."

"You had a vasectomy, too?"

"No." Bryan lowered his voice. "Nicole's getting pregnant is highly unlikely. She has some medical things going on, and we both had accepted that. We weren't even looking to have children. Then Tricia comes from out of nowhere with Gerald, and both of us were apprehensive at first, but we became attached to him very quickly. I think he filled a void for both of us.

"Now we're back where we started," Bryan continued. "I'm not a father anymore. Nicole isn't a mother anymore, and Gerald doesn't have a father."

"Yes, he does," Garrett corrected him.

"I'm sorry," Bryan said. "I didn't mean that. I wasn't thinking."

"I know," Garrett said. "Listen, you have another week before Gerald is scheduled to come for another visit. We can think of a way to tell him this without shattering his whole world."

"No. We don't have a week," Bryan said. "Gerald is here now."

"He's here?"

"Not here at the house," Bryan said, calming his father. "Not right now anyway. He's at the park with some other kids and Aunt Maggie."

"That's the preacher's wife?"

"Yes," Bryan explained further. "I went to Tallahassee last night to pick him up, because I found out that he was at home with his great-grandmother who was wheelchair-bound and not capable of caring for him."

"Where's his mama?"

"Who knows?" Bryan said, cringing at the thought of Tricia. "She's on some pleasure trip."

"How did you find out that he wasn't your son?"

"He told me about the party. He kept saying that he saw me at his fourth birthday party, and that was the last time he had seen me. I kept prying because I knew that I didn't know about him until a few weeks ago, and therefore I couldn't have been at his party. He kept insisting that it was me and that I had given him a Lakers jersey.

"Then it became clear when he said that I looked older then and had plaits and wore a beard. That's when it hit me like a freight train. It was you. To a four-year-old kid, the two of us could easily be the same person nearly nine years ago. I knew that you used to wear locks and pull them back in a ponytail. I figured he mistook the locks for plaits."

"At the time of his party, I was wearing my hair plaited, actually," Garrett said. "My goodness," he continued. "That really was nine years ago, and I've not seen that boy since. I went on the road after that day, and I met Geneva a couple of weeks later. When I called Tricia to tell her that I was seeing someone else, she was fighting mad," he continued.

"I was never in love with Tricia. I don't think I was ever in love with any of the women in my life before Geneva. Tricia always was jealous and a bit crazy acting, but she just went totally off when I broke up with her. She started stalking me and harassing Geneva. One morning, she was just standing out on my front lawn smoking a cigarette in the middle of the night. That's when I got the restraining order.

"I hated to do that because she had my kid, and I told her that I would take care of him. She told me that I'd never see him again if I didn't come back to her. She was about to drive Geneva crazy. The madness went on for about three years before I just concluded that it wasn't worth losing my family over. I took Geneva, Vivica, and Angela, and we moved to a secluded area of Orlando, changed our phone number to a private one, and I haven't heard from her since."

"Well, I guess she decided that I was the next best thing," Bryan said.

"Son, I'm so sorry," Garrett said. "I never once thought that my mistakes would affect you. I always felt like I was the only one that would get hurt if things somehow went wrong in one of my relationships. I thought about stuff like catching sexually transmitted diseases and getting girls pregnant, but I never thought that your family would be threatened because of something that I did."

"I don't have the time or the energy to blame you for this," Bryan said. "I just need to figure out what to do from this point on. There's a boy out there who has, for the past two months, thought I was his father. I'm going to have to tell him that I'm not."

"Excuse me," Pastor Gaines said as he opened the bedroom door and walked in with the others following close behind. "Nicole just came up with an idea that just might work. It's not going to be easy, but it just might work."

"I'm all ears," Bryan said.

"I was just thinking that we should fight for custody of Gerald," Nicole said. "Hear me out." She held up her hand to stop Bryan from interrupting. "What Tricia has been doing is illegal. Because she demanded money from us, it's extortion, and I'm sure it qualifies as child neglect or endangerment that she leaves Gerald alone or with an invalid caretaker."

"Nicole. . ." Bryan shook his head.

"We can't send him back to her," Nicole said. "He's just a child, and he can't protect himself from a crazy mother. Garrett, do something." She broke into tears. "He's your son. Don't let him go back."

"Come here," Bryan said, and he stood and pulled her close to him.

"I'll do whatever I can to help," Garrett said. "I can't take custody from her, because I haven't been there for him. But if you want to fight for custody, I'll back you. I have police reports and a restraining order that can be submitted as evidence. Geneva has tapes with messages that were left on our machine, and she even has a couple of letters that we found stuck in our door before we moved."

"Please, Bryan," Nicole pleaded. "Please don't let him go back without a fight."

"You have all of our support," Melvin said.

"I can be a witness that she threatened Nicole at work and about the hang-up phone calls," Sharon offered.

"Uncle Charles," Bryan said, "what do you think?"

"It's up to the two of you," Pastor Gaines told the couple. "I can't advise you on whether you should go through with this or not. But if you do, just make sure that everything is done legally."

"I think it's time to talk to Gerald," Bryan said.

"I'll call Maggie," his uncle said, and he left the room.

"I need a minute with Nicole," Bryan told the others.

After they had left and closed the door behind them, Bryan handed Nicole some tissues from the nightstand and held her hand in his.

"Sweetheart, are you sure this is what you want to do?"

"Yes."

"We would be taking on full responsibility of Gerald."

"Bryan, we've been through this before, remember? We were talking about taking him on full-time for at least a year."

"I know," Bryan said. "But that was taking him on as our child. It's different now. Now, he's my brother. That makes him your brother-in-law. Before, you talked about being able to be a mother to my son. That won't be the case now."

"I know," Nicole said. "I can't pretend that I'm not just a little disappointed in that. But just like with the first situation, this one isn't Gerald's fault either. He still needs guidance, love, and support. We can give that to him in a way that his mother can't."

"And you're completely sure?"

"Yes, Bryan. I'm completely sure."

"Okay, then," Bryan said. "We'll go for it."

"Thank you," Nicole said as she hugged him.

"No, sweetheart," he said. "Thank you."

By the time Sister Gaines arrived with the children, Bryan had arranged for his father to remain in their bedroom. All of the others left and went to Melvin and Sharon's house to give them the privacy that they needed.

"Is this about the party?" Gerald asked as soon as the others left.

"That's a part of it," Bryan said. "Sit down here between me and Ms. Nicole."

"I'm sorry," Gerald apologized as he sat. "I wouldn't have ever said nothing to Todd if I had known it was going to cause trouble."

"We're glad that you told Todd," Bryan said. "And we're glad that Todd told us. I mean, in a way we're sad, but it was for the best."

"Can we just pretend that it never happened?" he asked.

"No, Gerald. We can't. If we pretend it never happened, you'll continue thinking that you have the whole truth, and you don't."

"You're still going to say that you weren't there, aren't you?" he asked as he looked despondently at Bryan.

"Yes, I am going to say that," Bryan said. "Not because I'm trying to pretend that I wasn't there, but because I really wasn't there."

"But . . ." Gerald began.

Bryan stopped him. "Listen to me Gerald. I have never had long plaits or worn my hair in a ponytail. I've never had a beard other than this thin one that I have right now. I've never bought a Lakers jersey, because I've never been a Lakers fan. It wasn't me at the party."

"Okay," he said, as though not wanting to discuss it any longer.

"No, Gerald. It's not okay. I need you to understand something. I'm not trying to make you think you're crazy or that you dreamed up this whole story. I believe you."

"You do?"

"Yes, I do. I believe that all of those things happened at your party. As a matter of fact, I know they did. I know because I've spoken to the man who had the long plaits in a ponytail and a beard. I've spoken to the man who loves the Lakers. He told me that it happened. It just wasn't me."

"But he said he was my daddy," Gerald said. "Why would he say that? And if it wasn't you, why do you look so much like him?"

"He said he was your daddy because he is." Bryan choked back tears. "I look so much like him because he's my daddy too."

Gerald looked at Bryan in confusion for a moment. Bryan could tell that he didn't quite understand.

"What?" Gerald asked.

"Sit right there," Bryan said. "I'll be back in a second."

"What's he talking about?" Bryan heard Gerald whisper to Nicole as he walked toward the bedroom door.

Garrett was already in tears as Bryan joined him in the bedroom.

"Is it time?" he asked.

"Yeah." Bryan nodded, wiping his own eyes.

"God help me," Garrett said as he took a deep breath.

"Get yourself together," Bryan said. "We can't fall apart here."

"Okay, I'm ready," Garrett said as he rubbed his hands through his beard and straightened his shoulders.

The two men walked slowly into the living room, where Nicole was assuring Gerald that everything was going to be all right. She held her breath as she saw them walk in.

"Gerald," Bryan called.

Time seemed to stop as Gerald turned to face the two men. His body began to visibly tremble as he stared into the face of the man in his distant memory. He tightened his grip on Nicole's hand as he swallowed hard and attempted to find his voice.

"Who's that?" he whispered.

"This is Garrett Walker," Bryan said, as Garrett covered his face to hide his tears.

"Your daddy?" Gerald whispered.

"Yes," Bryan said in a trembling voice. "And yours."

"But you're my daddy." Gerald's lips trembled as he

tried to fight tears.

"Look at him, Gerald," Bryan said. "Look at the beard. Look at the ponytail."

"But you're my daddy," he repeated as a river of tears streamed down his face.

"I'm sorry," Garrett said. "I'm so sorry, son."

"Gerald." Bryan sat next to him and held his face in his hands. "When you told me the story last night and you described the man, I knew it wasn't me. I knew that there had been a terrible mix-up. The things your mother said weren't true. I never knew about you, and I never knew your mother. I'm not your father."

"She said you were my daddy," he wailed.

"I know," Bryan said. "It wasn't the truth. I don't mean to talk bad about your mother, but the fact is that she tricked me, and she tricked you. She tricked all of us. Garrett is your father, not me."

Garrett knelt on the floor beside Gerald and placed his hands on the boy's knees.

"You've grown so much, son," he began. "I don't have no excuses. There were reasons, but I could have done more. I should have been there for you, but I wasn't. I should have fought for the right to spend time with you, but I didn't. I wish I could turn back the hands of time and live my life all over again, but I can't. I made some terrible mistakes in my life, and two of them were not being around for you and not being around for your big brother here. I was too much of a coward and too selfish to fight for you and your other siblings as I should have. All I can say is that I'm sorry."

The boy buried his face in Nicole's chest and cried as she held him tightly.

"Gerald, do you understand any of this? Do you understand what we're saying here?" Bryan asked.

349

He nodded yes.

"Everything is going to be okay," Bryan assured him. "We're still going to take care of you. You're still family, and we still love you. You still want to spend time with us, right?"

"Yes," he said through tears.

"Good, because we want that, too. It doesn't matter that you're not my son. You're my brother, and I still want to share my life with you. Okay?"

"Okay," he said, gasping as he tried to catch his breath.

"We need your help with something, Gerald," Bryan said. "We need to get your mother some help."

"Why?" he asked.

"We think she's sick," Bryan said. "I don't mean physically sick, but we think that she needs to talk to someone about why she told us all those things that weren't true. I may need you to talk to someone, too. Do you think you can do that?"

"What am I supposed to tell them?"

"The truth, that's all. Whatever questions they ask you, all you have to do is tell the truth."

"But she'll burn me if . . ." he began before catching himself.

Bryan, Nicole, and Garrett froze at the boy's words.

"She'll *what?*" Bryan shouted.

"Nothing," he said.

"Oh, Jesus," Nicole said.

"Finish the sentence, Gerald," Bryan said. "Burn you if what?"

"Come on, son," Garrett said. "It's okay. We won't let nobody hurt you."

"Burn me if I say the wrong thing," he said slowly.

"Burn you where?" Nicole asked as she frantically

began lifting his shirt and looking at his back and stomach.

"Right here." He pointed below the cheek of his right buttock.

"Stand up," Bryan said.

Bryan slowly pulled Gerald's pants down to his knees and turned him around to see the back of his leg.

"We've gotta do something!" Garrett said.

About three inches below his buttock was a burn mark about five inches long that stretched across the back of his thigh.

"Let me see," Nicole said as she turned him around.

"Just low enough so that it won't hamper him sitting, and just high enough so that it can't be seen when he wears shorts," Bryan said.

"How many times has she done this?" Nicole asked.

"I don't know," Gerald said.

"Where else have you been burned?" Garrett asked.

"Nowhere. It's always the same place. Please don't tell her that I showed you this," he whimpered.

"Don't you worry about a thing," Bryan said.

"What did she do this with?" Nicole asked.

"The thing that she curls her hair with."

"When was the last time she did it?" Nicole asked. "It looks recent."

"Monday."

"Why?" Bryan asked. "What did you do that she thought was bad enough for this?"

"I told y'all that I didn't want braids."

"Oh, God," Nicole said, and she buried her face in her hands.

"I really need you to talk to some people for me, Gerald," Bryan said as he helped him pull his pants back up. "It's the only way that we're going to be able to protect you and get your mother some help."

"She's going to be mad at me," he said tearfully.

"Son," Garrett said, "none of us are going to let her hurt you."

"You have to trust us," Bryan added. "Remember I said I'd never lie to you. I won't let her hurt you anymore. You have to believe and trust me. Okay?"

"Okay," he whispered.

CHAPTER TWENTY-SEVEN

The atmosphere in the Walker household was solemn on Sunday morning. In an attempt to lighten Gerald's mood, Todd had spent the night with him in his room. The laughter and chatter that generally came from the room when Todd stayed over was absent on Saturday night.

Nicole called the police to their home after they had questioned Gerald concerning the burn. He quietly told the police his story of abuse and neglect and then stood silently and despondently as they took pictures of his injury. If that weren't enough, he also accompanied Bryan and Nicole to their attorney's office as they filed custody papers and Bryan and Garrett to a private doctor for a paternity test.

After Garrett left for Orlando, the family shared a quiet dinner, and Gerald asked permission to go to bed. After going upstairs to say prayers with Gerald, Bryan stayed with him until he fell asleep. Todd went to bed shortly thereafter.

Before the police had left, they told Bryan that they would contact the Tallahassee Police Department and issue a warrant for Tricia's arrest. They would pick her up as soon as she returned from her trip on Tuesday.

Bryan's tossing and turning during the night kept Nicole awake. She moved closer to him, held him tightly, and spoke in his ear softly as he tried to hide the silent tears that streamed down his cheeks. Her love and comfort felt good, and he woke up and turned to face her. She held him in her arms for the rest of the night.

Because they slept later than usual, they were late getting to Sunday morning service. The praise and worship had already begun, but their usual seats on the row with Melvin and Sharon were vacant and waiting.

Pastor Gaines had apparently already alerted the church on what had happened the day before with the Walker family. Just before he began his message, he asked that everyone stand and hold hands as they prayed for the family's strength. After the prayer, the pastor proceeded to deliver a moving sermon that stirred many of the listeners.

The altar prayer that ended the service was just what the family needed. The floor of the sanctuary filled with gatherers as Pastor Gaines called for as many of the members that could to come closer to the pulpit area. The prayer was heartfelt and refreshing. Bryan, Nicole, and Gerald wept as they held each other close.

Not wanting to discuss the issues at hand, the three of them linked hands and headed for the exit doors following the dismissal. The sight of Garrett and his family walking toward them from the rear of the church stopped them in their tracks.

Garrett greeted them.

"Hi," Bryan said as Nicole happily embraced her father-in-law. "I didn't know you were here," Bryan continued.

"We are," he said. "It's been a long time since we've been in church, but I enjoyed the program that you all had here today."

"I'm glad," Bryan said. "I'm glad you could come."

"Me too," Garrett said as he and Bryan embraced.

"Oh," he said as he stepped aside. "This is my wife, Geneva, and my daughters, Vivica and Angela."

"It's nice to meet you all," Bryan said, and he and Nicole gave them hugs.

"This is my oldest son, Bryan," Garrett proudly told his family, "and his wife, Nicole. And this is my youngest son, Gerald."

"It is so wonderful to finally meet you all," Geneva said, smiling. "Garrett has told me so much about you," she told Bryan. "It's really a pleasure. It's a pleasure to meet all of you."

Geneva was a tall, dark, and thin woman, much like Bryan's mother, Teresa, and Gerald's mother, Tricia. There was a definite pattern in the type of woman that Garrett was attracted to.

"Thank you," Bryan said. "I've heard a lot about you all too over the past week. You're as lovely as he said," Bryan concluded, and his father's stepdaughters blushed and smiled.

"We'd love it if you all joined us for dinner," Nicole said. "Can you spend a little time with us at one of our fine restaurants before heading back to Orlando?"

"Absolutely." Garrett smiled as he rubbed Gerald's head.

Melvin and Sharon joined them as they walked out onto the church grounds. Suddenly, the screeching of tires caused several of the members to direct their attention to the parking lot.

"Who do you think you are?" Tricia demanded as she stormed across the lawn.

"Oh my God," Nicole gasped, and she quickly tucked Gerald behind her.

"Get your hands off my son," she ordered, toward Nicole. "You ain't had no right to come barreling up in my house and take him. This is not his week to be here."

"Don't you even try it," Bryan said through clenched teeth as he stepped in front of Nicole and grabbed Tricia's wrist.

Sharon returned inside and alerted Pastor Gaines, who came rushing out of the sanctuary to see what was going on. Gerald clung to Nicole's waist in fear of what might happen.

"Let her go, son," Pastor Gaines told Bryan as he stepped forward.

"Get over here, Gerald," Tricia demanded as she saw him hiding behind Nicole.

"Now!" she ordered when he didn't respond to her previous demand.

"Take him inside," Pastor Gaines told his wife.

"You can't do that," Tricia demanded as Sister Gaines took his hand and rushed him inside. "That's my son!" Tricia yelled. "Gerald, you get back here!"

"We know about your little scheme, Tricia," Bryan said as he finally released her arm. "We know the whole story."

"What are you talking about?" She swore.

"Watch your language," Pastor Gaines ordered. "You're on God's property."

"I want my son," she said.

"*Your* son?" Bryan asked.

"All right, *our* son," she said. "You took him without

356

permission from me. Now give him back before I go to the police."

"*Our* son?" Bryan asked with increasing anger.

"Yes, *our* son," Tricia said in confusion.

"You mean, our son?" Garrett stepped forward.

The sight of Garrett nearly knocked Tricia off her feet. She stumbled backwards and gasped as she looked from Garrett to Bryan. It was clearly apparent that she was not prepared for the situation she now faced.

"What are you doing here?" she said in a weak voice. "And what is she doing here?" she pointed at Geneva.

"I can't believe even you would stoop this low, Tricia," Garrett said.

"Give me my son before I call the police," she said as she continued backing away.

"Don't bother," Sharon said as she walked through the crowd. "I already did."

"Give me my son!" she yelled as tears welled in her eyes.

"You should be ashamed of yourself," Nicole said angrily as she walked forward.

"You shut up!" Tricia swore again. "I ain't listening to nothing you got to say."

"I will not shut up," Nicole said the sound of sirens blaring in the distance. "And you will listen to me. You think you can just come out of nowhere and destroy my family with your lies and deception? You accused my husband of impregnating you and leaving you to fend for yourself," she said as angry tears slowly streamed down her face.

"You said he sent friends to your home to threaten to kill you if you told anyone. You called my house and disrupted my family life with your accusations. You called my job and disrupted my workflow with your lies. You

357

used a beautiful, innocent child to get back at a man who you hated, and in the process you crushed the heart of the man I love."

"Nicole," Bryan said as he saw her anger and frustration mounting.

"That is my husband, and you crossed the line," Nicole continued. "Your sick, twisted lies could have destroyed my family and my home. You are so hateful and spiteful that you abused and misused your own child," she continued through her tears as the police cars pulled onto the church lot and the policemen approached cautiously.

"I love my family," Nicole said, trembling with emotion as the remaining congregation stood back and listened. "I know you don't have a clue what it feels like to love beyond measure, but that's what I have for this man, and I take offense to the fact that you would try to tear up my home. You abused your own child! So don't you dare tell me to shut up, Tricia Smart," Nicole concluded between clenched teeth. "You've had the upper hand in my life for too long already. I've sat back and held my peace while you rampaged on and on with fictitious stories about your past with the man I love, because I felt the need to keep peace between the two of you for Gerald's sake. Well, no more! Do you hear me? You will not destroy my life! You will not destroy my father-in-law's life, and you will not destroy Gerald's life!"

"Nicole!" Bryan called as he watched her collapse to the ground and lay motionless.

Two of the policemen handcuffed Tricia and dragged her to the patrol car as she kicked and fought. The other two rushed by Nicole's side and called for emergency help as Bryan cradled her head in his arms. Several members scampered to get wet towels while Pastor Gaines prayed silently over her limp body.

Hours later, Nicole opened her eyes to find Bryan standing by the side of her hospital bed and holding her hand.

"She's awake," he said to one of the nurses that stood in the room.

"Bryan?" she called weakly.

"Yes, sweetie. I'm here," he said as he stroked her forehead.

"Where am I?"

"You're in the hospital. You passed out on the church grounds. Do you remember?"

"No," she said. "But I had a really bad dream."

"You did?"

"I dreamed that Tricia came and tried to take Gerald. She had gotten back from her trip early, and she came and tried to take him, but the police arrested her before she could."

"It wasn't a dream," he said. "It really happened, and you really let her have it."

"I did?"

"Yes. It happened after the service today."

"She didn't take him, did she?" she asked, worried.

"No." Bryan smiled. "He's in the waiting room right down the hall with Melvin, Sharon, Uncle Charles, Aunt Maggie, my dad, his wife, and the girls. Let me run out and tell them that you're awake. It's right down the hall. I'll be right back."

"Okay," she said as he dashed out of the room.

"Well, Ms. Thing," Dr. Sims said as she walked into the room. "Glad to see you're awake."

"Dr. Sims," Nicole said as she rubbed her eyes. "What are you doing here?"

"I'm a doctor. It's the hospital. You're my patient. Where else would I be?"

"But you're a GYN."

"I know what I am, Nicole." She laughed. "I just wanted to make it seem like I was as important as, say, a surgeon or something. I'm here because they called me in. Where did Bryan run off to?"

"He went to tell our friends that I am all right."

"Hi, Dr. Sims," Bryan said as he returned.

"Hi, Bryan" Dr. Sims smiled.

"How is she?"

"Looks like she'll live," the doctor said.

"Can she go home?"

"If she does well through the night, Dr. Shivley will release her tomorrow."

"You're not her doctor?" Bryan asked.

"Just for the GYN-related stuff," she said as she looked at her chart. It seems that her blood pressure went through the roof there for a minute."

"Yeah, she was a bit upset."

"These readings say she was a lot more than a bit upset."

"I've been under a lot of stress lately," Nicole said. "We've had a lot of personal issues. It's had my head spinning and my stomach upset so much lately. I guess it just all came to a head today."

"It won't happen again," Bryan said. "I think we got to the root of the problem today. I'll make sure it doesn't happen again."

"You make sure you do that," Dr. Sims said. "By the way, Nicole," she added, "have you been taking that medicine that I prescribed for you? I noticed that you didn't come back for a refill."

"No." Nicole shook her head apologetically. "I've just been so preoccupied with other stuff that I've neglected taking it for the past several weeks."

"Have you had another period since the last time when you came to me?"

"No," Nicole admitted. "Everything was going so well. I guess I messed it up. I'll just have to start over again and hope for the best. I'm sorry, Dr. Sims. I'll start back on the medication as soon as I get back home."

"No, no," Dr. Sims said. "There's no need. I'm going to change the prescription anyway."

"Okay," Nicole said. "I promise, I'll take it."

"You'd better," Dr. Sims said.

"She will," Bryan added.

"How much do you love her, Bryan?" Dr. Sims suddenly asked.

"What?"

"How much do you love this woman?"

"I couldn't calculate that, Dr. Sims. I love her with all my heart. You know that. Why do you ask?"

"Because after a few months, you may have to cut back hours at the office and spend more time with her."

"Why?" Bryan asked.

"What's wrong with me, Dr. Sims?" Nicole tried to sit up.

"All of the symptoms that you've been having for the past couple of months have been magnified by stress, but stress alone hasn't been the cause of them," she said as she ripped the page from her prescription pad and handed it to Bryan.

"Make sure she takes one capsule every day for the next seven months. You two are having a baby."

"What?" Nicole gasped.

"She's pregnant?" Bryan asked with widened eyes as he looked at the prescription for prenatal vitamins.

"She's pregnant," Dr. Sims smiled.

"She's pregnant?" Bryan asked louder. He then unexpectedly picked Dr. Sims up and spun her around before placing her back on the floor.

"She's pregnant," the doctor repeated with a laugh.

"You're pregnant," Bryan said. He leaned over the bed rail and kissed her lips.

"We're having a baby," Nicole said through tears as Bryan headed for the door.

The excited father-to-be ran out into the hall and faced the direction of the waiting room.

"She's pregnant!" he yelled. "Nicole is pregnant! We're having a baby!"

Nicole laughed and cried when she heard his announcement followed by her family and friends cheering from the nearby waiting room as Bryan ran back into the room. Even patients and visitors in neighboring rooms joined in the rejoicing at the sound of the happy future father sharing his news with the world.

"Congratulations," Dr. Sims said with a laugh. "And lower your voice before you have us all thrown out of here," she added as she hit his arm with the clipboard before leaving the couple alone.

"We're having a baby," Bryan whispered through his own tears. He gently touched her stomach and kissed the tears from her cheeks.

"I know." Nicole smiled while touching his face and guiding his lips to touch hers for a soft, lingering kiss.

"We're having a baby," he said again, and he leaned in closer and hugged her warmly.

"I love you," he whispered in her ear.

"I love you too," Nicole whispered back.

The Negro National Anthem

Lift every voice and sing
Till earth and heaven ring,
Ring with the harmonies of Liberty;
Let our rejoicing rise
High as the listening skies,
Let it resound loud as the rolling sea.
Sing a song full of the faith that the dark past has taught us,
Sing a song full of the hope that the present has brought us,
Facing the rising sun of our new day begun
Let us march on till victory is won.

LIFT EVERY VOICE

So begins the Black National Anthem, by James Weldon Johnson in 1900. Lift Every Voice is the name of the joint imprint of The Institute for Black Family Development and Moody Publishers.
Our vision is to advance the cause of Christ through publishing African-American Christians who educate, edify, and disciple Christians in the church community through quality books written for African Americans.

The Institute for Black Family Development is a national Christian organization. It offers degreed and nondegreed training nationally and internationally to established and emerging leaders from churches and Christian organizations. To learn more about The Institute for Black Family Development write us at:

15151 Faust
Detroit, Michigan 48223

Since 1894, *Moody Publishers* has been dedicated to equip and motivate people to advance the cause of Christ by publishing evangelical Christian literature and other media for all ages, around the world. Because we are a ministry of the Moody Bible Institute of Chicago, a portion of the proceeds from the sale of this book go to train the next generation of Christian leaders. If we may serve you in any way in your spiritual journey toward understanding Christ and the Christian life, please contact us at:

820 N. LaSalle Blvd.
Chicago, Illinois 60610
www.moodypublishers.com

A LOVE SO STRONG TEAM

ACQUIRING EDITOR
Cynthia Ballenger

COPY EDITOR
Tanya Harper

BACK COVER COPY
Becky Armstrong

COVER DESIGN
Lydell Jackson

COVER PHOTO
Photo Disc/Getty Images, Inc.

INTERIOR DESIGN
Ragont Design

PRINTING AND BINDING
Color House Graphics

The typeface for the text of this book is
Sabon